The Three Admirals

W. H. G. Kingston

"The Three Admirals"

By

W.H.G. Kingston

1875

Chapter One.

The Dragon off the Bonins—A conversation between Tom Rogers and Archie Gordon—Gerald Desmond on the sick-list—Threatenings of a typhoon—It strikes the ship—She runs before it—The ship hove to—The bowsprit carried away—A marine Will-o'-the-wisp—Enter a bay in one of the Bonin Islands—Tom, Gerald, and Billy get leave to visit the shore—A beautiful cavern—Land on the island—Their discoveries—Fishing—Interrupted by sharks—A picnic—Boat drifts away from the shore—Tom swims off—Narrow escape from a shark—See the ship in the offing—Pull after her—A hurricane coming on—Fearful danger when re-entering the harbour.

Her Majesty's corvette *Dragon*, lately commanded by our old friend Jack Rogers, who had been superseded by Commander Rawson, was on her passage across the wide Pacific, bound for Esquimault harbour, Vancouver's Island, from Japan, to which she had been sent with despatches.

The wind being fair, the screw was at rest, and she was under all sail, looking as trim and taunt a little man-of-war as a sailor's heart could desire. Her stay in Japan had been short, so that no leave had been granted, and even the officers had seen little of the country and people; though, as they hoped to return before long, that did not much matter. As it was of no great importance that the *Dragon* should soon get back to Vancouver's Island, Commander Rawson had received directions to visit the Ladrone Islands, somewhat to the southward of his course, in order to obtain particulars of an outrage, said to have been committed on an English subject by some of the mongrel inhabitants of those islands, which have for some centuries belonged to Spain.

The smooth sea shone brightly in the rays of the sun, undimmed by cloud or mist. In all directions the snowy wings of sea fowl could be seen, now dipping towards the ocean, now rising into the blue ether, showing that land was at no great distance. As the wind was from the northward, the air was cool, though the shady side of the ship was generally sought for by the watch on deck, except by a few whose heads seemed impervious to the hot rays of a tropical sun.

Two midshipmen were slowly pacing the port side of the quarter-deck, where a few feet of shade afforded them shelter from the heat. The one, a somewhat short, well-knit lad, with open countenance, well tanned, and blue laughing eyes, his whole appearance giving promise of strength and activity; the other, a tall youth with sandy hair, and pleasant features well freckled. Though tall, he was too well built to be called lanky, and showed that he possessed both strength and activity.

"I say, Archie, I do envy those fellows of the *Eolus* going on to China; they will see all sorts of fun, for the Celestials are sure not to give in in a hurry. The *Eoluses* will have the same sort of work that my brother Jack and your cousin Murray went through in the last Chinese war, when they were midshipmen."

The speaker was Tom Rogers, the youngest brother of Captain Jack Rogers; his companion was Archie Gordon, Captain Alick Murray's cousin.

"Gerald was dreadfully cut up at not being able to remain on board the *Eolus*, and having instead to come back with us to return home; but Captain Adair's letter was peremptory, and, as the newspapers say, I hope that he will hear of something to his advantage. Gerald would have been better pleased had his uncle let him know why he was sent for."

"He has no great cause to complain, seeing that the climate of China is none of the most delectable, and he would have run the risk of being shot into the bargain," observed Archie. "I wish that I had the chance of going home, and finding myself the possessor of a tidy fortune with a title."

"But then there's the honour and glory, and the fun, and the pig-tails to be captured, and the loot, and the chance of serving in a naval brigade and seeing some work on shore, just as the *Shannon's* people did in India, with a fair prospect of promotion at the end of it."

"If a body happens not to be shot, ye ken," observed Archie, who, though every bit as eager as Tom for the sort of work he described, took a pleasure in differing in opinion from him whenever he could.

"We will not, however, bother poor Desmond about the subject until he is well again," said Tom. "I really believe that he fell sick through vexation, though he was happy enough to be with us once more."

"He is much better to-day," remarked Archie, "and I hope by to-morrow that the doctor will let him come on deck again, although he may not be fit for duty for a day or two more."

Mr Mildmay, the first lieutenant, who was officer of the watch, paced the deck, spyglass in hand, now and then going on to the bridge and sweeping the horizon with his glass, while he frequently called to the look-outs on the forecastle and fore-yardarm to keep their eyes open. Jos Green, the master, was also continually there, or else consulting the chart in his cabin, for that part of the ocean was comparatively little known, and cruel reefs might exist, not marked down.

"The first lieutenant and the master seem very fidgety," remarked Tom.

"So would we be, I suspect, if the responsibility of navigating the ship rested with us," answered Archie. "After all, no one suffers by being sufficiently careful; that's the rule my cousin gave me when I first came to sea."

"And a very good rule it is, too, no doubt about that," observed Tom. "My brother Jack is as careful of his ship, and everything connected with her, as an old lady is of her best silk gown on a Sunday morning, though any one, to hear him talk, would suppose that he was the most harum-scarum fellow alive, always excepting his old shipmate, Captain Adair. He is, however, staid and steady enough in reality. I was very glad to hear that he got his post rank at the same time as my brother Jack did; and now the three old messmates, as they delight to call themselves, are post-captains, and will some day, I hope, be admirals. I wish, however, that they had not to wait so long. Your grave cousin Murray is as fit to be an admiral now as he will be twenty years hence, and, unless not a few fine fellows die off, it will take the best part of that time for any of them to get their flag."

"It is encouragement for us, though," observed Archie; "for if they have all been posted without any great amount of interest, we may hope to get promoted in consequence of our good conduct."

"Yes, but then remember that they have seen a great deal of service, and should the piping times of peace return, we may find it a hard matter to get employed and be able to exhibit our good conduct."

"Weel, mon, we'll hope for the best, and may be some other nation will kindly think fit to come to fisticuffs with old England, and give us something to do," said Archie.

"There's every chance of that, I should think," said Tom. Just then seven bells struck in the afternoon watch. "I'll go and see how Gerald is getting on, before I have to come on deck again; it's dull work for him lying all by himself."

Tom found his old messmate, whose cot was slung a little way outside the berth, so that he might have the advantage of the air coming down the after-hatchway, sucking lustily at an orange which he grasped in one hand, while he held a book in the other. He was so absorbed in its perusal that he did not notice Tom. Suddenly he burst into a loud fit of laughter.

"Capital fun; I should have liked to have seen it!" he exclaimed; "soused over head and ears a second time. Ah, ah, ah!"

"What's the joke?" asked Tom.

"I've just got to where old Peregrine Wiffle tumbles into the water a second time, when he is showing how he saw the small fish playing under the wharf, and was picked up with a boat-hook." Tom and Gerald had a good laugh together.

"You don't seem very bad," observed Tom.

"No; the fever, or whatever it was, that had got hold of me, has cut its stick, though I don't feel quite as nimble as I ought to be," answered Gerald. "I believe that the disappointment of not going to China, and the thinking over what my uncle Terence can want me home for, had more to do with it than the climate, the hot sun, or anything else, and I intend to ask the doctor to let me go on deck to-morrow, by which time I shall have finished my book, and I want to have a look at any of the islands we may happen to pass. There are some curious shaped ones, I am told."

"Yes; we have sighted some. One seemed to rise three or four hundred feet in a pointed peak, right out of the water, and it was not, I should say, an eighth of a mile in circumference. It is marked on the chart as Lot's wife. A solitary existence she must lead all by herself."

"Whereabouts are we?" asked Desmond.

"At noon, when we were passing that curious rock, our latitude was 29 degrees north, and our longitude 14 degrees east. We shall next sight the Bonin Islands, or Rosario, which is another lofty island, little more than a rock, standing up out of the sea."

"Do ask the doctor if I may get up, Tom; I should be sorry to pass these places without having a look at them," exclaimed Desmond. "I can finish my book by-and-by."

Just then the officer spoken of, Mr Hussey, came out from the gun-room. He was a short, somewhat stout gentleman, with a good-natured expression of countenance, and a merry twinkle in the eye, which showed that he could enjoy a joke, and was likely to utter many a one himself. His naturally florid complexion was deepened into a still more ruddy hue by exposure to the hot suns of the tropics.

"Do, doctor, let me get up; your physic has done me an immense deal of good, and I feel quite well already," said Desmond.

The doctor felt his pulse. "You get up!" he exclaimed. "What do you think yourself made of?" trying to look grave.

"Arrah, shure, sugar and spice and all that's nice! that's what midshipmen are made of. But shure, doctor dear, you will not keep me here, stewing by myself, when I might be enjoying the pure air of heaven?—for I really am well, doctor."

"You mean to say that you have finished your book, and have got tired of lying in bed," was the reply. "Well, if you promise to be a good boy and keep in the shade, you may dress and go on deck, but I cannot undertake to scratch you off the sick-list yet."

"Thank you, sir," said Desmond; "I will do everything you tell me, and take as much medicine as you think fit to prescribe. I do not want to do duty yet, as I've got a hundred pages more of 'Tom Cringle's Log' to read, and I cannot gallop over a book as some people do."

"Well, well, possibly the ship may manage to take care of itself without you," said the doctor, as he passed on.

Whereupon Desmond began to put on his clothes, a task which he accomplished with Tom's assistance. He felt himself, however, much weaker than he had expected, as he made his way upon deck, though he tried hard to show that he was himself again. He received a friendly greeting from his messmates, and Mr Mildmay congratulated him on being able once more to make his appearance.

There was plenty to amuse those who had a taste for natural history even when no land was in sight, and the doctor, who was a great naturalist, was constantly on the *qui vive*, for the sea teemed with squid, medusae, polypi, and flying-fish. Several of the latter came through the ports, when there was a general scramble for them, the midshipmen, who were on the watch and the most active, coming in for the largest share. A short time afterwards the unhappy fish made an appearance, well fried, on their mess-table. Whales, too, were sporting in all directions, tempted to the locality by the abundance of food which the before-named creatures afforded. Several old whalers among the crew could scarcely restrain their impatience, and, could they have obtained leave, would have gone off with such gear as they could have prepared to attack the monsters of the deep.

Since the *Dragon* had left Japan, the weather had been remarkably fine, with calms and light winds. But the calms lasted scarcely long enough to have the fires lighted before the ship was again under sail. That evening, however, a long heavy swell began to come from the north-east; the undulations rapidly increasing in size, making the ship roll from side to side, until her chains touched the water. Desmond, in common with two or three of his messmates, and most of the ship's boys and marines, began to feel very uncomfortable.

"What's going to happen?" he asked; "I'm mighty quare about the region of the stomach."

"I suppose we are going to have a gale of wind, as a change," answered Tom, who had never been ill since he first came to sea.

"We shall have to shorten sail, I've a notion, before long, to be prepared for blustering Boreas, when he thinks fit to visit us."

The whole appearance of the sky and sea quickly changed. The wildfowl, which had been hovering around the ship, winged their flight to the nearest islands where shelter could be found. The atmosphere was pervaded with a peculiar glare by the rays of the sun coming through the clouds of a dull ochreous red, giving the ocean, the ship, her canvas and sides, the same unnatural tint.

As the summits of the swells, till now as smooth as glass, rose higher and higher, they formed crests of foam, which sparkled in the ruddy light, like masses of jewels. Hitherto there had not been sufficient wind to steady the ship as she made her way amid the heaving billows. Mr Jay, the second lieutenant, was now the officer of the watch; he made a sign to Tom.

"Rogers," he said, "go and tell the commander that the weather is getting much worse."

"Be quick about it, too," exclaimed Green; "there is no time to lose."

Commander Rawson was quickly on deck. After taking a rapid glance round, he shouted out, "All hands shorten sail."

The watch below came tumbling up on deck. The topsails were lowered, and the topmen, like bees, swiftly swarmed aloft, laying out on the yardarms.

"Hold on by your teeth and eyelids, Billy," said Tom to his old friend Billy Blueblazes, as he sprang up to his station in the main-top. The canvas was speedily reduced to closely-reefed fore and main-topsails and fore-staysail. It was hard work to hold on, for the ship rolled even more violently than before. The wind, however, did not come as soon as was expected, but it was impossible to say at what moment it might strike her. That it would come with no ordinary strength, and without further warning, there was every reason to believe.

The crew, having performed their task, were called down on deck. There was something in the appearance of the sea and sky, and the heaviness of the atmosphere, which made even the toughest old seaman feel an extraordinary depression of spirits, though he might not have suspected the cause.

"Faith! I'm sorry I did not remain quietly in my cot," said Desmond; "it seems to me as if the world were coming to an end. I should not be surprised to see flames spouting up out of the sea. It looks as if some big fires were burning away under it."

"Don't you ken, Gerald, that the water would be putting the fire out," observed Archie; "though from the appearance of some of those islands there has been fire enough below them at one time or other. They have all been raised up out of the ocean by volcanic agency."

"I am not disposed to dispute the truth of your remark," said Desmond; "I only wish the sea would get quiet, and let us glide comfortably over it, instead of kicking up such a disturbance."

While the midshipmen were speaking, the ship had continued her uneasy course, slowly rising to the summit of a huge billow and then gliding down into the deep trough.

Suddenly a loud roar was heard, and it seemed as if some mighty monster of the deep had struck a prodigious blow on the side of the ship. Over she heeled until the water rushed in at her lee ports.

"Up with the helm. Furl the main-topsail. Take another reef in the fore-topsail. We must run before it," cried the commander, hoping to steer clear of any islands or reefs which might be ahead.

The ship quickly rose to an even keel, and dashed forward amid the foaming seas, rolling, however, even more violently than before. So rapidly did the waves follow, that many struck her stern; not, however, before her dead lights had been closed. So tremendous were some of the blows, that it seemed as if her masts would be shaken out of her. The doctor and purser, who were sitting in the gun room, were thrown off their seats sprawling under the table, fully believing that the ship had struck a rock, and that all hands would soon be struggling for their lives.

As soon as things could be got to rights, Tom helped Desmond below, and he was glad enough to again turn into his hammock, which he had before been so anxious to quit.

"Shure we have got Harry Cane aboard of us, Mr Rogers," observed Tim Nolan, who was in Tom's watch, and took the liberty of an old shipmate to address his officer with a freedom on which others would not have ventured. They were both stationed together on the forecastle, looking out ahead.

"I wish that the gentleman would be good enough to take himself off, then," answered Tom, "or he may be playing us a scurvy trick, by sending our craft on some of the ugly reefs which abound hereabouts."

"We'll be after keeping a bright look-out for that, sir," said Tim.

"We may be on a reef before we can see it," observed Tom. "For my part, if I did not believe that Providence was steering us, I should not be at all comfortable."

The ship continued to drive on before the gale. The second lieutenant came forward, but he had to confess that his eyes were of little value to pierce the dark gloom ahead. The foam-crested waves could alone be seen, rapidly rising and falling. Tom's eyes ached. He was not sorry when he was relieved. Still, neither he nor any one else felt inclined to go below; no one could tell what might happen. The thick clouds hung down like a dark canopy, apparently just above the masts' heads. The thunder, which had been rumbling in the distance, now began to roar loudly, while flashes of forked lightning came zig-zagging through the air, threatening every instant to strike the ship. But, though they played round on all sides, none touched her. The commander had ordered the fires to be got up, so that the ship might be under steam, ready for any emergency.

Hour after hour the typhoon continued to howl even more fiercely than at first. Frequently a blast would strike the ship, making her tremble as if some solid mass had been hurled against her. Then there would come a lull for a few seconds, then another blast would suddenly strike her in a way that made every plank shake throughout her frame. Even the most hardy on board wished for day. The morning light brought no abatement of the gale.

Onward went the ship, now plunging into a vast hollow, which threatened to engulf her; now she rose rapidly to the top of another sea, while on either side they appeared to be vying with each other, which could leap the highest and accomplish her destruction.

The officers were gathered aft, the men in the waist, holding on firmly to the stanchions, or anything to which they could secure themselves. Each time that the ship plunged her head into the seas, the masts bent, as if every moment they would go by the board. At length a lull came, and the commander, having consulted with Green, fearing dangers ahead, determined to bring the ship to, an operation attended by considerable risk, as a sea striking her at the moment might sweep her deck. A favourable opportunity was waited for. The crew stood ready to lower the fore-topsail and hoist the main-topsail, which had been closely reefed. Both tasks were accomplished; the officers were anxiously watching the seas as the ship rode over them, but happily she was safely rounded to, and now lay with her main-topsail to the mast, though scarcely had she got into that position, than a fierce foam-crested sea, roaring up, struck her bows and deluged her decks, but shaking herself clear, like a thing of life, she sprang forward, while the water rushed through the ports. The lull continued, and many hoped that the gale was breaking; but in less than an hour another furious squall struck the ship, and nearly laid her over on her beam ends. Once more she rose, her stout canvas having stood the severe trial to which it had been put, and she rode with comparative ease for a few minutes.

The seas, however, seemed to become more broken than ever. A prodigious one came roaring towards the weather bow. The *Dragon* appeared to see her danger, and struggled to avoid it, but the next instant she pitched headlong into a deep hollow, when another monstrous wave, rising apparently half as high as the foretop, fell completely down on her deck. For a few seconds, her commander and his officers feared that she would never again rise. No orders could be issued, and nothing could be done. The crew stood silently at their stations, not uttering a word, or showing that they felt the fearful predicament in which they were placed.

The ship remained, as it were, fixed in the sea; then with a sudden jerk she burst her way through it, but her stout bowsprit was broken short off, and the next sea threw the wreck of it across the forecastle. The commander's voice was now heard in tones vying with the howling of the gale. The crew, obedient to his orders, rushed forward to secure the bowsprit with lashings; while the boatswain, with another gang, lost not a moment in setting up fresh stays, to prevent the foremast being carried away.

This, with the loss of one of the boats, and the forepart of the bulwarks stove in, were the chief damages hitherto received by the *Dragon* during the gale. It was not over, however. Again the sun set, and the wind continued to rage with unabated fury. The watch below had been ordered to turn in, but few of the officers had done so, and, though tired out, still remained on deck. Tom and Archie were standing aft, close together, when the latter suddenly grasped Tom by the arm.

"Oh, mon! what's that?" he exclaimed, pointing to the main-topmast head, which appeared crowned by a ball of pale fire.

"It has a curious appearance; though I never saw it before, my brother Jack has told me about it. It is a sort of Jack-o'-lantern, or Will-o'-the-wisp, or, as Gerald once called it, 'Saint Vitus' dance.' I believe he meant to say Saint Elmo's fire."

While the midshipmen were gazing up, the flame descended rapidly down the mast, running first along the main topgallant yardarm, then returning, down it came, to the main-topsail yard, where it glided out to the extreme end. Here it rested for some seconds, as if it had not made up its mind what next to do. Presently back it came to the mast, and darted out to the lee yardarm. It had not yet finished its journey. Once more gliding back, it ascended the mast, when it made its way by the main-topmast stay, on to the foremast and there went gliding backwards and forwards along the yard.

"I wish it would come down on deck, and then we might have a chance of catching it," said Tom. "I have read somewhere that a man going aloft with a bucket, clapped it over the light, and brought it down a prisoner. It is a sort of gas which is driven about through the air until it finds something to rest on. Why it goes moving up and down in that curious way I don't know, nor does anybody else, I believe. I wish the doctor were on deck,—he would tell us."

"Shall I call him?" asked Archie.

"I don't think he would thank you," said Tom. "Let him rest in quiet; perhaps before he can get on his clothes the fire will have disappeared."

Tom was right. In another minute the luminous ball, gathering itself into a point, shot upwards and vanished.

"That's a good sign," they heard Green observe to the first lieutenant; "we shall have the gale breaking before long."

Before the watch was out the hurricane had sensibly decreased, showing that the master was right in his prognostication. The sea continued, however, to tumble the ship about terribly until the morning dawned, when the clouds began to disperse, and as the sun rose they appeared to fly before his burning rays. By noon the sky was perfectly clear, when, an observation having been taken, the commander determined to run under the lee of one of the Bonin Islands, which were sighted shortly afterwards. Steam had been got up, and the vessel made rapid way, though she continued to roll considerably, moved by the now glass-like swell, which still came in from the north-east, showing that, although a calm rested on the waters where she was, a storm raged in another part of the ocean.

Several islands were now seen rising out of the water on the port bow, and as the *Dragon* drew near trees could be distinguished on the hills, showing that they were not as barren as they appeared to be at a distance. Rounding the southern end of one of them, she went on at half speed, feeling her way with the lead until she opened a sheltered bay between two high projecting points. Running in she brought up within a quarter of a mile from the shore in perfectly still water. Everybody was glad enough to be at rest after the tumbling about they had had during the last few days. They were not allowed, however, to enjoy many minutes' quiet; all hands were speedily set to work to repair damages.

"We should be thankful that we have escaped so easily," observed Archie Gordon, who had been surveying the shore through his telescope. "Look there, Tom, at those tall trees stretched on the ground with their roots in the air; it must have taken a pretty hard blow to break them down. I can see some stumps sticking up, showing that others have been snapped off by the wind. It is a mercy that we weathered it out as well as we did."

Tom took the glass. "I should have been sorry to have been under them," he answered, "and I only hope that no poor fellows were living on shore, or they would have run great risk of being crushed. It makes me think of the old song—

> "'A strong nor'-wester's blowing, Bill;
>   Hark I don't ye hear it roar now?
> Lord help 'em, how I pities them
>   Unhappy folks on shore now!'

"I hope the commander will let us take a run on shore, however, before we sail."

In the course of a couple of days the repairs were nearly finished, but as there was a good deal of painting to be done, the commander resolved to remain at anchor another day. Green and the second lieutenant had been employed during the time in surveying the island, but their surveys were not complete.

"I say, Gerald, we must get our trip some way or other," said Tom to Desmond. "You'd be the better for a run ashore, and I'm sure, if you suggested the idea to the doctor, he will say so, and get Mr Mildmay to let us have a boat."

Gerald followed Tom's advice.

"Of course, my boy," answered the good-natured doctor; "if you find anything curious, remember to bring it off for me."

"That I will, sir," said Tom.

The doctor having spoken to the first lieutenant, Tom went up boldly and asked for the use of the jolly-boat.

"You can have her; but remember you must be on board again in good time," answered Mr Mildmay.

Tom and his party were quickly ready, carrying some fishing-lines, as well as some baskets to bring off any wild fruit they might happen to find. Tom and Gerald were below making their preparations, when Billy Blueblazes came out of the gun-room.

"Holloa!" he exclaimed; "I've got leave to go with you. I suppose you'll take some grub?"

"We'll be afther finding that on shore," answered Desmond; "game, or fish, and fruit. I propose we carry a couple of muskets; we shall be sure to find something or other."

"Elephants or rhinoceroses," suggested Billy.

"Not quite such big beasts as they are," answered Tom. "We should find them rather too cumbrous to stow away in our game-bags."

"But we'll take some bread, and rum, and some cold beef—they are not likely to grow on the island, at all events; or potatoes either, or a pot to boil them in," remarked Desmond.

The articles they fancied would be required were quickly collected.

"Shure, if we haven't forgotten the powder and shot!" exclaimed Desmond, as they were committing the things to the charge of Tim Nolan, who was to accompany them, that he might stow them away in the boat. Pat Casey, the other Irishman who had been saved from the savages, with Jerry Bird, formed the crew of the boat. Bird and Nolan were tried, steady men. Casey, who was accustomed to a savage life, might be useful in searching for fruits or any animals which might be found in the island. He was also a first-rate fisherman, having had plenty of experience during his residence with the Indians.

The party shoved off soon after the second lieutenant and master had left the ship.

"The only thing I'm sorry for is that Archie is not with us," said Tom. "However, we are sure to have plenty of fun of some sort or other."

At the further end of the bay was a small piece of sandy beach, towards which Tom steered the boat. As there was no surf, they ran her up on it, and stepped out without difficulty. A nearer acquaintance, however, showed them that the country was not of so tempting a character as they had at first supposed. There were a few trees close to the beach, some of which had been broken in two by the storm, and now lay prostrate on the ground. Even larger trees, a species of mahogany, lay uprooted in all directions, so that they found it very difficult to make their way among them. Still, by dint of climbing over the fallen trunks, and cutting a road through the brushwood, they had made some progress, when they discovered a circle of rocky hills, in many places almost precipitous. It seemed almost hopeless to attempt climbing over them, especially as Desmond acknowledged that he "did not feel very well up to that sort of work," and they would have had likewise to carry their muskets, provisions and cooking utensils.

"As we have not much time to lose, I propose that we go back to the boat, and try and find another landing-place further along the coast," said Tom.

His plan was agreed to; and launching the boat, they again took to their oars. After rounding a rocky point, which formed the eastern side of the bay, they pulled along for some distance in the hopes of finding another landing-place, from whence they could make their way into the interior. As there was no surf, and the sea was perfectly smooth, they kept close in with the land. In many places high cliffs rose precipitously out of the water. As they pulled along at the foot of one of these cliffs, Tom shouted out—

"Holloa! there's a big cavern directly ahead of us; the water seems to run right up into it, and I should not be surprised if we could get up some distance in the boat."

They stopped rowing, to survey the mouth of the cavern. It appeared to be upwards of thirty feet in height and almost of the same width. Everybody, of course, was eager to explore the cavern; and rowing gently, that no risk might be run of knocking the bows of the boat against a rock, they made their way into the cavern. By just keeping the oars moving, the boat glided on. Ahead, all was darkness, so that it was impossible to ascertain how far the cave penetrated into the land. As soon as their eyes got accustomed to the subdued light which existed at a distance of thirty or forty feet from the entrance, the beauties of the grotto began to dawn on their sight. Glittering stalactites, of a thousand fantastic forms, hung down from the high and vaulted roof, while at either side appeared columns and arches like those of some ancient temple, tinted with numberless delicate hues, the extreme points of the stalactites glittering like bright gems as they were reached by the reflected rays of the sun, which penetrated far down into the depths beneath, illuminating every object below its glassy surface. So beautifully clear was the water, that when the party in the boat looked over the sides, they could see right down to the bottom of the cavern, which appeared to consist of masses of rock, forming caves and hollows, covered with the richest marine vegetation. Here were corals of various tints, blue and yellow, red and white: amid them the ocean fan expanded its vast leaves; from the lowest depths sprang up the sea-green stems of the fucus, twining round columns which sank far down, and afforded them support. Here feathery tufts of green vegetables floated upwards in the clear water, while others of various strange shapes and hues formed recesses and arches, twisted and knotted in a variety of ways. Fish, of varied forms and brilliant colours, darted in and out among the openings, some rising close up to the boat, as if curious to ascertain the character of the visitors to their submarine palace.

"I wish the doctor were here to tell us their names," exclaimed Tom. "Look there, at those odd creatures. What can they be?" The fish at which he pointed were flat, of an oval form, and of a rich silvery colour, delicately striped downwards with azure bands. They swam in a perpendicular position, aided by two long and slender fins, one curving upwards from the back, of a considerable length, and the other curving downwards from the opposite side. There were many others differing in form, but all of the most beautiful colours, darting and gliding in and out, but, being apparently of a less curious or more timid disposition than those which had excited Tom's astonishment, did not venture near the boat. There were cray-fish, too, of large size, and enormous crabs, and star-fish, and sea-urchins, and bivalves of various sorts clinging to the rocks, with open mouths, to catch any unwary creatures coming within their reach.

After enjoying the scene for some time, by giving a few strokes with their oars the midshipmen allowed the boat to proceed further up the cavern. Most of the party were hanging over the water with their noses just above the surface, some with their hands trying to catch any of the fish which might venture near, when a cry from Tim made them spring up.

"Shure, he'll be afther catching some of us, if we don't look out," exclaimed the Irishman, and at that moment they saw rising out of the far depths of the cavern an enormous shark, his eyes glaring like two glowing coals, as with open jaws he came nearer and nearer the boat.

"He'll be after swallowing the whole of us," cried Tim. "Back water! back water!" To the Irishman the shark probably appeared much larger than it really was.

"He won't do us any harm; but just keep the oars out of the water," said Tom, who was, of course, obeyed, and the shark glided alongside the boat, which he kept eyeing with suspicious glances.

"Would you be afther wishing to have one of us?" asked Desmond. "Then I hope you'll be mistaken; unless, Billy, you wish to be kind to the baste, and let him have your arm as a treat."

"Thank you," said Billy; "I'd rather not. It wouldn't give him much trouble to bite it off, though."

"We must not be disappointed in our expectation of exploring the cavern by a brute like that," exclaimed Tom. "Hand me the boat-hook." Standing up, he struck the point with all his might against the nose of the monster, which at that instant sank with a suddenness which made Tom lose his balance, and had not Desmond and Billy seized him he would have been overboard.

"He's more afraid of us than we are of him," said Tom. "Now let us get as far up the cavern as we can."

They pulled cautiously on, Tim standing up in the bows, and feeling ahead with the boat-hook. The mouth of the cavern seemed to grow smaller and smaller, until only a point of light remained. Suddenly Pat Casey, who was pulling with Jerry Bird, declared that he felt something seize the blade of his oar.

"It's the shark, perhaps," said Tom. "We have the muskets ready. I'll give him a shot, and that will make him keep his distance. Wait until he tries it again."

Tom took the musket, and stood up ready to fire.

"There! he's got my oar in his jaws," cried Pat.

Tom fired. The flash revealed for an instant the sides and roof of the cavern, which seemed to glitter as if studded with thousands of jewels, while ahead all was pitchy darkness, showing that they had not yet got to the extremity. The sound of the report, greatly increased in loudness, went echoing amid the arches and pillars, until it died away in the far distance, proving the great extent of the cavern.

Whether the shark was hit or not, it was impossible to say; but the bullet tore off the point of Pat's oar, showing that Tom had taken good aim.

Jerry Bird now suggested to the midshipmen that it would be prudent to pull back, as without torches they could not see where they were going. There might be, for what they could tell to the contrary, some big sea monster squatting up at the further end, who might crunch them up without ceremony.

Though Tom had no apprehensions on that score, he agreed to return, proposing, should the *Dragon* remain at anchor another day, to explore the cave with a supply of torches. The boat was accordingly cautiously pulled round, and made her way towards the mouth. It was curious to watch the arch growing higher and higher, and the light gradually increasing. They had almost reached the entrance, when, on either side, not one, but several sharks, came gliding up. One, bolder and bigger than the rest, seized the blade of an oar, crunching off the end; and the other men had to keep a watchful eye to save theirs from being destroyed. Tom fired the other musket, and declared that the bullet went through the shark's head. As the monster did not appear the worse for it, Desmond and Billy doubted the fact. Not until Tom had fired several times, and the boat had got to a considerable distance from the cavern, did the sharks leave her.

"There's one thing certain: that's not a place to bathe in, nor would it be pleasant to tumble overboard hereabouts," observed Tom, gravely. "I never can see those black monsters, with their wicked eyes, floating near and looking up at one, without feeling uncomfortable."

They had to row farther than they expected. At last they saw a narrow opening in a reef of rocks, within which they made out a small bay, with a sandy shore, where they could land with ease and draw up the boat. The country beyond, too, looked far more tempting than they had yet seen. The water in the passage was deep, so that they had no difficulty in making their way into the bay. As yet they had seen nothing of the second lieutenant's and the master's boats, which, supposing the island to be of small size, they had expected to meet coming round from the opposite side.

"We shall probably see them if we cut directly across the island," observed Tom.

They were not disappointed in the bay. The beach was exactly what they wished for. They hauled the boat up, and agreed that she could be left without danger.

"But I hope you fellows are not going to begin a long march without some food," observed Billy, who was noted for his excellent appetite. "We have no game, nor have we caught any fish. It's lucky that we brought some food, as I advised."

Wood was collected, and a fire quickly made. As they had brought cold meat and bread with them, they had only their potatoes to cook. This operation was superintended by Tim, while the rest of the party searched for any other productions of the island which might add to their repast. They had not gone far when Tom exclaimed—

"Why, there are some cocoa-nut trees, and very fine ones, too. I thought there were none on the island."

"They are cocoa-nut trees, sure enough," said Desmond, "and with cocoa-nuts growing on them. How to get them down is the question, for the stems are too stout to allow us to swarm up."

"'Where there's a will there's a way'; up we must climb, some way or other," said Tom, who never liked to be beaten.

On reaching the spot, they found not only cocoa-nut trees, but yams and bananas, covering the ground in the wildest profusion, the latter climbing up the surrounding branches, from which the ripe fruit hung temptingly down.

On examining further, they discovered the remains of a fence, showing that the ground had been enclosed, for the purpose of forming a garden, at some probably distant period.

"Bless the man whoever planted these," said Jerry Bird; "he had a thought for any poor fellows who might be wrecked here some day or other. If others would do the same at all the desert islands they visit, the lives of many castaway seamen might be saved."

The yams, from growing wild, were not likely to be worth much, but the bananas, notwithstanding the latitude, appeared to be very fine. In vain, however, they gazed up at the cocoa-nuts. Jerry, though an active man, vowed that he could not attempt to reach the top unless they could get a rope over one of the branches. While they were discussing the matter, Pat Casey, who had been helping Tim, came up, having also caught sight of the cocoa-nut trees from a distance.

"Bedad, I'll be afther doing it," he exclaimed; and running back to the boat, he returned with three or four fathoms of rope. This he twisted into a huge grummet round the tree, leaving space enough for his own body to get in also. Then slipping it behind his waist, he began to swarm up, shoving the rope on the opposite side of the tree each time he moved on, as high as his shoulders. In a wonderfully short time he reached the top of the tree.

"Stand from under," he shouted out, as he threw down a cocoa-nut, which very nearly hit Billy, who had not attended to his warning. Several cocoa-nuts split by their fall, but Billy, rushing forward, seized one of them before all the milk had run out. This example was followed by the rest: Seeing this, Pat secured several about his neck, and then getting into his grummet he descended. That one tree gave them as many nuts as they could require.

"We ought not to take more than we want," said Tom; "though before we shove off, we will get a supply for the ship."

Tim now shouted out that the "taters" were cooked, and returning to the camp-fire, the party enjoyed a very satisfactory repast with the aid of the bananas and cocoa-nuts. After this they made their way for some distance inland, passing large forests of tamanas, or mahogany trees, which appeared to cover the greater part of the island. Excepting in the deserted plantation, they could discover no other fruit-bearing trees or roots, but they observed traces of some wild animals, which Pat asserted must be hogs.

As there was some risk of losing themselves, and there was nothing to induce them to continue their ramble, they returned to the boat. Desmond, seconded by Billy, now proposed that they should set to work to fish, that they might carry a supply with them on board.

Tom agreed, and Pat having collected a quantity of crabs which he found among the rocks, to serve as bait, they once more embarked. They pulled out towards the mouth of the bay, just inside of a high reef, which completely shut out the sea from their view. Here, so clear was the water, that although fully three fathoms deep, the bottom could be clearly seen, covered with masses of coloured coral and sea-weeds of various shades and tints. Amid them they observed beautiful fish of all sizes and tints, gliding in all directions, now disappearing under some cavern, now darting again into sight.

"As the creatures can see us and our lines, we shall have no chance of catching any," said Tom.

"Just try, your honour," exclaimed Pat; "they're mighty hungry bastes, and not accustomed to the look of white faces, so that they will not know what we're afther."

The hooks were accordingly baited with crabs, and scarcely was the first line let down than a big fish caught it, and was immediately hauled up.

"I told you so," cried Pat exultingly; "we shall have as many as we like to catch."

All were now eager to get their lines overboard, and no sooner had the hooks sunk towards the bottom than the fish, attracted by the tempting bait, dashed forward and seized them.

"We'll mighty soon have a boat load," exclaimed Pat, as fish after fish was hauled in.

Suddenly a change came over the scene. From out of a cavern, far down below the reef, a huge form appeared, very similar to the monster which had attacked the boat in the stalactite cave. Rapidly and noiselessly it glided up, and before Billy, who just then felt a bite, saw its approach, it had seized the fish which had bitten at his hook. Billy gave a pull, expecting to haul up his fish, and very nearly got his fingers cut through by his line, as the shark, finding something tickling his throat, darted off with it. Bird, seeing what had happened, cut the line, and away dashed the shark. The monster had put the other fish to flight, and it was some time before they returned. Scarcely had they assembled, and a few more had been caught, than, other sharks appearing, the lines were immediately drawn up, to save them from the fate Billy's had met with. As these pirates of the deep appeared, the smaller fish darted off in all directions.

"Shure, it matters very little to them whether they are caught by one of us or by those black brutes, excepting for the honour of the thing, and the pleasure of tasting a crab's leg before they die," observed Desmond.

These interruptions prevented the party taking note of time. They had got no small number of fish, still they were eager to catch a boat load; and Tom, who ought to have looked at his watch, forgot to do so.

Thus hour after hour passed by, until they all began to get hungry, when Desmond proposed going on shore and cooking some of their fish. The idea was too good a one to meet with dissenting voices; and returning to the beach, they quickly made up their fire, the embers of which had remained burning, and soon had three or four fine fish roasting on sticks round it, under the superintendence of Pat Casey. So busy were they with this interesting occupation, that no one had observed the changed appearance of the sky. The fish were, as Pat declared, "just done to a turn," and Tom and Desmond and Billy were served, the latter having filled his mouth with a dainty morsel, when they were startled by the booming sound of a gun. Another followed. It was evidently fired for their recall.

"We ought to have got back before this," exclaimed Tom, starting up and looking seawards.

The rest followed him, carrying the cooked fish down to the beach. What was their dismay to find, on reaching it, that the boat, which had been hauled up, had been floated by the rapidly rising tide, while a strong gust of wind had driven her a considerable distance from the shore, from which she was drifting further and further off.

Not a moment was to be lost. Tom felt that he had been guilty of an act of indiscretion in remaining so long on shore, and in not having seen that the boat was properly secured. He had not forgotten those huge monsters of sharks, which had been prowling about, but there was only one way by which the boat could be regained. Somebody must swim off to her. These thoughts rapidly passed through his mind. The swim itself was nothing; he had often swum ten times further without fatigue. But those sharks! He recollected the shudder which had passed through him as he had seen them approach the boat not two hours before. Without saying anything, he had quickly thrown off his clothes.

"Shout, all of you, as loud as you can," he exclaimed. "Good-bye, Desmond; good-bye, Billy," he said, shaking hands. "If I am swallowed by one of those brutes, say it happened while I was doing my duty."

Without another word, Tom plunged in, and the rest of the party, rushing forward up to their knees, began splashing the water about, and shouting at the top of their voices.

"I cannot let him go alone," said Jerry Bird, as soon as he saw what the midshipman was about. Throwing off his jacket and shirt, he followed Tom, shouting out lustily.

"I am coming, Mr Rogers," he cried; "you climb in on one side of the boat, and I will on the other."

Tom was within a couple of fathoms of the boat, when to his horror he saw a dark fin, just rising above the water. It was stationary, however. Perhaps the savage brute was merely surveying the boat, and wondering what strange creature it was.

Tom, undaunted by the sight, swam on. He might manage to scramble on board before the shark caught sight of him.

"Do not lose heart, Bird," he cried out, for he guessed that his companion would have seen the shark's fin; "the chances are that he won't attack two of us."

A few strokes more, and Tom had got hold of the gunwale of the boat; Jerry had seized that on the other side.

Tom, being in no way fatigued, easily held himself up, and, having got his left leg over, was about to drag up the other, when Jerry threw himself in and tilted the boat over to the side he was on. It was a fortunate movement, for the shark ran his snout against the side, missing Tom's foot almost by a hair's breadth. Tom felt the brute's head strike against the boat, and well knew what had happened. It made him draw his breath quickly; but he had work before him. Without stopping a moment, he and Jerry, seizing the oars, rapidly pulled the boat back to the beach. Their companions gave way to a hearty cheer as they reached it.

"Thank Heaven, you have escaped," said Desmond. "I saw what happened; my heart sank so low that I thought it would never get up again to its right place. However, 'a miss is as good as a mile'; now the sooner we are away from this the better."

Tom's and Jerry's clothes having been handed into the boat, they dressed themselves, while the rest of the party pulled down the bay.

"I vote we eat the fish while it's warm," said Billy Blueblazes, whose appetite (as Gerald used to say of him) "no dangers could daunt."

"Just hand me a slice, and I'll eat it as I pull." This proposal was seconded by the looks of the men, and Tom accordingly passed portions, with some biscuit, forward. The crew ate the fish with gusto. They were wise in so doing, as they might have a long pull before them. Another and another gun was heard.

"Those guns were not fired in the harbour," observed Tom; "the ship must have put to sea."

Gerald agreed with him; but as yet the reef, which ran across the mouth of the bay, concealed her from sight. The wind had lately been blowing from all quarters—now down the harbour, now directly across it—until at length a heavy squall came in through the entrance.

"We shall have a strong wind in our teeth, and a pretty heavy pull," observed Tom to Gerald. "I wish we had not spent so much time here; and I shall justly get the blame, if anything happens."

"It won't much matter who gets the blame if we happen to be all drowned," answered Gerald. "However, as we were known to have gone in this direction, the captain will probably stand along the shore to pick us up; and the chances are that we shall be safe on board within an hour or so."

The men had now to bend their backs to the oars to force the boat over the heavy seas which came rolling in through the narrow entrance. Under other circumstances, Tom would have put back and waited for an improvement in the weather; but the signal of recall was peremptory, and he considered it his duty to try and get on board at all risks. The sea, which had been so calm when they pulled along the coast, was now tossed into heavy foam-crested billows, which came rolling on in rapid succession, bursting with loud roars against the rock-bound shore, and casting sheets of spray over the reef.

"We must heave our cargo overboard," said Tom, when he saw the heavy seas come tumbling in. "The lighter the boat is the better."

The fish, with which they hoped to regale their shipmates, were quickly thrown overboard.

"Shure, a fine feast we are giving to the sharks," observed Desmond, as he was engaged in the work. They retained, however, a dozen or so of the cocoa-nuts, in case they might be required for food. So slow was the progress they made against the sea and wind, that it was almost dusk before they got clear of the land. Tom had been keeping a look-out to the westward, the side on which he expected the ship to appear.

"There she is," he exclaimed at length; "but she is under sail, standing to the south-east, and I see no smoke coming out of her funnel."

Gerald agreed with Tom that such was the case. They asked Jerry Bird, the oldest seaman on board, to give his opinion.

"You're right, sir," he said; "to my mind something has happened to the machinery. Either the shaft or the piston rod is broken, and they cannot get the screw to work. The commander, of course, did not like to remain in the bay, with the chance of a hurricane blowing right into it; and so he got up the steam, and was probably standing along the shore to look out for us, when the accident, whatever it was, happened; and the only chance he had of saving the ship was to go about and stand on the course he is now doing. Maybe he will come about again before long to look for us."

Tom and Gerald were very sure that the commander would not desert them, at the same time they felt far from comfortable at seeing the ship at so great a distance off. The wind was rapidly increasing; the seas came rolling in far more heavily than before, while the spray from their foaming crests being sent over the boat, soon thoroughly wetted through all hands. This, of course, no one cared much about; the question was whether their small boat would live in the furious sea they were likely to encounter before they got on board. If Jerry Bird was right, the ship herself must endeavour to get a good offing from the island in case a hurricane should come on. Of that there now seemed every probability. The gloom of night had rapidly increased, and now they could only distinguish the ship from the light which she showed over her quarter. Was it intended for a signal to them, or had the other two boats not yet returned to her? As the night advanced, the weather became worse and worse.

"It's that old rascal Harry Cane at his tricks again," cried Tim; "I wish that he had waited a bit, and let us get comfortably on board."

"Never complain, Tim," observed Pat; "maybe we shall be glad that we haven't left the boat; we have got a harbour under our lee, and plenty of grub on shore, and that's what many a poor fellow has wished for, and not been able to find."

Tom and Gerald were excessively anxious to get on board, and determined to persevere as long as they possibly could. The men strained at their oars with hearty good will. Now the boat mounted one sea, rapidly to descend into the trough of another. Tom steered her carefully, keeping her head to the seas. He full well knew that at any moment one of the heavy tops of those seas falling on board might swamp her. Bird frequently looked over his shoulder with an anxious glance.

"Beg pardon, Mr Rogers, but it won't do," he said at length; "the keener we put about and run back into the harbour, the better chance we shall have of living through this night; what has happened to the ship I cannot tell. But, while it's blowing like this, dead on shore, we shan't get on board to-night or to-morrow either."

Tom and Gerald at length saw that Jerry Bird was right. They could no longer distinguish the *Dragon's* lights. Either a thick mist had arisen, or she had got too far off for them to be seen; indeed, the shore itself, as the boat sank into the hollow of the sea, was invisible.

"We must look out for a smooth, and pull the boat round, lads," cried Tom.

"Arrah! shure, that will be a hard matter to find," said Tim Nolan, as if to himself.

Watching for an opportunity, Tom, when in the trough of the sea, got the boat round. "Give way, lads! give way!" he shouted out. Not that there was any necessity for saying that; the men knew well enough that their lives depended on their pulling as hard as they could. Any moment a sea, rolling up astern, might break over them. Tom stood up to look out for the entrance to the harbour, which he believed they must be approaching, but he could see nothing but one unbroken line of foam bursting over the reef. The land rose from the shores of the bay. On the highest part Tom recollected having observed a large clump of tamana trees, which, as they had pulled down the harbour, he had noted as a good land-mark for entering. In daylight it could easily be seen, but in the darkness he could scarcely hope to make it out against the sky, while the boat tumbled and rolled about in the way she was now doing. Still, it was their only hope; should she strike a reef on either side of the entrance, she must in an instant be dashed to pieces, and all hands be washed amidst the foaming breakers.

"Now, Desmond, use your eyes as you never have before, and try and see that clump of trees, or find out the passage."

Gerald strained his eyes. "I think I see a dark spot almost ahead," he said at length.

"If you do, that must be the entrance," observed Tom. "I can see no other; it is our only chance; the boat will not live long in the sea which is now getting up."

Tom steered towards the point Gerald indicated. On sped the boat. The loud roar of the breakers as they neared the shore almost deafened them, and Gerald, though sitting next to Tom, had to shout to make him hear.

"That's the passage, I'm sure of it," he cried out.

"You're right," answered Tom. "Give way, lads!" The boat rushed on. A tremendous sea, with a huge crest of foam, came roaring up astern, and threatened to overwhelm her. The men saw it, and redoubled their efforts. On either side rose a wall of white foam dashing directly over the rocks beneath which they had been fishing. An instant later and the boat would have been swamped; but on she flew, surrounded by spray, and in another minute was floating in comparatively smooth water within the sheltering reef. At that moment the hurricane burst forth, sending the breakers flying in sheets over the reef, howling fearfully as it went rushing amid the trees of the forest, tearing off huge limbs, and laying many low, while vivid flashes of lightning were followed by peals of rattling thunder, adding yet further to the wild uproar of the elements.

"Thank Heaven, we are safe!" exclaimed Gerald.

"We may rightly acknowledge that; but what has become of the other boats and the old barkey?" said Tom.

Chapter Two.

Land—Bury the boat—Take shelter under a rock—The hurricane rages—The night passes by—Desmond shoots at a wild beast—Storm abates—No ship—Boat missing—Boat discovered—Tim's pork chops—Digging out the boat—Pat charged by a wild boar—Flag-staff set up—No ship appears—A hut built—Explore the island—Miss the hogs, but kill some birds—Preparations for the voyage—Turtle—Billy's exploit—Leaky condition of the boat—Search for pitch—Tom and Desmond set out to explore the island.

Tom steered the boat up the bay towards the beach they had so lately left. It no longer afforded an easy landing place, for the waves came rolling in, even through the narrow entrance, creating a surf on the sandy shore, and scarcely had her stern touched the beach than a sea burst on board, not only wetting every one through, but nearly washing several articles out of her. All hands therefore jumped out.

"Now, lads, a long pull, a strong pull, and a pull all together," cried Tim. In another minute the boat was hauled up the beach, and they began taking out the things and carrying them to the spot where they had left their fire burning. Fortunately, the muskets and ammunition, though wet, had been saved, as had the articles of value in the boat, together with a compass which Tom had thoughtfully brought, although they had hitherto had no use for it. The ashes of their fire were still alight, but they at once found that the exposed beach was not the spot where they would exactly wish to encamp.

"We must find some sheltered place, where we can put up our tent," said Tom to Desmond. "A high overhanging rock would suit us best, but it won't do to be under these tall mahogany trees, which may at any moment crash down upon our heads, and we have already had a specimen of how they are likely to behave."

"I'd rather get into a snug cavern, if we can discover one," said Desmond. "But how is that to be found in the dark?"

"I'll soon twist up a couple of torches such as I used to make when I was Prime Minister of the Cannibal Islands," cried Pat Casey. "I think we could find our way to the left, where I saw some big rocks this morning, and I should not be surprised to find tolerable shelter under them."

"We ought to be there as soon as possible," observed Tom, "for we shall probably have the rain down upon us before many minutes are over,—and the hurricane has only just begun, we must remember. Get your torches made as soon as you can. Before we leave this we must look after the boat, and haul her farther up the beach; it is impossible to say how high the water may rise with a hurricane setting on the shore."

They accordingly hurried back and ran the boat some feet farther up, but beyond that they found it impossible to move her.

"If we leave her as she is, she'll sure to be blown away," observed Jerry Bird. "If I may advise, sir, I'd make a sort of dock all round her, and fill her up with sand, so as to sink her in it. It will cost us some little trouble to clear it out again, but it will be better than having her knocked to pieces."

Tom and Desmond highly approved of Jerry's proposal. All hands, therefore, set to work with the boat stretchers to make the dock, which was very easily and quickly accomplished. They then filled her up with sand, almost to the gunwale.

"She will be steady enough now, sir," said Jerry.

As soon as the work was finished, they returned to their former encampment, carrying the boat's mast, yards, sails, and oars with them, to assist in forming a tent, while the rest of her gear they placed for safety high up on the bank. Pat had quickly twisted up some torches from the fibre of the cocoa-nuts, and now loading themselves with all their property, they set out, he leading the way. Scarcely had they commenced their march, than they felt themselves almost taken off their feet; a loud crash was heard, and down fell a large tree, close to where they were, torn up by the roots. Happily they were on the weather side. They hurried on, keeping as much as possible in the open ground. Another blast came with redoubled fury, almost blowing out Pat's torches, which burnt, indeed, with so much rapidity, that there seemed but little probability of their being able to reach the point towards which they were steering, by their light. They had not gone far when two torches had burnt out. Heavily laden as they were, they could not move very fast. Tim Nolan alone was staggering under the boat's sail, an oar, a musket, and a basket of provisions. Jerry Bird had the breaker of water hung at his back, and was equally heavily laden.

It was a great relief to Tom when he heard Pat shout out, "Here are the rocks, though not the sign of a cave can I see."

"Perhaps, if we skirt along them, we may find a still more sheltered place than this," observed Tom.

The party accordingly moved on, and just as Pat announced that his torch was beginning to burn his fingers, they found themselves in a recess of the rocks, where they were well sheltered from the wind, although they would obtain no protection from the rain when it should begin to fall. The end of the torch afforded them sufficient light to collect sticks for a fire, and by its light they were able to put up their tent. The side of the rock affording a back, it was made to slope from the rock down to the ground, so that the heaviest rain would run off. There was just room for all hands to get under it, closely packed; and after the fatigues of the day, they were very thankful to obtain such shelter. As far, indeed, as they themselves were concerned, they had no reason to complain. They had shelter, fire, food, and water.

"Let us see what you have brought, Billy?" said Gerald.

Billy produced three fish, which he had hung over his back. "I thought that we should want something for supper, and it is always wise to carry one's grub with one," he observed.

"Much obliged to you for your forethought," said Gerald; and Tim and Pat were summoned to cook the fish. The fire had been made up close under the rock, so that it was not much influenced by the wind. In a short time Tim announced that the supper was ready, "smoking hot," when a bottle of rum was produced from the provision basket.

"Now, lads," said Tom, as he poured out the liquor. "I do not want to stint you of your grog, but recollect that we have but a small supply, and my belief is that it may be many days before we get back to the ship, so a glass apiece is all I can give you."

The grog was mixed, and the seamen, with their young officers, sat round the fire, thinking just then very little of the past or future. The fish were pronounced excellent; while they sipped their grog one or the other alternately spun a yarn or sang a song. Tom Rogers must be excepted. He felt his responsibility as commanding the party, and he could not get over the consciousness that he ought to have returned at an earlier hour to the ship. This thought weighed down his spirits, although he tried not to allow his companions to discover his uneasiness. He felt also very anxious about the ship. If Jerry Bird was right in supposing that an accident had happened to the machinery, she might, during the hurricane, be exposed to the greatest possible danger; and if she was wrecked, they might have to remain for many months on the island, before they could find an opportunity of escaping.

Tom, before he came to sea, had often read about living on a desert island with one or two pleasant companions, and had thought that it would be very good fun. When the reality rose vividly before him, he could not but confess that he would rather be keeping watch on board, with a prospect of returning home to see his father, mother, and friends. When, however, it came to his turn to sing, he trolled forth, in his rich deep voice, "Cease, rude Boreas," or some other sea song of the same character, as if he had no anxious thoughts to trouble him. The blazing fire which they kept up served to dry their clothes.

When, about an hour later, the rain came down, as it is wont to do in the tropics, they all crept under the tent, taking care to carry the muskets and such things as would be damaged by the wet with them. Tom, in spite of his fatigue, lay awake for some time. He was thankful that they were safe on shore, and had been able to find a sheltered position for their encampment. The wind roared and howled in the most terrific manner among the forest trees. The very earth seemed to shake, as if it would topple down the high rock above them; but although branches, and sometimes large shrubs, torn up by the roots, flew over their heads, none fell on their tent. Sometimes, for several minutes together, crash succeeded crash, as huge trees were levelled with the ground. Then there would come a lull, and the wind would whistle mournfully, or rather moan, but only to recommence roaring more lustily than ever.

Tom wondered how his companions could sleep so soundly amid the uproar. The light of the fire, which came through the side of the tent, fell on their forms stretched out with their heads against the rock; while, in the lulls of the tempest, he could hear them all snoring away in concert. He was sufficiently well acquainted with the natural history of the Pacific Islands to be aware that there were no wild beasts to interfere with them, excepting the hogs, whose traces they had seen; and he had every reason to believe that the island was uninhabited. He thought it possible, however, that the rocks at the top of the cliff, loosened by the hurricane, might come tumbling down on their heads; but as only earth and small branches had hitherto fallen, he hoped that they would continue in their places. At all events, even should he and his companions move away, they were not likely to find more secure shelter. Should refuge be sought under the trees, they might prove still more treacherous. He kept an eye on the fire, fearing that a sudden blast might whisk the embers into the tent; but, as the canvas was thoroughly wet, that would take some time to burn. He got up two or three times, and, by standing with his back against the cliff, he avoided the rain which poured in torrents scarcely more than a foot in front of him. Excepting where the glare of the fire was cast upon the white tent on one side, the black rocks on the other, and the shrubs in front, all was pitchy darkness, though, on looking upwards, he could distinguish the tops of the trees waving to and fro against the sky. "I pray that the dear old *Dragon* may have escaped this!" he ejaculated more than once, as the hurricane, with apparently renewed strength, again and again hurled itself against the island. At length Desmond roused up.

"You must have had your two hours' watch or more. Tom," he said. "Just lie down and get a snooze; we may have a long pull before us, and there won't be much room for sleeping in the boat."

Tom, not sorry to be relieved, lay down, while Desmond took his place.

How long Tom had been sleeping he could not tell, when he and the rest of the party were aroused by a shot fired close to their oars, and, looking up, they saw Desmond with the musket at his shoulder, which he had just discharged.

"What did you fire at?" asked Tom.

"At a bear, or a wolf, or some big baste or other, to be shure," answered Desmond. "Whatever it was we shall find out, for it cannot be far off. I hit it, I am certain of that, for it gave a terrible growl, and bolted back into the bushes."

The fire had by this time almost burnt out, giving forth a faint glow, which scarcely afforded light sufficient to see any objects except those close to them, so that it would be useless to attempt searching for the wild beast which Desmond asserted he had shot. He acknowledged that he had dropped asleep, and that, on suddenly awakening, he had seen the animal's eyes glaring at him not ten yards off. Tom, on looking at his watch by the declining light of the fire, saw that it was nearly dawn. A change for the better had occurred. The strength of the hurricane had much abated, though the tree tops still waved backwards and forwards as the wind whistled and howled amid the branches, but it was with abated breath, while the rain had completely ceased. On looking up, small spaces in the clouds could be seen, through which, here and there, a star glittered brightly.

Jerry Bird, who ought to have been on the watch before, now took Desmond's place, and the party settled down again to wait for morning. Sailors are accustomed to short snatches of sleep. Even half an hour or less of rest was not to be despised, so that in less than a minute they all again had their eyes closed in happy forgetfulness of where they were. Tom required no calling; he had scarcely forgotten in his sleep what had happened, and no sooner had the pale light of early morn driven away the darkness of night, than, opening his eyes, he crept out of the tent over Bird, who had just dropped off. "I will let the rest sleep on, and see how things look," he said to himself. As he made his way over the fallen trunks towards the bay, he kept looking out to discover some accessible part of the hill, by which he might climb to the summit of the rock, under whose shelter they had slept, and which he supposed to be the highest point thereabouts, in order that he might obtain a wide view of the ocean around. He at length found a part, from whence by a little climbing he might reach the top of the hill. He had began his ascent, when he heard Desmond's voice shouting to him, and sitting down he waited for his messmate to come up. The rock was more rugged and uneven than they had at first supposed. Sometimes Desmond helped him up to a ledge, then he hauled Desmond after him. Here and there shrubs grew in the crevices of the rock, which assisted them in their ascent. At last they stood together on the top. On casting their eyes around, they could nowhere see the ship; indeed, they scarcely expected that she would have been in sight. As far as the eye could range to the southward and eastward, foam-crested giant waves leaped up and down, but already their motion was becoming less rapid, and they seemed to be tumbling lazily and slowly against each other, as if weary of their late exertions, though the breakers incessantly burst on the rocky coast, sending masses of foam flying far inland.

"Even should the ship appear, we are not likely to be able to get out to her to-day," observed Desmond, pointing to the entrance of the bay, through which the seas came tossing and foaming. "It seems a wonder how we got through last night."

"We may indeed be thankful to heaven that we were not swamped," said Tom; "but I should not be surprised if we find, within a few hours, should the ship appear, that we can get off to her. There has scarcely been time for the sea to go down since the hurricane ceased blowing; I do hope that the other boats got on board, or they will have run great risk of being lost."

"Perhaps our shipmates landed," observed Desmond; "and we shall meet them before long. I should be very glad to know for certain that Archie and Jos Green and Mr Joy are safe, though it is a terrible thing to think that the ship may have been cast away."

"We will hope for the best," answered Tom; "and now we will go down and see how the boat has fared. I am somewhat anxious about her, though I don't see how we could have secured her better than we did."

The descent was nearly as difficult as the climb up the hill, and they ran a great risk, when leaping from rock to rock, of slipping off and tumbling a dozen or more feet at a time down to the next level. They had nearly reached the bottom, when they saw Billy Blueblazes and Jerry Bird looking up towards them. The countenances of both wore an aspect of dismay.

"What has happened?" asked Tom.

"The boat has gone!" answered Billy; "we can't see her anywhere, not even a bit of her wreck."

"Faith! that's bad news," exclaimed Desmond; "but did you look everywhere? for, remember, everywhere means a good wide space."

"No, we did not go right up to the spot, for there was no use in doing that," answered Billy.

"Then we will, and perhaps we may discover some signs which may indicate the direction in which she has been driven," said Tom.

They accordingly set off. Tom observed what Billy had failed to do, that the shape of the beach was greatly altered, the wind having driven the sand far higher up than usual, so that in some parts it had risen to the height of the bank on which grass and shrubs grew. Indeed, a portion of the grassy ground had itself been covered up by the sand.

"What shall we do without the boat?" cried Billy; "we shall have to spend our lives here, I suppose, if the ship has been lost, and the men say that they think she had very little chance of escaping."

"I hope they are wrong in their conjectures," answered Tom; "and as for the boat, I am not quite so certain that she is lost, although we may have some trouble in finding her."

On arriving at that part of the beach where the boat had been left, Tom looked round in every direction, and examined carefully the bushes and herbage along the edge of the beach.

"If she was driven in this direction, she would have broken some of these bushes, but they do not appear to have been injured," he observed. "Now, let us see whereabouts she lay. Do you think you can tell, Bird?" The seaman examined the ground.

"I remember coming through just such a clump of bushes as these, directly after I left her; and look there, sir, there is her rudder and a stretcher," and he enumerated other articles belonging to the boat. Then stepping back, he said, "I'm sure it was just hereabouts where she lay."

"Then, depend upon it, here we shall find her. Don't you see the sand has blown over her, and she is safe enough within it. To save ourselves trouble, we will dig a line parallel with the beach, and another at right angles, and the chances are we shall strike some part of her gunwale before long."

"Shall I go and call the other men?" asked Billy.

"They are cooking the breakfast, sir," observed Bird.

"Let them go on by all means," said Tom; "if we find the boat we will come back afterwards and dig her up."

They immediately set to work, under Tom's directions, but the sand had risen even higher than they had supposed, and as they had only the boat's stretchers and their hands to work with, it was a slow business.

"I've thought, sir, of a quicker way of finding her than this," observed Jerry; and taking his axe, he cut a short pole with a sharp point, and ran it down though the sand, along the line which Tom had marked out. "There's something here, sir," he cried out at length, and forthwith a hole was dug at the spot. Jerry then plunged down his hand. "No doubt about it, sir; there's the boat's side, and if the weight of the sand has not bulged her out, she will be all to rights."

"I have no fear on that score," observed Tom. "The sand has probably driven up around her, and afforded her sides support. I am very thankful that we took the precaution of banking her up as we did, or I am pretty sure that she would have been rolled over and over, and knocked to pieces."

The party having satisfied themselves as to the safety of the boat, returned to their camp, where they found Tim and Pat busily engaged over a huge fire in cooking pork chops.

"Why, where did these come from?" asked Tom.

"Shure, sir, they are from a porker which we found in the bush. It's my belief it's the very baste Mr Desmond shot last night. He was not quite dead, and showed some fight, but we finished him, and cut him up in a jiffy."

"I congratulate you on your success," said Tom.

"To tell you the truth," said Desmond, "I was half dreaming at the time; and I was not quite sure this morning whether I had shot anything or not, but I'm mighty glad to find that my dream has come true."

The pork chops were found very satisfactory, and it was still more so to know that there was an abundance of animal food in the island; for if there was one hog, there would to a certainty be many more; at the same time, they would have prevented the increase of roots which would otherwise have afforded nourishment.

"As hogs live here, there, are probably acorns and nuts of various sorts, so that even should the cocoa-nuts and bananas run short, we need be under no apprehension of wanting vegetable diet," said Tom to Desmond. "Again I say we have good reason to be thankful that we have landed on an island so abounding in provisions."

"I wish we had brought off some tea, coffee, and sugar," said Billy. "I should have enjoyed my breakfast much more."

"Be thankful for what you have got," observed Tom.

Before setting out to commence the digging up of the boat, Tom suggested that they should form some rough spades, without which the operation would be a very tedious one. They had fortunately brought with them two axes for cutting fire-wood, and with these Jerry and Pat managed to chop out from the fallen branches six rough spades. They would have finished them off in better style had Tom allowed them. Having ascertained the exact position of the boat, by running down a pointed stick, they commenced operations. They were much surprised at the enormous pit they had to dig before they even reached the gunwale of the boat. The digging was easy enough; the labour consisted in heaving the sand to a sufficient distance. All hands were getting very hungry. Billy, as usual, was the first to cry out.

"What do you say to dinner, Rogers?"

Tom looked at his watch, and directed Pat to go to the camp and prepare dinner, while the rest continued to work as before. It took them till noon to clear away the sand as far down as the gunwale, as of course it was necessary to dig a much wider space all round the boat than simply her width. The sun, too, had now become excessively hot, and the only coverings they had for their heads were straw hats.

Tom suggested that they should stick some large leaves or small branches into the bands, by which means a more effectual shelter could be formed for their heads. In spite of the heat, they returned with good appetites to the camp.

"Bedad, it's fortunate we have got anything to eat at all," exclaimed Pat, as they approached. "Just as I came up, what should I see but a couple of porkers poking their noses into the tent; in another minute they would have got hold of the meat and fish I had hung up ready for cooking. I would have turned them into pork pretty quickly, but before I could get hold of a musket, they had scampered away back into the woods; but we'll be even with them before long. When I went to look for the rest of the hog, if the bastes hadn't eaten up their brother, barring the hide, and that they had been quarrelling over, by the way it was torn to pieces." There was an ample supply of pork, and fish, and bananas, cocoa-nuts and vegetables, for that day's dinner Tom had to consider what provision should be made for supper, and the next day. Eager as he was to get the boat dug out, in case the ship should appear, he would not allow his companions to work for a couple of hours or more, for fear of their suffering from a stroke of the sun, whose fierce rays beat down with terrific force on the sand. Pat, who was well inured to a far greater heat, under the line itself, in the meantime took one of the muskets, "to try and kill some game," he said, "or one of the porkers which had lately paid him a visit."

The rest of the party lay down in the shade under the rock, to prepare themselves for their afternoon's work. Pat had been absent for some time, and a couple of shots had been heard; but lately no sound had reached them, when again they heard a report at no great distance. Presently he was seen scampering along, a big boar close at his heels. It appeared as if the next instant the creature's tusks would have run into him, when he seized the branch of a free and threw himself up upon it, while the animal ripped off the hem of his broad trousers. Luckily the canvas gave way, or Pat would have been brought to the ground. The boar looked up at his late opponent as if he still meditated vengeance; but suddenly seeing the party under the cliff, he came towards them, tearing up the ground in his fury, with his sharp tusks. Fortunately the other musket was loaded.

"Stand by, for advance or flight," cried Tom, seizing the weapon. Bird grasped the boat-hook, while Desmond and Tim each took an axe, Billy, having no arms, fulfilled the latter part of the order, by beginning to climb up a ledge of the rock on one side of the cliff. It was a moment of dreadful suspense, for, should Tom miss, he well knew that the boar's tusks might, in the next instant, pierce him through. Fortunately the animal caught sight of Billy as he was climbing up the cliff. This for a moment distracted his attention, and, instead of coming directly at Tom and his companions, it swerved a little on one side. Seeing, however, that Billy had got beyond its reach, it once more came galloping towards them, singling out Jerry, who was the most conspicuous object, for its attack. Tom waited until it got within twelve feet, when he fired. The bullet hit the animal, but did not stop it. Jerry sprang on one side to avoid its charge, and then drove his boat-hook into its neck, bearing it to the ground. On this Tim and Desmond sprang forward, and, before it could again rise, dealt it several heavy strokes with their axes, preventing it from committing any further mischief.

"Hurrah; you've finished the baste, I hope," cried Pat, who had been watching the proceedings from his bough, and now came hurrying forward.

"I'd somehow or other missed a couple of pigs, when I caught sight of this big fellow taking a snooze in the sun. I was creeping up to him, when he opened his wicked eyes, and if I hadn't taken to my heels he would have had his tusks through and through me. At last I stopped behind a free and gave him a shot; but he didn't mind it at all, at all, by reason that the bullet flew over his head, and I had again to run for it. However, 'All's well that ends well,' and, sure, we will be having him for supper, with the greatest pleasure in the world."

After this specimen of rat's sportsmanlike qualities, Tom resolved not to trust him with the musket again, as it was necessary carefully to husband their powder and shot. As, however, Pat possessed very good qualifications for a butcher, he was left to cut up the boar, while the rest of the party returned to the boat, he being directed to rejoin them as soon as he had secured the joints.

Digging out the boat was severe labour, as to prevent the sand slipping back it had to be thrown several feet on either side of the boat. They then had to cut a channel down to the water. Tom soon saw that they could not hope to get their boat afloat for another whole day at the soonest. Diligently as they worked, the sun was sinking rapidly towards the horizon before the boat was free of sand. They examined her anxiously, fearing that her sides might have been forced out; but, as far as they could ascertain, she had received no material injury.

"We must take another look-out for the ship, before it gets dark," exclaimed Tom; and he and Desmond set off to ascend the hill, from whence they could obtain an extensive view of the ocean around them. In vain they strained their eyes; no sail was in sight—not a speck appeared above the horizon. The sea was rolling in lazy undulations, here and there flecked with foam, which sparkled brightly in the rays of the setting sun, while the sea-fowl were once more venturing forth from their rocky homes in search of prey.

"She must have run a long distance before the gale, and it will take her some time to beat back," observed Tom. "We must not give her up yet."

"I should think not, indeed," answered Desmond. "It would have been rather inconvenient if she had come, and we had not got the boat afloat. However, we must manage to get a signal-staff set up to-morrow morning, in case she should appear, that they may know where we are, and send in to help us."

Tom agreed with Desmond, and they accordingly arranged to cut a flag-staff the first thing the next day, and manufacture a flag which might be seen from the ship. Descending the rock, they returned to their companions, who were still hard at work. Pat, however, had been sent back, to light the fire and prepare supper. The party continued digging in the sand until darkness at length compelled them to give over. They had no little difficulty in making their way back to the camp, until their eyes were gladdened by the sight of Pat's blazing fire.

"We must compliment you on your pork chops," exclaimed Billy, holding up the remains of one which he had been discussing with the help of his clasp knife. "I'll trouble you for another, as soon as it's done brown."

"You're welcome to it, sir; and, bedad, I'm mighty better pleased to be cooking his hams, than for him to have had his tusks through mine," answered Pat.

The supper was pronounced excellent, though they had nothing but cold water from a neighbouring rivulet with which to wash it down. Tim suggested that a thimbleful of rum would be mighty pleasant.

Tom refused to serve out any of their limited supply, having determined to keep it in case of emergency. Although he did not express his fears to his companions, he could not help dreading that some accident might have happened to the *Dragon*. The night passed quickly away. As soon as it was daylight Tom and Desmond ascended to their look-out place. They were again doomed to disappointment. The sea had become perfectly calm, a light air occasionally only rippling the surface.

"It will take her a good many hours to get up to our island, even if she is now only just out of sight," observed Tom. "Still we must get a flag-staff set up, in case she should appear before we can launch the boat, and we shall be fortunate if we can do that before night." As soon as breakfast was over, Tom having told the men what was wanted, all hands went in search of a tree fit for the purpose. None, however, were discovered. At last it was agreed that a young cocoa-nut tree must be cut down. This was soon done by Jerry and Tim, while the rest recommenced their attempt to free the boat. All hands were required to get the flag-staff to the top of the rock and set it up. The three men offered their handkerchiefs, which with others belonging to the midshipmen formed a tolerably sized flag. As they had no halyards, it was fixed with rope yarns to the top of the staff, before it was set up. A crevice was found in the rock, into which it was driven, and fixed on either side with large stones.

"That will show clearly enough where we are, and if they can count the number of handkerchiefs, they will know we are all right," observed Desmond.

"I trust that the ship will come," said Tom, though he could not throw much confidence into his tone. "Now, lads, we must go back and dig away at our boat. I should like to see her afloat to-night or early to-morrow morning."

In spite of the heat, they toiled on, not even returning to the camp for dinner; Pat instead being sent to bring provisions and water. Notwithstanding their perseverance, the work was not finished when Tom set off alone to have another look out from Flag-staff Hill. He was soon seen coming back.

"Not a sign of her," he said; and taking up his spade he resumed his labours. A heap of sand still remained between the boat and the water, that had to be removed before she could be launched.

"We must get rollers under her, or it will be more than we can do to drag her into the water," observed Jerry, as he stamped his foot into the soft yielding sand under her keel.

"You are right," said Tom, "and we must make them the first thing in the morning."

The songs sung and yarns spun that evening were not so cheerful as they had been; indeed, all hands were so sleepy that they were glad to turn in as soon as supper was over. Tom hoped against hope, that the next morning the ship would appear, had no accident happened to her. Even without her machinery she would surely be able to beat up to the island by this time.

Tom was at the flag-staff as soon as the light enabled him to see his way up the hill. He waited, gazing anxiously at the horizon, while the ruddy glow which suffused itself over the sky, announced the rising of the sun. But no sail appeared. "She will not come at all," he exclaimed to himself; "she must have been driven on the rocks during that fearful night, and probably all hands have perished. Poor Archie, I wish he had come with us, and I am very, very sorry for all the rest."

Tom, however, well knew that he must not give way to his melancholy forebodings, and that, at all events, it was his duty to try and keep up the spirits of his companions. On returning to the tent he put on as unconcerned a countenance as possible, and sat down to breakfast as if he had nothing on his mind. The high flavour of the pork showed him that they must, in the first place, look out for another hog, and some means must be found for preserving it. Pat asserted that the hams were still very good, and Tom suggested that they should be immediately smoked, until salt could be scraped from the rocks, or obtained by evaporation. "You see we have got plenty to do, and even if we spend a month here, we shall have no time to be idle," he observed.

Jerry and Tim, before they recommenced digging, cut with their axes a number of rollers, which were then placed under the boat's keel, when with renewed ardour all hands set to work to clear away the intervening sand. It took, however, much longer than they had expected, and another day was drawing to a close before they could attempt to begin launching her. She was moved, however, but a few feet cut of the hollow in which she had been imbedded, as there was no object to be gained that night by putting her in the water, although the bay was now so smooth that she might have floated in perfect safety.

Tom made his usual visit to Flag-staff Hill, and came back with the same report as on the previous evening.

"Before we launch our boat," he said, when he rejoined the party at breakfast, "we must dismantle our tent; and indeed it is not wise to wear out our sail by using it as a roof. We may want it, and we shall certainly require the oars. I therefore propose, should the ship not appear by noon, to build a hut in the place of the tent, and we shall then have shelter, should we require it, at night. We cannot tell what we may need. The hurricane season is not yet over, we may depend upon that. We came in for the first blow, and there may be several others before the weather becomes settled."

"What! Do you think the ship's not coming back for us?" asked Billy, in an anxious tone. "I should like to change my clothes, and I wish we had some tea and sugar, and some hard tack, and pepper, mustard, and all sorts of things."

"As to the ship's coming back, it's possible she may not," observed Tom. "If she does not, we must manage to do without the things we should like to have, and make the best of those we have got."

"That's the right sort of philosophy," observed Jerry Bird, who knew that he might take a liberty which another man might not, and talk freely to his officers.

As soon as breakfast was over, the oars and gear of the boat were carried down to the beach, when, with the help of rollers, she was, all hands hauling together, after some labour, run into the water.

As Tom had feared might be the case, it was soon discovered that, either from the hot atmosphere or the pressure to which she had been subjected, she leaked considerably. The leaks, however, it was hoped, would partially fill up, though she would require some fresh caulking, and a coat of tar, or some substitute, if tar was not to be procured. The hour of noon approached, and, in spite of the heat, Tom and Desmond climbed to the flag-staff. They looked around the horizon, and then at each other.

"I am afraid she will not come at all," exclaimed Desmond.

"I feared as much from the first," answered Tom.

"Then what do you propose doing?" asked Desmond. "I don't wish to have to live on here month after month, or for what we can tell year after year, while our fellows are fighting the Chinese, and all the rest of the world, perhaps."

"No, nor do I," said Tom. "We must fit our boat as well as we can for sea, and try and make our way, either back to Japan, or to the Ladrones, to which we were bound; but, as I said before, it won't do to put to sea until the hurricane season is over. Even in fine weather it will be a pretty long trip in an open boat; but people have gone as far, or much farther, and what others have done we can do."

"I am ready for anything you think best," answered Desmond, "and I am sure the rest will be, but we must try and fit the boat for a long voyage, and the sooner we set about it the better."

"It will be a difficult job to do that without tools," observed Tom.

"Faith, I forgot that," remarked Desmond. "Still, as you often say, 'Where there's a will there's a way.' As we shall want our sail, we must try and manufacture some thick matting instead of canvas, to fix over the bows to raise the gunwale a foot or two, to keep out the sea. Then for provisions, we shall have to salt down as many hogs as we can kill, dry a stock of yams, and carry our water in cocoa-nut shells."

45

"I am glad, Gerald, that you have thought about the matter; that's just what I was going to propose," said Tom.

"Of course," cried Gerald. "I have been thinking of that and a number of other things besides while I was digging in the sand, though I did not like to talk about them until the time came for action."

Thus the two midshipmen discussed their plans for the future. On their return to the camp, as the time fixed upon by Tom had passed and the ship had not arrived, the tent was dismantled and Tom set the men to work to cut poles of sufficient length to serve for rafters and uprights. Their tent had answered so well that it was agreed that the hut should have a roof of the same shape. The walls were formed by closely interlacing the uprights with creepers, which also served to bind on the large pandanus leaves which they used for covering the roof. The hut being nearly completed, Tom and Desmond set out, armed with their muskets, to try and kill a hog or some small game. Billy wanted to go, but Tom advised him to remain and assist in finishing the hut.

"If one of those fellows were to run at you, what could you do without a weapon of some sort?"

"But I'd take the boat-hook," said Billy.

"A wild bear would be afther laughing at it in your hands," observed Desmond.

Though they saw several hogs, which animals seemed to abound in the island, they were unable to get near enough to obtain a fair shot. While in search of hogs, their object was also to explore the island. They made their way across to the northern side. It consisted of deep indentations and high rocks, to the top of one of which they climbed; they could make out in the far distance another island to the north of them. Though they narrowly scanned the ocean in every direction, no sail was to be seen.

"I am determined not to give her up altogether," said Tom; "but still, if she has escaped shipwreck, I cannot account for the commander not coming to look for us. My only idea is that by some mistake or other he supposes we were lost, and that being driven a long way to the southward, he does not think it worth while to come so far out of his course."

On their way back they caught sight of a large number of good-sized birds perched thickly in a tree, apparently intending to roost there for the night. Having drawn their bullets, they loaded with small shot, and firing into the midst of the birds, they brought down a dozen, which proved to be a species of pigeon.

"We have got something for supper, at all events," cried Desmond as he ran to pick up the birds and to finish off a few which were still fluttering on the ground.

Their ill-success in hog-hunting made them determine the next day to go out fishing in the boat. It need not be said that either Tom or Desmond paid periodical visits to the flag-staff. So often had they been disappointed that they at last gave up all expectation of seeing the ship. Their fishing excursion, though not as successful as the first, had produced a good supply of fish, some of which they ate fresh and the rest they dried in the sun and smoked over a wood fire. They had, however, to keep baling nearly the whole of the time. This satisfied them that they must caulk the boat before they could venture out to sea in her. All hands were now busily employed in a variety of ways. Pat had woven some baskets with long grass, and Billy and Tim, each carrying one, went out in search of salt, of which they found a plentiful supply in the hollows of the rocks, close down to the sea.

Tom and Desmond searched in all directions for trees which might yield pitch or a gum of some description which would serve to pay over the outside of the boat, but they searched in vain.

"We must find some substitute for pitch, or we cannot accomplish our voyage, that's very certain," said Tom.

The boat was constantly kept wet; at last they tried sinking her for several hours together, but her planks would not swell sufficiently to stop the leaks. They were almost in despair.

"Had we only a good supply of powder, we might live in luxury on fish, flesh, and fowl, with plenty of vegetables; but without the powder, should we get a continuance of had weather, we may be reduced to the vegetable diet," said Desmond, as they were sitting round the fire at supper.

"As to the hogs, we may be pretty sure of catching them," observed Pat; "we can soon find out their runs, and by digging pitfalls it won't be long before a porker will find his way in."

"Then the sooner you can manage to dig a pitfall and catch a porker the better," said Tom.

"That will be the very thing I'll set about to-morrow morning, with Tim as my mate," answered Pat.

Tim agreed, and so it was arranged.

"I should like to get half a dozen hogs well salted and smoked, so that there may be no fear of the meat turning bad," said Tom; "we cannot tell how long our voyage may last, and it will not do for us to run short of provisions if we can help it. We must also catch and cure a supply of fish, and they, with the yams, will serve us for provisions. Nothing else will be likely to keep, though perhaps we may obtain birds and vegetables at some of the islands we may pass."

"But it won't do to land, sir, unless we know the people who inhabit them," said Pat. "Where I was living so long they would have knocked any visitors on the head and eaten them up, to a certainty."

"My belief is that the people on this side of the equator are generally well disposed towards strangers," said Tom. "I heard the commander say so only a short time ago, and he had been reading some books on the subject." So altogether Tom was persuaded and imbued his companions with the same idea that the proposed voyage could be performed without any extraordinary risk, and all hands looked forward to the time when they might venture to commence it—not that they were tired of remaining on the island— but even the men had no wish to spend their days there, and the midshipmen were naturally anxious to be employed on active service. Next morning, Tom, having gone as usual to the flag-staff to take a look out, as he was descending, saw several dark objects moving on the sand of the bay below him. Some were far up on the dry sand, others nearer the water. "Those must be turtle," he said to himself; "we may catch some of them if we are quick about it, before they return to the water." He hurried back to the camp and told his companions what he had seen. They all followed him as fast as they could scamper towards the bay. Each man got hold of a stick or weapon of some sort. The instinct of the turtle telling them that enemies were approaching, those farthest up the beach began to make their way, vigorously working their fins, towards the water. Tom and Desmond, who were ahead, managed to get their sticks under a good-sized one, which they turned over without much difficulty, and they then attacked three others in succession, throwing them over on their backs. The rest of the party had now come up. Jerry and Tim, in the same way, turned over two more. Their success encouraged Billy, who, being ambitious, tackled a big fellow, which was scrambling away at a great rate towards the water. Billy, who was as courageous as a lion, seized hold of its fins, and in an instant he was covered over with showers of sand thrown up by its other fin, while the turtle showed no disposition to stop. Billy shouted to his companions to come and help him. Pat, who though the last on the field, having just turned a turtle, rushed forward and seized the big fellow by the other fin; but the creature had got good way and was not to be stopped by the united efforts of the midshipman and the Irish sailor, who in another instant were dragged into the water. It was still too shallow for the turtle to swim, but it used its four flappers with so much effect against its two assailants, as to give them a thorough shower-bath.

"We must have him; help, help!" shouted Billy; "don't let him go, Pat!"

"That I'll not, shure!" answered Pat, who maintained his hold like grim death to the hind flapper. "Tim, me darlin', be quick here, or the baste will be off. Jerry, man, lend a hand."

"Rogers, Desmond, do come and help, or the fellow will get away after all our trouble," shouted Billy.

Thus summoned, the whole party came to the assistance of the two heroes, Tim in his eagerness toppling over on his nose in the shallow water. He quickly, however, recovered himself, and he and Jerry seizing one of the fore flappers, and Tom and Gerald the other. They managed to stop the progress of the unfortunate turtle, though not until they had all been well wetted.

With a heave they turned the turtle over and dragged it up again on the dry beach. By this time nearly all the other turtle had escaped; but another big fellow had just got into the water, and was paddling off, when Pat in his eagerness threw himself upon it, shouting to his companions for help. Billy dashed forward, when Pat at the same moment contrived to turn over the turtle, but, unhappily for poor Billy, his foot slipping, down he fell with the turtle on the top of him; though his head was above water, the turtle almost smothered him with water and sand, which its flappers sent flying into his face.

"Help, help!" he kept crying out. Pat, in his efforts to release the midshipman, also slipped down under the turtle, which was all the time working itself into deep water, and dragging its assailants, who still held on, with it.

Tom and Gerald, however, came to their rescue; but already the turtle had got into water of sufficient depth to enable it to recover its proper position, and with such good effect did it use its flappers, that, in spite of the exertions of the midshipmen and Pat, who had to choose between being drawn into deep water at a risk of being drowned or seized by a lurking shark, or losing their prize, they instinctively let go, and the turtle diving, joined its more fortunate companions who had escaped. As, however, more turtle had been caught than the party could possibly eat, they had no cause to complain.

"Hurrah! I don't mind the wetting," cried Billy, as he shook himself like a spaniel on coming out of the water. "We shall live for many a day like aldermen."

"There's little chance of our eating them up before they turn bad," observed Desmond.

"You need not fear that, sir," said Pat; "we will build a house for them, where they will live as happy as princes till we want to cook them?" His plan was to form an enclosure with a roof over it to protect the turtle from the rays of the sun, and to keep them well supplied with wet sea-weed.

"I wonder I did not at once think about that," said Tom. "We will do as you propose immediately."

The axes were soon at work, and the enclosure was formed of sufficient size to contain all their turtle, before they returned to breakfast, dragging with them one of the smaller turtle, which was destined to serve them as food for the day. They had turtle steaks for, breakfast, turtle soup for dinner, and turtle again at night.

"It is a pity we have not some port wine, and cayenne pepper, and some lemons," cried Billy.

"We have no cause to complain, since we have abundance of salt," said Tom. "For my part, I think we have every reason to be thankful for the ample supply of food with which we have been provided."

As day after day went by the hope that the *Dragon* would return became fainter and fainter. Tom made up his mind that if they were to escape from the island, they must perform the voyage in the boat; but as he examined her again and again he could not help confessing that she was but ill-suited for the undertaking in her present state. Whenever they went out fishing they had to keep constantly baling, so that they ran a great risk of going down. He had no anxiety about provisions, though there would be a difficulty in preserving them sufficiently to stand the constant exposure to the sun and wet. That risk must, however, be run. He charged Pat and Tim to thoroughly salt and smoke the pork and fish. He directed them also to clear out a number of cocoa-nuts to serve as bottles for holding water. Pat had succeeded in catching two hogs in his pit-fall, and when the subject of carrying water was discussed, he offered to sew up the skins, so as to form two big leathern bottles.

"Where will you find the needles and thread to sew them up?" asked Tom.

"The needles! shure, I'd be afther makin' them from bone, and there would be no difficulty in finding the thread."

Though Tom allowed all preparations to go on, his mind was not at all easy in regard to the condition of the boat, and Desmond agreed with him that, unless her leaks could be stopped, it would be madness to put to sea.

While the men, therefore, continued working at their several tasks Tom had assigned to them, assisted by Billy, who was not fond of long walks, he and Desmond continued their search for pitch or something which would answer as a substitute. Desmond had heard of pitch springs, and looked about for them for some time, until Tom recollected that such were alone found in volcanic regions, and that they could only expect to discover some vegetable substance.

At last they determined to explore the whole of the island, which would occupy them some two or tree days.

Taking one of the muskets, they filled their wallets—which Pat lad manufactured for them of plaited grass—with a store of dried yams, salt pork, and fish, which they carried in case they should be unsuccessful in obtaining game. They charged Billy, should the *Dragon* appear, to fire off the musket left behind, and also to light a beacon fire on the summit of Flag-staff Hill, the smoke of which they would probably be able to distinguish from any part of the island. Bidding farewell to their companions, they first directed their course towards the south-east end of the island, which, as it had a rocky and barren appearance, they had not yet visited.

Chapter Three.

Tom and Desmond discover a wreck—Horrible scene—Find tools and stores on board—Return with their treasures to the camp—Visit the wreck in their boat, and bring back stores—The boat fitted for sea—Last night on shore—Setting sail—Steer for Japan—Wind changes—Stand to the south—A long calm—Followed by a shark—A breeze, but against them—Running short of provisions—Reduced to yams and oil—Boat run down by a whaler—Desmond and Tim missing—Tom and Jerry find them.

Tom and Gerald trudged manfully forward on their survey of the island. The path was very uneven. They kept as near to the coast as they could, and frequently they could only make their way, on account of the ruggedness of the rocks, by turning inland. They had to clamber over fallen trunks or to cut a path with their axe through thick creepers. At other times they had to climb wild rocks and rugged hills, then to descend again, either into some valley running up from the shore or to the shore itself. Their object being, however, to examine the productions of the island, they generally kept away from the beach. They had made good eight or ten miles, when, ascending a rocky height, they obtained a view of the sea and a line of coast for some distance. Suddenly Tom stopped and put his hand on his companion's arm.

"Tell me, Desmond, what do you think is that dark object out there? It is curiously shaped, like—or, is it—"

"A vessel, to be sure," exclaimed Desmond, whose eyes had been turned towards the spot. "How could she have come there without our seeing her?"

"She may possibly have been there for some time," said Tom. "Certainly she must have been wrecked during a gale before we landed here, and she appears to be thrown high up on the rocks."

As they got up to the vessel, they saw that she had been driven on shore between two ledges, where she had remained fixed. It had probably been high tide when she was wrecked, as the water had completely left her. After much difficulty, by scrambling along over the rocks, the midshipmen got alongside, then hauled themselves on board by some ropes which were hanging over the bows. The vessel was a fore-top-sail schooner. Her masts were still standing, and her canvas was hoisted, though torn to tatters, now fluttering in the breeze. A horrible odour came up from the main hold as they went aft, and on looking down what was their horror to see three bodies, one apparently a white seaman, from his dress, the other two evidently blacks, from the few rags still hanging to their remains. The two midshipmen anxious to accomplish the survey of the vessel, hastened aft. About the companion hatch and on the bulwarks, the wood had been chipped off, as if by bullets, and there were other signs that a severe struggle had taken place at some time or other on board. They descended the companion ladder; at the foot were stains of blood, traces of which were discovered on the steps. They expected, from the odour which pervaded the whole vessel, to find some festering body in the cabin, but no human being, either dead or alive, was there. They discovered, however, what had evidently been the captain's log-book, by which it was shown that the vessel was the *Ark*, of Brisbane, Queensland, and that she had been engaged in carrying labourers from various islands to serve as apprentices for three years in that colony. How she had come thus far north it was impossible to say. The last entry in the log showed that she was in the latitude of the Caroline group; so that if she had been deserted there, she must have drifted several hundred miles. Tom and Desmond concluded that the blacks must have risen on the white crew, and that the latter, after defending themselves desperately, must have been overcome, while the former had probably swum on shore. One thing was certain, that a terrible tragedy had been enacted on board. The dead bodies below could tell no tales; probably they had fallen in the struggle and been left there by their companions. Perhaps the blacks, after murdering the crew, had steered to the northward, fancying that their own islands lay in that direction.

"We may suppose anything we like," said Tom; "but we shall not get nearer the truth. However, we will take care of the log, and see if anything more can be got out of it. We will see now if the vessel contains anything likely to be useful, and if there is, we must send and fetch it without delay, as another gale might knock her to pieces."

Before they could further continue their search they had to come up and take fresh air; and they then again descended into the little cabin. No sooner had they commenced their search than they found a set of carpenter's tools, some parcels of nails, and several other articles which they required for repairing their boat.

"These are indeed treasures," said Tom, as he examined them. "Now, if we can only find a cask of tar, we shall be fortunate."

"That most likely is forward, or in the hold," said Desmond.

"Ugh! I don't like having to go into the hold," said Tom; "but we must go down, if we do not find what we want forward."

Nearly all the articles they wanted most were in the after cabin: a quadrant, a chart, canvas and rope, sail-maker's needles, twine—indeed, almost everything they could possibly require. They at once placed, ready for packing up, the things which were of the most value to them, such as some of the tools, the quadrant, and chart, a spy-glass, and other articles. They then, as they were unwilling to remain longer on board than was necessary, made their way forward. Almost one of the first objects which their eyes encountered as they examined the fore hold was a cask of tar, which had been got up apparently for use; there were also oil, turpentine, white lead, and brushes.

"I only wish we had time and skill, and we might, instead of repairing our own boat, have built another better fitted for our intended voyage. Perhaps we could get the vessel off?" suggested Desmond.

"You would not say that if you saw her at high tide, when the water must flow in and out of her, for her bottom is like a sieve," answered Tom. "We must not think of launching her, or of building another boat; but we may improve our craft, so as to make her thoroughly seaworthy."

As the tackles were at hand, they at once hoisted the tar-barrel on deck; but by this time it was impossible to remain longer on board, and therefore, doing up the more valuable articles in two parcels, Tom having first descended, Desmond lowered them over the side to him. Altogether their packages weighed a good deal; but, delighted with their acquisition, they trudged along right merrily, hoping to get back before night.

"We shall astonish them," exclaimed Desmond, "when they see us and the things we have brought."

They had no little difficulty in getting back, and had frequently to stop and rest; but eager to join their comrades, they persevered, and at length, as night closed on them, they caught sight of the welcome fire under the cliff. Pat had just concocted their potful of turtle soup, and had some yams roasting in the embers. He and the rest could scarcely believe their eyes when they saw the treasures Tom and Desmond had brought. The men were all eager to set off the next day. Tom, however, determined to go in the boat, as there was a landing-place not far off, and the weather promised to be fine. Next morning they accordingly launched their boat, carrying several cocoa-nut shells with which to bale her out, not forgetting to take also a supply of provisions.

The wind was off the land, the water smooth; and setting the sail, they skimmed merrily along outside the reefs, keeping a bright look out for any which might be just below the surface.

The only disagreeable part of the expedition was the necessity of keeping two bands constantly baling. This showed how utterly impossible it would have been to have attempted the proposed voyage before the boat had been repaired. They found a sandy beach about a quarter of a mile from the wreck. Here they hauled the boat up, and all hands at once eagerly hastened on board. Pat suggested that the first thing to be done was to bury the bodies, so that they might search the hold without inconvenience; and he and Tim agreed to perform the disagreeable task. Having found an old sail, they placed the remains in it. Among the articles on board were a couple of spades, so that having dragged the bodies to a piece of soft ground inside the rocks, they quickly dug a grave, in which the white man and the blacks were placed together.

"They'll not fight there," said Tim, "whatever they may have done while they had life in them."

The hold was then washed down, after which some cases of gunpowder having been found, Tom devoted a portion to fumigating the hold. They were now able to search the vessel thoroughly. Almost everything they could possibly require was discovered in her. Still Tim was seen searching about, as eagerly as at first. At length he gave a shout.

"Hurrah!" he cried out, "here is the treasure, my boys;" and he produced a box of tobacco, in which was still a considerable portion of its original contents. "It will serve us for many a day to come."

Some pipes were also found, and Tom at once gave the men leave to take a smoke, for which they were truly grateful after the unpleasant duty they had performed. The midshipmen in the mean time were engaged in selecting the articles which they considered would be of the most use, so that should any accident happen to the wreck before they could return, they might at all events have secured the most necessary things.

In Tom's eyes the cask of tar was the most valuable. The voyage had apparently been a long one, as nearly all the provisions had been exhausted. A small barrel of biscuit, with a few pieces of beef at the bottom of a cask, were almost the only provisions remaining on board. There was, however, some tea, coffee, and sugar, and they did not forget to carry off some cooking utensils, as well as a few cups, plates, a tea-pot, some knives and forks, as also several articles of clothing, which would enable them to enjoy the luxury of a change of linen.

Tom at first thought of shifting their head-quarters to the little bay where their boat was drawn up; but on consideration, as it was in an exposed situation, he and Desmond agreed to return to their original camp. They found a sufficient amount of planking to raise the boat's gunwales, and to put a small deck forward and some lockers aft. Altogether they were highly satisfied with the treasures they had obtained, and having laden their boat, they once more put off. The wind again favouring them, they had a pleasant sail back to the bay. It was night by the time they landed their stores and had conveyed the articles of food to their encampment.

Tom and Desmond were in much better spirits than they had been before. They had now, as they could make their boat seaworthy, great hopes of performing their intended voyage. They had a good store of provisions, with a compass, chart, quadrant, and almanac, so that they could direct their course in any direction which was considered advisable. They were still in some doubt whether they should go on to the Ladrones or steer for Japan. In the latter case they would be likely to fall in with an English man-of-war, but the voyage must be difficult, and they finally decided to be guided by the winds and the state of the weather.

Japan was certainly nearer, but they might make a port at which no Englishmen were settled, and it was very uncertain how they might be treated by the natives. They hoped, too, that the *Dragon* might have escaped and managed to reach the Ladrones, where, as she would without doubt remain some time, they might be able to rejoin her.

None of the party, unfortunately, had much practical knowledge of carpentering. Pat, from having lived so long among the savages, was the most skilful and accustomed to turn his hand to all sorts of work. They trusted, however, for success to the right exercise of their wits. They had to make a couple more trips to the wreck, to bring away various articles which they thought might be of use. They then, without further loss of time, commenced operations.

The first task was to fix on a false keel, about half a foot in depth, to enable the boat to sail closer to the wind than she would otherwise have been able to do. It took some time, as they were greatly afraid of injuring the original keel. Fortunately, they had found some long screws, which much assisted them.

"I have a bright idea," said Tom, as they were about to begin. "We'll nail on a length in the first place two inches deep, which we can firmly secure with iron hoops to the side of the keel, and into that we can run our screws, so that there will be no risk of splitting the keel."

This plan was carried out.

"To my mind, no carpenter could have done it better," exclaimed Jerry, as he surveyed the work.

The fore-part of the boat was next decked over, a piece of canvas being nailed down on the top of it, and well painted, thus rendering it perfectly water-tight. On the same principle they formed some large lockers aft, and another amidships, in which their heavier previsions could be stored.

These being made water-tight, would materially assist in keeping the boat afloat should a heavy sea break on board of her. The gunwale was then raised a foot all round, and a bulwark placed athwartships, abaft the forecastle deck, from which, extending some feet further aft, a sliding hatch was fitted, so that in reality their boat was half decked over. They lastly gave her a thick coat of tar outside, and two coats of paint all over inside. She was rigged with a mainsail, a mizen, and a foresail, to which they added a sliding bowsprit, so that a jib could be set in light winds, with a flying gaff topsail. Having plenty of canvas and spars, they also fitted a square sail; some sand-bags served for ballast, although the stores they intended to take would reader them at first unnecessary. Tom had, however, half a dozen spare ones made, which could be filled from the beach of any island at which they might touch, as their stores became exhausted. Altogether the craft was made thoroughly seaworthy. They had been working hard all day, the last touch was given, and after a critical examination she was pronounced complete.

"Now, lads, we will launch her," cried Tom.

By means of the rollers placed under her keel, this was done without much difficulty, and all hands jumped on board. Ballast was then placed in her, and she was found not to make a drop of water.

"For my part," exclaimed Tom, anxious to encourage the rest, "I should be ready to sail right across the Pacific in her."

"And so should I," cried Billy and Desmond in chorus.

"Pardon me for saying it, sir; there are two things we cannot carry enough of to do that—water and fresh provisions," said Jerry Bird, the oldest seaman of the party. "If we did not meet with a hurricane or too heavy a gale for the boat, we might of course get across. Such voyages have been performed before now, but no man would willingly undertake one if it could be avoided."

These observations of Jerry set Tom thinking. "We must calculate the quantity of water we can carry, and go on an allowance from the first," he said to Desmond. "We must do the same also with regard to our yams and all our other provisions, or, after all the pains we have taken, we might run short, which would not be pleasant."

"I should think not," remarked Billy. "I don't mind how long we remain in the boat, but I should not like to be on short commons."

The weather promising to be fine, the boat was anchored close in shore, being also secured by an additional warp fastened to a stake driven into the ground. Their intention was to carry their provisions and stores on board the next morning and immediately sail. With the writing materials he had found on board the schooner, Tom wrote a short account of their adventures, and their intentions as to their *future* proceedings, and corked the paper up in a bottle. This they lashed carefully to a stake close to the flag-staff, which they felt sure would be visited should any vessel come off the island.

"At all events, our friends will some day or other learn what has become of us if we are lost," said Desmond.

"Oh, pray don't talk about that," cried Billy; "I can't bear to think about, anything so dreadful."

It was some time before Tom, who felt the responsibility of the undertaking resting on his shoulders, could go to sleep. He thought over what had to be done, and how he should act under the various circumstances which might occur.

Just as the first streaks of dawn appeared in the sky, he awoke. He immediately got up and went out to look at the state of the weather. As far as he could judge, from the sheltered position of the hut, it was as fine as it had been for some days past. "Thank Heaven, we shall commence our voyage under favourable auspices, at all events," he said to himself. Then he shouted—

"Rouse up there, rouse up!" His companions were quickly on foot. Billy wanted to have breakfast immediately. Tom would not hear of it.

"No, no, we must get the cargo on board, and then we will take our last breakfast on the beach," he answered.

The party now loaded themselves with the various articles which were to be taken from the hut. The heavier stores had been housed close to the beach. Tom took a look round to see that nothing was left behind. They then all set off to the boat, which floated in the calm water of the bay. Some time was occupied in loading her and stowing the stores judiciously away, so that those first required might be uppermost. Their live stock were the last articles carried on board, consisting of a couple of turtle, which they hoped would live and serve them for fresh provisions. The survivors of those in the pen they allowed to scramble back into the water, a proceeding at which Billy sighed deeply.

"Can't we tow them after us," he said, "or haul them on board as we might want them, or during calms make them tow us?"

"Bosh!" was the only answer Tom made to Billy's remark. It was with considerable anxiety that Tom watched the depth to which the stores, as they were placed on board, gradually brought down the boat. They had still more water in cocoa-nuts and pigskins to bring on board. He, soon saw that should they meet with bad weather they might have to heave overboard a considerable portion; still, as long as the sea remained smooth, she was not considered much overloaded.

Pat having lighted a fire on the beach, the party sat down to take their last breakfast on the shore. It was a hearty one, it may be supposed, as after this they could not venture to have more than one hot meal in the day. They had found a small cooking apparatus on board the wreck, which could be heated either by an oil-lamp or by wood chips.

"All hands on board," cried Tom at length. He stood the last on the beach. Having a gain cast an eye around to see that nothing was left behind, he once more gave a look at the boat. "She is indeed deep in the water—almost too deep," he said to himself. "She will, however, I trust, weather any gale we are likely to meet with. We must, at all events, run the risk, and trust to providence to take care of us."

Having cast off the warp, Tom waded out to the boat and got on board. Before giving the order to weigh anchor, he saw that everything was properly stowed, and that the chart, quadrant, and compass were in the locker ready for use. The wind in the bay was very light, but by the colour of the water outside, it could be seen that a breeze was blowing, though from what quarter it was difficult to determine.

"Now, lads, we will get up the anchor and pull away into the offing, though one cheer before we go for our island home."

A cheerful hurrah burst from the lips of the party, the anchor was lifted and stowed, and the oars being got out, they pulled merrily down the harbour. The entrance to the passage was as smooth as the rest of the bay. Having at length got well into the offing, Tom and Desmond had to decide in which direction to steer. The chart showed them Guam, the principal of the Ladrone Islands, much further off than Yokohama, on the coast of Japan, towards which they proposed steering. The wind, too, was from the north-east, and should it continue from the same point, they might reach some place in the latter islands, much sooner than they could hope to arrive at Guam. Still, as they had taken it into their heads that the *Dragon* would touch at Guam, they were far more inclined to go there than to Japan. When Tom, however, considered the risk of running short of water and of fresh provisions, he decided that they ought to attempt to reach Japan. Desmond agreed with him, and he accordingly at once put the boat's head to the north-west. The wind was so light that both the jib and gaff-topsail were set, and the boat which, at a distance, would have looked like a little cutter, stood well up to her canvas.

"She will do it, sir," said Jerry Bird. "She is going better than four knots an hour now, and if there comes a stiff breeze, we shall get six out of her."

Tom was not quite so sanguine as to that; indeed, when he came to heave a log which he had fitted, he found that she was making really only three and a half knots, though that, considering the lightness of the wind, was very good. The little island on which they had spent so many days drew gradually astern. They could see others away to the northward. They concluded that they were also uninhabited, or, if there were any people on them, that they were not likely to afford them any assistance. At last the island itself faded from sight, and as the sun went down they floated in the midst of a watery circle. Tom, with Desmond and Jerry Bird, had taken the helm one after another, for Billy had had no experience, and neither of the other men could be trusted to steer by the compass. As it got dark Tom wisely took in the gaff-topsail and jib, while he kept a hand always ready to lower the mainsail, should a sudden squall strike the boat. There appeared to be little chance, however, of that, for scarcely had the sun gone down than the wind fell to a perfect calm, and the boat lay motionless on the water.

"Don't you think it would be well to take to the oars?" asked Desmond.

"If we were certain of making good our passage in this direction. I should say so, but before exerting our strength we must see from which quarter the wind will next blow. It may be in our teeth, and all our labour will have been in vain."

Tom divided the crew into two watches: he, Billy, and Pat taking one; Desmond, with Jerry Bird and Tim, being in the other. Tom took the first watch, as he had an idea that the weather would change before midnight.

"You need not sit up, Billy," he said. "If you are wanted I'll call you. Tim will tend the main halyards and keep a look-out forward."

Billy, who was always ready for a *caulk*, lay down in the stern sheets. Tim kept himself awake by alternately singing snatches of Irish songs and whistling. Tom himself had some difficulty in keeping awake. He had lighted the binnacle lamp, by which he saw that the boat's head was turned now to one, now to another point of the compass. Several times he got up to look about; though no sailing vessel could near them, a steamer might, and often and often he fancied he heard the sound of one in the distance. Hour after hour passed by; he looked at his watch, which had fortunately kept good time. At midnight he roused up Desmond, charging him to keep a good look out for any sudden squall. "Which way it may come it is impossible to say, but I think very likely from the point for which we are steering," he observed.

Bird was of the same opinion. "We'll not be caught napping, sir," he said, as Tom lay down, thankful for the prospect of getting some rest. Desmond managed to keep awake, and amused himself by listening to Pat Casey's yarns, which were so extraordinary that Desmond fancied he must be drawing upon his imagination, though he did not think fit to say so. The middle watch passed away much as the first had done. Now and then a whale or some vast fish was heard blowing or splashing in the water, but nothing could be seen, the sound travelling over the smooth surface to a great distance.

"We will let the first watch have their sleep out," said Desmond. "It is a pity to rouse them up until daylight, though you, Pat, can lie down."

"Shure, it's only my tongue that's been kept hard at work, and that will get along very well without any rest, so with your leave I'll sit up and keep Jerry company," answered the Irishman.

Scarcely an hour after this, Desmond, who fancied he was awake, was sitting near the tiller, with his hand placed mechanically on it, when he felt it suddenly move. There was a rushing sound, the boat heeled slowly over. Tom, who even in his sleep felt the movement, jumped up, and finding the boat heeling over, "Let go the main-sheet," he shouted to Pat, who, being in the land of dreams, had neglected to lower away on the main halyards. Once aroused, he quickly obeyed the order, and the boat happily righted. Fortunately, the stores being well stowed, nothing shifted, or it might have gone hard with them. Tom's first act was to look at the compass. The wind, as he had expected, was from the north-west. Desmond was keeping the boat close on the starboard tack, heading away to the southward of west.

"I was afraid so," exclaimed Tom. "However, we will try what we can do. Perhaps it will shift again to its old quarter; but if it holds as it now does, we shall have a dead beat to Yokohama, and it may be many a long day before we get there. We will give it a fair trial, however, in case the wind should change."

Daylight soon came. Tom gazed anxiously around.

"We will heave to and go to breakfast. Should the wind continue as it is for a couple of hours, we will then bear up at once and run for Guam. It is a sign to us that that must be our destination."

Having boiled their kettle, they took their first breakfast on board the boat.

"Follow my example, and make a good one," said Billy. "If it comes on to blow, and we should have to heave any of our cargo overboard, it is as well to save as much as possible."

The men, at all events, were inclined to follow the midshipman's advice; and after breakfast Tom got out his chart and pricked off their course and present position.

"With this wind we shall soon sight the Bonins, so that we shall not have lost much time. We shall, I hope, make Bailey Islands before dark; after that our course must be south by east, which will carry us clear of several rocks and reefs to the westward, and I hope that if we have a good breeze we may sight one of the more northern of the Ladrones in the course of a week or ten days, and Guam is about three hundred miles further south."

Desmond fully agreed to Tom's proposal, and the time they had fixed on having arrived, and the wind blowing as strongly and steadily as ever, the helm was put up, and the boat was steered on the proposed course. Although the Bonins were seen, night came on before they sighted Bailey Islands; and Tom, afraid of running on them in the dark, steered more to the eastward than he otherwise would have done.

Before the first watch was set he addressed his companions, urging them one and all to keep a vigilant look out ahead, both day and night. "We have not the advantage, recollect, of a large vessel, when a rock or reef may be seen from the mast-head," he observed. "Should there be any sea running, the first intimation we may have of our danger may be by finding ourselves on the top of a coral rock. We must be always ready, at a moment's notice, to alter our course, and get out the oars should the wind fail us. By that means we may escape the dangers we must expect to meet with. Remember, the chart we have got is an old one and may be inaccurate, so that it would be unwise to trust completely to it."

"Very important remarks, and I hope the men in my watch will remember them, as I shall myself," said Desmond.

Though the wind was fair, they ran on all night, under the main-sail, foresail, and mizzen, in case they should suddenly have to haul up to avoid any danger upon which they might be running. "As soon as we have daylight we will set the square sail, and make up for lost time," said Tom. The wind held fair, but towards morning it began to fall, and by daybreak it was again perfectly calm.

"Suppose the wind springs up next time from the southward, are we to run north?" asked Billy.

"Wait until that time comes," answered Tom. "We have now laid a course for Guam, and Guam I hope we shall reach some day or other."

As the sun rose the heat became very great, increased by the glare from the ocean, which shone like a sheet of burnished gold. Having a second suit of sails, Tom had the mainsail rigged as an awning, which, as the sun got higher, served to shelter their heads, and to prevent the risk of a sunstroke. The awning, however, could only be kept up as long as it remained calm, when it was of course most required. Although some progress might have been made by rowing, Tom was unwilling to fatigue his crew, thinking it better to husband their strength for any emergency which might occur. At the usual hour Tom piped to breakfast, which was made to last as long as possible. Tom's great difficulty was to find occupation for all hands. Unfortunately they had no books except the nautical almanac, which was not interesting reading. Yarn spinning is very well in the evening when men have done their work, but few can go on all day either as listeners or narrators. Even singing songs becomes somewhat monotonous, especially when the list is small and the singers have already trolled them forth over and over again. Their chief amusement was watching the coveys of flying-fish which rose every now and then from the ocean, and darted through the air, their bright scales glittering in the sun. Occasionally a whale spouted forth a jet of vapour and spray with a loud noise like that emitted by the safety valve of a steam engine; while albicores, bonitos; and dolphins, with various other fish, could be seen here and there, sporting and tumbling, as they came to the surface, sending a circle of wavelets extending far and wide around. Sea birds also flew through the blue ether, their wings appearing of snowy whiteness as they caught the rays of the sun in their rapid flight.

Jerry Bird proposed getting out the oars. "Maybe, sir, if we pull on for a few hours we may fall in with some craft becalmed; and though we may wish to continue the voyage in our boat, we may have a talk with her people, hear the news, and maybe get a glass of grog."

"Or slice of plum pudding, or pot of jam," put in Billy.

As there appeared to be no signs of a breeze springing up, Tom agreed to Jerry's proposal, and the oars were got out, Billy taking one of them, at which Gerald promised to take a spell when he got tired. Heavily laden, however, as the boat was, they could scarcely send her ahead at the rate of two knots an hour; but even that was something; and supposing they could row for fifteen hours, night and day, thirty miles might be made good during the four and twenty.

Jerry, to keep up the spirits of his companions, led off with a song, when Tim and Pat followed him; and thus they continued until Tom piped to dinner. They indeed seemed much happier than when doing nothing. As soon as dinner was over they again took to the oars, and pulled on steadily until dark; but no land was seen, nor was a sail in sight. Indeed, so limited was their horizon, that they were likely to pass low islands without observing them. The night was as calm as the day; but, as the men required sleep, Tom kept only two oars going. When the sun rose the next morning it shone on the same polished surface as on the previous day.

"Not an air in the heavens," said Jerry, in answer to Tom's inquiries, as he rose from his sleeping-place in the stern sheets; "and, to my mind, there won't be."

"We must have patience," said Tom, preparing to take a morning bath by jumping overboard.

"Be careful, sir, and look out for sharks," observed Jerry. "I would not, if I were you, go far from the boat."

"I will follow your advice. Keep the oars splashing, and that will frighten them off, if any are near," said Tom.

Plunging in, the midshipmen swam round and round the boat several times. Billy jumped overboard, but being of opinion that he was likely to prove a tempting morsel to Jack Shark, very quickly begged Jerry to help him on board again. The midshipmen having dressed themselves, the men imitated their example. They were splashing about round the beat, when Pat shouted out—

"Bear a hand; get on board, mates. I caught sight of the fin of a big fellow not twenty fathoms off; he'll be after trying the taste of our legs, if we don't look sharp."

The midshipmen stood ready to help in the men, for they also had seen the ominous black fin. Jerry, who had an especial dread of sharks, quickly threw himself over the gunwale, with the assistance of Tom, while Desmond and Billy helped up Tim. Pat, who was farthest out, caught hold of the bobstay and was hoisting himself on board by the jibboom, when a cry of dismay escaped him.

"He nearly had me, the baste; for I felt his jaws touch my foot."

That this was not imagination was proved by the blood running from Pat's heel, where the lips, though fortunately not the teeth of the monster, had struck him. A second later, and Pat's foot would have been off to a certainty. The shark was directly afterwards seen swimming alongside the boat and casting a malicious leer at those on board.

"It will be a lesson to us in future not to swim away from the side," observed Tom.

"It will be a lesson for me not to go overboard at all," said Billy. "*I've* no fancy to become food for a shark."

Another night passed. Tom found at noon the next day that, instead of thirty, they had not made good twenty miles. The fact was that at times they were not rowing at all; at others only two oars were going, when not more than one mile an hour was made, and even when four were rowing, they had to exert themselves to move the boat at the rate of two knots an hour. Still progress was being made. They should in time reach the most northern of the Ladrones, where they might venture on shore without fear of being killed and eaten, as would certainly be their lot on any of the islands further to the south-west. Rowing all day under a burning sun is not conducive to health, and though none of the party were actually ill, they began to long for a breeze, which would send them more rapidly on their course; while their spirits, which had hitherto been kept up, also flagged considerably. Each day, too, they made less progress than on the former one, a sign that their strength was somewhat failing. They had hitherto had an ample supply of food. The salt junk found on board the wreck had been kept to be used only in case of necessity. Of their turtle, one had been killed, and they had feasted on it for a couple of days, until the remainder grew bad, and they were compelled to throw it overboard. One morning Pat, who had taken charge of the animals, announced that the other was dead, having died during the night, and that unless it was quickly eaten it would be lost. This proved to be the case, especially to Billy's regret, who saw the tempting morsels swallowed by the shark, which had, since its first appearance, followed the boat. The still more alarming announcement was that several of their hams, which they had fancied so well cured, were also getting bad. Some were consigned to the maw of the voracious shark, though others, which were only slightly tainted, were kept until the continued heat rendered them uneatable. Pat could not make it out, but it was discovered on examination that neither the smoke nor salt had penetrated to any depth, and that they would have done better to have cut the meat in thin strips and attempted thus to preserve it.

"Well, we shall have fish enough and roots, before we attack the junk; we must husband the biscuit and other things," observed Tom.

He accordingly put all hands on an allowance. It was with no small anxiety that he examined the cured fish, which he was grieved to find emitted far from a pleasant odour; still, as it was at present eatable, he continued to serve it out.

"It is not often I have known a calm last so long as this," exclaimed Jerry, when a whole week had passed, and not a breath of air had filled their sails. "We would have been better off on shore had we known what was coming."

"We should not grumble," observed Tom. "We have got upwards of a hundred miles to the southward; when a breeze does come we shall have so much less distance to make."

"But the food and the water, sir?" exclaimed Jerry.

"We must touch at the nearest island we sight and obtain a fresh supply," was the answer.

Day after day the shark had followed the boat, and while his hideous snout was seen, or that triangular fin of his, it would have been useless to put over a fishing-line, as it would certainly have been carried off. When, however, the fresh provisions ran short, Gerald and Tom determined to try and get rid of their fearful foe. The three men and Billy, who, though fat and short, pulled a very good oar, were rowing as men do who have been at the task many hours, in a sort of mechanical fashion, when Tom exclaimed—

"Load the muskets, Desmond, and if we cannot kill that brute astern, and get a few slices out of his carcase, we will, at all events, drive him away."

The muskets had been kept clean and ready for use. They were soon loaded, when the midshipmen, bringing the weapons to their shoulders, took, as they thought, a steady aim and fired. The shark instantly sank out of sight. Whether they had hit him or not, they could not tell, but it was possible that the bullets, being deflected by the water, had glanced clear of his head. They at once reloaded, expecting that he would return; but though they looked down into the clear water astern and on either side, the monster was nowhere to be seen.

"He won't trouble us again," said Desmond. "I feel pretty sure my bullet went into him."

"And I think mine did," said Tom; "but neither could have killed him, or he would have floated up."

"Then the sooner we get out the lines and try and catch some fish for supper the better," exclaimed Billy.

Taking off the heavy leads, two of the lines were baited with pieces of rancid pork and allowed to tow astern. The lines had been out for some time, but not a bite had been obtained.

"Perhaps the lines are not deep enough, or the bait is not as good as it should be," observed Desmond, beginning to haul in upon his line. He had got it in a third of the length, when he felt it torn from his grasp, and he caught sight of a monster running off with it. The next instant, as Desmond had the line round the thwart, it snapped short off. Away went hook and line. Directly after, Tom's line, hanging over the other quarter, without any warning was snapped off.

"It's that brute of a shark come back again," cried Tom. "Get the muskets, Desmond, and if we can entice him near, we will settle him this time."

"He's too knowing for that, sir," observed Jerry. "You may fire away every shot you've got—he'd see them coming, and be out of the way before they reach him."

Tom, not believing this, determined to try once more. He got out another piece of pork, and fastened it to the end of one of the broken lines.

"The hooks will puzzle his inside," said Desmond, "when he begins to feel them. He'll think twice before he has another bite."

The muskets were loaded, and the midshipmen standing up, kept their eyes closely watching the bait, which floated on the surface, two or three fathoms astern.

"There he comes," cried Desmond. And as the shark, turning on his back, exposed the white of his belly, they both fired. The brute disappeared, and so did the bait, sinking like a rocket until lost to sight.

"We have finished him this time, at all events," cried Desmond. "He'll not take any more of our hooks."

"Yes, but we have lost the slices out of his back," cried Billy; "and, unless we can now catch some fish, we shall be on short commons for supper."

Hoping that they should not be again troubled by the shark, fresh lines were got out. No fish, however, took the bait; either none came near, or it was not suited to their tastes. Supper consequently consisted only of biscuits and tea; but the warm tea was a great comfort after the heat of the day. The watch kept the lines down all night, but still without success. Two more days went by with little variation. Now and then their hopes were raised seeing a ripple far away on the surface; but, if caused by wind, it died away before it reached them. They were now on a short allowance of water; that in the skins had either evaporated or leaked out, the store in the cocoa-nuts had soon been exhausted, and they had only the boat's breaker, on which they had already commenced. A few biscuits and a portion of the salt beef, which was at the best scarcely eatable, and possessed but slightly nutritive qualities, alone remained. Still they had enough to keep them alive for three or four days, perhaps for longer; but before that time, should a breeze spring up, they might at all events reach Faralon de Pajaros, the most northern of the Ladrones. There were other small islands marked down to the westward, one of which they might sight; and, if so, Tom determined to land, and try to obtain water and any food they might be able to find. They would most likely be able to get shellfish from the rocks, which would be an improvement on the junk. It was night. Desmond had the watch, and Tom was lying down fast asleep. He was aroused by hearing Desmond sing out, "A breeze! a breeze! All hands make sail!" Tom in a moment was on his feet. He looked around him and up at the stars.

"From which quarter does it come?" he asked.

The binnacle lamp had not been lighted. A light was soon struck. Tom examined the compass. "It is dead against us," he exclaimed, with almost a groan.

"It is coming on very strong too, sir," observed Jerry. "It would be better not to set the mainsail, until we see what happens."

As Jerry had feared, the wind became stronger, and they presently had as much as the boat could stagger under, with only her mizzen and foresail set. The sea, however, was not as heavy as might have been expected. Tom kept the boat's head close to it, and she rode easily over the fast-rising billows. The hatch, which had hitherto been of no use, was shipped, and kept out the seas which occasionally broke on board. The boat was much lighter than when she had started; indeed, as Jerry observed, "she would have been the better for a few more sand-bags in her bottom." Tom was delighted at her behaviour.

"She rides beautifully over the seas," he exclaimed. "I should have been sorry not to have given her a trial. The wind will very likely change before long, and we shall have a quick run to Faralon. I wish that I knew more about it, but if we can get water and cocoa-nuts and shellfish there, we must not complain. We can afterwards make our way without difficulty to Guam, having plenty of islands to stop at in our course."

Tom said this to keep up his own spirits and those of his companions. They had not as yet begun to suffer from hunger, but he well knew that they should in a few days unless they could reach land. They had none of them calculated on the contingency which had occurred. The gale continued all day. At night the sea went down, and the wind fell considerably, but still blew from the southward. The boat was put about, as Tom and Desmond agreed that they must try and beat up to Faralon, which they might hope to sight in two or three days at the utmost. By daylight the wind had fallen sufficiently to enable them to set all sail, but they agreed that it would have been better to have had a dead calm, so that they might have pulled the boat in the direction they wished to go. At present, however, there was too much wind to enable them to do that.

Tom, who had hitherto bravely kept up his spirits, began to feel far from happy, although he did his best not to allow his companions to discover this. He could not help reflecting that in three or four days their water and provisions must come almost to an end. They had not enough now, even to keep up their strength, and it might still take two or three weeks before they could reach an island inhabited by civilised people. He, however, did his best not to communicate his feelings to his companions.

"I wish we had gone to Japan," exclaimed Billy Blueblazes. "We should have been there long ago, and I don't like these short commons—that I don't."

"I acted for the best," answered Tom. He could not say another word: he felt more for his companions than himself.

The two Irishmen were looking very woe-begone. All Pat's fun had left him; he had just strength enough to tend the jib sheets. Tim was stationed at the foresail, while Jerry stood by the main halyards.

Tom and Desmond, who had never played tricks with their constitutions, which were remarkably good ones, suffered much less than the rest, but even they felt themselves growing weaker and weaker. They had each day taken an observation. According to the chart they were nearly up to Faralon, but no land appeared in sight.

Each day Tom had lessened the allowance of food and water; he now took stock of what remained. Half a dozen yams had been discovered, and these, beaten up with some oil, were all they had to sustain life. It was nauseous at best, but they ate it greedily. Another night came on; the sea was tolerably smooth, the sky was overcast, and a thick mist arose, although it still blew very fresh. The boat was kept under easy sail, close-hauled. Tom had the first watch with Billy and Pat. It was unusually dark, so that it was with difficulty that he could see the length of the boat. Before night came on Tom had again examined the chart.

"I am convinced that by noon—perhaps earlier—to-morrow at latest, we shall see land," he said.

"I agree with you," exclaimed Desmond. "On the strength of it, I propose that we have a glass of grog apiece."

"You'll not be afther laughin' at us, shure, Mr Desmond?" said Tim. "If we could but have a dhrop of the creature, it would cheer our hearts mightily."

"Indeed, I am not," said Desmond, producing the bottle from one of the after lockers. It was but a quarter full of rum, but even the small portion mixed with water which Desmond served out was sufficient to restore energy, to the almost exhausted party. The remainder he carefully put by for the next day. After this the watch below lay down and went to sleep.

Tom sat at the helm. Every now and then he told Pat to keep a bright look out.

"Arrah, sir, it will be a hard matter to do that, since I cannot see half a fathom before my nose."

"There cannot be much use in looking out," said Billy. "If we were near the land we should have seen it before dark; and as we have not fallen in with a single vessel since we left the Bonins, we are not likely to meet with one to-night."

"That's not sound reasoning, Billy," answered Tom. "We must, until the fog lifts, make more use of our ears than our eyes. We may hear breakers ahead in time to avoid them if we listen attentively."

74

They were silent for some time. Tom's chief object in speaking was to keep his companions awake.

"Billy," he said, after some time, "did you hear anything?"

"Yes; I fancied I heard a bell strike."

"More than once?"

"Yes; four times."

"So did I," said Tom; and he took out his watch, intending to look at it by the light of the binnacle lamp, when at that instant the lamp went out. The oil had been exhausted, and there was no more in the can. Pat, he had reason to fear, had taken a pull at it unperceived.

He struck a match, and saw it was just ten o'clock. There could be no doubt, then, that the bell they heard was that on board a ship; still it was so faint that she was probably a long way off.

Tom could now only steer by the wind, which, however, he believed was holding steady. He had settled with Desmond to go about at four bells, and to keep on the starboard tack until midnight, then again to go about. He had just ordered Pat to let fly the jib sheet, and had put down the helm, when, as the boat was in stays, Pat sang out—

"A sail right ahead!" What was Tom's horror at that instant to see a vast pyramid of sail towering above him. The next moment a crash was heard; the stranger's stem struck the boat's bow. At the sound Desmond and Jerry sprang to their feet. Instinctively they knew that they had been run down, and simultaneously they uttered shouts of "Help, help!" Ropes were hove to them by the look-out men on the stranger's forecastle. Tom put one into the hands of Billy, who was too much alarmed to know what to do, while he himself grasped another. Pat had caught hold of the dolphin striker, and was making his way up to the bowsprit. Jerry grasped another rope, and all three swarmed up until they met friendly hands to assist them. Tom supposed that Desmond and Tim were following, but, as he looked back, what was his dismay to see the boat drifting away. The crash he had heard convinced him that her side must have been stove in, and that she must sink almost immediately.

"There are two men clinging to the craft you ran down, sir. In mercy's sake, lower a boat and pick them up," he shouted out.

"Aye, aye," was the answer.

And he thankfully heard the order given to shorten sail and bring the ship to the wind. Rushing aft, he found a party of men preparing to lower a boat. He begged to go in her. Before she was in the water Jerry joined him, and, together with three other hands, they shoved off. He then saw that she was a whaleboat. One of the men, an officer he concluded, took the steering oar.

"Desmond! Tim!" he shouted out.

No answer came. The boat must have gone down, but they could both swim well.

"Do you know the bearings?" he asked of the mate.

"Aye, aye! I guess I do," was the answer. "We will give them another hail presently."

The boat pulled on. Then Tom, standing up again, halloed, the rest of the party joining him. An answer came from right ahead. Tom recognised Desmond's voice. With renewed zeal they pulled on and looked around. Tom could distinguish the boat through the gloom, just above the water.

"Bear a hand," shouted Desmond again, and they were up to the boat.

She had gone almost over, her side being only above water. Desmond was clinging to it.

"Here, take him off first," he said; and the crew of the whaleboat lifted Tim on board. Desmond sprang after him. Scarcely had they got clear of the wreck of the boat than she went down.

"Thank Heaven, you are safe," exclaimed Tom, as he rung Desmond's hand, as if they had been long parted. "Did you not hear our first hail?"

"No; I suppose it was when I was dragging poor Tim up. He got a blow on the head, I think, and was very nearly slipping off. As the boat broke clear of the ship I was on the point of hauling myself up, but I could not bear to desert him."

"Just like you," said Tom. "I hope he will recover."

"No fear of that. We Irishmen have good hard heads. If there is a doctor on board he will soon bring him round."

"Have you a doctor on board?" asked Tom of the mate.

"I guess we have; a smart man he is, too," answered the mate. "Are there any more of you to pick up?"

"No, thank you," replied Tom; "all the officers and ship's company of our craft have been rescued."

"What craft was she?" asked the mate.

"The jolly-boat of her Majesty's ship *Dragon*," answered Tom.

"And how did you happen to be out here?" Tom explained that they had lost their ship, and that they were steering for Guam, where they expected to find her.

"I guess you'll not do that, for we put in there a week ago, and there was no British man-of-war there at that time."

This was unsatisfactory news. The mate had not time to ask many more questions before the boat was alongside. Tom and Desmond, on reaching the deck, found the master, who informed him that he was Captain Paul Sibley—that the ship by which the boat had been run down was the whaler *Columbia*, of Boston. "I am very sorry for the accident," he added, "but I do not see that any one was to blame. It could not be helped. We could not see you, and you could not see us, and of course the weakest went to the wall, or rather to the bottom. However, now you are on board, you are welcome to remain until we can put you on board your ship, or set you on shore wherever you wish to land. I guess it won't be on any of the Solomon Islands of New Hebrides, where they have an ugly fancy for eating their visitors."

77

"Thank you," answered Tom. "If our ship is not at Guam, where we expect to find her, we must consider at what other place it would be best to land, so that as soon as possible we may get on board a ship of war."

"Well, well, there, is no hurry," answered the captain. "And just now, the best thing you can do is to get off your wet clothes and turn in. I will have some shakedowns made up for you young gentlemen in my state cabin, while your three men can go forward, and the doctor will look after the one with the broken head."

Tom, Gerald, and Billy thanked the good-natured captain for his kind offer, but hinted that, as they had had nothing but mashed yams and oil for the last two days, they should be thankful for something to eat.

"Not very pleasant fare. It's an ill wind that blows nobody good; so, though I ran you down, you are better off than you would have been starving on such food as that, I guess. Here, Peter, light the galley fire, and get some food as quick as possible. Hot tea in the mean time; and look after the men forward—they want food as much as their officers."

The black steward, who had been asleep, came out rubbing his eyes, and hurried to obey the orders he had received; while the captain ushered his guests into the cabin, and soon produced three blankets.

"There, strip off your wet duds, and wrap yourselves in these," he said, "while I make up your beds."

The three midshipmen, weary and hungry as they were, indulged in a laugh, as they sat with the blankets over them, like three Indian squaws looking at each other, while the kind captain completed the arrangements he had promised.

The steward quickly returned with a pot of hot tea, and the captain produced a box of American crackers, which soon took off the edge of their appetites.

"There, lie down now, until Peter is able to bring you mere substantial fare," said the captain.

They followed his advice, Billy carrying a handful of crackers with him, munching which he soon fell fast asleep. They were roused up, it seemed to them, a moment afterwards by the steward, who announced that supper was on the table; when they again, not *unwillingly*, wrapped in their blankets, sat down to discuss some basins of hot soup and slices of cold beef, which, as Billy observed, "was a great improvement on the raw salt junk, which had so long been their only substantial fare."

At length the captain, observing that all three were nodding over the table, advised them to return to their beds; and scarcely had they put their heads on their pillows, than they were fast asleep.

Chapter Four.

Kindly treated on board the American whaler—Looking out for whales—A whale killed—Cutting in and trying out—The master goes off in chase—The second mate lost overboard—Sandwich Islander endeavours to save him—The boats disappear—No appearance of the master and first mate—A gale—The boatswain assumes command and plays the tyrant—Will not search for the captain—Hides the nautical instruments—The boatswain dashes Tom's quadrant to the deck—Night—The midshipmen turn in—The ship strikes—Boatswain and crew put off—Leave Tom and his companions on the wreck—Weather moderates—Land seen—They build a raft—Voyage to the shore—See a savage on it—Turns out to be Pat Casey—Night on shore.

When Tom Rogers at length awoke, he found the captain, Doctor Locock (the surgeon), and the first mate seated at dinner.

"Well, young gentlemen, do you find yourselves well enough to join us?" asked the former.

"Yes, sir," said Tom, slipping into his clothes, which he found perfectly dried by his side. He aroused his companions, and they were all three soon seated at table, where plates had been laid for them. They were thankful to hear from the doctor that Tim, though still in his hammock, was in a fair way of recovery, and would be on deck in a day or two.

They now gave a fuller account of their adventures than they had done on the previous night. The possible loss of the *Dragon* was discussed, and from the captain and mate's observations the midshipmen's hopes were somewhat raised that she might have escaped shipwreck. Their opinion was that, as her machinery was damaged, she would have run to Hong-kong, the nearest place at which it could be repaired; and that it would take several weeks before she could get back to the Bonins to look for them. That their captain would return they felt sure, unless he was convinced that they were lost.

"At all events, as we are about to fish off there, we will take a look round the neighbouring islands on the chance of discovering the wreck, and rescuing any of her people who may have escaped," said the master. "If we fail in that, we may fall in with a British man-of-war, and you shall be put on board. If not, we will land you at Yokohama or Kagoshima, from whence you can without difficulty get to Hong-kong."

Tom, as spokesman, thanked the captain for his kindness, adding, "I feel sure that the British consul at any place at which you may land us will reimburse you for the expense to which you may be put on our account."

"We won't talk about that, my young friend," answered the American captain. "We will set off the loss of your boat against that; and I am only too happy to have saved your lives, and to have rendered any service in my power to British officers in distress, for I tell you it is my belief that you would all have starved before you got to Guam, or any other island at which you could have landed in the Ladrones."

"I guess that they don't value midshipmen at a long figure in your service," observed the mate, as if he doubted that the *Dragon* would return to look for them.

"That depends on the sort of midshipmen they happen to be," answered Tom, putting on a modest air. "We flatter ourselves that we are not likely to be neglected. Now, if we happened to have all been like Billy Blueblazes there, who, from the quantity of beef he consumes, is undoubtedly a heavy cost to her Majesty, our captain might have considered it his duty to leave us to find our own grub for the future, and thus save our beloved country a heavy expense."

"I see," said the mate with a wink, discovering that Tom was not a person out of whom he could take much change. "And pray may I ask if that young gentleman's name is really Billy Blueblazes? It's a curious sounding one, at all events."

"It's the name by which he is known among us, at all events," answered Tom. "The captain may in his supreme wisdom call him Mr William Blewitt, or when he is gazetted, on obtaining his lieutenancy, he may possibly be designated by the last-mentioned appellation; but Billy Blueblazes he will be called by his messmates while he remains afloat."

The midshipmen went for a short time on deck, where they found Jerry and Pat, who seemed well pleased at the way they had been treated by the crew, who, though rough enough in appearance, were far less so than the seamen of many merchant vessels.

"They have, howsumever, already tried to persuade Pat and me to join them, as they have lost two or three men since they came out; but you know, Mr Rogers, that an old man-of-war's man is not likely to desert his flag, and least of all to join a greasy, stinking whaler," said Jerry in a whisper, not wishing to be overheard.

Tom and Gerald paid Tim a visit, and found him almost himself again. "If it had not been for you, Mr Desmond, I should have lost the number of my mess—that I know; and though I cannot make a fine speech about it, you know that an Irishman's heart can be grateful. If you ever come to Barry Shingle, there is an old mother I've got; and a couple of sisters, who will be showing you what they think of the matter. I have been thinking, as I lay here, what a sorrowing there would have been if you had not held on to me after I got that crack on the skull."

On returning to the deck, Tom and Desmond found Billy Blueblazes fast asleep on the companion hatch; and as they could scarcely keep their own eyes open, they followed the captain's advice and turned in, where they quickly forgot what had happened and where they were. They awoke up for a short time to take supper, and very soon went off to sleep again. Indeed, even Tom felt that he required sound rest for two or three nights, to set him up after the hardships he had gone through.

The voyage of the *Columbia* had hitherto been fortunate; she had, however, lost two of her boats stove in, and three hands drowned. She was already half full, and Captain Sibley hoped in the course of a few more months to be able to return home. The midshipmen were politely and kindly treated, and agreed that they ought to be thankful at finding themselves so well off. They were anxious, before leaving the ship, to see a whale captured, and to witness the operation of cutting out and trying in, which the doctor described to them.

Hitherto it had been almost calm since they came on board. The ship had but slightly changed her position; still a look-out was kept for whales, as at any moment one might appear. The midshipmen were asleep, when one morning, just at daybreak, they were aroused by the sound of feet hurrying overhead, and springing on deck, they saw the crew busily engaged in lowering two of the boats.

"There! and there again!" shouted the look-out, meaning that a whale, which he had some time before seen, had come to the surface was spouting. Tom immediately sprang into the rigging, and on looking out, he saw a whale spouting about a mile to windward. In less than a minute after the people had come on deck half dressed, the boats started away with six men in each, including the headsman and boat's steerer. The captain went as headsman in one, and the first mate in the other. The water bubbled and hissed under the bows of the boats, as the eager crews urged them forward.

"I wish I had gone in one," cried Tom.

"So do I," said Desmond; "but I doubt whether we should have found ourselves of much use, and as the captain would have considered us in the way, we should have had very little chance. However, we can see the fun, and if we get a breeze we may beat the ship up to the whale."

The boats made good way, but before they got near enough to fire their harpoons into the monster, it sank beneath the surface.

"The whale has disappeared! How provoking!" cried Desmond.

"Don't suppose that. Depend upon it, the captain has not given up the chase yet. The whale must soon come to the surface again to breathe," said Tom.

He was right. The whale rose at no great distance from where it had gone down, and somewhat nearer the ship. The boats were quickly up to it, and before it had done spouting, two harpoons, with a deadly force, were shot into its side. The boats backed off speedily to return to strike into it a number of lances. The whale, feeling a sudden pain, lifted up its flukes and disappeared. The line was quickly run out, and before long the creature again came to the surface and attempted to swim away from its foes; but it had not gone far, before it began furiously to lash the water with its flukes, beating it into a mass of foam and blood. The boats kept clear, their crews well knowing that one blow of that mighty tail would dash their boats to splinters. It was the last effort of the monster, which soon rolled over on its side perfectly dead. A cheer from the boats' crews, which was heard over the water, announced their success, when, securing tow-ropes to the whale, they dragged it alongside without loss of time, and the operation of cutting out was commenced.

Two of the crew descended with sharp spades, when they cut off the head of the whale, which was at once secured under the counter. A large hook being then fastened in a hole cut in the blubber at the head end of the animal, the operator commenced cutting off a strip about three feet broad, in a spiral direction, and a tackle having been fixed to the hook, this was drawn up on board, the body of the whale turning round and round. As the blubber was thus hoisted up, it was cut into pieces, known, as blanket pieces, and thrown into huge cauldrons arranged along the deck. As soon as the carcase was stripped of this, its outer coating, it was allowed to float away, and the spermaceti oil in the head astern was dipped out with small buckets at the end of poles, until the whole was extracted. This oil, the most valuable part of the whale, was then boiled separately, and stowed in casks. Now commenced the operation of trying out. Fires were lighted under the huge try-pots, the crisp membranous parts of the blanket, after the oil had been extracted, serving as fuel. The blubber was boiled until the oil rose to the surface, when it was skimmed off and placed in casks. In daylight the men thus employed looked grim enough, but at night, as they worked away, stripped to their waists, the fire casting a glare over their smoke-begrimed figures, they seemed more like a group of demons engaged in some diabolical work, than human beings. The midshipmen could scarcely recognise those with whom they had been talking familiarly the day before.

The whale, which was a large one, gave, the captain told them, eighty barrels of oil. It took the crew upwards of two days to try out and stow away that quantity.

"I should have to be precious hard up before I turned whaler," observed Billy Blueblazes. "It is hot work at night, but it must be terrible in a calm, with the blazing sun beating down on the poor fellows' heads."

Several days passed away after this before another whale was seen. A breeze, however, having sprung up, the ship stood to the northward. There was some sea on and the weather looked changeable, when one afternoon, as Tom and Gerald were enjoying a read at some of the captain's books in the cabin, Billy rushed in, exclaiming—

"Here's a school of whales close to us. Come up and have a look at them, or perhaps they will be off."

Sure enough, when the midshipmen came on deck, they saw half a dozen or more whales spouting together, which, as the captain told them, were young bull whales. The crew were standing ready to lower the boats as soon as they should get the captain's order. The weather appeared to clear a little, and eager to obtain one or more of the frolicsome monsters, he determined, in spite of the threatening aspect of the weather, to go off in chase. He, as before, went in one boat, and the first mate in the other. The boats were, however, apparently seen by the whales, which immediately separated and went off in different directions. One, however, after making several turns, came directly towards the captain's boat.

"'Faith! I wish we were with him," exclaimed Desmond. "He is sure to have that one."

The captain, making a sign to his men not to move their oars, waited silently for the young bull, which came close up without discovering its foe. When at length it did so, it swerved on one side, at that moment receiving the deadly weapon just behind its hump. No sooner did the whale feel the pain than, apparently terror-stricken, it seemed unable to move; but as the captain was again about to fire, suddenly recovering itself, it darted off like an arrow, spinning the boat so quickly round that she was nearly upset.

Away went the whale dead to windward, towing the boat at a rate of nearly fifteen miles an hour, right against a head sea which, as she ploughed through it, was formed in a high bank of surf on either side, while she was almost concealed by the showers of spray flying over her. The second mate, who was at some distance, seeing the whale coming, pulled up in time to shoot his weapon into its side, when both boats, being fast, were towed almost as rapidly as had been the captain's. In vain the boats attempted to haul up closer, so as to strike their lances more deeply into the animal.

Tom and Gerald, borrowing spy-glasses, ran aloft to watch the proceedings, but at so great a speed had the whale gone that, in a short time, neither it nor the beats could be seen by the naked eye. From the mast-head the midshipmen could just observe three objects like specks upon the ocean, and at length they entirely disappeared beyond the horizon. The wind had now freshened.

"We must go and lend a hand," said Tom, "as I suppose the second mate will beat the ship up to the boats."

They accordingly descended; but before they were half-way down, the fearful cry reached their ears of "A man overboard!" On looking astern they saw him struggling in the waves. Who he was they could not tell. Hastening to the deck, they found the helm put down, the hands raising tacks and sheets to bring the ship about. In the mean time some oars and a hen-coop had been hove into the sea, but the man, whoever he was, seemed to have very little notion of swimming, as his efforts to reach them were unavailing. Tom's first impulse was to leap overboard. Gerald, holding him back, exclaimed, "You could not save the poor fellow; he would carry you down, if you attempted to get near him."

"But I could tow the hen-coop up to him," said Tom.

"Stay where you are, young gentleman," said the doctor. "See! there is a man gone to his assistance;" and they then caught sight of a Sandwich Islander in the water. He had slipped quietly overboard and was making his way towards the drowning man. Just then the sun dipped beneath the horizon, looking angry and red, while the sky threatened a stormy night. Only one small boat remained, which was lowered immediately; the ship was brought to, and Tom, with Desmond, Jerry, and two of the crew, jumped into her; but by this time they had lost sight both of the drowning man and the Sandwich Islander. The sea, which was every moment getting up, broke over the bows of the boat as they pulled towards the spot where the men were last seen.

"Who is the poor fellow?" asked Tom of one of the crew.

"Our second mate. He has been queer for some time, and I don't expect we shall find him."

This was painful intelligence. Tom felt it his duty to persevere. At length they heard a cry. It came from the Sandwich Islander. They could not see him, but they caught sight of a hen-coop, which assisted them in directing their course. Just then Tom, who had taken the bow oar, standing up to look out, saw two heads. "We shall be in time, even now. Pull away!" he sang out.

The mate had apparently got hold of an oar.

"I see him," shouted Tom to the Sandwich Islander. "Wait another minute, and we will take you on board;" and he pointed towards the mate. They were not twelve fathoms from him, when a loud shriek escaped him, and, letting go the oar, he threw up his arms and sank from sight. They pulled round, still hoping that he might re-appear, but it was in vain. The Sandwich Islander came swimming rapidly up to them, and without waiting for assistance threw himself over the bows.

"A shark got him," he said; "and would have had me in another minute."

It was not without some danger of being swamped that the boat regained the ship's side. Until the return of the captain and first mate the ship was under the command of Mr Betts, the boatswain, who appeared to be a rough hand; although Tom concluded that he was a good seaman, who would act for the best, and endeavour to get up to the boats and take the officers on board. Tom at once offered his and his companions' services to work the ship. Indeed, she was so short-handed that without their assistance she could with difficulty even be put about.

"I suppose those who are eating the owner's bread should work for the owner," was the gruff answer, as if he declined the offer for himself.

This, however, mattered very little to Tom. As the wind increased he felt more and more anxious for the fate of the absent ones. In order not to miss them, it was necessary to make short boards, so that all hands were kept constantly at work, putting the ship about every quarter of an hour, while lanterns were hung over the weather side to show her whereabouts should the boats have got clear of the whale. The gale became stronger and stronger. The canvas was taken in, until the ship was under closely reefed topsails. The sea got up more and more, frequently breaking over her bows, so that it seemed too probable that the boats, before they could reach her, would be swamped. Already it would be a difficult matter for them to get alongside. Tom, having discovered that there were some blue lights on board, burnt one every now and then, hoping that they might be seen and encourage the crews of the wave-tossed boats. The surgeon told him that he still had some hopes that they might escape, as boats had often done in a heavy sea, by hanging on under the lee of a dead whale, which served as a breakwater.

"In that case we must take care not to go too far, or we may get to windward of them, and they might not venture to leave the shelter which the whale affords them," observed Tom. On this he proposed to the boatswain to "heave to."

"We are not up to them yet," was the answer. "I was at sea before you were born, young gentleman. Leave me to judge what is best to be done."

Tom made no reply. "We have got a queer character to deal with," he observed to Desmond. "However, we must try to manage him, although it will be a serious matter to us, as well as all on board, if we do not recover the poor captain and mate."

No one turned in; indeed, all hands were required to put the ship about, and all night long she was kept on tack and tack without any answering signal. The doctor continued to fire at intervals one of the six-pounder guns on deck, but no signal was heard in return. When morning broke, the boatswain at length consented to heave to. Neither of the boats had been seen, and those on board began to despair. The gale showed no signs of abatement, while the sea had continued to increase. High-tossing waves, crested with foam, rose up around, while the sky was obscured by dense masses of dark clouds.

"Will your whaleboats live in a sea like this?" asked Tom of the boatswain, who in his character as commanding officer was standing aft.

"I guess they could, young man, if they are handled as we know how to handle them," was the answer.

"Then we may still hope to find the captain and mate," observed Desmond.

"If that whale did not smash up one of the boats with her flukes. If he did, twelve people would prove a heavy cargo in a sea like this, and she is likely enough to have been swamped."

"I am afraid that some such accident must have occurred," observed Tom.

"I guess you may not be far wrong," was the unsatisfactory remark.

On going into the cabin for breakfast they found Doctor Locock resting his head on his hands, with his elbows on the table.

"Poor Captain Sibley! He and those with him are gone, I fear. I would have given all I possess to save him. A kinder-hearted man never commanded a ship. His poor wife and children! And the second mate gone! Only that rough diamond in charge, without men enough to handle the ship. It will prove a very serious matter to us, I fear, young gentlemen, even should we ride out the present gale and bad weather continue."

"With our party of six we shall have no difficulty in managing the ship," observed Tom. "My eldest messmate and I are thorough navigators; and though we cannot assist in following up the object of the voyage, we shall be able to take her into a port where she can obtain another master, with more officers and men. I should propose steering for Hong-kong, where we are certain to fall in with American merchantmen, and probably a man-of-war; but, before we leave this neighbourhood, I should wish to make a thorough search for the missing boats. Notwithstanding what the boatswain says, I am not satisfied that they are lost."

"Do you think it possible that they can have escaped?" asked the surgeon, looking up.

"I think it possible, though I dare not say it is probable," answered Tom. "They may have killed the whale and hung on under the lee of its body, or they may have run before the wind and succeeded in reaching one of the small islands to the eastward. The weather has been so thick that they might easily have passed us without discovering our signals."

These remarks of Tom's greatly cheered the poor surgeon, who grieved for the loss of his friend the captain, and he was also naturally very anxious about his own fate.

"With any other man than Betts I should have less fear; but I know him to be an obstinate, self-opinionated, unprincipled fellow, and very ignorant at the same time," he observed. "If he were utterly ignorant of navigation there would be less danger; but he knows something about it, and has an idea that he is a first-rate navigator, and fully capable of taking charge of the ship."

"We must take our observations and keep our reckoning carefully, and we may then be able to correct his errors," said Tom.

As he spoke, a gruff voice was heard to exclaim, "What's that you say?" and the boatswain, who had been standing at the door of the cabin, walked in, casting furious glances at the doctor and the three midshipmen.

"So you think I know nothing about navigation, do you?" exclaimed the man. "I'll soon show you what I know, and as this cabin is mine, unless you can keep civil tongues in your heads, out you shall go and find berths forward."

Tom, remembering that a soft answer turneth away wrath, replied, "We have no wish to dispute your authority, Mr Betts, and shall be glad to give you all the assistance in our power. If the captain were here, and both the mates had been lost, he would have wished us to take observations and help him navigate the ship."

"The captain was one man, and I am another. He might have liked what won't suit my fancy. So now, as I'm captain, I'll beg you to keep your hands in your pockets until you receive my orders to take them out. You understand me?" Desmond, who was not so much inclined to keep his temper as Tom, was firing up at the boatswain's impudence, when Tom put his hand on his mouth, and turning to the boatswain, said, "Very well, Mr Betts; we understand each other.

But without boats, even if my people were able to help, you could not attempt to catch any more whales, and you have not even a sufficient number of men to take the ship home, so that you must put into a port to get fresh hands. If you take my advice you will, as soon as the gale is over, shape a course for Hong-kong, but before we leave this part of the ocean I would strongly urge you to make a diligent search in all directions for the boats."

"We might as well look for a needle in a bundle of hay. The boats are swamped, I'm sure of that, and don't intend to lose time by hunting for what we shall never find," answered the boatswain, as he took the captain's seat at the table.

Tom had considerable difficulty in restraining Desmond from saying anything which might irritate the man. Billy ate his breakfast in silence, stowing away an ample supply of provender to be ready for all emergencies. The doctor made no remark, fearful lest anything he might say should irritate the boatswain, whom he knew was capable of any act of tyranny.

As soon as the meal was over, Tom and Desmond went on deck.

"I wouldn't give way to that fellow," exclaimed the latter. "He'll be wanting us to take the ship round Cape Horn to Boston, and then get the credit of bringing her home himself. The best thing we can do is to clap him in irons and take command ourselves. The doctor would side with us, and so would two or three of the ship's company, if not all of them; for, depend upon it, they must be aware that he is no navigator, and would not wish to trust the craft to him."

Tom, who was averse to this proceeding, replied, "It might turn out very well if we were first to fall in with a British man-of-war; but suppose we met an American, we might be accused of running away with the ship. Rest assured that the boatswain and some of the men would be ready to swear to anything which would suit their own purposes."

"I would risk that," said Desmond. "The doctor's word would be taken before that of the boatswain, and any American officer would at once see that our statement was the true one."

"Suppose we were to fail in our attempt to seize the boatswain, he would murder us all, or at all events clap us in irons, and accuse us of mutiny and an attempt to seize the ship."

"Arrah! now, what's come over you, Tom?" exclaimed Desmond. "You'll not persuade me that you're afraid of carrying out my plan."

"No," answered Tom, smiling. "I only want to look at both sides of the case, as Archie Gordon would have done if he were with us. I fully agree with you, that if the fellow refuses to go to Hong-kong we must compel him by some means or other; but, it would be wrong in us to seize the ship unless we are assured of the incapacity of the boatswain, by which her safety and the lives of all on board would be imperilled. In that case we should be justified in acting as you propose."

"And isn't he incompetent?" exclaimed Desmond. "The doctor says so. If he had been a good navigator he would not have been serving as boatswain."

"If he will agree to go to Hong-kong or Sydney, or even to the Sandwich Islands, and let us assist him in navigating the ship, well and good, as we can leave her at any of those places, and he can obtain a fresh crew."

Tom's remarks satisfied Desmond that they ought to wait and see how the boatswain would act. A look-out was kept in every direction for the boats, but hours went by and still they did not appear. As the day drew on the wind began to abate, and the sea proportionately to go down. The boatswain had turned into the captain's berth and gone to sleep, and no one felt inclined to awaken him. Tom, Desmond, or Billy were constantly going to the mast-head to look out for the missing boats, still hoping that they might appear. Desmond had gone into the cabin, where he heard the boatswain snoring loudly.

He returned on deck.

"Now would be our time to seize the fellow," he said to Tom. "The doctor has a brace of pistols and a fowling-piece. I found another brace in the first mate's berth. I will speak to Jerry, and he can easily let Tim and Pat know what we are doing. Peter, I am certain, would side with us by the way he looked when he saw the boatswain take the captain's seat. The rest of the men would be very easily won over; and if not, after we have clapped the boatswain in irons, we must make them prisoners. We can easily tackle the watch on deck, and then master those below as they come up."

"Your plan is a good one, and I dare say would succeed, but I hope we shall not have to carry it out," said Tom. "We have had no proof that the boatswain will not act reasonably, and I again repeat that I do not consider we should be justified in taking the ship from him until he has shown by his conduct that he is likely to endanger our lives, and the rest of those on board."

The midshipmen had the after part of the deck to themselves, while the ship was hove to. Only two of the crew could be seen; one of them was the boatswain's mats, who, with the carpenter, were the only men remaining on board capable of taking charge of a watch.

Tom and Desmond were now wishing that the boatswain would come up, in order that they might learn in what direction they were to steer. They were both indeed getting so sleepy that they could scarcely keep their eyes open, and much longed to lie down, even for a couple of hours. At last the boatswain made his appearance.

"May I ask, Mr Betts, what you intend doing?" said Tom, in as polite a tone as he could command.

"What's that to you?" asked the boatswain, gruffly. "You are only passengers, and will have to go where the ship goes."

"I had no intention of dictating to you," replied Tom; "but because we are passengers, we naturally wish to learn when we are likely to get on shore."

"That must depend upon circumstances," said the boatswain, evasively. "I am in command of this ship, and intend to keep it, unless the captain and mate should come on board."

"We are perfectly ready to obey you, and to assist you in carrying the ship, either to Hong-kong, or Honolulu in the Sandwich Islands, or Sydney, where you may obtain fresh hands to take her home, and all I ask is that you will tell me for which of these ports you intend to steer."

"I have not made up my mind upon the matter," answered the boatswain.

"Perhaps you expect that we may still find the captain and boats crews; and if we were to work to windward during the night, and run back to-morrow over the same course, we may fall in with them, should they have kept afloat during the gale," said Tom suggestively, for he was afraid of saying that this was the course he would advise.

"Wait until you see what I do," said the boatswain. "As you may be wanted on deck, I advise you to turn in and get some sleep; the ship is hove to now, and for what I can tell, hove to she will remain for some hours longer."

Tom and Desmond agreed that they had better follow the boatswain's advice, and accordingly they went below. They found Billy Blueblazes snoring away, not troubling himself about what was likely to happen. Throwing themselves on their beds, they were both in another minute fast asleep. They expected to have been called to keep watch; but no one arousing them, fatigued as they were, they slept on until daylight. Tom was the first to awaken; he roused up Desmond and Billy, and all three went on deck together, where they found that the wind had again freshened up from the old quarter, and that the ship was standing close hauled to the eastward. The carpenter had charge of the deck, but they could get nothing out of him. The doctor soon afterwards came up. Tom inquired whether he knew the boatswain's intentions?

"He has not thought fit to enlighten me, but I conclude from the course he is steering that he intends visiting the Sandwich Islands," was the answer.

"I wish that he had thought fit to steer in the opposite direction," observed Tom. "However, we may perhaps find one of our ships there, and should then have no reason to complain."

"I hope that you will keep to your intention of taking an observation every day, and ascertaining our position," said the doctor, in a low voice, so that he might not be overheard.

"You may depend upon that," answered Tom.

"I conclude that you can tell whereabouts we now are?" said the doctor.

"Not unless I can learn at what hour sail was made and we began to stand on our present course," was the reply.

When Tom inquired of the carpenter, he received an evasive answer, and on going forward to learn from Jerry, Tim, or Pat, they all said that they had gone below at night, and had not been roused up. Some of the crew replied that it was in the first watch, others that it was in the middle watch.

"At all events, I hope to ascertain our latitude if the weather clears, and perhaps we may get an observation in the afternoon, or a lunar at night," said Tom. "But a good look-out must be kept ahead, for I know that there are numerous small islands and reefs, one of which may bring us up if we are not careful."

The doctor assisted the midshipmen to search for a sextant and nautical almanack, but, to their surprise, neither were to be found. "The chronometer was," the doctor said, "he knew, in the captain's cabin;" and they at last began to suspect that the boatswain had managed to get hold of the mate's as well as the captain's sextant and charts, and had shut them up in the cabin he had appropriated. What his object was in so doing it was difficult to say, unless he thought that he should keep the midshipmen more in his power by preventing them from knowing whereabouts they were.

Just before breakfast the boatswain came out of his cabin, carefully locking the door behind him. After remaining on deck some time, he returned and took his seat without uttering a word either to the surgeon or to the midshipmen, although he swore away at Peter for not being quick enough in bringing him what he asked for. Tom took no notice of this, but after waiting some time, said in his usual polite way —

"I should be much obliged to you, Mr Betts, if you can supply me with a sextant, and the use of the chronometer, as I should like to ascertain our position."

"Then you won't be obliged to me, for I don't intend to let you have them," answered the boatswain. "I can take care of this ship, and I won't have any one interfering with me."

"I do not wish to interfere," said Tom. "I only desire to take an observation for my own satisfaction."

"Then you won't have the satisfaction," said the boatswain. Desmond bit his lip, and Tom expected to hear him every moment say something, which would be sure to enrage the boatswain.

"At all events, if I can get a look at a chart, I shall be able to calculate where we are although that may not prevent this obstinate fellow from running the ship on a reef, and it will be a mercy if that is not her fate," thought Tom.

"I believe the man has gone out of his mind," said Desmond, when he found himself alone with his two messmates. "It is a pity we did not put him in irons at first, and we might now have been on our way to Hong-kong."

"We did what was right," observed Tom, "and whatever happens that will be a satisfaction."

They hunted about for a chart, but the boatswain had locked that up also, and refused to allow Tom to look at it. The wind continued tolerably steady during the day, though the weather looked unsettled, and the sea appeared again to be getting up. As the ship was kept under her topsails and spanker, with two reefs down, no fresh sail was made, and the boatswain did not order the midshipmen to perform any duty. The doctor seemed to feel the loss of the captain very much. He had until that morning entertained a hope of finding him, but this he now abandoned, and having no confidence in the boatswain's skill as a navigator, he seemed to have made up his mind that the ship would be cast away, and that all on board would be lost. He had hitherto appeared to be of a cheerful disposition, but he now sat all day moodily in his cabin, with a book before him, although his eye scarcely glanced at its pages. Tom and

Gerald tried to induce him to come on deck, but he shook his head, declaring that he did not feel able to walk. Billy endeavoured to amuse him by telling him one of his funny stories, but not a smile came over the poor doctor's face. At dinner the midshipmen had all the conversation to themselves. The boatswain did not address even a word to them. This did not, however, disconcert them in the least, and they continued talking away as if there was no such person present, so that he was well pleased to get up and go on deck.

The same weather continued for a couple of days. The boatswain kept a watch on the midshipmen to prevent them taking an observation. Billy, however, found a quadrant in the second mate's cabin, and watching his opportunity when Mr Betts was below, brought it up on deck to Tom and Gerald. They had fortunately carefully compared their watches with the chronometer, and the doctor had concealed a nautical almanack.

"Arrah!" exclaimed Desmond; "we shall be able to make something of an observation, although not as correct as we should wish."

Tom took the quadrant and was looking through it, when he suddenly felt it dashed from his hand, and falling on deck it was broken. Turning round he saw Mr Betts, who had stolen up behind him.

"So you fancy I cannot navigate the ship, do you; and must needs try and take an observation yourself? Do you and your mates try that prank again, and I'll land you all on the first island we sight, where you may follow your own pleasure, if the savages don't knock you on the head and eat you; and if some one doesn't take you off, which is not very likely, there you will remain to the end of your days."

Gerald was beginning to answer this rude address, when Tom stopped him.

"We do not wish to have a dispute with you, Mr Betts, though we have a perfect right to take an observation, or to do anything else which does not interfere with the discipline of the ship," said Tom, as he turned away, feeling that it was better to avoid any dispute with the boatswain.

Tom accordingly signing to his companions, they all left the deck, allowing the boatswain to pace up and down by himself.

Towards evening he sent the steward to them, and told them that he expected all three to keep the middle watch.

"Your men will have the first watch," he said, "and I would advise you to be on deck directly you are called."

As there was no reason to object to this they agreed to do as the boatswain wished. They accordingly turned in for the first part of the night. They had been asleep some time when a fearful crash was heard. They, all three being awake, quickly slipped into their clothes.

"I knew it would be so," exclaimed the doctor, whom they met in the cabin; "we shall none of us see another sunrise."

"I hope things won't be so bad as that," said Tom; "the ship seems to be moving forward; perhaps she has merely touched a coral reef and has scraped clear. We will go on deck and ascertain how matters stand."

The cries and shouts which reached the cabin showed that something serious had happened. Scarcely had Tom and his companions gained the deck, than again the ship struck with greater force than before, every timber quivering from stem to stern. The foremast went by the board, carrying with it the main-topmast, when a sea striking the ship swept over her. The wild shrieks for help which followed showed that some of the crew had been borne away.

"Can you see land?" asked Desmond of Tom.

"No; we are on a coral reef, and our chances of escape are very small."

Just then they heard the boatswain shouting out to the crew to lower a boat, the only one remaining.

"Don't let us go in her," said Tom; "if the ship holds together, we shall be better off where we are: when daylight comes we can form a raft, and if there is any land near we may get there on it."

Both Desmond and Billy agreed to do as Tom proposed.

Just then Jerry came up. "I'll stick by you, whatever you intend doing," he answered, when Tom told him what he proposed.

In the mean time, the boatswain, with the survivors of the crew, had lowered the boat, and were throwing various things into her. Jerry made out Tim and Pat among the people about to go off.

"Where are you going to?" he shouted. "Mr Rogers says he'll stick by the wreck, and you'll not be deserting him, I hope?"

"That I'll not. Tim Nolan is not the man to desert his officer," answered Tim, as he made his way to the after part of the ship, where Jerry was. Pat either did not hear Jerry, or determined to go off in the boat if he could. The doctor and Peter, who had come on deck, seemed undecided. It was evident from the dislike Peter had for the boatswain that he was unwilling to accompany him. The boatswain, with six other men, who alone remained of the crew, disappeared over the side into the boat. The doctor, seized by a sudden impulse, rushed to the side of the ship, shouting—

"Take me with you! take me with you!" but the oars had been got out, the boat shoved off, and was already tossing among the broken water on the lee of the ship, several fathoms off.

"You are safer on the wreck than in that boat," said Tom, as the doctor came back.

"Dat you are, Massa Locock," said Peter. "See dare where de boat go."

Through the gloom the boat could just be distinguished, surrounded by leaping masses of foaming water. The party on board watched her with anxious eyes, until she disappeared in the darkness.

"Hark!" cried Peter. "Me tink I hear a shriek; dat come from de boat; depen' upon it we no see her 'gan."

As, however, she must have been by this time a long way to leeward, Tom thought it impossible that any human voice could have come up against the wind still blowing as it did. Tom and Desmond, with the rest of the party, discussed the probability as to where they were. They must have passed over a sunken reef, on which the ship had first struck, and had then run right on to another part of the reef, somewhat higher, where she had become fixed. This was probably on the inner or lee side. Though the sea broke over the fore part of the ship, the after part was tolerably dry, and hopes were entertained that she would hold together for some hours, and, should the wind go down, perhaps for days, which would enable them to provide for their safety. After the doctor had sufficiently recovered to take part in the discussion, he suggested that perhaps she might be got off.

"You wouldn't say that, sir, if you had been forward when she struck," answered Jerry. "She is entirely stove in, and must have twelve or fourteen feet of water in her by this time. It will be a hard job before long to get any provisions."

"Then the sooner we set about it the better," said Tom, "if we can manage to find our way in the dark."

"De lamp in de cabin is still 'light—me get him," said Peter, who soon returned, carefully shading the lamp, when he, Jerry, and Tim made their way below, hoping to reach the fore hold, where the bulk of the provisions were stowed. They were, however, very soon convinced that it would be utterly impossible to get up anything until the tide had fallen, as the sea was rushing in at the bows, and completely flooding the hold.

"Then we must try what we can do at daylight, for at present it would be useless to attempt getting anything up. We will see, however, what is to be found in the afterpart of the ship."

Peter recollected that there were some eases of biscuits and other articles, which it was necessary to keep dry. His report encouraged Tom to hope that they should not starve.

"Now, my lads, the first thing we have to do is to collect all the spars and loose plank we can get hold of, to form a raft. We are likely to find land either on one side or the other, perhaps not far off, though we are unable to see it now, and we must manage to reach it and carry provisions for our support, as we are not likely to find much more than cocoa-nuts and fish. One satisfactory thing is that the people hereabouts are not cannibals, and are generally disposed to be friendly to white men, so that if the island we may reach is inhabited we are not likely to be ill-treated."

Tom by these remarks and by keeping up his own spirits, prevented his companions from losing theirs. Even the doctor began to hope that they might escape. All hands now set to work to collect materials for the raft as far as could be done in the dark, and to drag them up to the weather side of the quarter-deck, where there was not much risk of their being carried away. Altogether they managed to secure a number of spars and pieces of the bulwarks and a good supply of rope of various sizes. The cabin bulk-heads with other portions of the vessel which could easily be torn away would give them wood enough to make a raft of sufficient size to carry the whole party as well as provisions. By lashing underneath two rows of casks, it would be sufficiently buoyant.

They were thus employed until daylight, when Tom, who had sprung up to the poop to look out, exclaimed—"A ship in sight! a ship in sight! she's only just hull down."

His shout brought the rest of the party up around him, and all were eagerly looking out in the direction be pointed. As daylight increased, Tim began to rub his eyes—

"Arrah now, ill-luck to it; but my ship has just turned into a white rock," he cried out. "Shure but it's a mighty disappointment."

The expectation of speedy deliverance was thus suddenly destroyed; but the shipwrecked party continued looking round on every side, in the hope of discovering land. The light yet further increasing, Tom's countenance brightened as he observed what looked like the masts of a ship rising, far off, out of the water.

"Why, I believe those are three cocoa-nut trees," he cried out cheerfully. "I see several others away to the eastward."

"If there are cocoa-nut trees, there must be land too, for they don't grow out of the sea," said Billy, "and I hope we may be able to get there."

"You need not doubt about our doing that," said Tom.

This announcement raised every one's spirits. The weather had much moderated. The sea between the reef on which the ship lay and the land was tolerably smooth.

The forlorn party began to cheer up. All now began to feel hungry. "I'll tell you what it is: if we don't get something to eat soon, I for one shall die of inanition," exclaimed Billy. "I can't stand starving at the best of times, and I am suffering dreadfully."

"We will see what can be done, Billy," said Tom, and as if it was a matter of course, he told Peter to get breakfast ready.

"Yes, massa officer, me soon do dat same," answered the black, grinning and looking towards where the caboose had lately stood. "Me try what can do in de cabin," he added, diving below.

Though the caboose had been washed away Peter managed to light a fire in the cabin stove and to cook a tolerable breakfast, of which all thankfully partook.

"'Faith! we're not so badly off after all," observed Gerald. "If the boatswain and the poor fellows with him had stuck to the ship, they might all have been alive now and have reached land without difficulty."

Immediately after breakfast they began to put the raft together, which Tom determined to form of an oblong shape like a catamaran, so that it might, should the wind be fair, be sailed or propelled by paddles towards the shore. As the distance was considerable, it was important to make it as strong as possible, to stand any amount of sea they were likely to meet with before they reached the shore. It took upwards of an hour to form the frame-work and deck it. They then, having cut away the bulwarks, launched it overboard with capstan bars. The water under the lee of the wreck was tolerably smooth, so that the raft remained alongside without injury. They had next to lash the casks below it. This was a more difficult operation, as it was necessary to secure them firmly in their proper positions, a row on each side, head to head. When it was completed, the platform floated well out of the water.

Three oars only could be found on board, so that they had to form paddles by nailing boards on to the ends of short spars. The next work was to rig the masts. Tom and Desmond agreed to have two masts with a bowsprit, so that they might be able to sail with the wind abeam. The masts were firmly fixed by means of blocks nailed to the deck, and they were set up with stays. By noon the raft was completed. The midshipmen surveyed her with considerable satisfaction.

"I for one should not mind sailing in her anywhere, provided she was well provisioned," said Billy Blueblazes. "I don't see why we should not try to fetch the Ladrones, if we don't find ourselves very comfortable where we are going."

"I would strongly advise you not to make the attempt, young gentlemen," said the doctor, with a groan, he not being as well satisfied with the appearance of the raft as his younger companions.

"We shall see how she will behave when she has her cargo on board, and we get under way," said Tom.

"Don't you think we had better have some dinner before we shove off?" asked Billy; "it won't do to be going away without our grub, as it may be some time before we reach the shore."

Billy's proposal was agreed to, although Tom strongly recommended that there should be no unnecessary delay. While Peter was preparing dinner, all the stores which could be collected were placed on the raft and lashed securely down amidships. The principal provisions found aft were biscuits, tins of potted meats, a few preserves, coffee, tea, sugar, and five well-cured hams.

"We are pretty well off as it is," said Desmond; "but don't let us go without firearms."

The doctor had a fowling-piece, and muskets and pistols enough were found to arm each of the rest of the party. With a good supply of ammunition they would thus, should they meet with hostile savages, be able to keep them at bay.

They had already secured provisions sufficient to last them for several weeks. As it was important, however, to obtain some of a more substantial character, Jerry and Tim volunteered to dive down into the fore hold to try and get up some casks of beef. This, after some labour and no little risk of drowning themselves, they succeeded in doing, and two casks of beef were hoisted on deck. They fortunately came upon two casks, one of flour the other of rice, which, although damaged by the water, might be dried on shore in the sun, and rendered eatable. These accordingly were added to their provisions. Two cases of wine and a small keg of spirits were also put on board. Peter added to these some cooking utensils, with cups, plates, knives, and forks. At length, Tom declared that the raft would carry no more. It was high time indeed to set off, as it might take them until dark to reach the land in sight.

"Let me advise you, gentlemen, to carry some clothing and blankets; they will not weigh much, and we may want them," observed the doctor.

His advice was followed.

"We must get on board and shove off," cried Tom, at last.

His messmates and the men obeyed him, being fully as eager as he was. The doctor was below; he presently appeared with his medicine chest and instrument case, which were handed down.

"Why, we are going off without a chart or nautical instrument!" exclaimed Tom, reminded of his negligence by seeing the doctor's cases.

He and Desmond returned on board and found the chart, sextant, and chronometer, which the boatswain had fortunately not carried off.

"The raft is as fully laden as she should be," observed Tom to Desmond; "we should arrange what things to heave overboard, if it comes on to blow and she cannot carry them all."

"The doctor's physic, cases, and instruments, I should say," answered Desmond; "however, I hope we shall not have to do that. The weather looks promising. As the wind is fair, we may soon reach the land."

These remarks were made on deck. The two midshipmen now sprang on board the raft. Tom gave the order to cast off, and all hands getting out the oars and paddles, the raft began to move away from the wreck. The foresail was now set, then the mainsail with the jib, Tom steering with a long oar, the raft glided rapidly and smoothly over the water. Their voyage was thus far well commenced, but Tom and Desmond could not help recollecting their late adventure in the boat, and how narrowly they had escaped perishing from hunger, although they had been so well supplied with provisions when they started. While Tom steered, Billy remained aft to tend the main-sheet, and Desmond, with Jerry, stood forward to keep a look-out for any reefs which might not have sufficient water on them to allow the raft to pass over. No dangers, however, as yet appeared ahead. They were apparently in the centre of a large circular reef, of which the island they hoped to gain formed a portion. They expected to find a beach on which they might run the raft, and land their cargo without difficulty. They were, however, too far off as yet to ascertain its character. Of its existence they could only tell by seeing the cocoa-nut trees growing on it. It was evidently very low. Of its extent they were unable to form an opinion.

"My fear is that we shall find no water on it, and in that case we must search for another," observed the doctor.

"You forget the milk in the cocoa-nuts," said Desmond, laughing.

"We should very soon exhaust that," answered the doctor, in a gloomy tone.

"But we don't know yet that we shall not find water," answered Desmond; "I can already make out the land extending a couple of miles north and south, and if it was not higher than we at first supposed, we should not see it even yet."

"If any volcanic agency has been at work, we may then hope to find water," observed the doctor, brightening a little; "but I confess that I cannot see the land."

The doctor, however, was near-sighted. The question next arose whether there were any inhabitants, and if so, whether they were likely to prove friendly.

"I should say that if white kidnappers from your colonies have visited them, they are likely to be anything but friendly, and we shall probably have to fight for our lives," said the doctor.

"But, my dear sir, we don't know whether there are any inhabitants," said Desmond. "Let us look at the bright side of things we have escaped with our lives, and have abundance of provisions. Why should we make ourselves more unhappy than is necessary?"

The wind occasionally dropped, when the oars and paddles were put in motion, and the raft continued its course steadily towards the land. Even when the wind blew the freshest she moved but slowly, so that for a long time it appeared as if she would not reach the shore before dark. As they looked astern, however, they found that they had sunk the wreck almost out of sight. The doctor fancied she must have gone down, as he could not distinguish her. The wind, however, again freshened, and Jerry asserted that the raft was going at the rate of three knots an hour.

At length the land was clearly seen in some places, at the further side of the island especially, rising to a considerable height in ridges and hillocks.

"No fear now, doctor, about not finding water," observed Desmond. "Volcanic agency must have been at work to throw up those hills, and I begin to see low trees or shrubs. It may turn out to be after all a fertile spot, though not a very picturesque one, I grant."

"If it affords us rest to our feet, and vegetable productions to keep scurvy at a distance, with an ample supply of water, we shall have reason to be thankful," said the doctor, whose spirits rose as he was persuaded that his worst anticipations would not be fulfilled.

The sun was now getting low, and it would be dark before they could reach the shore. Desmond and Jerry both declared that they could see no sign of breakers, and just before the sun dipped beneath the horizon his rays shone on a white sandy beach, which promised to afford them an easy landing-place. On one point, however, the doctor's mind was not satisfied. "What if the island is inhabited by savages? And if it supplies food and water, it is very likely to be the case," he observed.

"We must try and make friends with them, or, if they will not be friends, keep them at a distance; depend upon it they will be civil enough when they see our firearms," answered Desmond.

"Inhabited? I'm sure it is," exclaimed Jerry, suddenly. "Look there! there's a fellow dancing away on the top of that hillock. He sees us; the chances are a score or two more black fellows like him are hidden away, who will be down upon us as we step on shore."

Desmond at the same time saw the savage, and told Tom.

"Well, there is but one as yet," said Tom; "perhaps, however, it may be prudent to load a couple of the muskets, though one will be sufficient, depend upon it, to keep them at bay."

As the raft approached the shore, the gestures of the savage appeared to become more and more frantic, but the gloom of evening soon rendered his form indistinct, although he could still be seen against the sky. The breeze having once more almost died away, the paddles were again got out. The raft neared the shore. There was, they saw, a little surf, but not sufficient to endanger the raft and cargo. In a few minutes more the beach would be reached. The savage had disappeared, but a voice was heard, evidently shouting to them.

"Bedad! but the savage is Pat Casey!" exclaimed Tim, who recognised his countryman's voice, and, as the raft touched the beach, Pat rushed forward, and grasped the hands of Jerry and Tim, who sprang overboard to assist in securing it. The rest of the party quickly followed, as it was important to lighten the raft as soon as possible.

"Where are the other men?" asked the doctor. "We thought you were all lost soon after you left the wreck."

"Sure, so they all were entirely but myself," answered Pat; "and how I came on shore is more than I can tell, except that I'm after supposing I held on to the bottom of the boat, and this morning I found myself high and dry on the beach. I'm mighty glad to see you all, and you are welcome to the island."

"Are there any savages?" asked the doctor.

"Barring myself, no, your honour," answered Pat, with a laugh. "They would have been down upon me before now if there had been any, but not a soul have I set eyes on since I came ashore."

However, there was no time for talking, as it was important at once to land the cargo. The whole party, aided by Pat, immediately set about performing this task. Everything was got on shore without damage. The raft itself was then secured by the strongest ropes they possessed to the trunk of a cocoa-nut tree, which fortunately grew near. Pat had collected wood for a fire, though he had forgotten that he did not possess the means of igniting it. But some matches having been fortunately brought among other things, a bright blaze was soon produced. By its light, at the doctor's suggestion, a tent was formed with the sails of the raft and some spare canvas, large enough to afford shelter to the whole party.

Peter and Pat had been, in the mean time, busily engaged in preparing supper, to which all hands were ready to do justice.

"Dare, gentl'm," exclaimed Peter, as he placed some slices of fried ham before the doctor and midshipmen; "you no get better dan dis in de bes' hotel in Boston. Per'aps you tink de cook is worth glass ob grog?"

Tom took the hint, and divided a couple of bottles of wine among the party, which assisted to put them in good spirits. They sat round the fire, yarns were told and songs were sung, but their heads soon began to nod, and they were glad to seek the shelter of the tent. As the island was uninhabited, Tom did not consider it necessary to set a watch; indeed, had any one of the party made the attempt, the probabilities were that he would have been unable to keep his eyes open.

Chapter Five.

Search for and find the boat—Return in her to the wreck—
Find more stores, and build a raft—Carry it to the shore, and
go back to break up the wreck for building a vessel—Once
more getting back they find the doctor working at a still—
Another trip—It comes on to blow hard—Reach shore—The
still successful—The gale increases—Its effects on the
wreck—More stores saved—Seeds found and sown—A flag-
staff set up—Plans for their proposed vessel—Engaged in
shooting and fishing—Discover a marine poultry-yard—
Billy and the eggs—Successful fishing—Seeds sown.

Tom, who was always the first on foot, roused up his companions.

"Do let a fellow have his sleep out," murmured Billy; "we have got
nothing to do."

"We've plenty to do," answered Tom. "We've got to look out for
water, and if we find it to build a hut, and ascertain what food the
island produces, and try to go back to the wreck and bring off more
stores, and put up a flag-staff, and fifty other things."

"Well, I didn't think of all that," said Billy, sitting up. "Dear me, dear
me! here we are, on another desert island; with the chances of
remaining all our born days."

"Better than being at the bottom of the sea, or crunched up by
sharks," observed Desmond, "or than being cast on shore among
cannibals, who would have cooked and eaten us at the first
opportunity. It is not a barren island either, for there are cocoa-nut
trees, and there may be other fruits or roots. We shall probably also
be able to catch plenty of fish."

"If we could get hold of some fine fat turtle, it would be more to the
purpose," said Billy. "Pat makes capital turtle soup. I'm glad he
escaped."

"I am afraid the turtle have done laying their eggs by this time,"
observed the doctor. "They only come on shore for that purpose, and

we are not likely to catch them otherwise, so you must give up all thoughts of revelling on turtle."

While Peter prepared breakfast, Pat climbed one of the cocoa-nut trees, and sent down nuts enough to afford each of the party a refreshing draught of liquid. It could not properly be called milk, as it had not yet assumed its white appearance, which it does only after the nut is perfectly ripe. It was welcome, notwithstanding. Though a small cask of water had been brought on shore, Tom wisely wished to husband it until a spring had been discovered. About this the doctor was very doubtful, and Pat, whom he questioned on the subject, stated that he had not discovered any signs of water.

"I should have wished to search for water the first thing," observed Tom; "but whether it is to be found or not, it is most important that we should ascertain whether the boat was washed up on the beach, and if she can be repaired to enable us to return to the wreck."

"Can you show us where you came on shore, Pat?"

"Bedad, sir, I've been wandering up and down so many times, that I am not quite certain; but it's my belief that if she is to be found anywhere, it will be away to the northward, for I didn't see her at the other end."

"Then we will set off without delay," said Tom; and taking Pat, he and Desmond, with Jerry Bird, commenced a search for the boat in the direction Pat mentioned.

The sandy beach was divided in many places by masses of coral extending some distance into the water, among which the boat might easily be concealed. Had she, however, been thrown on any of them, she would, Tom feared, in all probability be knocked to pieces. The surprising thing was that Pat had not seen her. It appeared from his account that when he had partially recovered his senses, finding himself on shore, he had set off in a confused state of mind, without knowing where he was going, and that some time must have elapsed before he came entirely to himself.

"Suppose we do not recover the boat, how are we to visit the wreck?" asked Desmond.

"We must build a smaller raft out of the large one, which we can much more easily manage; and should the weather continue calm, as there appears to be no strong current likely to drive us away, we may, I think, without much risk easily make the trip there and back," answered Tom.

"But how are we to carry a cargo?" inquired Desmond.

"We must form another raft on board, and the materials will serve for building our hut," was the answer.

"Then you think we shall have to remain some time on the island?" said Desmond.

"Of course; it may be for months or years, or we may get off in a few days or weeks. Had we a good carpenter among us, we might have built a vessel from the wreck, should she hold together long enough for us to bring a good portion of her planking and timber ashore; but I am very certain that none of us are capable of that, although we have a stock of carpenter's tools."

"There is nothing like trying," said Desmond. "I have seen ships being built; and if we can obtain timber, we might manage in time to put one together large enough to carry us at once to Guam or to the Sandwich Islands."

"We will hear what the doctor says. What do you think about it, Bird?"

"Well, sir, I have helped to rig many a craft, but cannot say that I ever worked as a shipwright, though I am ready to try my hand at that or anything else, and 'where there's a will there's a way.'"

"What do you say, Pat?" asked Tom.

"As to that, Mr Rogers, when a man has been a Prime Minister, he ought to think himself fit for anything; and sooner than live on a dissolute island all me life, I'd undertake to build a ninety-gun ship, if I had the materials."

The answers of the two seamen made Tom think that Desmond's proposal was, at all events, worth consideration.

"Well, if we find we can get timber enough from the wreck, I don't see why we should not make the attempt," he said, after turning over the matter in his mind.

"I'll undertake that we can build a vessel of ten or fifteen tons, which will carry us to the Sandwich Islands," observed Desmond, confidently. "I have got the idea in my head, though I cannot promise that she will be much of a clipper, but she shall keep afloat, beat to windward, and stand a pretty heavy sea."

Tom and Desmond discussed the matter as they walked along. Presently Pat, who had started on ahead, cried out, "Arrah! here she is, all right, if not all tight," and he pointed to a little sandy bay, almost at the extreme northern end of the island. There lay the boat on the beach. She had narrowly missed being swept round the island, when she would in all probability have been lost unless some counter current, on the lee side, had driven her back. She had escaped also another danger, that of being dashed to pieces against a rugged ledge close to which she must have passed. The party hurried up to her to ascertain what damage she had received. The surf had evidently turned her over, and but little water remained in her. At first sight she appeared to be uninjured.

"I was afraid so," said Tom, as he was going round her, and put his hand through a hole in the bows. "The water ran out here; perhaps she would have suffered more if she had not been thus damaged. If she's stove in nowhere else, we shall be able to repair her." This was apparently the only damage the boat had received.

"I am not surprised that she should have been swamped with so many men in her, in the heavy sea there was running when those unhappy men put off," observed Tom. "We shall have to bring our tools and materials here. And now let us see if any oars have been cast on shore." They hunted about, but the oars, being so much lighter than the boat, had either been swept round the north end of the island or thrown on some other part of the shore.

Having hauled the boat up, they returned towards the camp. Tom and Desmond were very anxious to repair the boat and visit the wreck before night-fall, in case the weather should change and she should go to pieces. As they walked along they discussed the best plan for repairing the boat. Desmond suggested that they should first nail on pieces of well-greased canvas, and then fix over that two or more lengths from the staves of one of the casks.

"But where's the grease to come from? I'm afraid we have none," observed Tom.

"We've got a piece of bacon, and there would be grease enough from that for the purpose," answered Desmond.

Their conversation was interrupted by a shout from Jerry Bird, who held up an oar which he had found floating close in by the shore under one of the ledges. This, with the three oars they already possessed, and one of the long paddles to steer by, would enable them to shove off as soon as they could patch up the boat. The doctor's spirits rose considerably when he heard that the boat had been discovered, and he consented to remain on shore with Tim and Peter, while the rest of the party returned to the wreck—he undertaking to search for water.

"You must not be alarmed if we do not come back to-night," said Tom; "for, if the weather promises to be fine, it may be better to build a large raft, on which we can tow ashore all the stores we can obtain."

"Remember, Rogers, to bring one of the tripods, the smith's forge and tools, and some piping; for should we fail to discover water, I may be able to construct a still, by which we may obtain as much fresh water as we require."

"A capital idea," exclaimed Tom. "I didn't think of that."

"'Necessity is the mother of invention,'" answered the doctor. "I never worked as a smith, but I know the principles on which a still is constructed, and I hope that I shall be able to put one up; if, however, we can find water, we may be saved the trouble, and employ our labour for other purposes."

As they would have no time on board to spare for cooking, Tom had a supply of food, sufficient for a couple of days, put up, with a bottle of water and a few cocoa-nuts, in case they might be unable to get at the water on board. Thus laden with the materials for repairing the boat, they went back to where she lay, accompanied by Billy. Tom had begged the doctor to light a fire at night, in case the weather should come on bad and they might have to return sooner than they intended.

Desmond's plan was carried out. Bird had brought some oakum, which was forced in between the seams with a chisel, and as the party surveyed their work, they had reason to hope that the boat would at all events swim.

They watched the result, however, with no little anxiety, as, having run her down the beach, she was once more afloat. She leaked slightly, but Desmond declared that it was not through the place where she had been repaired, and they found after getting some distance from the shore that they could easily bale out the water which made its way in. Tom had brought the compass, and believing that he knew the bearings of the wreck, he steered a course which would soon bring them in sight of her. The sea was so calm that he did not suppose it possible she could have gone to pieces, and as they pulled on, he looked out eagerly for her. At length he made out a dark object rising out of the blue sea almost due west of the island.

"There she is!" he exclaimed; "we shall be on board of her in an hour."

The crew gave way, and in less than the time mentioned they were alongside. She appeared to be exactly in the condition they had left her. The boat having been carefully secured, they climbed up her side. The first thing to be obtained was a cask of fresh water, which they were fortunate in finding; it was at once got up and placed on deck. It would take too long to describe the various articles which were obtained. Among them were the smith's forge, some piping and the tripod, which the doctor especially asked for. For some of them Jerry or Pat dived into the hold. Others were found on the spar-deck and the after part of the ship, where they were got up without difficulty. Tom and Gerald, when they came on deck, frequently took a glance around to see how the weather looked, and were satisfied that there was every appearance of its holding fine. They accordingly made up their minds to remain during the night. Having collected all the stores which such a raft as they intended to build could carry, they at once commenced forming one. The mizzen and part of the mainmast still remained standing; Tom proposed forming shears and trying to hoist out the former; but as this was found impracticable, they cut both the masts away, to serve as the main beams of their raft. Several more spars were got up, and they then began cutting away the spar-deck. They worked on until it was dark, when Pat cooked some supper—the first food they had eaten since the morning.

"Now, we shall want some sleep," said Tom; "but though the ship won't run away with us, it will be prudent to keep watch in case bad weather should come on; although it looks very fine at present, we should not trust to that. I'll keep the first watch; you, Desmond, take the middle; and Bird shall have the morning watch. We will excuse Billy, because it is just possible he may fall asleep and tumble overboard, or at all events forget to call us, and Pat requires another night's rest after his night on the bottom of the boat and the hard work he has done to-day."

Tom, in reality, did not wish to trust Pat entirely, thinking it very possible that as soon as they were all below he would stow himself away and go to sleep. The deck cabin being free from water, the party were far more comfortably off than they would have been on shore. The deck having too great an inclination to afford a good walk, Tom managed to keep awake by holding on to the weather bulwarks, and moving backwards and forwards, constantly looking to windward for any change of weather. Though, after all the trouble they had taken, they would have been sorry to lose the various things they had found on board, it would have been unwise to have risked remaining on the wreck should the wind get up. The sky, however, was perfectly clear, the stars shone out brilliantly, undimmed by the slightest vapour, while scarcely a breath of wind disturbed the surface of the now slumbering ocean.

"We shall want a breeze to-morrow to carry us to the shore, though I hope it will remain calm as at present until then," thought Tom. He very frequently had the greatest difficulty in keeping his eyes open, but he succeeded. He calculated that it was about midnight when he went below, and finding that it was time, roused up Gerald. "Do not let sleep overtake you, old fellow," he said. "I found it a hard matter to keep my eyes open."

"Yes, but mine have been shut for four hours," said Desmond. "I'll look after the ship, and depend upon it as soon as my watch is out I'll rouse up Jerry."

115

The middle watch passed away as calmly as the first, and Jerry, after taking a look round, declared his belief that the day would be as fine as the former. According to Tom's orders, all hands were aroused at daybreak, and they immediately set to work on the raft, which was completed and launched overboard before they knocked off for breakfast. Empty casks were then got under it, and masts set up. As the wind was fair, they had only to rig a couple of large lugs, which answered every purpose. They had next to load their raft; the water was perfectly smooth, and it was hauled under the side, where this was easily done, though they had to lower many of the heavier articles on it with a tackle. Tom directed Desmond and Jerry to go ahead in the boat, while Billy and Pat remained on board to help with the raft. As the day advanced, a steady breeze arose, and the raft, heavy as it was, made great progress, helped by the boat, towards the shore. As towards evening they neared the beach, they saw their companions anxiously waiting for them. The doctor's face looked even longer than usual.

"What's the matter?" asked Tom, as he shook hands.

"We have found no water," answered the doctor; "and if you have not brought materials for making a still, we are doomed."

"But I hope we have brought everything you want, doctor," replied Tom.

"Thank Heaven! our lives may then be preserved," said the doctor. "I was almost afraid to ask the question."

"We have got even more than we expected," said Desmond; "and should the weather hold fine, we may hope, in the course of two or three trips, to get wood enough for our proposed craft."

There was no time for talking, however. All hands set to work to unload the raft; the doctor, who was now in better spirits, hauling away with might and main, to get the more heavy articles up the beach before dark. Not only was everything already on shore, but the two rafts taken to pieces, and dragged up likewise.

The weather continued so fine that Tom and Desmond determined, before hauling up the boat, to go back to the wreck for further stores, and to bring away as many rafts of timber as they could obtain. The doctor said he must remain on shore to work at the still. For his assistants he chose Billy Blueblazes and Peter the black. Billy was not ingenious, but, as the doctor observed, "he could collect wood and blow the bellows."

Billy was at first indignant on being told that he was thus to be employed, but after due reflection he came to the conclusion that it would be easier work than tearing off planking from the wreck, or pulling an oar under a hot sun for several hours each day. The first thing to be done was to set up the forge. All hands had turned out at daybreak, so that the doctor was able to begin work before the boat party shoved off.

It took them two hours to get to the wreck. They had hard work before them. First they made a thorough search for all remaining provisions, iron-work, canvas, ropes, and blocks. These were placed aft, ready for lowering on to the raft as soon as one could be put together. Sailors naturally feel it a somewhat melancholy task to break up a ship. It seems as if all hope of its being of further use is gone, but probably the party did not trouble themselves with any sentimental ideas on the subject just then; all they thought of was the best, way to tear up the planking, and to secure as much timber as possible. They indeed were cheered with the thoughts that they should be able to build a trim little craft out of the battered hull, to carry them to some place from whence they could once more get back to Old England. For hours they laboured away with sledge-hammers, crowbars, and saws. The bowsprit was first got out, then all the remaining portions of the bulwarks wore cut away. They then commenced on the upper deck, and as the planks were torn up they were lowered overboard and lashed alongside.

"To my mind, a pretty strong gale would save us a mighty deal of trouble," observed Tim, as he was working away. "The say in a few hours would do more work than we can get through in as many days."

"Very likely, my boy," observed Jerry; "but where would all the timber go to? it would not come floating of its own accord to our landing-place, and I suspect it would not be of much use when it got there. Let us be thankful for the calm weather, and work away while it lasts."

After some hours' labour, a sufficient quantity of wood had been obtained to form a large raft. It was of a much rougher description than the two former ones, but still buoyant enough to carry the remaining stores. Among other things they had brought a kedge anchor and a hawser. They had, however, forgotten that there were no spars remaining to serve as masts or yards; it was necessary, therefore, to tow the raft. By the time all was ready, it was so late that it would be impossible to reach the shore before dark, and Tom had omitted to charge the doctor to keep up a fire by which they might steer to the landing-place.

"Well, never mind, we will begin our voyage," he said, "and when it gets dark we will anchor the raft and return for it in the morning. Should bad weather come on, the chances are that the timber, at all events, will be washed on shore, though we may lose the stores; but that will not matter so much, although we may be compelled to reduce the dimensions of our craft." Tom and Jerry took charge of the raft, having contrived two large paddles to propel it, while Desmond and the rest went in the boat and pulled ahead. More progress was made than had been expected, as a slight current set towards the shore, and they had performed half the distance before it grew dark. The night also was very fine, and as Desmond had a compass in the boat and had taken the bearings of the harbour, he was able to steer for it. The doctor had not forgotten them. In a short time, catching sight of a fire blazing up brightly, which they knew must be burning close to the beach, they continued their course. It was, however, past ten o'clock before they reached the shore, where they found the doctor and his companions ready to receive them.

"You have not been idle, I see; nor have I," he exclaimed. "I have made good progress with my still, and I hope to get it into working order early to-morrow."

Tom hoped that the doctor would not be disappointed in his expectations, for on examining the water he found that they had sufficient, at the rate at which it was consumed, to last only two or three days more. He determined, therefore, to place the party on an allowance, in case the still should not succeed.

"You need not be afraid of that," observed the doctor; "if we do not obtain the fresh water by to-morrow evening, I will undertake to drink a gallon of salt water. Will that satisfy you?"

"I should think so," answered Tom, laughing. "I have no doubt of your success; but some accident may happen, and it is as well to be on the safe side."

Another trip was made the next day to the wreck, and as the party were able to devote the whole of their strength to the work of breaking up the vessel, they got out a larger quantity of wood than on the previous day, including several of the timbers, which, sawn through, would make the ribs of their proposed vessel. As the day drew on, the weather gave signs of changing. Tom had intended remaining until even a later hour than before, for as the doctor had promised to keep a fire blazing on the beach, the voyage could be performed as well during the dark as the day-time. But, about two o'clock the wind began to get up, and the ocean, hitherto shining like a mirror in the rays of the sun, was seen to be rippled over with wavelets, which gradually increased in size, while the dash of the water against the weather side of the wreck sounded louder and louder.

"We shall have it blowing strong before night, Mr Desmond," observed Jerry; "and I am thinking it would be prudent if Mr Rogers were to order us to shove off, and to make the best of our way to the shore."

Desmond reported what Jerry had said to Tom, who at once saw the wisdom of the advice.

The timber which had been got out was forthwith fastened together. A spar to serve as a mast, with a square sail, had been brought off, and these being rigged the voyage was commenced.

The wind increased and sent the raft along at a rapid rate, considering its form and weight, Tom, as before, steering it. Sometimes, indeed, those at the oars had little work to do except to assist in guiding the raft. At last Tom ordered them to cast off end keep alongside, in case he and Jerry might be washed away by the fast-rising seas which occasionally swept almost over the raft, so that the water was up to their knees. Gerald at length advised Tom to come into the boat and to let the raft find its way as it best could to the shore.

"No, no," answered Tom; "as long as I can steer it I will, and try to carry it safely on to the beach; should it strike the coral rocks, the timbers may be injured and of no service."

As the raft neared the island, Jerry every now and then took a look astern. "There won't be much of the ship left by to-morrow morning, but I hope that a good part of her will come on shore, and if we can get this lot safe on the beach we shall have timber enough for building our craft and some to spare for fire-wood."

Though the wind blew stronger and stronger, Tom stuck to the raft, and was rewarded for his perseverance by carrying it, just before dark, safely on to the beach.

"Welcome back, my young friends. I shall not have to drink the gallon of salt water," exclaimed the doctor, producing a jug. "Just taste that."

All the party pronounced the product of the still excellent, and as they had had nothing to drink since they had left the wreck, they were glad to obtain it.

After taking a few hurried mouthfuls of food they set to work to drag up the materials of the raft, lest the sea might carry them off during the night. The task accomplished, they at length lay down in the tent, which the doctor had rendered more tenable than it otherwise would have been by putting up a close paling on the weather side. Fortunately no rain fell, but the wind, which as the night advanced blew with great force, found its way in through the crevices.

In the morning the ocean was covered with tossing foam-crested waves, which as they rolled in broke with a continuous roar on the rocky shore. They soon had evidence of the effect of the gale on the wreck. Fragments of various sizes and casks of oil were seen floating in all directions, the larger portion drifting towards the northern end of the island. Some came right into the bay, and were at once secured; others struck the coral rocks, and were soon ground into small pieces. Jerry proposed going along the shore, accompanied by Tim and Pat, in order to pick up whatever they could find. They might save not only timber but casks and cases from the hold, which, from being under water, they had been unable to get up. The rest of the party in the mean time commenced building the hut. They first selected such timber and planking as would be of no use to the vessel. The discomfort they had endured the previous night made them anxious to secure sufficient shelter before the rain should come on, as in that exposed situation they could not trust to the protection of the tent. The roof, however, they intended to form with canvas, as they had enough for the purpose, and it would answer better than anything else they could obtain. Peter prepared dinner for all the party.

"But there is more here than we want," observed the doctor, looking into the pot; "we must be economical in the use of our provisions."

"Neber fear, massa," answered Peter; "dey all come back in good time. Dey smell dis at de oder end ob de island."

Peter was right in his conjectures. Just as he was about to serve out the stew, Jerry and his companions made their appearance. They reported that they had hauled up several good-sized pieces of wreck, three casks of oil, a barrel of flour, and two of beef or pork.

"Very good," observed the doctor; "we shall not run short of provisions; but I should have been glad to hear that you had found a case or two containing lime-juice. We must look out for vegetables of some sort, or we may not keep scurvy at bay."

"Shure, doesn't this island grow taters?" asked Tim.

"I'm afraid not," answered the doctor.

"Thin it must be a poor place, and I'll not wish to spend the remainder of me days here," answered Tim, with one of his inimitable grimaces.

"Though there are not potatoes, there may be roots of some sort, and we have not yet examined all the cases which we brought out of the cabin. If I recollect rightly, some seeds were sent on board before we sailed, though fortunately we had no opportunity of making use of them," observed the doctor.

A search was at once instituted, and the box the doctor spoke of discovered; it contained cabbage, lettuce, onion, carrot, turnip, and several other kinds of seeds.

"The onions, in our case, will prove the most valuable, as they will have grown to some size before the vessel has been completed, and we can carry them to sea with us. They are the most certain specific against scurvy," said the doctor.

These remarks were made while the officers and men sat together at breakfast. They were all in good spirits, thankful that they were so well supplied with everything they could possibly require. Had it not been for the doctor, however, how different would have been their condition! In a day or two they would have been suffering all the horrors of thirst, and must ultimately have perished miserably, but now they could obtain as much fresh water as they could require for drinking and cooking.

"One thing, however, we must remember, that our provisions will in time come to an end," observed Tom. "We must use the most perishable first and keep the best preserved for our voyage."

"But we shall be able to catch fish, and we need not go on short commons, I hope," said Billy.

"You shall have all you catch," said Desmond, laughing; "but have we any hooks?"

"Lashings, sir," answered Tim. "I found a bag full in the carpenter's store-room, and threw them down among the other things."

The hooks and lines were soon discovered, but at present there was too much work to be done to allow any one to go fishing. The hut was very soon finished. It was placed with its back to the wind.

There were plenty of spars, which, without cutting, served for rafters, and over them were stretched a couple of sails, lashed securely down, so that no ordinary hurricane could have blown them away. In front, sheltered from the wind, were established the two fires, one for cooking, the other for the still. To give a sufficient supply of water, it was necessary to keep the latter always alight.

Gerald, who had been the first to propose building a vessel, was anxious to lay down the keel.

"I should be as eager as you are, did I not think that we may possibly be taken off by some passing vessel," said Tom. "As soon as the gale is over we must set up a flag-staff, and a good tall one too, so that it may be seen at a long distance, as no vessel is likely, intentionally, to come near these reefs."

"But we've only got an American flag, and I should not like to be taken for a Yankee," exclaimed Desmond, without considering what he was saying.

"Young gentleman," exclaimed the doctor, bristling up, "you might sail under a less honoured flag, and fight under it too, let me tell you! It is one which has made itself respected in every sea, and will ever be found on the side of freedom and justice."

"I beg your pardon, doctor," answered Desmond. "If I was not an English midshipman, I should be perfectly ready to become an American commodore, and I fully believe your navy, for its size, is superior to that of any other nation under the sun."

"Well, well, my young friend, we all of us have our national prejudices, and it is right that we should, provided we do not bring them too prominently forward. You may think England the tallest country in the world, and I may consider the United States taller still, but it is as well not to be measuring heights, or we may both have to come down a peg or two."

"Come," said Tom, "let us set up the flag-staff and hoist the stars and stripes, and should one of Uncle Sam's ships come by, we will hand over the island as a free gift in exchange for our passage to any part of the world for which she may be bound."

It did not take long to form a flag-staff and to fit it with rigging: the chief difficulty was to dig a hole of sufficient depth in the coral rock in which to step it. This, however, was at last done, and the wind having fallen, before the evening the flag-staff was fixed, and with a hearty cheer, led by the doctor, the stars and stripes were run up to the top. The flag was, however, hauled down again at sunset. Tom also had a quantity of wood collected and piled up on the highest point near the flag-staff, so that should a ship at any time in the evening be seen in the offing, it might be lit to attract attention. One of the brass guns which had beer brought on shore was placed on its carriage near the flag-staff, so that it might be fired if necessary.

"We have had a good day's work, and I propose that to-morrow we lay down the keel of our vessel," said Desmond.

To this Tom readily agreed; and the two midshipmen, with the doctor, sat up until a late hour, discussing the subject and drawing plans for their proposed craft. They had a couple of adzes, three axes, and two augers, but only five of the party could be engaged on the building; indeed, it would have been dangerous to have entrusted some of them with such tools. Billy to a certainty would have cut off his toes, and neither Tom nor Desmond were accustomed to their use, although they knew what it was necessary to do. To form the keel was simple work enough, to shape the timbers properly required the greatest skill.

Here the doctor was superior to the rest. He chose a level part of the sand, on which he drew the form of the timbers, and the rest of the party executed the plans he gave them. As the timbers had to be out in two, a saw-pit was dug, at which Billy was doomed to work as under-sawyer, a task which Desmond assured him he performed to perfection. By the end of the first day the keel was put down and the stem and stern-post set up.

"I have other work, which must not be neglected, my friends," said the doctor, when the party were collected at supper. "We must look after fresh provisions. Perhaps, Rogers, you or Desmond will take your guns and shoot some birds to-morrow; there are large numbers, I see, at the further end of the island. They may prove wholesome, if not palatable food. I don't know who are the best fishermen among you, but I would advise that two should go out every day in the boat fishing, so that we may not trespass on our salt provisions."

"Pat Casey is the most skilful fisherman among us, and he with another of our party will do as you suggest, doctor," said Tom.

Tom and Desmond accordingly, who had wished to explore the end of the island not hitherto visited, set off with their guns the next morning. They had not gone far when they found themselves among numbers of birds, a large portion of which had made their nests on the ground. It appeared that for some reason or other they had selected the southern end of the island. Most of them were so tame that they refused to move, and attacked the midshipmen's legs with their beaks. Among them were gannets, sooty terns, and tropical birds in large numbers. The gannets sat on their eggs croaking hoarsely, not moving even when the midshipmen attempted to catch them. There were also frigate birds which had built their nests, in the lower trees, of a few sticks roughly put together. They sat for some time watching the trespassers on their domain, then spreading their wings flew off, inflating their blood-red bladders, which were of the size of the largest cocoa-nuts, to aid them in their ascent though the air.

"We need not expend any powder and shot on these fellows," observed Desmond; "and all we have to do is to wring the necks of as many as we want for our use, and take the eggs."

"Let us ascertain how long the eggs have been sat upon, or we may have the trouble of carrying them for nothing," answered Tom.

They went forward, expecting to get beyond the region of birds, but instead, the nests grew thicker and thicker; indeed, the midshipmen's progress was almost stopped at times, as they had to dodge in and out and skip here and there to avoid the attacks made on their legs.

"We need have no fear of starving, although we might in time get tired of poultry," said Desmond.

At last they came to a lower part of the island, over which the sea occasionally washed. It had been avoided by the wise birds, but still had its inhabitants. Whole armies of soldier-crabs were marching about in every direction with their shells on their backs, as well as common crabs on the watch for lizard or snake-like creatures which ventured among them. Sometimes, when a big crab had got hold of one of these, and its attention was occupied in carrying off its prey, a frigate bird would pounce down and seize it, carrying both it and its captive off to its nest.

The midshipmen were so amused that they could not tell how time passed, until hunger and the hot sun reminded them that it was the time when dinner would be ready; and passing through the "farm-yard," as Desmond called it, they secured as many birds as they could carry and also filled their pockets with the freshest-looking eggs they could find. Desmond, giving a wink to Tom, put among them a couple from a nest over which the mother bird had fought stoutly, and which certainly did not look very fresh. "I can almost hear it croak," he said, placing an egg to his ear. "I intend these as a *bonne-bouche* for Billy. We won't show the others, and will make him suppose that we especially favour him by bringing these, knowing how fond he is of eggs."

Gerald kept to his intention. As nobody was in the hut when they got back, they hid away all the eggs with the exception of two, which Desmond so kindly selected for his messmate. Peter was engaged in cooking, and having his stew ready, he shouted to announce the fact.

They hurried in, for all were hungry and eager again to begin work. Tom and Desmond showed their birds, and described the numbers they had met with.

"Did you bring any eggs?" asked the doctor; "they can be cooked at once, and are likely to prove better flavoured than the birds themselves."

"Yes," said Desmond, "we brought as many as our pockets will hold, and we will hand them over to Peter directly, but I want to give Billy some first, as he is especially fond of eggs; he will value them the more if he thinks that nobody else has them."

Saying this, he handed them to Peter to put them under the ashes.

"There," he exclaimed when Billy appeared, "we know how you like eggs, and so we brought a couple, and whenever we go out again we will try and find some more."

Billy watched the eggs eagerly, until Peter declared that they were sufficiently cooked.

"Doctor, won't you have one?" asked Billy, politely, when Peter handed them to him.

126

"No, thank you," answered the doctor; "I am content with this stew."

Billy very reluctantly felt himself called upon to offer an egg to Tom and Desmond; but they both declined.

"Then I suppose I must eat them myself," said Billy, beginning to break the shell. He went on until the operation was performed, when he clapped the end into his mouth.

"Horrible!" he exclaimed, spitting the contents out. "If I haven't bitten off a bird's head!"

"Try the other, Billy," said Desmond; "that may not be so mature."

Billy, not suspecting a trick, commenced on the second egg, when Desmond, running into the hut, produced the rest they had brought, which Peter slipped under the ashes. Billy looked several times at the second egg; he was going to put it into his mouth when he bethought him of his knife. No sooner had he cut into it, than he threw it away, exclaiming—

"I do believe, Desmond, that you brought those on purpose; you have almost spoilt my appetite."

"Then I have done more than anything else has ever accomplished," answered Desmond, laughing. "Never mind, Billy, you shall have the freshest of those eggs cooking under the ashes if you can regain your appetite."

"I think I shall be able to do that, but I think I will take some stew in the mean time."

The rest of the eggs were fresh, but the doctor advised that they should collect a supply at once, before the birds had sat too long on them, as probably the greater number had by this time done laying.

In the afternoon Pat went off in the boat a short distance, and in less than an hour caught more fish than the party could consume. The doctor had been too busily employed hitherto, but he, having set each man to work, started at the same time in search of vegetables. He came back with a bag filled with small green leaves.

"I have found nothing except the cocoa-nuts very palatable, but until our garden seeds come up this will prove of greater value than any roots likely to be discovered. I was not aware that it was to be found in so low a latitude. It is a species of sorrel; it seems placed here by Providence for the especial use of seamen, as it is most efficacious in preventing scurvy. All sea officers should be acquainted with it, as it grows on nearly every uninhabited island."

As soon as it became too dark to work on the vessel, all hands turned to for the purpose of breaking up a plot for forming the proposed garden close to the hut, that the seeds might be put in without delay. They again went to work the following morning before daybreak, and in a short time a sufficient space was cleared and broken up for the intended object; as there were no animals, all that was necessary was to run a few sticks into the ground to mark the spot.

"Now," said the doctor, "if Providence so wills it, we may live here for the next ten or twenty years, should we fail to build a craft in which we can venture to sea."

"I am not afraid about that," said Desmond, "and I hope by the time the crop of vegetables is up, that we may have our craft afloat, and ready to sail for the Sandwich Islands, or Hong-kong."

Chapter Six.

Progress made in building a vessel—Tools break—Signal kept flying—A sail seen—The flying beacon—A night of suspense—Signal guns fired—An answering gun heard—A man-of-war steamer in sight—A boat comes on shore—Tom and his friends get on board HMS Bellona, Captain Murray, and find Captain Rogers—Fall in with a dismasted junk—Jonathan Jull and his wife—Suspicious appearance of junk—Jull and his wife taken on board the Bellona—The junk blows up and founders—The Bellona proceeds on her course—Pass a reef—A wreck seen—Visited—Supposed to be the Dragon—No one found on shore—Bellona reaches Hong-kong—Jull disappears—Captain Rogers assumes command of the Empress.

The midshipmen and doctor had been somewhat over sanguine in regard to the rapidity with which the proposed craft could be built. They had not taken into account the damage the tools would receive from unskilful hands. They were constantly striking bolts and nails with their adzes and hatchets, blunting the edges. One of their two augers broke, and they had reason to fear that the second was injured. Tim Nolan cut himself badly, and was unable to work for several days. Two of the party were obliged to go off and fish for some hours, as the fish caught on one day were unfit for food on the next. Several of the ribs, from being unscientifically shaped, had to be taken down and reformed. Two or three were split so as to render them useless. Tom and the doctor, who were the architects, exerted all their wits, for practical skill they had none, and they often regretted the want of such training.

"If every sea officer were to serve for a few months in a dockyard, he would gain a knowledge which would be useful under our circumstances, at all events," observed the doctor.

Still, by dint of sawing and chopping, they got a dozen ribs cut out and fixed in their places. They improved too, and, Gerald declared, "would have got on like a house on fire," had not one of the adzes been totally disabled by the constant grinding which it required to restore the edge. An axe also broke, and they had now only three tools for executing the rougher work, beside some large chisels; but they found smoothing down with these was a very slow process.

The doctor was constantly charging Jerry and Tim to be careful when using the took. He was especially anxious about the auger. "If that goes we shall be brought pretty well to a standstill, for I doubt if I can replace it," he remarked. At last he determined not to let it out of his own hands, and to bore all the bolt holes himself.

One day, however, as he was working away, a crack was heard, the auger refused to advance. He drew it out; the tip had broken. Examining it with a look of dismay, he sighed deeply, "Our shipbuilding must come to an end, I fear, unless we can replace this simple instrument."

"We will try, however, and see what we can accomplish in the forge," said Tom.

"You forget that it is steel," observed the doctor; "it will be difficult to soften it and afterwards to restore its temper."

"We can but try," repeated Tom; "a day or two won't make much difference, and we can go on with the other parts of the vessel in the mean time."

Tom was not disappointed; after repeated experiments he and the doctor succeeded in putting a head to the auger, and their success encouraged them to repair the first which had been broken; but they found that neither worked as well as they had done before. At last, however, they again broke.

Neither Tom nor Desmond were made of stuff which could easily be defeated.

"We must try again," said Tom. "I have heard of a missionary in the South Seas who built a vessel entirely by himself, without a single white man to help him, in the course of three or four months. He had to begin without tools, and with only a ship's anchor and chain cable, and trees still growing in the forest. He set up a forge, manufactured tools, saws, and axes, then taught the natives to use them. They cut down trees, which they sawed up. He made ropes out of fibre, and sails from matting; and the necessary iron-work, of which there was very little in the whole craft, was formed from the remainder of the old anchor; yet that vessel performed long voyages and during several years visited numerous islands in the Pacific.

Surely if one man can accomplish such a work, we ought to be ashamed of ourselves if, with materials all ready to our hands, we cannot build such a craft as we want."

"Yes, my friend; but the missionary you speak of—the late lamented Williams, who was murdered not far off to the west of us—was a practical mechanic. He had studied blacksmith's work before he left England, and must have possessed a large amount of mechanical talent, such as none of us can boast of."

Encouraged by Tom, the doctor recovered his spirits, and once more their shipbuilding progressed at fair speed. The main beams had been fixed up, and the skeleton was almost complete, but as yet not a plank had been fixed on. This, however, appeared to them comparatively easy work, and no one entertained a doubt of the success of their undertaking. Regular discipline had been maintained all the time. At daybreak Tom or Desmond visited the hill, hoisted the flag, and took a look round. In the evening, when the flag was hauled down, generally two went up, in case a distant sail might escape the observation of one, and be discovered by the other, when they intended to light the beacon fire, in the hopes of attracting her attention.

Billy Blueblazes, who had got a sharp pair of eyes, whatever might be said about his wits, had one evening accompanied Desmond. They stood for some minutes scanning the horizon, but not a speck was visible in the blue sky except here and there, where a sea-fowl was winging its way towards the shore.

"It would save us a great deal of trouble if a vessel would come," observed Billy. "If we could build a steamer it would be very well; but we may be becalmed for days together, and I should not like to go through what we had to endure in the boat—mashed yams and oil. Bah! I've not got the taste out of my mouth yet."

"You've put a good many things into it, though, since then," said Desmond. "For my part, after we have done so much, I should be almost disappointed if we were to be taken off before our craft was finished. I should not exactly wish to go round Cape Horn in her, but I would go anywhere else. I hope Rogers will decide on sailing for Hong-kong."

"At all events, I wish she was finished, for I am tired of that sawing work," cried Billy.

"Well, Billy, we will haul down the flag, as there appears to be nothing in sight; but before we go, just swarm up the flag-staff, and take another look round; the horizon is remarkably clear, and you might see a ship's royals, even though they were but just above it."

Billy did as Desmond asked him to do. Presently he took off his cap, and waving it, shouted —

"A sail! a sail! to the eastward!"

"Are you certain of it?" asked Desmond.

"As sure as if I had it in my hand," answered Billy. "A ship's royals, I am certain of it. I think, too, she is standing this way."

"Come down, then," said Desmond, "and I'll have a look out through the glass." He had a telescope slung at his back. He swarmed up until he reached the head of the shrouds, when, securing himself, he brought his glass to bear in the direction Billy had pointed.

"You are right, Billy," he exclaimed, after taking a steady look through it. "I can make out the fore, main, and the head of the mizzen royals. A large ship too, and, as you say, she is standing this way, with the wind from the eastward. She will not pass far from this either." Having taken another steady glance through the glass, Desmond descended; indeed, the thickening gloom by this time almost shut out the sail from sight. He and Billy hurried back to the camp.

"Hurrah! hurrah!" they shouted out in one breath. "There is a ship coming to take us off!"

The rest of the party were incredulous until Desmond fully described the appearance of the sail. "And now let us get the beacon fire alight," he exclaimed.

"No great hurry for that," said Tom.

"It could not be seen for some time, but we will carry up a supply of fuel to keep it burning all night. There may be a sail, but you cannot be positive she is standing this way, or if she is she may alter her course, which will carry her to a distance from us," said the doctor.

"But I can be positive that she is standing this way," exclaimed Desmond. "She may alter her course, but our fire will be seen."

At the doctor's suggestion, one of the oil barrels was rolled up that the contents might increase the flame. Every one was eager to light the beacon fire; even Billy forgot to propose that they should first eat their supper.

The doctor remarked that as the ship was drawing near they should send up a long spar, placed horizon tally with a burning mass at the end of it, which from its greater height might be seen further off than the fire on the ground.

His plan was adopted; the signal halyards were strong enough for the purpose, and by means of a line at the other end it could be hoisted without risk of burning the shrouds. He quickly manufactured a fusee, so that the mass would not blaze up until the yard was fixed. The material to be fired was composed of oakum mixed with gunpowder, canvas saturated with oil, and bundles of shavings kept together with pieces of iron hoop. Tom gave the word to hoist away, and "the flying beacon," as Desmond called it, soon afterwards burst forth into a bright flame. The fire below was then lighted, and as it blazed up it cast a lurid glare over the whole island, on the ribs of their vessel, their hut below the tall cocoa-nut trees, and the lower shrubs. At the same instant loud screams were heard—the birds, startled by the unusual appearance, mounted into the air, numbers flying towards the fire, and the party on the hill had to use sticks to keep them off, as they darted here and there, blinded by the light. More and more fuel was added, and as soon as the doctor's flying beacon had burnt out, another of the same description was hoisted.

"Well, if they don't see our fire they must be all asleep on board the stranger," said Desmond.

"No fear of that," remarked the doctor; "in these seas, with reefs on every side, depend upon it a bright look-out will be kept, or no ship could get across with safety."

"If she stood on, as you supposed she was steering, she must be by this time near enough to hear our gun," said Tom. "Bring up powder and wadding, Bird."

Jerry eagerly hastened to obey the order. The gun was fired every five minutes, although it was not likely, as the sound had to travel against the wind, that it would be heard for some time on board the ship. Most of the party had forgotten all about supper, until Billy exclaimed: "If I don't get some provender, I shall collapse."

As the rest acknowledged that they were much in the same state, Peter and Pat were sent to bring up a supply of food.

"Let there be plenty," said Billy; "we need not be on short commons now, I hope!"

The supper was discussed by the light of the fire. Tom in the mean time could not refrain from now and then looking out for an answering signal.

Hours went by, and all remained dark as before round the island. As to sleeping, few would have closed their eyes even had they gone back to the hut.

Tom had kept his watch in his hand to time the firing. The gun had just been discharged and all was again silent, when, as he was about again to give the order to fire, there came down on the breeze the boom of a heavy gun.

"No doubt about the sort of piece that comes from, sir," exclaimed Jerry. "The craft away there is a man-of-war, or I'm no sailor."

"I think so too," cried Tom; "they must have noticed our signals, and I don't think the ship will pass by without sending on shore."

"We might go off to her in our boat," said Jerry.

"We should have a difficulty in finding her at night, so we shall be wise to remain until the morning," answered Tom; "the wind is very light and she is probably still a long way off, for I could not see the flash of her gun."

Notwithstanding their belief that they were discovered, the party on the island still kept their beacon fire blazing, and fired the gun at intervals.

At length, pretty well tired out, all hands turned in with the exception of two, who remained to keep up the fire and discharge the gun every ten minutes.

Tom awoke at dawn of day and hurried up to join Desmond, who was keeping the morning watch.

"Where is she?" he exclaimed eagerly.

"That is more than I can tell," answered Desmond. "I expected to see her close to, and to have had a boat come on shore by this time."

"The mist hides her from us; see how it sweeps over the water from the northward. As the sun rises depend upon it we shall see her," observed Tom.

Still Desmond was in doubt; the mist was so light that he had not hitherto observed it, and his eyes were dazzled by the glare of the fire, which was still burning. Tom ran up the flag, so that it might be seen the moment the mist should disperse. In a short time they were joined by the rest of the party, who in various tones expressed their disappointment at not seeing the stranger.

Presently the sun rose, and in a few seconds the veil lifted, disclosing a large ship, her bulwarks just rising above the horizon.

"She is a man-of-war steamer," said Tom, who had been the first to take a look at her through the telescope. "She's English too, for she's just hoisted her ensign. There is smoke coming out of her funnel; she's getting up steam. Hurrah! we shall soon have her here."

The excitement after this became general and greater than ever. Tom and Desmond, however, were the only two of the party who witnessed the approach of the British man-of-war with unmitigated satisfaction. The men, having plenty of food, were in no hurry to go back to their routine of duty. The doctor and Peter would be among strangers, besides which the former, feeling assured that the vessel would in time be completed, was anxious to perform a voyage in a craft constructed under his own superintendence.

"The bother is, I shall have to keep that tiresome watch," murmured Billy. However, he did not express himself openly to his messmates on the subject.

The frigate came slowly on with the lead going and look-outs at frigate, although she might not carry more than six or eight guns. At length she got within about a mile of the island, when the screw was stopped and a boat lowered. There was only one landing-place on the lee side, close below the hill on which the flag-staff had been erected.

Tom, securing four handkerchiefs to the end of a spar, hastened down to it to guide the boat in. On she came, pulled by six strong arms, a lieutenant and midshipman in the stern sheets. Tom, Desmond, and Billy stood ready to receive the strangers. The boat was quickly run up on the beach, when the officers stepped on shore.

The lieutenant, observing the three midshipmen's tattered uniforms, advanced towards them, and inquired as he shook hands, "Has an American man-of-war been cast away here?"

"No, sir; but an American whaler was wrecked here a few weeks ago."

"Then who are you, and how came you here?" asked the lieutenant.

Tom in a few words narrated their adventures, and then asked, "And what is your ship, sir?"

"The *Bellona*, Captain Murray—"

"What! Captain Alick Murray?" exclaimed Tom. "I served with him. He is my brother Jack's greatest friend."

"Are you Captain Rogers's brother? That is extraordinary," exclaimed the lieutenant, "for he is a passenger with us, going out to command the *Empress* in the China seas."

"My brother Jack on board! That is good news."

Tom now doing the honours, introduced the lieutenant to Dr Locock.

"Of course Captain Murray will be most happy to receive you on board, with any of the survivors of the whaler's crew," said the lieutenant.

"I am much obliged to you; there is but one, and I shall be glad to embrace the opportunity of visiting China," answered the doctor.

The lieutenant had received orders to return as soon as possible, but Tom begged him to come and see the vessel they had commenced building; though he had made up his mind to try and get Jack to come on shore also, as he was ambitious to show their handiwork to him.

"You deserve great credit for the attempt," said the lieutenant, as he examined the structure; "but I congratulate you on escaping the necessity of making a voyage in her, for had she touched a rock, it is probable that she would have gone to pieces."

After this remark Tom felt less anxiety to exhibit the vessel to his brother Jack. The lieutenant now repeated that his orders were to return immediately. The doctor merely requested that he might be allowed to take his medicine case, instruments, and clothes.

"I shall be happy to let you have as many things as the boat will carry," said the lieutenant; "but as the captain is in a hurry to continue the voyage, he may be unwilling to send ashore again for any other articles."

The boat was soon loaded with the doctor's property, the nautical instruments, and the clothing which the men had appropriated, and then rapidly made her way towards the *Bellona*. The doctor had written a note, which he left in the hut, stating the name of the vessel wrecked on the island, and the circumstances under which he and the only survivor of the crew, with a party of English officers and men, had quitted it. By his special request the stars and stripes were left flying.

As the midshipmen followed the lieutenant up the side, they saw the two captains standing on the quarter-deck, but even Jack did not recognise his own brother. Tom, lifting the remnant of his cap, went aft, and putting out his hand exclaimed —

"What, don't you know me, Jack?"

Captain Rogers looked at him for a few seconds, then wringing his hand said, "How did you come into this plight, my dear fellow?"

Tom of course explained what had happened, while Gerald and Billy were telling the same story to Captain Murray. Doctor Locock was of course well taken care of by the surgeon, and invited into the ward-room. Tom had a good deal to hear about family matters. Desmond and Billy Blueblazes were soon made at home by the other young gentlemen of the ship, while the men were equally cared for forward. Captain Murray did not think it worth while to send on shore for the small part of the whaler's cargo which had been saved, but he promised to give information to the first American man-of-war he might fall in with, that she might go for it if it was thought worth while.

The account which the midshipmen gave of the *Dragon* caused considerable anxiety. When Captain Murray heard that her machinery was out of order, he felt satisfied that she had gone on to Hong-kong, and as she would certainly be detained there for some time, she would not even yet be able to get back to the Bonins.

"Perhaps," observed Tom, "Commander Rawson fancies we are lost, and if so he is not likely to come and look for us."

The wind continuing light, the *Bellona* steered on, soon leaving the coral island far astern.

Shortly after they had got on board, Gerald asked Tom to try and learn from his brother the reasons why his uncle had sent for him home.

"One of them was, I conclude, that as he expected to get a command himself, he was anxious to have his nephew with him," answered Jack. "Another is that in consequence of the death of several persons, young Desmond is heir-at-law to a handsome estate and a title. His uncle thought it better to have him near at hand, instead of knocking about far away from home. There is likely to be a trial of some sort, but my friend Adair is very sanguine of success. It may be several years, however, before the matter is settled, as all depends upon the life of the present possessor, who, although somewhat old, is hale and hearty. But as he may possibly break his neck, or go out of the world suddenly by some other means, it is well that Desmond should be on the spot to claim his rights. I don't know whether Adair intended to let his nephew know this until his arrival, but as it was not told to me in confidence, I may mention it to you. However, use your own discretion in what you say to your friend—only do not let him be too sanguine; but it may perhaps make him take care of himself, which hitherto I suspect he has not been apt to do."

Tom promised to be very discreet in what he said to Gerald, so as not to disappoint him should he fail of success.

Towards the evening of the day the *Bellona* had left the coral island, a shout was heard from the look-out at the mast-head, "A rock on the starboard bow!" An officer, however, going aloft with his glass, pronounced it to be a dismasted vessel. The frigate was accordingly headed up towards her, and on a nearer approach, from her peculiar build, she was seen to be undoubtedly a Chinese or Japanese craft. It was at first supposed that no one was on board, but as the steamer neared, a flag was waved from the after part of the stranger.

The ship's way was accordingly stopped, and a boat was lowered. Captain Rogers volunteering to examine her, Tom accompanied him. As they approached they saw that she must have encountered bad weather, for not only had she lost her masts, but she had no boats, and a considerable portion of her upper works had been carried away, while her sides had a weather-worn appearance, as if she had been a long time knocking about at sea.

On getting on deck, one person only was to be seen, who, though dressed as a Chinese, had European features.

"I am thankful you have fallen in with us, gentlemen," he said, in good English, "for I don't know what would otherwise have become of this craft or us."

"Of us! Is there any one besides yourself on board?" asked Jack.

"Yes, I have my wife with me—we were passengers on board; when the junk was blown off the coast and lost her masts, the crew deserted in the boat, leaving us to our fate."

"Your wife! Where is she?" asked Jack.

"She is below, sir," was the answer; "but she is a foreigner, young, and timid, and was afraid to come on deck."

"What are you?—an Englishman?" inquired Jack.

"Well, as to that, I am more of an American, though I have been out in these seas so long that I cannot say I belong to any nation. Still, I have not forgotten my native tongue. I should be grateful if you would take us in tow, or supply me with spars and canvas, so that I might find my way back."

"That is more than you will be able to do, I suspect, with your craft knocked about as she is, and probably leaking not a little, even with the assistance of your wife," answered Jack. "As for taking you in tow, that is out of the question—we should drag the bows out of her; but if you will bring your wife and any property you possess on board, I can answer for it that the captain will give you a passage to Hong-kong or any other place at which we may touch where you desire to leave the ship. You are a seaman, I presume, from your undertaking to sail back the junk. What is your name, may I ask?" said Jack.

"Jonathan Jull, at your service."

"That name has a Yankee smack about it, certainly," observed Jack. "Well, Mr Jull, I'll overhaul the craft, and report her condition to the captain. He may possibly think fit to take her in tow, but I can make no promises on the subject. In the mean time prepare your wife for accompanying you on board."

While Jonathan Jull went into one of the after cabins, Jack and Tom, with two men who had come on board, went round the junk. She had a considerable amount of cargo on board, of a somewhat miscellaneous character. Jack ordered the well to be sounded. Tom and one of the men performed the operation, and reported three feet in the hold, a large amount of water for a flat-bottomed craft. They had not long continued their search when Tom exclaimed —

"Look here; these are suspicious-looking marks. I have already observed others. They are evidently caused by bullets. See, in several places pieces of wood have been chipped off, and here is a bullet sticking in the planking."

"What do you think of this, sir?" asked one of the men, pointing to some dark splashes on the deck and side of the vessel.

"That's blood; there can be no doubt about it. I suspect that there has been some foul work on board," observed Jack. "I wonder whether Mr Jull can account for the circumstance."

"He, at all events, will give his own version of the matter," remarked Tom.

On a further search other signs of violence were discovered. Jack began to suspect that the man's account of being deserted by the crew was not a true one. He resolved, however, before questioning him, to take him on board the *Bellona*, to let Captain Murray decide what to do. "It appears to me that unless several hands are placed on board to keep the vessel clear of water, she must sink in a day or two if towed by the ship; and that certainly Mr Jull, experienced seaman as he may be, even with the aid of his wife, cannot, even were the craft supplied with masts and sails, find his way back to China. He is far more likely to run on a coral reef, or purposely cast his vessel away on one of the many islands in these seas, and take up his abode there."

One thing was certain, there was something suspicions about the man. Captain Rogers and Tom now made their way to the main cabin, where what was their surprise to see a remarkably handsome young female bending over a chest, in which she was engaged in packing up various articles which Jonathan Jull, as he called himself, standing by, was handing to her. Her complexion and countenance, as well as her costume, showed her to be an oriental, probably a Malay, though her features were more refined than those of Malays in general. She rose as she saw the strangers enter the cabin, and unconsciously stood with her arms crossed on her bosom, gazing at them with her large lustrous eyes, which expressed more terror than satisfaction.

"I see that you are preparing to quit the vessel, Mr Jull," said Jack. "I must beg you to make haste and stow that chest, as we cannot remain much longer on board. Indeed, from her condition, it is impossible to say when she may go down."

The man, without at first answering, turned to the Malay girl, and spoke some words to her in her own language, on which she again knelt down and continued packing the chest. There were several cases which the man handed quickly to the girl, but the other things were chiefly articles of clothing, with two or three jewel-hilted daggers, a short sword, and a brace of long-barrelled, beautifully mounted pistols. He had been apparently not desirous to allow the English officers to see the contents of his chest. As soon as it was filled, having locked it, he produced a stout rope and lashed it in a seamanlike manner.

"Now, sir, my wife and I are ready," he said, throwing a cloak over the girl's head, with which she could conceal her features. "If your people will lend me a hand to get this chest into the boat, I shall be obliged," he continued. "As you say, sir, the craft is not very seaworthy, and since I made you out I have neglected to keep the pump going. I have been compelled to work at it for several hours every day, or the leak would soon have gained on me."

The man as he spoke seemed perfectly cool and collected, and not at all unwilling to go on board the ship of war. The chest, which was somewhat heavy, was lowered into the boat, with the aid of a tackle which the owner produced. He and his wife then followed, taking their seats in the stern sheets. As the boat pulled away from the junk Jack observed that she had sunk already much lower in the water than when he went on board, and seemed to be settling down astern.

"That craft has sprung a fresh leak since we saw her first," observed one of the crew, who had remained in the boat looking at the stranger. "I heard a curious noise as we were alongside, as if water was rushing in under the counter. We should have let you know if you hadn't come to the side with the chest."

These words were spoken loud enough to be heard aft. Tom fancied that he detected a peculiar expression pass over Jull's countenance, but the man immediately resumed his unconcerned look, and spoke to his wife as if endeavouring to quiet her apparent alarm.

The chest was hoisted on board, and the two persons who had been taken from the junk were allowed to seat themselves on it, while Jack made a report to Murray of his visit to the junk.

"Her cargo," he observed, "appears to be of considerable value, and it would be a pity to lose it."

"We might get some of the most valuable portion out of her, but we must not spend time about it," remarked Murray. "From your account, even were we to take her in tow, she is not likely to keep above water. We can afterwards examine this suspicious gentleman and his wife, although I doubt whether we shall get much out of them."

"We are not likely to get much out of the junk either," said Jack, pointing at her. "Look there!"

As he spoke the junk, towards which the frigate was steering, was seen to lift her bows, and immediately afterwards a loud report was heard; her stern and after decks were blown into fragments, and in a few seconds she disappeared beneath the surface.

"Our friend there had no intention that we should make a further examination of the craft," observed Jack. "Depend upon it, he had taken effectual measures to prevent us from doing so after he had secured in his chest the most valuable property on board."

"We have no proof that he was instrumental in her destruction, though the circumstances are suspicious," said Murray. "He will of course tell us what he thinks fit as to the cause of her sudden foundering and the explosion on board, while we are prevented from making any further examination of the signs of a conflict, which you suppose must have taken place. We will, however, try to get some information out of the man."

A few fragments of wood floating on the surface was all that remained of the junk, as the frigate, now again put on her proper course, passed over the spot where she had lately floated. Notwithstanding the suspicions which were entertained about Mr Jull, Captain Murray wishing to treat the man's wife with consideration, ordered a screen to be put up on the main-deck, where she might be in private and have the chest under her eye. He then sent for Mr Jull to come into the cabin, where he, with Jack and the first lieutenant, were seated.

Jonathan Jull persisted in the story he had given to Jack, stating that he had commanded an opium clipper, which had been cast away; and that he had simply taken a passage with his wife on board the junk to go to Shanghai, where he expected to find other employment. He glibly announced the name of his craft, the *Swallow*, as well as the names of his officers, and was running on with those of his crew when he was stopped.

"That is not necessary at present," observed Captain Murray. But Mr Jull seemed to be anxious that there should be no suspicion resting on him. He next mentioned her tonnage and armament, and indeed everything about her.

"All very good," said Captain Murray; "but can you account for the signs of violence which we observed on board the junk — the stains of blood, the chipped beams, the bullets sticking in the bulkheads?"

Captain Jull, as he announced himself, looked very much astonished. "You have observed, sir, what I failed to discover," he answered, "and I simply cannot account for the marks. If any violence occurred, it must have taken place before I went on board the junk. The crew appeared perfectly orderly, and only after the vessel had been dismasted, and they found her drifting away from the shore, did they take to their boats. For some reason, for which I cannot account, they refused to allow my wife and me to accompany them."

"Very well, Mr Jull; but can you account for the junk sinking so soon after you left her, and for the explosion?"

"She was leaking very much indeed, and probably a butt suddenly gave way," answered Captain Jull. "In regard to the explosion, my wife had lit a fire in a stove aft, and I suppose a cask of gunpowder must inadvertently have been left in the neighbourhood. But this is merely conjecture. She herself will tell you that she lit the fire."

It was very clear that the naval officers would not get any information from Captain Jull which he was unwilling to give them. Although there were several suspicious circumstances against him, Captain Murray did not feel justified in making him a prisoner, and he therefore allowed him to remain with his wife.

Tom and Gerald made themselves happy on board with their new shipmates, and Billy was always liked wherever he went, never being out of humour and having not the slightest objection to be laughed at, besides which he had a store of amusing anecdotes, and was able to spin a good yarn, and sing a merry song.

Tom had plenty to talk about to his brother Jack, who in course of time gave him all the news from home. Captain Rogers had been very unwilling to leave his wife, but the command of a ship having been offered him, he felt himself bound not to refuse. It had cost Murray also not a little to leave *Stella*.

"We shall have his magnificent little boy come to sea before long," said Jack. "How old it makes one! It seems to me only yesterday since I was a midshipman like you, Tom, and I can scarcely fancy myself even now a post-captain."

"I hope I shall not be a midshipman long," said Tom, "and that Desmond and Gordon will get promoted."

"There's little doubt about that," said Jack, "if there is anything to do in China, and I fully expect there will be something, for the government are sending out troops and more ships. The Chinese are too self-conceited to give in without a sound thrashing. By-the-by, have you told Desmond anything about his prospects?"

"No; I thought it might upset him," answered Tom. "I merely hinted that you had heard from his uncle that there was a possibility of his obtaining a fortune, but that there was some uncertainty, and as he did not cross question me much, I got off without committing myself."

Jack commended Tom's discretion. "It would be better indeed that he should hear the whole matter from his uncle, who will probably be sent out to China, where we shall meet him before long," observed Jack.

The ship had run on for a couple of days, the weather continuing calm and fine, though a favourable breeze would have been acceptable to save coal. About noon land was sighted on the starboard bow. The master stated that it was the Island of Dolores, very appropriately so called, as it consists of a small patch of land rising up amid a collection of coral reefs, which would prove the destruction of any unfortunate vessel driven on them. The *Bellona* had passed along the southern edge of the group, and the glasses of several of her officers had been turned towards the land to ascertain its appearance, when, just as they were leaving it on the starboard quarter, the look-out from aloft hailed the deck to say there was what appeared to him to be a wreck on an outer reef off the western side.

The master and second lieutenant, on going aloft, were convinced that such was the case, and the ship was accordingly headed in that direction at half speed, a bright look-out being kept for any dangers which might lie off at a distance from the reef below the water. As soon as the ship arrived abreast of the wreck, two boats were lowered, and sent off under the second lieutenant and master to examine and ascertain what she was, and, if possible, what had become of her crew. Captain Rogers and Tom went with the first-mentioned officer, and Desmond with the master. As there appeared to be a channel leading up to the island, Captain Murray directed the party in the boats, should no persons be found on board, to make their way to the shore and see whether any people were there or had been there lately.

The perfect calmness of the sea enabled the boats to get close up. As they got near, they saw from her shattered condition that it was not likely any one was remaining on board. When they were almost up to her, Jack exclaimed—

"She is a steamer, for I see some of her machinery above water, and a man-of-war too, and I very much fear that she is the *Dragon*."

"I am afraid that she is," said Tom. "That we shall soon learn, however, when we get on board, for I know every inch of her, and knocked about as she is, I should recognise something or other, which would put the matter beyond doubt."

The ship lay broadside on the reef. The stern had been completely knocked away, and nearly the entire part of the lower side, but the fore part had suffered less, although the bulwarks had been swept off, and the bowsprit had gone. Indeed, she greatly resembled the skeleton of a vast animal, with the head attached.

There was but little footing anywhere, but Tom and Desmond, getting over the rocks, scrambled up.

"Yes, this is the old craft; there is no doubt about it," said Tom, after they had made such a survey as was possible.

"I am very sure of it," answered Desmond. "If Bird or Nolan had come with us, they would have known this part of the ship even better than we do."

They were now joined by Captain Rogers, who was perfectly satisfied that they were right. For a few seconds he stood contemplating the sad remains of the once gallant vessel he had commanded. What his thoughts were may be imagined. Whether or not he heaved a sigh is not known, but Jack Rogers was not addicted to being sentimental.

"We must ascertain whether any of the poor fellows have escaped," he exclaimed, leading the way to the boat. "We will now carry out Captain Murray's directions, and visit the island."

The boats were accordingly steered for the shore. It required a careful look-out to keep in the right channel, so that the rocks, which appeared in all directions under water, might be avoided.

The shore was reached at last, but no one was seen, though fragments of the wreck were found scattered about and fixed in the crevices of the rocks. Here and there were pieces of casks, cases, and cabin furniture, but all were so shattered that it was impossible to recognise them.

The whole island was searched, but no huts had been put up. No remains of fires were seen—indeed, there were no signs of any one having landed; not even a skeleton was discovered.

"They must all have been lost, I fear," said Jack. "We can easily conceive, with a fierce gale blowing, what a fearful surf would be dashing over these rocks. Not a boat could live in it."

The other officers were of opinion that every one on board must have been lost.

"Poor Archie!" said Tom to Desmond; "there's one of us gone, then. I wish he had come in our boat, instead of accompanying the surveying expedition. Captain Murray will be very sorry when he hears it."

As time was of consequence, and there was no object in searching further, the boats put off and returned to the ship.

Captain Murray, while deeply regretting the loss of the *Dragon*, her officers, and crew, was especially grieved to believe that his young cousin, in whom he had taken so deep an interest, had perished also. Both officers and men, however, soon got over their sorrow for ship-mates and friends. They knew very well that such might be their own fate some day, though, as is natural to human beings, they hoped to escape it and die in their beds at a good old age, their fighting days over and their gallant deeds done.

The *Bellona* continued her course, passing through the Bashee Channel to the south of Formosa, when she had a clear run for Hong-kong. At length the lofty heights which extended from east to west along the entire length of the island came in sight, and the *Bellona* steered for Sulphur Channel, which lies between the larger island and the little island known as Green Island.

Steering through this channel, she entered the harbour of Victoria, which assumed a completely land-locked appearance, being shut in on one side by the Kowloon Peninsula and on the other by a point jutting off from the main land, the former being only about a mile from the town of Victoria.

The island of Hong-kong is of irregular shape, about nine miles long and three broad. Besides the centre ridge there are a series of high lands on either side of it. The Western end rises to the height of 1825 feet; Victoria Peak, at the foot of which stands the town of Victoria, creeping up the height from the beach. There are several other harbours—Ly-tum on the southern side, and another on the west known as Wong-ma-kok. On the western side of the neck of the peninsula which forms the latter harbour is the military station of Stanley, where barracks have been erected, as it was supposed that it would prove a healthy position from being exposed to the south-west monsoon.

The *Bellona* steamed up to an anchorage near Victoria. Among the ships in the harbour was the *Empress*, which Jack Rogers was destined to command. There were several vacancies, and Tom, Desmond, and Billy Blueblazes accompanied her captain, who intended to get them appointed to her. Bird, Nolan, and Casey were also entered on her books, and Peter, from having been well treated on board the *Bellona*, expressed his wish also to join; Jack, at Tom's recommendation, took him as his steward. Dr Locock, expressing his gratitude for the kindness he had received, went on shore, intending to remain until he could join an American ship, either a man-of-war or a merchantman.

No sooner was the anchor dropped than the ship was surrounded by Chinese boats with all sorts of provisions. Murray had not forgotten Captain Jull and his wife. Before Captain Rogers left the ship, he sent Tom to summon the man, intending to question him again to ascertain where he was going. Tom in a short time returned saying that Jull and his wife, with their chest, had disappeared, and no one could tell what had become of them, he must have managed, while the officers and men were busily engaged, to slip his chest through a port into a native boat alongside. No one had, however, seen him; his Chinese dress and the cloak his wife wore would have prevented them in the confusion from being observed.

"There is something not altogether right about that fellow, depend upon it," said Jack. "He had good reason for not wishing the junk to be brought into harbour, and he would have taken good care to destroy her even if we had had her in tow. We might have brought him to a trial for her loss, when very possibly he might have been recognised."

On mentioning the subject afterwards on shore, Murray learned that a large fleet of piratical junks were said to be commanded by an Englishman, but little was known about them, except from the depredations they committed on the Chinese merchant shipping, and occasionally on that of other nations, although they had hitherto avoided the risk of interfering with English vessels.

The first inquiry Murray and Rogers made, on coming on shore, was for the *Dragon*; but as neither she nor any of her crew had been heard of, their fears that she was the vessel they had discovered on the reef were confirmed.

The *Empress* had been some time on the coast, and the members of the midshipmen's berth were full of what they had seen and ready to impart the information to Tom and Desmond, who had heard little or nothing of what had taken place. They found several old acquaintances on board, among whom was Charley Roy, whom they had met frequently in the Black Sea. Charley could talk, and was not loth to make use of his talents.

"You fellows want to know all we have done and all we expect to do out here," he began, the very first day they were on board. "The Chinese, in my opinion, are the most obstinate fellows in the world; besides which they beat all others in cunning and deceit—at all events, their diplomatists do. They have a wonderful opinion of themselves, and don't know when they are beaten; Lord Elgin has found that out. You, of course, have heard of the thrashing we gave the Celestials at the Bogue Forts, Canton, Pekin, and dozens of other places, and of the expedition hundreds of miles up the big river, the Yang-tse-kiang, till we supposed that we had brought them to order, but they were still too clever for us, as you shall hear. You may have heard that Lord Elgin being desirous of going right up to Pekin to exchange the necessary ratifications of the lately formed treaty, a squadron of gun-boats was sent up to escort him. As soon as they arrived off the Peiho, the admiral sent an officer to announce the approach of the British ambassador, but the Chinese commander refused him permission to land. Of course this showed that they meant fighting."

"Before we commenced operations, however, a reconnoissance was made to ascertain what obstructions were in our way. In the first place we found that the forts, which before had been destroyed, were replaced by earthworks, mounting a large number of guns, and that the two forts higher up on the left bank were so placed as to rake any vessels which might advance abreast of the forts on the right, these forts being united by raised causeways. Right across the river also were no end of stakes and booms, some of iron, each several tons in weight, forked above and below so as to rip up any vessel striking them. There was also a boom composed of three stout cables, one of hemp and two of iron chain, while some hundred yards further on were two great rafts of timber, stretching one from each bank, a passage being left between them of scarcely sufficient width to allow even a gun-boat to pass through. In front of the line of forts were ditches and wide spaces of soft mud, over which it would be scarcely possible for storming parties to pass. The Chinese declared that these arrangements were simply made to prevent smuggling, and that they would be immediately removed.

"Another day passed, and no steps having been taken by the Celestials to do as they had promised, the admiral sent in word to say that if the obstructions were not removed he should take upon himself to do so by force. Having waited three days, he resolved to bombard the fort on the left. As our shot would have fallen into the town of Taku, the admiral sent an officer to advise the inhabitants to provide for their safety by leaving the place.

"They, however, replied that they did not receive orders from foreigners, and that if we touched the barriers the batteries would open fire upon us. Of course it now became necessary to attack the forts. Three of the larger ships and nine gun-boats were sent in two divisions to attack, in the first place, the Taku forts on the right bank, and one of the gun-boats was directed to pull up the stakes so as to afford a passage to the rest of the squadron. She at length succeeded and made her way up to the boom. The moment she struck it, the Chinese batteries opened on her with heavy guns. The other gun-boats took their stations astern of her. Two unfortunately got aground, one on the northern extremity and the other on the southern.

"The former, however, was notwithstanding still able to render some service against the forts further down the stream. In an hour one of the gun-boats was completely disabled; her commander killed, and out of a crew of forty men, nine only remained unhurt; the admiral himself, who was on board, being severely wounded. On this he shifted his flag into another vessel, with which he went close under the forts. Here he received a second wound, but still would not quit the fight. Unable to move, he took his place on the bridge, when the chain against which he was leaning was shot away, and he was thrown to the deck with such violence that one of his ribs was broken. Three times injured, it might have been supposed that he would have retired; but again shifting his flag to another vessel, he remained on deck in his cot, and directed the battle until, faint from loss of blood and pain, he consented to yield up command to the senior captain, who took his place.

"Still the battle continued; but three of our gun-boats were on shore and reduced to mere wrecks. We had, however, vessels and men sufficient to carry on the fight. At last it was determined to storm the forts. The soldiers, marines, and the blue-jackets detailed for the purpose were landed; the commander of an American man-of-war showing his sympathy by assisting with his boats in taking detachments of the storming party on shore. The tide, which had gone out, had left large banks of mud between the channel and the firm ground. Through this our men had to wade for many yards, covered, however, by the guns of the *Lee*, which opened fire for their protection. Scarcely, however, had they left the boats than every gun still serviceable in the fort, with numberless gingalls, rifles, and muskets, were directed upon them.

"One captain was mortally wounded, another severely hurt, and the colonel of the marines fell desperately wounded. The third in command still led on the storming party.

"The first ditch being nearly empty of water, was crossed, but a second, close under the walls of the fort, was full; and here, finding his immediate followers reduced to fifty men, while the larger party behind was almost exhausted, nearly 300 having been stricken down in their disastrous rush across the mud—he felt that it was his duty to wait for reinforcements. On sending back, however, for them, the commanding officer was obliged to refuse the request and to order him to retire, as there were no men to be spared. As it was, they were nearly cut off, for the tide rising, several boats had drifted up the stream. Some were taken possession of by the Chinese; but others were recovered. During the retreat the Chinese kept up a galling fire on our ranks, striking down many, who lay helpless in the mud until the returning tide put an end to their sufferings by washing over them.

"Not until past midnight did the commanders of the storming party, having collected all the men they could discover, embark in the last boat and return with heavy hearts to their ships. Six gun-boats were on shore, and it was feared that all would be lost; but the tide, rising higher than usual the next day, three were floated off, the others, however, remained immovable. Altogether we lost 80 men killed on the spot, and 350 wounded, many of whom died, among them being one of the most gallant officers in the service, Captain Vansittart.

"This disaster has shown us that, after all, when the Chinese have the advantage of strong fortifications, they are no contemptible enemies, and that it will not do to despise them. Of course, they are not to go unpunished for this last proceeding. As soon as the troops can be collected and the ships are ready, we expect to go back to Peiho to capture the Taku Forts and proceed on by land and water to Pekin, which, if the emperor will not give up, we are to bombard and take possession of. So you see you fellows have plenty of work before you. You need not be afraid of that."

Tom and Desmond, in return for the information they had received, had a still longer yarn to spin of the adventures they had gone through. Billy occasionally put in a word.

"The worst part of the business was when we were nearly starving and had to live on rotten yams and train oil. How would you fellows have liked that?" he asked.

"Not very pleasant," observed Charley Roy. "But you, Billy, don't appear to have suffered much from the fare you describe."

"I have had time to pick up again," answered Billy; "but I assure you that for many weeks afterwards I was as thin as a whipping-post."

Chapter Seven.

A visit to the tailor's, and a walk round Victoria—Tricks of
the coolies—A Chinese festival—Sail for Shanghai—An
unexpected meeting—Adventures of the Dragon's crew—A
walk through Shanghai—The midshipmen's ride into the
country—Their pleasure disagreeably interrupted—A ride
for life, and a narrow escape—Bring news of the approach of
the rebels—Regain their hotel—Aroused by the sound of
firing—Shanghai attacked by the rebels—The blue jackets
take part in the defence—Treachery defeated—Jerry saves
Tom's life—The rebels defeated—Return on board the
Empress—The Orion, Captain Adair, arrives from
England—Adair comes on board the Empress—Gerald's
anxiety—An astounding request—Captain Adair
communicates some interesting information to Desmond—
The fleet assembles, and the army lands on the shores of
China.

The fleet lay in readiness to proceed to Pe-chili, where it was
expected that they would find work to do, as the Taku Forts had to
be captured before the troops, now assembling in strong force, could
march on Pekin. In the mean time Captain Rogers took the
midshipmen on shore to obtain an outfit for them, which they much
required. With this object they repaired to the shop of Tung-Cheong,
the Buckmaster, of Victoria.

Mr Tung-Cheong came forward with a smiling countenance,
guessing, as he surveyed the tattered uniforms of the three
midshipmen, what they required.

"Me thinkee greatest tailor in the world. Thinkee nothing to make
coat'ees for three gentlemans," he observed, as he pointed to the
uniforms of every possible description hanging up in the shop. He at
once produced a midshipman's uniform, which he kept as a
specimen to show of what he was capable, and having taken their
measures, he promised that all three should be ready the following
evening, together with every other article they might please to order.
They, of course, wanted shirts, socks, caps, and shoes, swords and
belts, all of which, to their surprise, he had in stock—indeed, he
showed, like most of his countrymen, that he had a keen eye for

business, and would undertake to fit out a ship's company, from an admiral down to a powder-monkey.

Leaving the town, they climbed to the top of Victoria Peak, from whence they could look down on the harbour, which had the appearance of a picturesque lake, dotted over with vessels of every rig, while they obtained a good view of the town itself which extended along the shore for nearly four miles. Below on one side was the Kowloon Peninsula, now covered with military tents, while on the south side were seen numberless islands, with the wide expanse of the China Sea beyond.

"Now let us pay a visit to the Happy Valley," said Tom, as they descended the heights.

"It must be a pleasant place to live in. I should like to take up my abode there," observed Billy.

"Wait until you reach it before you form an opinion; it has a good many inhabitants already," observed Tom, who had heard all about the Wang-ne-chung from Charley Roy.

Billy changed his opinion when they got to the place, which is the burial ground of Hong-kong. On entering the Protestant cemetery, they saw a column erected to the memory of the officers and men of the 59th Regiment, which regiment, in the course of nine years, lost 644 persons, including a number of women and upwards of 100 children; the greater number cut down not by the weapons of the enemy, but by the pestiferous climate.

On their way to the town they met a soldier, holding a Chinaman by his pigtail, which he had twisted two or three times round his hand. On asking the Englishman what he was about to do with his prisoner, his reply was—

"Why, sir, this here chap is a coolie recruit; he has received his pay in advance, and was bolting, when I clapped eyes on him, and am taking him back to the barracks."

The coolie corps had just been raised to act as carriers to the regiments going to Pekin. Not being over troubled with honesty, the men took every opportunity of escaping as soon as they had received an advance, intending in many instances again to enlist.

On returning to the ship, Charley Roy told them of an incident, which had occurred just before. A number of coolies had been embarked on board a troop-ship, when one of them, who had purchased a quantity of pepper, started up and threw it into the eyes of the sentry placed over him, then dashing past the guard, leaped overboard, swam to a boat which was in waiting, and succeeded in making his escape.

While the midshipmen were at Hong-kong the great Chinese festival was going on; and as they had leave to go on shore, they had an opportunity of witnessing the proceedings.

One day they met a procession, consisting of some 3000 or 4000 people, many of them merchants and tradesmen, dressed in their gaudiest attire, extending upwards of a mile in length. There were bands of music and groups of figures, either carried on men's shoulders or wheeled along on platforms, representing various somewhat incomprehensible characters, but the chief attractions were three enormous dragons, each a hundred feet in length, which required thirty men to carry them.

In the evening an entertainment was given, open to all, without charge. It was in an enormous building erected for the purpose, composed of bamboo frame-work covered with matting. The interior was elegantly fitted up, and lighted by large numbers of glass chandeliers; the sides were richly decorated, and here were soon altars overhung with gorgeous drapery, and conservatories full of flowering plants, while concerts of vocal and instrumental music were going on in several parts of the building. There were also rooms where light refreshments, such as tea, coffee, and fruit, could be obtained without charge. Those who required more substantial fare could procure it at booths outside the large building, on very moderate payment. The midshipmen enjoyed themselves, and voted the Chinese very amusing, hospitable fellows.

At length the ships of war were ordered to the northward. The *Empress* was to call at Shanghai, at the southern entrance of the great river Yang-tse-kiang. Shanghai consists of a large English settlement and a Chinese city of considerable size. Soon after the *Empress* had come to anchor, a shore boat, pulled by Chinese, was seen approaching.

"She has English officers on board. Who can they be?" exclaimed Gerald, who was on the look-out at the gangway, to Tom. "I do believe! Can it be possible? Yes, I am nearly certain! There's Archie Gordon, Mr Joy, and there is Commander Rawson himself. Then the old *Dragon* must have escaped after all."

Tom sprang to the gangway, and waved his cap. This salute was replied to by those in the boat, which in another minute was alongside, and Commander Rawson, with the lieutenant and Archie, came on deck.

"We had given you up for lost," said Tom, as he shook hands with his brother midshipman.

"And we, to say the truth, had very little expectation of seeing you again," answered Archie. "How did you escape?"

"How did you find your way here?" asked Tom, without answering the question.

Before Archie could reply, Captain Rogers came on deck and welcomed the party. After exchanging a few words, the commander and lieutenant accompanied him into the cabin, while Archie was led off by his old shipmates into their berth. Before, however, he would give them an account of his adventures, he insisted on hearing about theirs, which of course occupied some time.

"And now," said Tom, "we want to hear your yarn. Was the *Dragon* lost? was it her we saw on the rocks, or was that some other unfortunate vessel?"

"She was the *Dragon*, there can be no doubt," answered Archie. "You remember the day at the Bonins when the hurricane suddenly sprang up. We had just got on board and were looking out for you, when the commander, considering that we should to a certainty be driven on shore if we remained where we were, ordered the steam to be got up, intending to run round and take you on board. We had not got far, however, when one of our boilers burst, killing half a dozen men and committing other damage. We had now to depend upon our canvas, while the hurricane was every instant increasing in strength. The ship, however, behaved very well. We ran on before the gale for four and twenty hours, when a lull coming on, the commander, wishing to get back to the Bonins, hauled the ship up. We had not, however, stood on long under close-reefed topsails, when a furious blast suddenly struck her, and in one fell swoop carried away all our masts. We managed, however, to get before the wind again by hoisting a sail on the stump of our foremast, and ran on, hoping to get under the lee of some island by the time the gale was over, where we might rig jury masts.

"Night came on; the hurricane was over. We were anxiously looking for daylight. Our belief was that we were a considerable distance from any island, when suddenly a loud crash was heard, and we had too sure evidence that the ship was on shore. Happily the sea had gone down, and although she struck heavily several times, we had hopes that she would hold together until we had made our escape. The commander, who was as cool as a cucumber, told us that although he could not get the ship off, seeing that already she had two or three holes in her bottom, our lives might all be preserved if we maintained discipline and exerted ourselves. When daylight came we found ourselves in sight of a small island, but it looked barren and inhospitable, with intervening reefs, over which the sea was breaking, so that we could have but little hope of reaching it. Outside, however, it was much calmer, but as the boats could not carry us all, the commander determined to build two or more rafts or catamarans which might convey all who could not go in the boats, and carry provisions and water.

"We hoped to reach the Loo-choo Islands, should we miss Grampus Island, half-way to them. The weather coming on perfectly fine, we were able to get three rafts rigged and the boats prepared for sea. The boats were to take the rafts in tow and keep within hailing distance, steering as the commander might direct. With a light wind from the eastward we shoved off from the wreck, without leaving a man behind. We made but slow progress, as the wind was light and the rafts towed somewhat heavily, still, we were all in good spirits, except that we regretted the loss of the ship and could not help thinking what had become of you fellows. We ran on for three days and then began to look out for Grampus Island, when the weather became threatening. As the barometer fell, so did our spirits. Had we all been in the boats, we might by this time have reached the shore, but of course they would not desert the rafts. The second lieutenant had charge of one raft, Josling another, and I volunteered to command the third. Even should a gale spring up, we did not altogether despair of navigating our rafts, so that we might run before it and lash ourselves down to escape being washed off.

"The wind blew stronger and stronger; the sea got up, and as night approached, matters were looking very disagreeable. The commander came round and spoke to those on the rafts, telling us what to do, and promising that the boats should remain by us should the worst come to the worst. The night was dark and squally. The catamarans rode over the sea better than was expected, although at times we scarcely expected to see another sunrise. When day at length broke, we were still in sight of each other, but there was no abatement in the gale, nor could land anywhere be discerned.

"Though we had weathered one night, from the experience we had had we earnestly hoped that we might not be exposed to a still severer gale, and yet there seemed every likelihood of the wind increasing. For my part, I began to think it was a pity those in the boats should expose themselves to greater danger by remaining by us, and was considering that we ought to urge the commander to leave us to make the best of our way, when a sail appeared in sight to the southward. As she stood towards us we made her out to be an American whaler. On coming up to us she hove to, when our commander went on board. We were, it may be supposed, not a little anxious to know what arrangements he would make with the master of the whaler. He was not long in settling matters. In a short time he made a signal for the other boats to come alongside, which they quickly did. The stores and the people not required for pulling were at once taken on board. The boats then came off to the rafts, when we all got into them and towed the rafts up to the ship. The stores were at once hoisted up, when the rafts were cast adrift, while our larger boats were allowed to tow astern, as they could not be taken on board. The American captain, who was bound to the coast of Japan in search of whales, agreed to land us at Yokohama.

"The voyage, however, was much longer than we expected. We were first of all caught in a heavy gale which came on that night, and were compelled to heave to, when we lost the boats towing astern. A day or two after this several whales were seen, which the captain was naturally anxious to catch. As he had plenty of hands on board, he put off with all his boats, and no less than three fish were killed. Then we had to cut them up and stow them away, which occupied the best part of a week. Scarcely was the operation concluded when two more whales were seen and taken, the American captain acknowledging that it was owing much to our assistance that he was able to secure such prizes.

"After this we had calms and light or contrary winds, so that our voyage was a protracted one. We had brought provisions and water, though they were nearly exhausted. What with so many men being on board, and the dirty condition of the whaler, it was a wonder that sickness did not break out among us so the doctor said, and so it would have done had not the people lived as much as possible on deck.

"The American captain fulfilled his promise, and landed us at Yokohama. We were detained there a considerable time before we could get across to this place. As soon as we arrived we sent word to Hong-kong of our safety, but I suppose the news had not reached that place before you sailed."

"Well, I am very glad, old fellow, that you and the rest have escaped," said Tom, "and I hope that we three shall be as fortunate as were my brother Jack and his two friends, when they were midshipmen."

The three newly re-united friends at once got leave to go on shore together with a few other midshipmen.

They first walked through the European settlement, which is handsomely laid out in streets running at right angles to each other. Many of the houses were well built, and stood in compounds like those in India. Strong wooden barriers had been put up at the beads of all the main streets, with loopholes in them, so that the place could be defended should the rebels succeed in capturing the native town beyond. This town is a short distance to the south of the European settlement. It was surrounded by a brick wall of about twenty-five feet in height, with an earthen embankment inside, forming a rampart six to ten feet wide. The parapet was two feet thick and seven high, containing embrasures for large gingalls three or four feet only apart. Between each gingall was a small hole in the parapet which held an earthen vessel filled with slaked lime, ready to be flung in the faces of an enemy attempting to escalade the walls. A considerable number of Chinese troops were stationed on the ramparts, with gay-coloured flags of various devices flying above their heads. It seemed curious that while the English were at war with the emperor, they should be in alliance with some part of his troops engaged in defending one of his towns against his rebel subjects.

"This is mighty dull work," exclaimed Gerald, after they had been wandering about the native town some time. "I vote that we get horses and take a gallop into the country. We shall have the fun of a ride, at all events, and perhaps see something curious."

"But suppose we fall in with the Tae-pings—that would not be pleasant; they would cut off our heads before we could explain who we were," observed Archie, who always took the cautious side.

"They look upon the English as friends, I believe," remarked Charley Roy. "They might, to be sure, take us prisoners and hold us as hostages; however, we must take care not to get near them, and by the last reports they were at Pow-shun, twenty miles off at least."

Notwithstanding the risk they might run, the votes were decidedly in favour of a ride if horses could be procured. The midshipmen for some time made inquiries where horses were to be let, in vain. At length they got a Chinaman to stop and try to understand what they wanted.

Gerald, jumping on Billy's back, sticking his heels into his sides and beating behind, the Chinaman signified that he comprehended their meaning, and led the way along several streets until they reached some stables containing a dozen Tartar ponies, sorry-looking half-starved animals. An old man with a long pig-tail, dressed in a blue serge shirt hanging over trousers of the same material, made his appearance, and again they had recourse to signs to ascertain whether he would let the horses, and how much they were to pay. To do this Tom produced some money, which he counted out into the hands of the old man, who immediately pocketed it, then saddled and bridled one of the ponies, thus giving the midshipmen to understand that he must be paid beforehand. As they had no objection to do this, the rest followed Tom's example.

"Take care no go near Tae-pings," said the old man, showing that he was accustomed to have dealings with the English, although his stock of words in that language was limited. The party, having been supplied with sticks instead of whips, set off in the direction of the west gate, which was wide open. As no enemy was near and it was supposed that the English officers were merely about to make a short circuit in the neighbourhood, they were allowed to pass unquestioned. As soon as they were clear of the walls, they put their horses into a gallop and dashed along at full speed, as if they were riding a race, laughing and shouting, to the great astonishment of the peasantry, who came out of their cottages to look at them. They had not gone far when they came upon a small pagoda-shaped edifice, about twenty feet in height. Seeing a man entering it carrying a small oblong bundle, wrapped round with bamboo straw, they followed him. Tom and Gerald, getting off their horses, entered the building. Round it were shelves, on which a number of similar bundles were seen; a pair of small feet sticking out of one of the bundles revealed to them the contents, and upon further inquiries from the man they ascertained that it was the "baby tower," in which the remains of infants whose parents were too poor to afford an ordinary funeral were deposited, and that when it was full it was cleared out by the municipal authorities.

"What wonderfully methodical people these Chinese are," said Archie; "but they certainly have curious ways of doing things."

The road over which they passed was well made and the country highly cultivated, with corn and paddy fields and gardens full of vegetables and fruit trees; ditches full of water to irrigate the ground ran in all directions, and over them were picturesque bridges, the larger ones of stone, and the others of wood or bamboo. People were at work in the fields, or employed in turning water-wheels, to raise the water to higher lands. The cottages were low, full of windows, deep caves, and so lightly built that it seemed as if a moderate gale would blow them away. The midshipmen had gone a considerable distance, much further, indeed, than they intended, but everything looked so peaceable that they could not fancy there was any risk, as they concluded that the rebels must be a long way off.

At last, getting hungry and thirsty, they looked about in the hopes of discovering a tea-house where they might obtain refreshments. Meeting a few peasants, as they seemed, by the road-side, they inquired by the usual language of signs where they could get something to eat. The men pointed to the west, and signified that they would soon come to a village where they could obtain what they wanted.

"Probably it is not much further; let us ride on," said Charley Roy.

They galloped forward, and were not mistaken, a good-sized village appeared in sight, and one of the first houses in it was of the description they were in search of. The host chin-chinned as they approached, and welcomed them to his establishment. Having fastened up their horses in a stable close at hand, where food and water were given them, they entered a tea house, and cakes, biscuits, and sweetmeats, with tea in wonderfully small cups, were at once placed before them.

"I say, I wonder whether the old fellow hasn't got something more substantial than this?" exclaimed Billy. "Some beef steaks and mutton chops, with a supply of vegetables, would be more to the purpose."

All the signs they made, however, produced nothing but a further supply of the same fare, which they despatched with a rapidity calculated to astonish their host, who was seen looking round at each of them and apparently calculating how much he should charge.

After their repast, they strolled out into the garden behind the house, containing arbours, miniature ponds filled with fish, canals crossed by bamboo bridges, and beds of tulips with other gay flowers. As there were no other visitors, they made themselves at home, lighted their cigars and took possession of the arbours, while Billy amused himself by trying to catch the fish with his hands as they swam up to gaze at the strange creature looking down upon them.

"This is really very jolly," said Desmond. "We will patronise our friend again if we come this way, although I wish I could make him understand that we want something better than cakes and tea."

They had been resting for some time, two or three of the party dropping off to sleep, when the sound of distant shouts and cries reached their ears. The noises grew louder and louder. Presently their host appeared at the door, gesticulating wildly, and pointing to the way they had come. Some straggling shots were heard.

"The place must be taken by the rebels, and as it is not our business to fight them, the best thing we can do is to make ourselves scarce," exclaimed Archie Gordon.

"We shall all be knocked on the head if we don't," cried Charley Roy, starting up. "Come, lads, the sooner we are on horseback the better."

Tom, shouting to his companions, led the way towards the house. The host had vanished, but they again caught sight of him hurrying off with a bundle under one arm, a box under the other, and a basket at his back. The doors were open, so they quickly rushed through the house towards the stables. The grooms had fled, fortunately not carrying off the steeds, which were munching away at their hay. To slip on the bridles and tighten up the girths did not take long.

"Now, boys," cried Tom, "discretion in this case is the best part of valour."

"We shall get preciously wigged by the first lieutenant if we lose our heads, for coming where we have no business to be," cried Gerald.

As they led out their horses, they saw people hurrying off in all directions across the fields, some scampering along the road they were about to follow. Behind them, at the further end of the village, came a confused multitude, but whether fugitives or pursuers they could not make out. One thing was certain, that if they delayed they would get into serious trouble, if not lose their lives.

"Mount, mount, and let us be off!" cried Tom. "Here, Billy, I will lend you a hand," and he lifted up his messmate, whose steed was somewhat restive, into his saddle; he then leaped on his own. Only a minute was lost before the midshipmen were all mounted, but that minute was of consequence.

The cries in their rear grew louder; several shots came whizzing past their ears.

"On! on!" shouted Tom. "I will bring up the rear," and, giving a whack to Billy's pony, he drew up for an instant to let the others pass him. They then altogether galloped on as fast as their steeds could move their nimble legs. Half-starved as the animals looked, they went at a good pace. Should their pursuers be on foot, they would very soon be beyond all danger of being shot. Tom occasionally turned to glance over his shoulder. Still the people behind, whoever they were, came rushing on, though as they were distanced they seemed to be more and more confused, until only a dark-coloured mass could be distinguished.

"We shall soon be beyond their reach," shouted Tom; "it won't do to pull up until we have distanced them thoroughly." Soon afterwards, as he looked again, he saw the dark mass divided, when he could distinguish sword blades flashing in the sun as they waved here and there.

"There are cavalry of some sort after us," he cried out. As far as he could judge at that distance, the horsemen were engaged in cutting down the native peasantry, whom they had overtaken unprepared for resistance.

"If we can make our horses go faster, we must do so," cried Tom. "Those fellows astern mean mischief, and we must keep well ahead, or they will be trying the sharpness of the sabres on our necks."

The party did not require this exhortation to do their best to make their steeds move forward faster, urging them on with rein and reiterated whacks on the back with their sticks. The hoofs of the animals clattered over the hard ground, sending up clouds of dust. The day was further advanced than they had supposed, but darkness would favour them should they find a road by which they might turn off and gain the city by another entrance.

"How far have we got to go?" inquired Desmond, shouting to Tom.

"That is more than I can tell; I know we came a good long way," answered Tom; "but our horses will carry us if we stick on their backs. Keep a good hand on your reins. Whatever you do, don't let them tumble down."

Though Tom encouraged his companions, he did not feel very sure that they would escape. He could distinguish flags and spears, as well as the sword blades. The horsemen behind them were becoming every instant more distinct. Much depended on the strength of their pursuers' horses. If these had already come a good way that morning they might be tired and soon knock up, but if they were fresh they might ere long overtake the midshipmen.

"If they overtake us, we must stand and make a fight for it," cried Tom.

"No doubt about that," answered Desmond. "It will never do to be cut down like sheep, running away."

"But as long as we can run we will," cried Tom. "If they do come up with us, my idea is that we should leap our horses over the ditch or fence, as may be most suitable, on our left, then wheel round and charge them if they attempt to follow us."

Roy and the rest agreed to Tom's proposal. "I don't think the cavalry have carbines, so that they cannot shoot us down at a distance, and our pistol bullets will reach farther than their lance points."

Tom had taken command of the party by tacit consent, and no one was disposed to dispute his authority. There was no time, however, for saying much. As they went along Tom had the satisfaction of observing that the enemy did not appear to be much, if at all, gaining upon them. This raised his hopes. They had already made good several miles, when Charley Roy proposed a halt, to breathe their horses and ascertain whether they were still pursued. Scarcely, however, had they stopped, than the clattering of their pursuers' horses' hoofs sounded in their ears, mingled with the shouts of the riders.

"We must push on, whether our nags like it or not," cried Tom; "if we can once distance them, the enemy are very likely to give up the chase, as they know they will run a risk of being cut off should they get too near the town."

Again the party galloped forward. Even their short halt enabled the Tae-pings to gain on them, and the rebels' voices sounded considerably louder.

"All right! they have no bow chasers, or we should have had them firing after us," cried Tom, laughing; "they will have had their ride for nothing, I hope, after all."

Two or three miles more were got over. The midshipmen began to look out for the lanterns on the city walls, which, by this time, they expected to see. Near, however, as they might be to a place of refuge, as their foes still continued the pursuit, they were not out of danger. Their steeds, too, were giving evident signs of being knocked up, and they had to keep their sticks going to make the poor animals move forward. Presently, down came Billy's horse, sending its rider clear over its head, Billy narrowly escaping a kick from the heels of the animal directly before him. Tom, without stopping to see what had become of Billy, pulled up, and fortunately succeeded in catching the animal's reins.

"Where are you, Billy?" he shouted out; "not hurt, I hope?"

"Not much, only on my knee," answered Billy, as he hobbled up and climbed again into his saddle.

The rest of the party, not seeing what had occurred, galloped on. Billy's horse, like his rider, had cut both its knees, and seemed very unwilling to continue the headlong race they had been so long running.

"You must make him get along," said Tom, applying his own stick to the animal's back. "I don't want my head cut off, and I don't want to leave you behind."

Short as had been the delay, it was of serious consequence, for when Tom looked round he could distinctly see the enemy coming after them. Billy, not being a good rider, cried out that he should be off again, as he had got one of his feet out of the stirrup.

"Never mind; hold on by your hands, and I'll lead your horse," cried Tom, seizing the rein. He had no wish to delay the rest of the party, so he did not shout out to them to stop, but he determined to push forward as long as the horses could keep on their legs. Billy in a short time succeeded in getting his foot into the stirrup.

"Now," said Tom, "if we have to leap, don't be pulling at the rein, but let your horse have his head, and you stick on like wax."

In the mean time the rest of the party pushed forward, Gerald was surprised that Tom did not answer a question; he shouted to him, still fancying that he was close behind.

"There's a light ahead," he cried out; "it must be on the walls, or else a house in the suburbs."

"If it was on the walls, it would appear higher," answered Archie, "What do you think, Tom?" he asked.

No reply came from Tom, and on looking round Roy discovered that both Tom and Billy were nowhere to be seen.

"We must wait for them," cried Archie; "we cannot leave them behind."

Before, however, he or his companions could pull up, a loud challenge was heard, and several shots came whizzing past them.

"If we stop or attempt to gallop back to look for them, we shall have another volley," said Roy. "I will ride forward slowly. That must be a piquet of the Indian regiment stationed outside the town. They mistake us for the enemy, and they may aim better the next time they fire." Without waiting for his companions' reply, Roy rode forward, shouting, "Friends, friends! English, English!" At length he came in sight of a party of men drawn across the road, and the English officer, advancing, inquired who he was. He explained that they were pursued by a body of cavalry, whom they supposed to be Tae-pings, and that he very much feared two of their companions had fallen into their hands.

The officer on this ordered his men to advance, but to be careful not to fire until he gave the word. Roy, riding forward, quickly overtook Archie and Gerald. On either side was a bank covered with shrubs, which would afford concealment in the dusk to the whole of the party. On seeing this, the officer told Roy to go a little distance further on and then to halt, and immediately he should hear the rebels advancing, to gallop back towards the town.

"You may, I hope, meet your friends, but if not, and they should have fallen into the hands of the rebels, we shall have a good chance of rescuing them."

"I understand, and will carry out your direction," said Roy, and the three midshipmen rode slowly back, hoping every instant to fall in with Tom and Billy. Their disappointment was bitter when they were nowhere to be seen. They had not, however, gone far, when they saw the Tae-ping horsemen moving rapidly towards them, but neither Tom nor his companions were visible. On this they immediately turned their horses' heads and galloped back, as they had been told to do, in the direction of the town, feeling dreadfully anxious as to the fate of their friends. They had got some little distance beyond the ambush when a rapid succession of shots told them that the Indian soldiers had opened their fire on the enemy. They at once pulled up, feeling sure that the Tae-pings would not venture to advance further. In this they were right, for as they returned they saw them in rapid flight, the soldiers still firing after them.

"You have saved our lives, I believe, sir," said Roy, addressing the officer, who had advanced to meet him. "What can have become of our companions?"

"I am afraid that the Tae-pings must have overtaken them, and too probably, immediately have cut them down, for they certainly were not with the party we got under our fire. My men tell me that they saw no English uniforms."

"If they were killed, they must be lying on the road," said Desmond, his heart sinking within him as he spoke. "We must go and look for them."

To this the officer made no objection, and sent forward five men with a sergeant. They proceeded even beyond where Tom and Billy had last been seen. Although they came on the dead bodies of several Tae-pings, who had been shot by the soldiers, they could discover no trace of their friends.

"Then they must have been carried off prisoners," observed Desmond. "However, that is better than had they been killed, as we may possibly recover them."

Any further search was useless; indeed, the officer was anxious to send back to the town to give notice that the Tae-pings were in the neighbourhood, and that a cavalry force had advanced so far without infantry to support them. The whole party accordingly returned to the house where the outpost was stationed. Gerald and Archie were so much cut up at the thought of Tom's loss—though, if the truth was known, they did not care so much about poor Billy,—that they felt scarcely able to ride back, and were glad to accept the lieutenant's offer of refreshment before they returned to the city.

"They'll be after cutting off the poor fellows' heads," cried Gerald. "How did we come to miss them? I would not have gone on if I hadn't thought they were close at our heels."

"Nor would I," said Archie; "it's some blundering of that fellow Billy Blueblazes. He must have tumbled off his horse, and Tom wouldn't leave him."

The lieutenant could give them very little consolation. The Tae-pings, from the reports received, committed the most horrible cruelties in the places they had taken, and when they captured Pow-shun they put to death indiscriminately men, women, and children; the defeated Imperialist troops having joined them and assisted in plundering the place.

"Our horses must be rested; it is time for us to be going back," said Roy at last.

Thanking the lieutenant, they again mounted. Just as they got outside the house they heard the sound of homes' hoofs.

"Don't fire!" cried the officer to his men. "These must be friends."

In another moment two horsemen were seen coming along the road, and Gerald, dashing forward, shouted out, "Hurrah! Why, it's Tom Rogers and Billy Blueblazes!"

Gerald was not mistaken, although their friends could scarcely be distinguished from the masses of mud which covered them and their steeds. Tom and Billy having received the congratulations of the party, and being introduced to the lieutenant, explained that finding the Tae-pings gaining upon them, they had leaped over a ditch bordered by trees, which concealed them from the view of their pursuers, and that they had then galloped along over the soft ground, having to scramble through a number of ditches, which were too wide to leap, until they, once more catching sight of the lights in the village, made their way back to the road.

As Tom and Billy were wet through, they declined to do more than stop and take a cup of hot tea, and the whole party then galloped on, as fast as their tired steeds could go, to the town, and managed to find their way back to the stable from which they had hired the horses.

The old man examined them with his lantern, exhibiting a rueful countenance, and shaking his head, muttering as he did so, "No good, no good!"

Tom tried to explain that if they had not ridden hard, he would never again have seen his horses; but probably the midshipman's explanations were not understood, as the owner of the animals still kept muttering, "No good, no good!"

"Well, as it was partly our fault for delaying so long, I propose that we pay the old fellow something more," said Tom.

All agreed, and: Mr Kay Chung's countenance brightened greatly when they handed him some more coin. On their way back they met several of the English inhabitants, to whom they reported that a force of Tae-pings was in the neighbourhood. Their news created no small amount of stir in the place. Information had already been received at head-quarters from the outposts, and immediately active preparations were made for the defence of the town, lest the enemy should advance during the night. Pretty well tired out, the midshipmen at last got back to the hotel where they settled to remain for the night, as it was too late by that time to return on board. Tom and Billy were not sorry to turn in, while a Chinese waiter undertook to get their jackets and trousers cleaned and polished up by the next morning.

Tom had been sleeping for several hours, when Gerald, followed by Roy, who had a different room, rushed in, exclaiming, "Rouse up, old fellows; something serious is going on. There's been tremendously heavy firing for the last ten minutes in the direction of the Chinese town, and there can be no doubt but that the Tae-pings are attacking the place. We are starting off to see the fun."

"Fun, do you call it!" said Archie, who had been awakened by Gerald's first exclamation. "It will be no fun if the rebels take Shanghai, and there is but a small garrison for its defence. As likely as not the Chinese will run away, or more probably fraternise with the Tae-pings."

"The marines and that Indian regiment are sufficient to drive back the enemy, and we shall have our own blue-jackets on shore, depend upon it, when Captain Rogers hears what is going forward," said Roy.

"Come, Tom, are you going with us? I suppose nothing will induce Billy to turn out, if he can help it."

"But my clothes, my clothes! that Chinese waiter Fau-ti has got them. I have nothing to put on."

"I will unearth him, and make him bring them to you," said Desmond; "and Billy's also, for he won't like to be left behind."

While Desmond went off to find the waiter, Billy, who was sitting up in bed, rubbing his eyes, asked what the row was about. On being told, he answered—

"Let them fight it out by themselves; I don't see why we should interfere," and lying down, he was about again to compose himself to sleep, when Roy and Archie, seizing the clothes, effectually roused him up. The firing was now heard closer than before, apparently extending over a considerable space. Billy, as much as he was disinclined to leave his bed, did not like to be left behind, and forgetting that his clothes had been taken away, began hunting for them.

"If you cannot find them, you must come as you are. Wrap yourself up in a sheet; you will help to scare the enemy, at all events," said Roy.

Desmond at last returned, followed by the waiter bringing the midshipmen's uniforms. Although they were not long dressing, some time had been spent, but it was not yet daylight. There was a general commotion going forward in the house, the other inmates calling to each other, and inquiring what was happening.

When the midshipmen got to the door of the house they found a large party collected, most of them with arms in hand and full of fight. For what they could tell to the contrary, however, the Tae-pings might already have scaled the walls. Just as they were setting off, the tramp of a large body of men was heard approaching. The midshipmen recognised Captain Rogers with the blue-jackets and marines of his ship, and several officers. Tom at once joined his brother, and confessed what they had been about, and how narrowly they had escaped being caught by the rebels.

"You were the means, however, of putting the garrison on the alert, for the messenger who came off with a request for me to land my men informed me that a party of midshipmen had brought in the intelligence of the approach of the enemy."

Tom was well pleased to hear this, as he hoped that he and his companions would escape the reprimand they expected to receive for having gone so far from the city. The sound of heavy guns was now heard, and a shot occasionally pitched into the ground at no great distance in front of them, showing that the enemy could not be far off outside the walls.

"They have not yet got inside, and we shall be in time to help drive them off before they succeed," said Jack.

A Chinese officer had been sent to guide the seamen to a part of the walls where the defenders most required support. Just as they arrived the guns pointed in that direction had ceased firing, and large bodies of men were seen through the gloom approaching with scaling ladders.

"We shall soon tumble those fellows over if they make the attempt to escalade the walls," said Tom.

The rebels, however, showed no want of pluck. In another instant the ladders were placed against the walls, and numbers of pig-tailed fellows, with broad hats, holding their shields above their heads, began to climb up, in spite of the hot fire which the marines and blue jackets poured down upon them. They had evidently not expected to meet with such a reception, supposing that the place was defended only by their own countrymen armed with matchlocks and spears. Along the whole line of the wall, at different points, the same scene was being enacted. Thousands of men were crowding forward, expecting by their numbers to overcome the limited garrison, but in every place they were met by the most determined courage, the civilians vying with the soldiers in repelling the foe.

Captain Rogers had ordered another party of seamen to join him under the second lieutenant as soon as the boats could bring them on shore, and finding the determined way in which the rebels were attacking the part of the walls he had been directed to defend, he sent back Tom and Desmond to hurry them forward. The midshipmen met the party about half-way, and Tom delivered the message. Under the belief that he knew the road, he led them through several narrow streets, when suddenly he discovered that he had made a mistake, but whether he ought to have kept more to the left or right, he could not tell.

Sharp firing, however, being heard to the right, he concluded that was the direction he ought to have taken. The party moved forward again at the double. The walls soon rose up before them, and the shot, which came down like hail, showed that the enemy were firing away as hard as ever. Just then, at the end of a short street they caught sight of a large body of men moving away from them.

"I wonder where those fellows can have come from?" remarked the lieutenant.

"They are making for the gate we rode out of yesterday," observed Tom.

"Probably the enemy are attacking it; we will go and assist, though they appear to be Chinese, and are not likely to make much of a stand," observed the lieutenant.

The seamen dashed forward, when just as they reached the gate, which was in front of them, it was thrown open, and the party they had seen, turning round, rushed back the way they had come, followed by many others who were streaming through the gate.

"There is some treachery at work here," exclaimed the lieutenant, and ordering his men to halt and fire, they poured a volley upon the advancing mass.

Before the rebels could recover from the confusion into which the unexpected shower of bullets had thrown them, the blue jackets were in their midst, cutting them down, knocking them over, or making them turn and try to escape through the gate. This put a stop to the further progress of those still outside, and the seamen, led by their gallant officer, fought their way up to the gate. Here a desperate struggle ensued. A big Tae-ping was on the point of cutting down Tom, when, a cutlass intervening, brought the Tae-ping with a blow on the head to the ground, and Tom saw his old shipmate, Jerry Bird, whom he had not before recognised, slashing away right and left by his side. The rebels at length having been forced out, the lieutenant ordered the gates to be shut. This was no easy matter, with the space on either side covered with the dead and wounded, but the seamen, hauling the bodies out of the way, at last succeeded.

One party remained to guard the gate, the other made prisoners of many as they could catch of those who had treacherously opened it. Tom, with Jerry Bird and three other men, was now sent to inform Captain Rogers of what had occurred, that he might despatch people to the other gates to prevent the same trick being played.

"You rendered me good service just now," said Tom to Jerry Bird, "in saving my head from the sword of that big Tae-ping. He would have cut me down to a certainty. I shall never forget it."

"Lor' bless you, sir, I'm as well pleased as you are; I wouldn't have had you killed, no, not to be made port admiral, and I hope, if ever there comes another occasion, I may do the same."

"Still, you have saved my life, and I should be grateful whether it was a pleasure to you or not," said Tom.

There was not much time for conversation, however. As they hurried on, they had to keep a look-out, lest they might be attacked by any of the traitors within the walls, who would have liked to have revenged themselves on those who had defeated their treacherous object. Several suspicious-looking characters approached, but dreading the cutlasses of the British seamen, they retired to a respectful distance. Tom and his party quickly made their way to the part of the walls where Captain Rogers and his men were stationed, and Tom delivered his message. On receiving it, Jack immediately despatched some of the midshipmen with the information to the officers commanding in the neighbourhood of the other gates, that they might be on their guard against any intended treachery.

The rebels, supposing that their friends had got inside the city, continued to make feints in all directions, to keep the garrison employed, fully believing that the place would in a short time be theirs. Along the whole line, as far as the eye could reach on either side appeared a rapid series of flames of fire, both from the summits of the walls and from below, as the defenders and their assailants exchanged fire.

The assault continued until daylight breaking exposed the rebels more clearly to view, and they, probably believing that they had no prospect of success, ceased firing along their whole line, and began rapidly to retreat. The officer in command, on seeing this, sent a considerable body of men out of the west gate, and pursued them for some distance, giving them a lesson it was not likely they would wish to have repeated. The Chinese soldiers cut off the heads of those they took. The English sailors contented themselves with depriving the fugitives of their pig-tails, generally giving them a probe in the back before they applied the final stroke. The whole ground for some distance was strewn with the dead, while under the walls they lay still more thickly, proving the desperation with which they fought, and the hot fire poured down upon them. Captain Rogers with his men remained on shore until it was ascertained that the rebels had retreated to Pow-shun, twenty miles off, and there appeared no probability of their returning. Information was received, however, that they were plundering the provinces in every direction, murdering the inhabitants, and committing every possible species of cruelty. An English regiment also arrived from Hong-kong to reinforce the garrison, when there was no longer the slightest fear that the rebels would succeed in taking the place.

Captain Rogers and his men had just returned on board the *Empress*, when a man-of-war was seen standing in for the anchorage. She made the signal *Orion*.

"Why, that's the ship to which your uncle Adair is said to be appointed," observed Archie to Gerald.

"I hope he has got her. I shall be very glad to see him, for a better fellow does not exist, and I shall then know all about the mysterious matter for which I was to go home," said Gerald.

The *Orion* brought up a short distance from the *Empress*. In less than half an hour a boat put off from her.

"There's no doubt about it; that's my uncle Adair," said Gerald, who was watching through his glass. "He's coming on board, so I feel like a young lady who is going to have a proposal made to her. I only hope now he has come out he won't insist on sending me home."

In a short time Captain Adair stepped up the side. Having been received with due honour, he was heartily welcomed by Captain Rogers, whom he accompanied, after he had shaken hands with his nephew, into the cabin.

"I'm not much wiser than I was before," observed Gerald; "but I suppose he will send for me soon."

Gerald, however, had to endure his suspense some time longer. Tom had faithfully kept the secret with which he was entrusted, so that Gerald had only a faint idea that some piece of good fortune was in store for him.

While the two captains were in conference, a handsome Chinese boat came off, and a mandarin of rank stepped on deck. He "chin-chinned" as the midshipmen drew up on either side of the gangway to do him honour, and the captains, hearing of his arrival, came out to receive him. He of course again "chin-chinned" to them, when, through an interpreter he had brought with him, he stated that "he had come to make a request which he hoped would not be denied."

Captain Rogers answered "that he should be happy to render any service that was in his power."

The mandarin replied, "that although he should consider the favour a great one, the trouble to him would not be so."

"Pray state, my friend, what it is," said Jack.

"Understand, that my beloved brother died a few days ago of a malignant fever, and that his body is now deposited in the Ning-foo Jos-house, outside the city walls. He belongs to Teit-sin, where his family reside, and as there is a difficulty in sending him by a merchant vessel, I shall feel deeply obliged if you will convey his coffin to that place, where it may be deposited with his august ancestors," was the answer.

Adair, when he heard what was said, could not refrain from bursting into a fit of laughter. Jack tried to compose his countenance as he told the mandarin that it was with much regret he must refuse his request, as the ship would not certainly get so far as Teit-sin, and that it was not usual for men-of-war to carry about dead bodies, except in rare instances; that when people died on board, they were buried at sea, and, especially for sanitary reasons, he could not receive that of a person who had died of a malignant fever.

In vain the mandarin pleaded that his brother was shut up tightly and would not cause the slightest annoyance. Jack was firm, and the mandarin had to return and allow his brother to remain in the Jos-house until navigation was opened. Terence had brought word for the *Empress* to proceed to the mouth of the Peiho in the Gulf of Pe-chili, as it had been resolved at once to recapture the Taku Forts and to march the army to Pekin, should the emperor not immediately yield to the demands of the British ambassador.

The summer had begun and the weather was remarkably fine. The two ships sailed along in company, getting up steam only when the wind fell light.

Gerald and Billy Blueblazes were transferred to the *Orion*, the berth of the *Bellona* being overcrowded. Some of the crew of the unfortunate *Dragon* were also sent to her, the remainder being kept on board to be distributed among other ships of the squadron, while most of the officers had gone on to Hong-kong with Commander Rawson, to await a passage home. Mr Joy joined the *Orion* in lieu of her third lieutenant, who was invalided. Gerald, as soon as he had an opportunity, having waited in vain for his uncle to speak on the subject, asked to be informed about the matter for which he had been sent for home.

"The uncertainties connected with it are so very great, that I have been unwilling to disturb your mind on the subject," answered Adair. "You know that you had a distant relative, Lord Saint Maur, who had a fine estate and numerous heirs to succeed him. One after the other, however, they have died. Immediately on hearing this I put the matter into the hands of a clever Dublin lawyer, who tells me that the direct descendants of the last lord having died, it is necessary to go several generations back, to a former Lord Saint Maur, of whom your grandfather was the lineal descendant, and that all the other lines having become extinct, you are the rightful heir to the title and estate. Other Desmonds, however, have appeared, who have made out a similar claim, and the question is who has the best. They have money, which, unfortunately, you have not; but our Dublin friend is so confident that he has undertaken the matter at his own risk. You, at all events, will lose nothing, and may gain your case; at the same time, I must confess I am not very sanguine on the subject. At first being so, I sent for you home, but after a time I arrived at a different conclusion, and would advise you not to think about the matter, though, if some day or other you succeed, well and good. It will be pleasant to be Viscount Saint Maur and owner of a fine estate, but perhaps you would not be much the happier. If you stick to the navy you will get promoted in due course, and it will be much the same thing to you a hundred years hence."

Gerald did not quite agree with his uncle in the philosophic view he took of the case; at the same time, he determined not to bother himself about the affair. He was sorry to be parted from Tom and Archie, and to have only Billy Blueblazes instead, the rest of his shipmates being strangers to him.

The *Bellona* and *Orion* had a quick run to the rendezvous off the Sha-la-tung shoal, about twenty miles from Pehtang. On their way, near the entrance to the gulf, they came up with the fleet conveying the troops intended to be disembarked near the mouth of the Peiho. It was a magnificent sight, as the clouds of canvas appeared covering the blue ocean, the ships' bows dashing up the spray, which sparkled in the sunshine as they clove their onward way. Among them were numerous steamers, but the wind being fair they were also under sail. The despatch vessels and gun-boats were moving about, enforcing orders and bringing up the slower craft. The ships as they arrived at their destination took up their position in line, according to the division, brigade, and regiment of the troops on board, all confusion being avoided by the admiral having furnished each captain with a plan showing the place in which he was to anchor. The next day the French fleet arrived, and the whole force moved nearer the shore. The smaller craft only could cross the bar of the Pehtang, at the mouth of which is a town of the same name.

Early on the morning of the first of August the signal was made for the gun-boats and the small steamers attached to the fleet to take as many troops as they could on board, and to tow boats carrying others, when the whole flotilla commenced steaming slowly towards Pehtang. As it would have been dangerous for the gun-boats to attack the forts in their crowded condition, they proceeded to a spot 2000 yards south of it.

The country presented anything but an attractive appearance, as all that could be seen was an extensive mud flat, with a raised causeway, running from Pehtang towards Taku, while deep ditches were cut for the purpose of drainage, and were likely to prove disagreeable places to cross. The boats of the men-of-war were employed also in landing the troops. Tom had command of one of the *Empress's* boats, and Gerald one of the *Orion's*, so that they had an opportunity of seeing what was going forward. As the boats approached, some Chinese soldiers showed themselves, but perceiving the strength of the force invading their country, wisely beat a retreat.

Among the first to approach the shore was the commander-in-chief. It was impossible to get close to the bank. He surveyed the extent of mud before him; then pulling off his shoes and stockings, and rolling up his trousers, he leaped overboard, his example being followed by his officers and men. Together they splashed and waded for upwards of half a mile through a horrible black mud. The French brigade landed on the left, and in the same manner in the neighbourhood, but finding somewhat harder ground, were the first to reach the causeway. A cavalry picquet now appeared on a drawbridge across the causeway, watching the movements of the allies, but they also, as the troops floundered on, mounted their horses and rode at a dignified pace southward towards Taka. The whole day was occupied in landing troops.

In the evening it was ascertained that the forts of Pehtang were abandoned. It was intended at once to march in and take possession, but private information was obtained from some of the Chinese that the garrison had left numerous infernal machines so placed with long fuses that they would explode among the troops on entering. The Chinaman who had given the information was at once compelled to point out where these horrible engines of destruction were hidden, and they were removed by some men sent forward for that purpose. The army which had now landed, if so it could be called, had to pass the night on the mud flats and causeway, destitute of water and food, without tents, and wet ground alone on which the men could stretch themselves. It was not a pleasant commencement of a campaign. Jack and Desmond agreed that they had reason to be thankful for having their own comfortable ship to sleep in.

The next morning at daybreak the gun-boats entered the river, and the troops advancing from their position occupied the town, the unhappy inhabitants being ejected to make room for them. It was one of the sad necessities of warfare that they were compelled to turn out the poor people. Children in arms, old men and women, who had not for years left their homes, were forced to seek for shelter, which was not to be found; and many of the men destroyed themselves and their families rather than expose them to the perils they would have to meet with. The English took up their quarters in one part of the town, the French in the other. It was said to have contained 20,000 inhabitants, but when it was abandoned by the army scarcely any were to be found. Among those who thus destroyed themselves was the man who had given the important information respecting the infernal machines, he and his whole family having put themselves to death. Although, except as volunteers, the blue-jackets and their officers had but little prospect of fighting, they had work enough to do in landing the troops and stores, they being thus engaged at all hours of the day and night for many days together.

"There is little honour or glory to be gained, that I can see, though we are very useful, I dare say," observed Desmond to Tom, after they had been in their boats for twelve hours on a stretch. "However, I don't mind if we can help the soldiers to lick the Celestials, who deserve a sound drubbing, at all events."

The soldiers were worse off than their sailor brethren. Rain came down, rendering the town almost uninhabitable by the horrible smells which arose, while the mud in many places was several feet deep. Such was the detestable spot in which the army was cooped up for nearly a fortnight.

The allied armies having captured the Taku Forts, the smaller steamers entered the river and greatly aided the army by conveying troops and stores to Teit-sin; but very few naval men saw anything of the subsequent operations, which terminated in the surrender of Pekin and the destruction of the emperor's summer palace, and the establishment of peace between the British and Chinese.

Chapter Eight.

Bellona and Empress in Victoria Harbour—A complaint of piracy—Mr Jull again—The two ships sail in search of his fleet of junks—Captain Po-ho goes as pilot—Fail in with Orion—Ordered to Japan—Expedition to attack a piratical fleet commanded by Jull—The pirate fleet sighted—Tom and Desmond sent in chase of junks—Tom hoards a junk, and has good reason for getting out of her again—Tom, pursuing the enemy, is captured—Billy pulls after the other boats—The first junk blows up—Vain search for Tom—Return to the Gnat—The fort and junks attacked—The Round Moon recovered—Jerry recognises Jull—The seamen and marines on shore prepare to attack the fort.

The Taku Forts had been captured, the march to Pekin accomplished, the summer palace destroyed, the pride of the emperor humbled, and once more peace was established.

Her Majesty's ships *Bellona* and *Empress* lay in Victoria Harbour, the broad pennant of Commodore Murray, for he had lately been raised to that rank, flying on board the former. He and Captain Rogers were seated in the cabin of his ship after dinner. The officers who had been the commodore's guests had retired, the midshipmen having previously received a polite hint to go on deck and ascertain which way the wind blew.

"I heartily hope we shall soon be ordered away from this most undelectable coast," observed Jack.

"So do I, in truth," answered Murray. "From what I hear, we shall soon be sent to Japan, which seems to be in a very unsettled state with the Mikado, Tycoon, and the Damios at loggerheads. If the latter especially are not put down, they will get the upper hand of their two spiritual and temporal sovereigns, and then set to work to murder each other, and the whole country will be thrown into a state of anarchy."

"I should be glad of something to do, at all events," said Jack. "The gun-boats have all the work nowadays, and as we have reduced the

Celestials to order there is not much prospect of our big ships being wanted."

"Had I a reason for proceeding in any definite direction I would sail to-morrow," observed the commodore; "but there is no object in cruising up and down the coast, expending coals and wearing out the ship."

"I am sometimes tempted to wish that steam power had never been introduced on board men-of-war when I think of our early days on the *Racer* in the Mediterranean, and the life we led on the coast of Africa and out here," said Jack. "After all, youngsters have the best of it."

"They certainly have few cares and responsibilities, and enjoy sounder sleep than those in command can do when at sea," observed Murray.

While they were speaking, Archie Gordon, cap in hand, entered the cabin, and addressing the commodore said, "A Chinaman has just come on board, sir, and as far as we can understand, desires to see you to report that his junk has some time ago been attacked and carried off by pirates."

"I will see him at once; let him come below," answered the commodore. "Request Mr Chin-ho, the interpreter, to come here."

"He has gone on shore, sir," replied the midshipman. In less than a minute Gordon returned, ushering in a stout-built Chinaman, dressed, to English eyes, in a very unnautical costume, but characteristic of that strange people.

"What have you got to say, my friend?" asked Murray, after the visitor had made the usual salutation and been requested to sit down, for Murray properly made it a rule to treat all the Chinese with due courtesy.

The stranger introduced himself as Po-ho, captain of the big junk *Round Moon*. As the curious jargon in which he made his statement would not be understood by most readers, we must give it in ordinary English.

"The *Round Moon* was lying in Swatow roads, in company with several other trading junks, when I, being asleep in my cabin, was awakened by a loud noise on deck, of shrieks and cries, clashing of swords, scuffling and thumps, as though men were falling. Rushing out to see what was the matter, what was my horror to discover that the deck was in the possession of strangers, and that most of my crew lay dead or dying. My mate with two or three others was still fighting bravely, not far from the cabin door, when I beheld an Englishman, Jull by name, whom I knew to be a fearful scoundrel, a sword covered with blood in his hand, and about to attack the mate and the others. Before I could run back and get my arms, Jull had killed the mate, and the rest were cut down. Seeing that I should share the same fate, I jumped through the cabin port into the water, intending to swim to a junk astern, when Jull, who had followed me into the cabin, discovering that I was overboard, fired at me, but missed. I thought that I should escape, but presently another shot struck me in the back; still I swam on, and reached the side of the junk.

"When I got on board, the first thing I saw was my ship with all sails set, standing out of the harbour. I wanted the captain of the junk who had picked me up to give chase, but he answered, 'No, no; Jull has got too many men and long guns.' Before I could say anything more I had fainted. When I came to myself, the *Round Moon* was out of sight. I have not seen her since, but wishing to recover her, I have not ceased inquiring about Jull at every place at which I have touched. A few days ago, as I was sailing from Chusan, I heard that Jull, in command of a large fleet of junks, had attacked and plundered a number of merchant vessels in that neighbourhood, and that he was even then at anchor with all his fleet in a channel between the island of Latea and that of Chusan. If you go at once northward with your steamers, you may arrive in time to catch him before he sails away. He has nearly thirty junks, carrying heavy guns and gingalls, and 500 or 600 men. Your steamers cannot get up the creek to attack him, and he is very likely to make his escape if he knows you are coming. You must, therefore, send in a large force, and be very careful how you approach, and as he fights with a rope round his neck, he will struggle to the last."

This narrative took a long time to deliver, as Mr Po-ho, though he professed to speak English fluently, had to search about for words to express himself, and Murray and Rogers had to cross-question him and make him repeat over and over again what he had said before they could comprehend his meaning. The above, however, as has been said, was the substance of his statement, reduced to plain English. Murray inquired whether Mr Po-ho, or rather Captain Po-ho, was ready to go as pilot. He jumped at the offer. Nothing would give him more satisfaction than to see Jull's head cut off.

"We will both go," said Murray. "Return on board, Jack; hoist the blue Peter, fire your guns to bring off any of your officers or men who may be on shore. I will do the same, and we will sail this very evening. Are you ready, Captain Po-ho?" The Chinaman's little eyes twinkled with satisfaction. "He would," he said, "send his boat back to let his friends know that he had found some generous Englishmen to avenge his loss, and expressed a hope that should his own junk be recovered, she would be restored to him."

That night the two ships, with most of their officers on board — with the exception of two or three, who, having gone to the other side of the island, were left on shore — were steaming northward. Just before they sighted Chusan, a vessel under all sail was seen standing from the north-east. As she approached she made the signal of the *Orion*, and that she had despatches for the commodore. The *Bellona's* way was therefore stopped, the *Empress* also waiting for her. In a short time Captain Adair came on board. He had come from Japan with the request that some of the ships on the station might be sent there at once to protect British interests, subjects, and property, which were in constant danger from the Damios. The commodore decided, however, that the matter was not so urgent as to prohibit his first looking after the pirate and his fleet, and resolved to carry out his object, taking the *Orion* with him. At Chusan, off which he called to obtain further information, he found a gun-boat, the *Gnat*, which, from her small size, would be able to play an important part in the expedition.

From the information furnished by Captain Po-ho, Murray learned that the pirate's stronghold was in the midst of several small islands, with four navigable channels between them leading up to it, and that to prevent the escape of the villains it would be necessary to watch the whole of them. The pirate also, Po-ho said, had a strong battery on shore, its guns commanding a deep bay, in which the junks were at anchor. Thus the boats in the expedition would be exposed to a hot fire, and should the junks be captured, they might immediately be sunk, before they could be carried off, by the guns of the fort, which was described as being very strong originally, and since it had been occupied by the pirates they had been employed in still further adding to the defences. It was said also that within was stored a large amount of merchandise, obtained by the pirates during several cruises. One thing appeared certain, that the piratical fleet was still at anchor off the fort. The commodore, having obtained all the necessary information, stood with his squadron late in the day towards the islands, so that he might not arrive off them until darkness would conceal his movements. Po-ho advised that three of the entrances should be guarded, each by one of the ships, and that the gun-boat and boats should proceed up the other to attack the pirates. This suggestion was adopted. Murray ordered three boats from each ship, with a strong body of blue-jackets, to rendezvous alongside the *Gnat*, which also carried the larger number of marines.

Captain Rogers, accompanied by Po-ho as pilot and interpreter, went on board the *Gnat* and took command. The three midshipmen had each charge of a boat, as had our old friend Jos Green, while the others were under command of lieutenants or mates. Tom was accompanied by Billy Blueblazes and Tim Nolan. The *Gnat*, taking the fleet of boats in tow, steered towards the entrance of the chief channel, up which the expedition was to proceed. As they neared it just before dawn, a rocket was seen to rise, forming an arch in the dark sky, its glittering drops shining brilliantly as they fell. It was fired apparently from the centre of the island, where the fort was supposed to be situated, as a signal to some of the junks which might have been at anchor near the entrance of one of the channels. As Captain Po-ho could not give a very exact account of the position of the fort, Captain Rogers thought it prudent to wait until daybreak before commencing the attack. Of the character of the enemy, however, he had no doubt, from the information obtained at Chusan. They were a daring band of pirates, who had long been the terror of traders.

The *Gnat*, having a long line of boats astern, made but slow way. A bright look-out was kept, lest any of the junks might attempt to steal out and escape; but none appeared. The rocket, however, was an evidence that some of the pirate fleet, at all events, were still inside. The entrance was at length gained. The shore on either side was so close that, had the enemy concealed themselves among the rocks and shrubs, they might greatly have annoyed the flotilla without the risk of much damage to themselves.

When morning broke the *Gnat* was approaching a long, low, rocky point, over which the masts of a considerable fleet of junks could be perceived. The steamer must at the same time have been discovered by the pirates, for the junks' sails were hoisted, and the wind favouring them, they stood away towards a channel in the opposite direction.

"The villains will soon find they have made a mistake, if they expect to get off that way," observed Tom to Blueblazes. "They will fall from the frying-pan into the fire. The shots from our ships will send every one of them to the bottom." Just then the *Gnat* grounded on a sand-bank, and the boats had to take to their oars while she made efforts to back off. While she was thus engaged, the junks were seen returning to their anchorage, sweeping along at a good speed.

"The rascals have discovered that they are caught in a trap, and, like rats driven into a corner, will fight desperately," said Tom. "We shall have some real work to do, Billy."

"I don't mind much about that, provided it will soon be over and we can get back to breakfast," answered the other midshipman. "I am terribly hungry already."

This delay enabled the greater part of the pirate fleet to get back to their anchorage, but the wind blowing stronger as the sun rose, three of them, unable to make headway against it, turned down another channel, expecting probably to escape in that direction, being thus unable to render any assistance to their companions.

On this Captain Rogers ordered three of the boats, of which Tom's was one, to go in chase of the fugitives and capture them, hoping, from the prisoners who might be taken, to ascertain the strength of the fort, so that he might devise the best way of attacking it. The second lieutenant of the *Empress* led the boats, Desmond's making the third. Away they pulled as hard as they could go. The pirates, seeing them coming, opened on them with their stern guns, and at the same time kept up a pretty hot fire with gingalls; but their shot generally flew over the boats, which, although the junks sailed well, were rapidly coming up with them.

"I will take the headmost; you board the other two," sang out the lieutenant, addressing Tom and Desmond.

In each boat, it should have been said, there were four marines, who, in return, fired at the junks, taking steady aim, and seldom failing to kill or wound some of their crews. The channel took several turnings, which would have been an advantage to the pursuers had they been acquainted with the navigation, but the fear of running on any rocks or sand-banks made them keep directly astern of the junks. Presently a shot struck one of Tom's men, and another knocked an oar to pieces. This of course caused some delay, and the boat dropped astern. On rounding a point Tom saw that the junk he had been ordered to board was in the act of running ashore in a small bay at the further side, while the other two junks continued their course, pursued by the lieutenant and Desmond. Tom considered it his duty to attack the one which could no longer escape him. He was soon alongside; but as he and his men clambered up on deck the pirates rushed forward, leaped down over the bows on to the beach, and began to make their way inland. Tom, on looking round from the more elevated position he had gained, discovered that the creek ran at the back of the fort, but how far off he could not tell.

"We must capture some of those fellows; Captain Rogers wants some prisoners," he sang out, and was about to lead the way over the bows when Tim Nolan exclaimed, "The villains have set their craft on fire. She'll be after goin' off like a sky-rocket in another minute."

"Back, back to the boat!" shouted Tom, seeing that Tim's words were likely to prove true.

The whole party quickly tumbled in, each man trying to be first. Tom was the last to leave his prize, and followed with no little reluctance. Shoving off, they pulled away in the direction they had before been going, to assist, if necessary, the other boats. They had not got far, however, when Tom caught sight of some of the pirates who had landed. They halted, and appeared as if they intended to return to the stranded junk. In their hurry they had thrown down their gingalls, and were armed only with their swords.

"We must have some of those fellows," cried Tom.

Steering in his boat, he jumped on shore, followed by the marines and four seamen, while he told Billy to remain in charge of the rest of the crew.

Off the little party dashed, hoping without difficulty to capture some of the pirates. The latter turned and fled, leading their pursuers to a distance from the boat. Tom imprudently was rushing on considerably ahead of his men when a volley fired from among some rocks laid three of their number low. The rest halted to return the fire of their concealed enemy, but, seeing no one, they let fly among the rooks, against which their bullets were flattened, without doing further execution. Before they could re-load a party of desperadoes sprang out, and seizing Tom, dragged him along with them. In vain Tom endeavoured to free himself, expecting every instant to feel the point of a sword, or its edge, at the back of his neck. The survivors of his party charged bravely, hoping to recover him; but another volley wounded two more, and, seeing that they would all be cut off, they retreated towards the boat. They would even now probably have been attacked had not Billy, showing unusual discretion on hearing the firing, landed with the rest of the men, and fired on the advancing pirates. What was his dismay to find that Tom was not among those returning.

"Where is Mr Rogers?" he exclaimed.

"The pirates, sir, have got hold of him," answered Tim, who had reluctantly returned. "If we are quick about it, and the rest can come with us, we can overtake them, and we will get back Mr Rogers, at all events."

Billy and the rest of the men could not resist this appeal, and were rushing forward when they came to the three men who had fallen. One was dead, but the other two were still living, though unable to walk. They entreated that they might be carried back to the boat; and Billy, finding that the pirates had disappeared, judged that there would be no use in pursuing them, and he remembered also that he had been directed to remain in the boat.

Notwithstanding, therefore, Nolan's remark, Billy ordered the men back to the boat. Just at that instant the junk, from which their attention had been diverted, and which had been in flames fore and aft, blew up with a loud explosion, portions of the fragments being scattered far and wide, many falling close to them.

"Shove off!" cried Billy; "not a moment must be lost."

His crew pulled away after the lieutenant and Desmond, in the hopes that should they have succeeded in taking the two junks, of obtaining their assistance and going in search of Tom. On getting round the point which hid them from sight, Billy discovered the junks, nearly a mile away, both on shore. As his boat got nearer he caught glimpses of the pirates running among the bushes, in the direction, as far as he could judge, of the fort. Both junks had, therefore, been captured. Billy only hoped that the pirates had not attempted the same trick they had played him, by laying trains to their magazines, although he half expected, before he reached the junks, to see them blow up into the air.

In his eagerness to save his other shipmates, he almost forgot poor Tom. "Give way, lads, give way!" he cried. "They will all be sent up like sky-rockets if we don't warn them in time."

The seamen made the boat fly over the water, understanding the danger as fully as he did.

As he got near he shouted out, "Back, back to the boats, or you will all be blown up!"

"No fear about that, now," answered Desmond, from the deck of the nearest junk. "We found a burning fusee, sure enough, but took good care to throw it overboard. Hallo! where's Rogers?" he exclaimed, looking down into the boat.

"Gone! The pirates have got hold of him, and may probably have cut his head off," answered Billy.

"Gone! His head out off!" cried Desmond, in an agony of grief, although scarcely believing his messmate's account; "How did you come away without him?"

"We could not help it," answered Billy, in a melancholy tone. "We should all have been killed if we had not. We have as it is lost two poor fellows knocked over, and four wounded. That shows that we did not give up the attempt to rescue Rogers while there was a chance of success."

"Pull round and report to Mr Norman what has occurred. I will go with you," said Desmond, jumping into Billy's boat.

The lieutenant was, of course, greatly grieved. "We must try and ascertain his fate, at all events. You did not see his head cut off?" he asked, turning to Billy.

"No, sir. We saw him in the pirates' hands. They were dragging him along."

"Then, perhaps they intend holding him as a hostage," observed Mr Norman. "The junks do not appear to have much in them; and so, for fear lest the pirates should get on board again, we will set them on fire, and pull back to where you lost Rogers."

Mr Norman at once gave the order, which the seamen executed with the delight of school-boys igniting huge bonfires, and then the three boats pulled back in the direction of the still burning junk. On reaching it Mr Norman landed his men, forming them in more regular order than Tom had done, four of the marines advancing in skirmishing order to feel the way.

No enemy, however, appeared; but being an experienced officer, he knew that they might be lurking at no great distance ahead, or concealed behind the brushwood either on the right hand or the left, so that they might attack him at any moment on the flank or get behind him and out off his retreat. Having advanced therefore a short distance, he ordered a halt, and getting close under a hill from the top of which he hoped to obtain a survey of the country, he climbed up it, accompanied by Desmond.

"There's the fort, sir," exclaimed the latter, "and I see a number of men going into it. If they have not cut off Rogers's head, they will be taking him in with them, and he'll run a great risk of being killed when the *Gnat* opens fire on the fort."

Mr Norman thought Desmond was right in his conjectures.

"Could not we make a dash at the rear of the fort? we might get in before the pirates know we were coming," said Desmond.

"With a stronger party I would try what we could do; but as the pirates must have been watching us, they would be prepared for an attack, and I very much doubt if we should succeed."

Desmond, though eager to try and rescue Tom, of whose death he was as yet far from being convinced, acknowledged to himself that his lieutenant was right. They remained a few minutes longer, taking a more perfect survey of the fortress and the surrounding country.

"If I mistake not, could we land on the right side of it, we might make our way, concealed by the mass of brushwood to the rear of the fort, and get close up to it before we are discovered, while the pirates, if they expect us to make the attempt, will be looking out for us over that open ground more to the left; but we must get back and communicate with Captain Rogers," observed the lieutenant.

Mr Norman, directly he came down from the hill, ordered his men to retreat. As soon as they were on board, the boats pulled away for the *Gnat* as fast as the crews could lay their backs to the oars, all knowing the importance of placing the wounded under the surgeon's care as soon as possible. Two poor fellows required no doctoring, but their bodies were carried, nevertheless, for the purpose of giving them, as Jack called it, "decent burial?"—in reality that they might be sewn up neatly in their hammocks, with a shot at their feet, to carry them down to the oozy bed of the ocean beyond the ken of the sharks.

The *Gnat* had just got off, and with the musquito fleet in tow was steaming up towards the pirates' stronghold. As Mr Norman's three boats passed within long range of the fort, several shots were fired at them without doing any damage, nor did the pirates make chase, which they might have done with a good chance of capturing their enemies.

At last the boats got alongside the *Gnat*. Captain Rogers received the account Mr Norman gave him with much concern.

"But is it certain that he is killed? Did any one see him fall?" he inquired.

"No, sir," answered Mr Norman. "We are confident that he was made prisoner; but the belief is that the pirates, in revenge for the destruction of their junks, would have cut off his head unless they were induced to hold him as a hostage."

"I trust that the latter is the case, and that we may manage to get him out of their hands," observed Captain Rogers. "But in my anxiety to save him I must not neglect my duty. We must attack these fellows without delay. Unfortunately they have had some time for preparations, and will give us more trouble than would have been the case had not this craft got on shore. I purpose, while the boats attack the junks, to land the marines and storm the fort."

Captain Adair having come on board, Captain Rogers directed him to accompany the marines with a small body of blue-jackets.

"I believe, sir, that we may be able to get to the rear of the fort from a landing-place I discovered as I came along," said Mr Norman. "While the *Gnat* and the boats are assaulting the fort, we may hope to approach undiscovered, and by coming suddenly on the pirates, should your brother be still alive, we may be able to rescue him before they have time to revenge themselves by killing him."

"I trust that you are right, Mr Norman, and that the poor fellow has escaped, although from the pirates not having sent off a flag of truce to treat for terms, I greatly fear that they have not kept him as an hostage."

While the *Gnat* sailed on Captain Rogers made the necessary arrangements for the attack. She, with two of the largest boats, were to bombard the fort, the rest of the flotilla were to board the junks, with the exception of the boats under Mr Norman, who was to land with their crews and some marines and attack the fort in the rear. Very little time longer elapsed before the *Gnat*, the leading vessel, got within range of the junks, which immediately began to blaze away with their guns and gingalls, she and her smaller consorts returning the fire with interest. Two large junks lay directly in the way; one, after the first round was fired, began to settle down so rapidly that many of the crew must have sunk with her, while the rest were seen swimming like a shoal of tadpoles towards the shore. The other, a fine-looking vessel, stood out longer.

"Fire at te deck, at te deck!" cried Po-ho; "she my ship; no sink her!"

A volley of musketry made the pirate crew quit the vessel and follow their companions on shore, while the *Round Moon* remained floating tranquilly, although Captain Murray fully expected to see her burst out into flames and blow up as the others had done. Po-ho entreated that he might go on board to prevent any such catastrophe; and he was allowed the dingy and a couple of men that he might take possession of his vessel. He might have been safer on board the *Gnat*, for several shot from the fort struck the junk as the man-of-war glided in between her and the shore. So close did the *Gnat* get that the guns of the fort, which were trained at too high an elevation, sent their shot over her; while the shells, round shot, and rockets, which she poured into the fort, were apparently producing havoc among its defenders. First one gun was silenced, then another, but the remainder continued blazing away, either at the gun-boat or at the other boats.

The report that Tom Rogers had been taken prisoner soon spread among the boats of the *Empress*, and from them to the boats of the other ships, no one exactly knowing how it had happened. There was a search on board each junk captured, in the hopes of discovering him, as junk after junk was taken. Several, however, which were farther from those first attacked, slipped their cables and tried to run on shore; some were overtaken before they had time to do so; others were set on fire by the pirates and blew up, and the remainder succeeded in effecting their purpose.

A good many of the prisoners, however, were taken, who either could not swim or had not time to make their escape. The British casualties were very small, as only two or three of the junks showed fight. One of the largest fired away until the boats were close up to her; she then cut her cable and made for the shore, still blazing away with her heavy guns, gingalls, and match-locks. Twice the crew were about to desert their guns and attempt to leap overboard, but were restrained by a fine-looking fellow in a Malay dress, who with his sword kept the men to their duty, cutting down two or three who showed signs of disobedience.

Jerry Bird was in one of the boats of the *Empress*, and catching sight of the pirate captain, he exclaimed, "Why, as I'm alive, that's no other than our friend Jonathan Jull! Hallo, Mr Jull, knock under; it's no use holding out!"

A fire-lock aimed at Jerry's head was the only answer made by the pirate chief. Fortunately the bullet merely cut off one of his love-locks, and the junk, already close to the shore, stood on. In another minute she touched the beach, when Jull, firing the last gun, set the example of deserting her, and leaping overboard, began to wade up the beach, surrounded by his men, towards the fort.

The British boats followed them, but as they got to the other side of the junk they were exposed to a hot fire from the fort. This, however, did not stop them. On they rushed, their lieutenant leading them, hoping to capture the pirate chief, and thus quickly put an end to the contest. Jull, however, had a very fast pair of legs, and he and his men were close up to the gate, when the gun-boats ceased firing and two rockets rose together, the signal agreed on to show that the party on shore were about to attack the fort.

In the mean time Captain Adair, with the marines, Lieutenant Norman, Desmond, and Gordon, had landed in a little sheltered bay, which had been discovered near the fort, and had pushed on without being perceived by the enemy. They advanced cautiously, feeling their way, in case of an ambush having been placed to attempt their destruction. All the time the continuous cannonade going on sounded in their ears.

Mr Norman had told Captain Adair that he had seen a number of people escaping from the junks, as well as others outside the fort, and that it would, therefore, be but prudent to be prepared for a surprise.

None, however, was made. The pirates had apparently assembled in their fort, determined to hold out to the last. They must have seen, however, that their case was desperate, when junk after junk was taken or destroyed, and that unless they possessed abundance of ammunition and provisions they must very soon have to surrender.

Chapter Nine.

Tom in the hands of the pirates—About to be killed when
rescued by Jull's young wife—Tom witnesses the fight from
the rock—The fort taken and Jull killed—Fugitives bring the
news—The young widow's philosophy—She makes Tom an
offer, who says he must ask his captain—Tom escorts the
widow on board the Gnat—Jack forbids the banns—Booty
removed—The widow engaged by Po-ho—The squadron
reaches Yokohama—Curious sights on shore—Expected
attack on Prince Satsuma—Squadron sails—The prince's
town bombarded and his fleet captured, proceedings which
bring him to reason and establish friendly relations between
the two countries.

We must now return to Tom Rogers. On finding himself in the hands
of the pirates, he expected nothing but instant death. His uniform,
however, showed them that they had got hold of an officer, and
always having an eye to business, they probably considered that
they might obtain a high ransom for him, or that if hard pressed, he
would prove a valuable hostage in their hands, and compel their
enemies to come to terms. On hearing the shouts of his companions
in the rear, he made several desperate efforts to escape, but, on
calmer reflection, the sight of a sword-blade held to the level of his
throat made him see the wisdom of desisting from any such
attempts.

On they dragged him to the rear of the fort; it was already in sight,
when the party were joined by the fugitives of the other two junks
which had been destroyed. They came boiling with rage at their
defeat, and on seeing an English officer in the power of their
companions, instantly prepared to kill him. A fierce-looking Malay,
whom Tom guessed was their captain, drew his sword and was
about to cut him down, when another party who had come out of the
fort, appeared on the scene. They were escorting, so it seemed, a
young female to a place of greater safety than the fort, which,
although the pirates might be victorious, would they knew be
exposed to showers of shot and shell. Tom instantly recognised the
girl as the young Malay wife of Jonathan Jull, their guest on board
the *Bellona*. As he had no desire to die, he immediately shouted out
to her, imploring her protection, and letting her know who he was.
In another moment the savage Malay would have cloven his head in

two, had not the Malay girl, answering to his appeal, sprung forward and placed herself in front of him, making violent gestures and vociferating vehemently. What she was saying Tom could only guess at, although he supposed she was insisting that his life should be spared.

"Thank you, thank you!" he said, taking her hand, and putting it to his lips. "You have saved my life this once, and I will do my best to protect you, if I get clear altogether."

The effect of the Malay girl's speech had been to appease the savage old captain, who at length stalked away at the head of his men towards the fort, leaving Tom with the Malay girl and the party escorting her, and some of the men who had captured him. Still Tom felt his position very insecure. At any moment, should the pirates be defeated, they might, in revenge, put him to death, and even should Jull lose his life, Tom thought his protectress might probably turn against him from the same motive. He did his best, however, to ingratiate himself with her.

As by this time the shot and shell were falling pretty thickly into the fort, some of the former occasionally flying over it and coming unpleasantly near the guard attending the Malay girl, they hurried her on, taking Tom with them. He was willing enough to go, as he would avoid the unnecessary danger he would otherwise have run had he been carried into the fort. The guard consisted only of about a dozen men, sufficient in number, however, to prevent Tom from making his escape. What they intended ultimately to do with him he could not ascertain, but he felt tolerably safe while with the Malay girl, who had already shown her willingness to befriend him. He talked away to her, although, as he could not speak a word of Malay and very few of Chinese, and she understood a very small number of English phrases, he found it a hard matter to make himself understood. "How can I prove my gratitude?" he thought; and he considered what present he could make her. He felt in his pockets; he could only find a few Chinese coins, a clasp knife, and a pencil-case—the latter being merely plated, and somewhat battered, was not very valuable. He then recollected there was a gold seal attached to his watch-chain. This he offered to her, but she smilingly put it back and showed him a variety of gold ornaments, which she produced from a bag by her side;—how come by, Tom did not ask.

Their conversation, such as it was, was interrupted by the increased roar of the guns, by which he guessed that the *Gnat* and the boats were hotly engaged with the fort and the fleet of junks. Tom observed several men climbing up to the top of a rock, from whence he judged that they could see what was going forward. He naturally felt very anxious to do the same, and made signs to the girl for her permission. She nodded her consent, and the pirates made no objection to his joining them. As, however, they watched the fight and saw junk after junk blow up, and others towed away by the boats, their countenances assumed a still deeper scowl than usual, while their hands ominously clutched their swords; still, they did not make any effort to molest him, and he was permitted by his guards to remain where he was and see the fight. At length he observed the large junk attacked by the boats, and, after a hot fight, run on shore. Shortly afterwards he caught sight of the marines appearing from under the shelter which had concealed them, and, with a party of blue-jackets, making a desperate assault on the rear of the fort towards the right hand. Slight preparations only had been made for its defence, and but scarcely a minute had elapsed before he saw the red-coats, flanked by the blue-jackets, climbing up the embankment, and bounding like red and blue balls over the parapet.

At first the pirates gave way, allowing the entrance of the whole force, and from the height he could clearly see all that was going forward in the inside. Before the victorious party had got half-way across they were met by a band of savage-looking fellows led by a big captain, who quickly rallied the fugitives. The pirate chief, for such Tom guessed he was, fought with the greatest desperation, but he and his men could not long withstand the points of the British bayonets, and the sharp edges of their cutlasses. Tom now saw the chief fall, with a dozen of his men round him, while the rest giving way, made their escape out by the left gate, and were seen scampering away in hot haste across the country.

Tom, as he saw this, felt himself in no very enviable position. The villains into whose hands he had fallen might revenge the death of their companions by murdering him, but he maintained as indifferent a manner as he could assume, while he watched the countenances of those surrounding him. He had the satisfaction of observing that instead of thinking of killing him, they themselves were evidently much alarmed. They were, indeed, completely separated from the fugitive pirates, and should they leave their cover, they would to a certainty be discovered by the victors, who now had possession of the fort, as they and Tom knew by seeing the British flag run up to the summit of the flag-staff on the fort. He was somewhat anxious to see what effect this would produce on the Malay girl and the rest of the party. Would any one venture to tell her that her husband was killed, or should he break the intelligence to her? She soon, however, apparently guessed from the exclamations of the pirates that the fort was captured, and might have suspected hat was her husband's fate. If such was the case, it did not appear to have any great effect upon her. She sat on the fallen trunk of a tree below the rock, maintaining the same composure as at first.

Tom now began to fear that the English would blow up the fort and embark without coming to look for him. "Sooner than they should do that I must try and make a run for it," he said to himself. "These fellows look so cowed that they will not dare to stop me. I must, however, first thank this young lady for having saved my life, and as she can have no object in keeping me a prisoner, I will tell her boldly what I intend doing, and ask her assistance."

Having formed this resolution, he descended the rock and approached the Malay girl.

"Things appear to have gone against my friends," she observed. "It was their misfortune, and cannot be helped."

"*Yes*, the English have possession of the fort, and have captured all the junks, so that I would advise your friends here to yield themselves prisoners, as the best way of saving their lives. I will intercede for them."

"A very good idea," remarked the girl. "If you will go at once I will accompany you."

"I shall be very glad of your society," answered Tom; "but what will these fellows do? They may try to stop us."

"I will order them to remain here until the English come and make them prisoners. Indeed, they cannot get away without being discovered, even if they wish it."

Tom, who was highly delighted at thus easily obtaining his liberty, agreed to the proposal. "Poor thing, she will be dreadfully cut up when she hears of her husband's death!" he thought.

As it might be dangerous to remain longer, lest the pirates should change their minds, Tom proposed to set off at once, and the Malay girl agreeing, they started together for the fort, none of the pirates attempting to stop them.

"I wonder whether I ought to tell her about her husband's death?" thought Tom; "but she will hear it soon enough when we get to the fort."

While he was discussing the matter in his own mind, she turned to him and said —

"They tell me my husband has been killed; if it is true, I hope that some of your people will take care of me. He was a dreadful tyrant; and now, after having lost all his wealth, he would have treated me even worse than before."

This remark showed Tom that all his sympathy had been thrown away. The young lady greatly puzzled him when she proposed that he should marry her. He was too polite to refuse at once, but remarked "that English midshipmen were not allowed to have wives on board, and that he would not think of such a thing without asking his captain's leave."

This appeared to satisfy her, and they continued walking along side by side very amicably, till Tom heard a voice exclaim, "Why, there's Tom Rogers, all alive and merry!"

Immediately several of his messmates rushed out of the fort to greet him. A party were at once despatched to make prisoners of the pirates who were hiding behind the rock, and who were shortly afterwards brought in.

Preparations were now made for destroying the pirates' strong hold. The prisoners were handcuffed and carried on board the junks, with a guard placed over them. The *Gnat* meantime got up her steam in readiness to tow out the captured junks. The Malay girl kept close to Tom, evidently considering him her protector, and he, of course, in gratitude, could do nothing less than attend to her, and as soon as a boat could be obtained he took her off to the *Gnat*. He explained her wishes to Jack.

"We must carry her to Chusan, where I dare say she will find friends," said Jack; "but you must let her understand that I cannot give you permission to make her your bride."

The girl pouted when she heard this, but being evidently of a philosophical turn of mind, soon appeared reconciled to her lot. A considerable amount of booty was found in the fort, the most valuable portion of which was embarked in the captured junks. In the mean time the guns of the fort, several of which were of brass, and of considerable value, were carried on board the gun-boat. Some powder having been landed and placed in advantageous positions for blowing up the fort, a train was laid, and as soon as all the party had embarked, it was fired.

The junks with the prisoners on board were taken in tow by the *Gnat*, while the other boats took charge of the rest of the junks. As the flotilla moved off, the fort blew up with a loud explosion, its fragments being scattered far around.

"I hope the lesson we have given the rascals will teach them in future to turn to more lawful occupations," observed Captain Rogers, as he witnessed the destruction of the fort.

"They will be at the same work in a few weeks, if they can cut out a junk, and find a fellow to lead them," said Adair, to whom the remark had been made. "Altogether we have had a good morning's work, and rendered some service to commerce by putting a stop for the present to the career of such desperadoes."

The flotilla having got clear of the passage, rejoined the larger ships, which, taking the junks in tow, steamed back to Chusan. Jack's chief puzzle was to know in what way to dispose of the Malay girl; but his anxiety was removed when Captain Po-ho, in due form, offered to marry her, an arrangement to which she appeared to have no objection. Jack was at all events very glad to get her out of the ship, as, to say the best of her, she was a determined coquette, and had turned the heads of half the midshipmen, and, it was whispered, of more than one of the lieutenants, during the short time she had been on board.

The prisoners were handed over to the Chinese authorities, to be dealt with according to law. Some lost their heads, others escaped, and the rest were turned over to the Chinese navy. The junks were sold for the benefit of the captors, with the exception of the *Round Moon*, which was delivered back with her cargo to Captain Po-ho, who, considering that he had regained his vessel and property, and a wife in addition, benefited more largely than anybody else by the expedition.

These arrangements having been made as quickly as possible, the commodore continued his course.

In about a week the squadron came to anchor before the lately built town of Yokohama. It stands on a dead flat, formerly a swamp, with bluffs of high land at each extremity, joined by a range of low and picturesquely wooded hills in the form of a horse shoe. Beyond these hills, some fifty miles away, rising to the height of 14,000 feet above the sea, towers the truncated cone of Fasiama. At the southern extremity was seen a long two-storied bungalow, serving as the British legation. Although some time before the followers of one of the principal damios had wantonly murdered an Englishman, the people were friendly to foreigners, who did not hesitate to ride out into the country.

The three captains the following day went on shore to see as much as they could of the country and its curious inhabitants, and those fortunate individuals, the three midshipmen, with some of their messmates, were invited to accompany them.

The foreign settlement was soon inspected, as there was but little to see in it, beyond its bungalow-looking buildings and gardens. They then went into the adjoining Japanese town. It greatly resembled that of some of the northern cities of China, the principal streets being broad, with neat and clean-looking shops. These greatly resembled those of China, except that the Japanese used neither tables, chairs, nor counters. Those in the main street contained lacquer ware, carvings in ivory, bronzes, some very beautiful porcelain, and a variety of toys.

Strange sights were witnessed. Females of no exalted rank were carried about in a basket-like litter, sitting cramped up in a most uncomfortable posture. The basket, which is called a "cango," is suspended from a pole, borne on the shoulders of two men. Ladies and gentlemen of higher rank were seen going about in palanquins, which were smaller, than those used in India. They were formed of wicker work, and covered outside with lacquer. They also were supported by poles on the shoulders of bearers. None of the gentlemen, who sat their horses with apparently such wonderful dignity, really guided them, though they held their bridles in their hands—a groom always leading their gaily-caparisoned steeds. The soldiers, however, of whom a troop was always in attendance on any "damio," or great lord, of course, managed their horses themselves.

The naval officers encountered a party of these gentlemen, and knowing the importance of avoiding any cause of dispute, managed in good time to get out of their way. The "betos," for so the horse-soldiers are called, cast fierce glances at the strangers. Gerald, ever inclined to merriment, could scarcely refrain from laughing as he watched them passing by.

"Well, those fellows are the thinnest-clothed rascals I have ever seen. Look, Tom, at their braided coats, they fit as tight as their skins. See what curious devices they have on them, both back and front. Look at that fellow with the big dragon—the head and fore part on his chest, its body and tail coming round his back, in blue, red, and yellow colours!"

"Why, that is his skin which is thus tattoed over in that curious fashion," answered Tom. "Not a shred of a coat has he got. See, every one of them has some device marked on him, and they are all in the same style of uniform."

"Take care, lads; don't speak so loud; or should the fellow see that you are laughing or talking about them, they may fancy you are insulting them, and disagreeable consequences may ensue," cried Jack.

The three captains accordingly turned their horses' heads and rode off in a different direction to that which the damio and his followers had taken.

On returning on board, the captains received a summons from the admiral, desiring to see them on important business. Having got themselves up in full fig, as required on such occasions, they pulled away for the flag-ship.

"There is something in the wind, depend upon it!" observed one of the midshipmen to Tom. "Did the captain say anything about it to you?"

"I don't think he knows himself; but if he did, he would not tell me sooner than anybody else," answered Tom. "I'll tell you what I heard him and Captain Adair speaking about, and I shouldn't be surprised if what they are now meeting for is connected with it."

Most of the occupants of the midshipmen's birth were assembled at tea.

"Well, Rogers, what is it?" exclaimed several voices.

"Most of us have heard of Prince Satsuma, a mighty magnificent three-tailed Bashaw, the chief lord and owner of the city of Kagosima and the adjacent parts. He, it appears, or one of his bare-backed followers, some time ago murdered, without any rhyme or reason, an English merchant, who happened to be riding along the high road. Of course the British Government demanded satisfaction: the punishment of the murderer, and a good round sum as compensation to his bereaved family. These very moderate terms the prince doesn't seem inclined to agree to, and we are, therefore, ordered here to impress him with the necessity of doing so, and, if he does not, we are to batter down his town, to take possession of his fleet—for it is said that he has got one—and to make such other reprisals as may be deemed expedient to bring him to reason. I heard the captain say that he paid a visit with one of the principal merchants residing here, who has transactions with the prince, to a Japanese official of high rank in the place—I forget his name—and that during the conversation the matter under dispute was introduced. A Japanese who speaks English very well was present to act as interpreter. The great aim of this official seemed to be to induce the British squadron not to go to Kagosima, and he entreated the captain to visit another official, the prince's chief envoy. This, he said, could not be done without permission of the admiral, but, if granted, he would willingly do as he was requested. No sooner had the interpreter translated the captain's reply than the great man, taking out writing materials from a box, seated himself on the floor, and began scribbling away on a scroll of paper, in wonderfully large characters, a note to the envoy. As line after line was finished he rolled it up, and then, with due formality, handed it to the captain, who had the curiosity to measure it, and what do you think was its length? Why, six feet at the very least. Official documents, by the same rule, must be thirty or forty feet long, according to their importance."

"Can you tell us the length of a lover's *billet-doux*?" asked the assistant surgeon.

"That depends very much on the excess of his ardour, and what he has got to say," answered Tom; "though, from what I've heard, I don't think the Japanese are addicted to writing love-letters."

"And what happened next?"

"That's more than I can tell, though I believe that the letter was delivered and answered, with a hint to Prince Satsuma that whatever might be said, he had better look sharp and yield to our demands, or that he might expect to have his town tumbling about his ears. The British envoy and admiral have been waiting a reply, and I suspect that it has arrived and is not satisfactory; consequently we shall proceed immediately to teach the haughty damio that Englishmen are not to be murdered with impunity. These Japanese will be like the Chinese until they are taught better. They fancy that their castles are impregnable, and as they have never been attacked, except by each other, that they can beat off an English squadron with perfect ease."

This information given by Tom afforded intense satisfaction, and all hands waited with considerable anxiety to hear how soon they might expect to exchange shots with the Japanese. They had heard that the batteries they were likely to be engaged with were somewhat of a formidable character, having already fired on an American and French man-of-war and inflicted considerable damage; the American indeed, being unsupported, narrowly escaped destruction. The captain, on his return, brought intelligence which confirmed their hopes. The emperor had, however, sent a document fifteen feet in length, earnestly requesting that the expedition might be put off; but as he gave no guarantee that by so doing a satisfactory result would be arrived at, the British envoy kept to his determination of immediately enforcing the demands of his government.

Early the following morning, the official gentlemen having embarked on board the flag-ship, the signal was made for the squadron to weigh, and the ships, steaming out of the harbour, shaped a course for the Bay of Kagosima. The distance was considerable, the voyage occupied four days, during which all preparations were made for the expected attack on the capital of the Prince of Satsuma. At last, through a wide entrance they steamed into the beautiful Bay of Kagosima, where they came to anchor some miles below the town, intending to wait there until the following morning.

The midshipmen, as might be supposed, during the evening talked over the work they expected to be engaged in the next day. Some thought that they should land and storm the town, others that the admiral would be content with bombarding it at a distance.

"One thing I know that if there is work to be done my brother Jack is the man to go in and do it," observed Tom to Desmond. "We are certain, therefore, to see the best part of the fun, whatever it may be."

"I don't think my uncle Captain Adair will be far astern of him if he has a chance," said Desmond, for he very properly always stuck up for his relative.

One thing only was generally known, that the admiral had orders to bombard the place and burn it down if the Japanese did not accede unconditionally to all demands made on them. The weather did not look so promising as could have been wished, but still hopes were entertained that it would allow the ships to take up their positions.

At an early hour the next morning, the signal was made for weighing, and the squadron steamed up the bay until they arrived off the town to be attacked, when they again dropped anchor. It was no trifling work in which they were about to engage, for they could see a long line of fortifications extending across the whole front of the city, the flag of Prince Satsuma flying from one of them. The guns, however, remained silent.

"We shall soon knock that place to pieces," said Billy Blueblazes, as he surveyed it with a look of contempt.

"Don't be too sure of that," answered Tom; "there are some pretty heavy guns inside those forts, and the Japanese know how to handle them too."

Still the guns did not open fire, and in a short time a boat was seen putting off from the shore. She contained a party of two-sworded officials, who came on board the flag-ship, where Captain Murray and Archie happened at the time to be. Archie afterwards related all he saw and heard.

One of the principal of the two-sworded gentlemen inquired, with an air of surprise, "why the ships of war had come uninvited to the town?" adding that he concluded the ships had brought a letter from the British Government on some subject or other.

"You are perfectly correct there," was the answer. "It is a letter, insisting that all the demands which have been made should be complied with within twenty-four hours, if not, you see the guns which our ships carry; we have shells and rockets and other missiles of warfare, and we shall be compelled to let them fly pretty thickly about your ears."

"But the prince is fifty miles off, and it is impossible to get an answer within the time specified."

"Then we will make the time thirty hours. Your posts can perform the distance in that time, and take care that they do not dally on the way."

The Japanese chief official smiled blandly, and then said that it would facilitate matters if the admiral and the *chargé d'affaires* would come on shore to discuss the matter in an amicable manner within the city, where a palace had been prepared for their reception.

"The Japanese must think us very green if they suppose us to be caught in that fashion," remarked one of the officers standing by, when he heard the interpreter give the invitation.

The Japanese official pressed the offer in the most bland and courteous manner, pointing out the great advantage which would be gained by more quickly bringing affairs to a conclusion.

The admiral, however, was not to be caught, and he had good reason to congratulate himself that he did not accept it, when it was reported that the Japanese intended as soon as he and the envoy had got inside the castle to lift the drawbridges and to send word on board the squadron that should a shot be fired the prisoners would be instantly beheaded.

The interview at length came to a conclusion, and the two-sworded officials took their departure for the shore. Within the time specified they returned with a long rigmarole letter, which was of course anything but satisfactory. They looked very much surprised when ordered to return on shore with an intimation that no further communication would be held with the prince unless under a flag of truce.

In the mean time a boat expedition had been ordered to proceed further up the gulf to ascertain what had become of the fleet of vessels which the prince was said to possess. Tom and Desmond had the satisfaction of going in one of the boats, their hopes being raised that some work would be cut out for them.

The scenery presented on either shore was magnificent, while the weather continued fine. No ships were, however, seen until they had got about seven miles up, when they came in sight of three large steamers, with the flag of the prince flying on board.

It was hoped that these would be at once captured and held in pledge until the demands of the British were complied with; but the officer in command having been directed simply to make a reconnaissance, ordered the boats to be put about, and they returned to the squadron. They found that the Japanese officials had been going backwards and forwards, evidently with the intention, for some reason or other, of spinning out the time. That the Japanese intended hostilities was manifest enough, for they began to assemble large bodies of men in their batteries, and to point the whole of their guns, numbering some seventy or eighty, upon the squadron. Shortly after this, five large junks were warped out of the inner harbour, and anchored out of the line of fire. Later in the day, a number of Japanese boats came out of the harbour, and as they approached the squadron, they were seen to be filled with soldiers, although, at the same time they contained a few water melons, fowls, and eggs, apparently intended to represent the provisions with which the Japanese had promised to supply the ships. Instead of coming alongside, however, they merely pulled round the squadron, evidently for the purpose of counting the number of guns, that the garrisons of the forts might be satisfied how far superior a force they themselves possessed.

The best scene of all, however, was a visit from a damio, or person of high rank, who came off with a guard of forty men. He had the impudence to ask to come on board the flag-ship with his guard, and, perhaps greatly to his surprise, this was granted, but he looked very much astonished when he saw a body of marines drawn up on the opposite side of the deck, who in a few seconds would have sent him and his guard of honour flying headlong into the water had they shown any hostile intentions.

Of this the two-sworded official was evidently very well aware judging by the nervous expression on his countenance. As soon as he could find an excuse for doing so—glad enough to get out of the ship—he hurried away. Before he was half-way down the companion ladder, the admiral hoisted the signal to the squadron to get up steam and to be ready to weigh anchor at a moment's notice. The reason of his doing so was evident, for it was seen that the Japanese had been training their guns to bear directly on the squadron, under the belief that they were going to remain where they were to be shot at.

The admiral then issued another order, directing five of the smaller vessels of the squadron to proceed up the gulf and take possession of the three steamers which had been discovered by the boats.

"We shall have some fun now, at all events," exclaimed Tom to Desmond, who, with himself and a boat's crew, had been sent on board one of the gun-boats short of hands. "If they do not fight they will run, and we shall have the amusement of making chase. It will be better fun than battering away at the walls, which, in my opinion, is a sort of work affording very little satisfaction to any one."

The men-of-war, immediately getting under way, proceeded up the gulf. They steamed on at full speed, and soon came in sight of the three Japanese steamers, which, however, showed no inclination either to fight or run away. This was somewhat of a disappointment. No sooner did the men-of-war approach, then they hauled down their flags and tamely submitted to be carried off, when they were brought to, just out of range of the guns of the fort, their crews and other persons found on board being taken out of them.

"The admiral is speaking to us, sir," said Desmond, who was acting as signal midshipman on board the *Empress*.

Captain Rogers quickly turned over the leaves of the signal book. "Engage north battery, until signal to form line of battle is thrown out." Jack immediately gave the order to slip the cable, and steam having been got up, the ship moved away towards the spot she was directed to occupy, opening her fire without loss of time on the battery, which replied in earnest, with well-directed shots. Several struck her hull, while others, flying between her masts, cut away her rigging. This only made her crew work with greater zeal, in the hopes of soon silencing the battery. That, however, was not easily done, for the Japanese were evidently handling their guns well, and were not to be driven from them.

Desmond kept his glass directed towards the flag-ship, to report any signals which might be made. Tom was attending to his duty at the guns. Billy Blueblazes was standing near Desmond, ready to convey the captain's orders. A shot passed unpleasantly near his head.

"A miss is as good as a mile," remarked Desmond, as Billy bobbed, looking rather pale.

"I hope no other will come nearer than that," said Billy, recovering himself and trying to laugh.

Just then a shot struck the end of Desmond's telescope, shattering it to pieces, and carrying the instrument out of his hands, a fragment striking Billy on the cheek and drawing blood, but not inflicting any serious wound. The same shot took off the head of a man who was at the moment coming aft, at the other side of the deck.

"Now, that's not fair!" exclaimed Billy; "aiming at me on purpose."

"Then go and get me another spy-glass, and afterwards ask the doctor to stick a plaster on your cheek," said Desmond. "You'll be out of harm's way there, and have the honour of being reported wounded, which will be pleasanter than being in the other list, though it may not tend so much to your fame."

Billy gladly hurried off, holding his handkerchief to his face and speedily returned with the telescope, with which Desmond, as coolly as before, continued to watch the mast-heads of the flag-ship. It was warm work, for already two men had been killed and several wounded, not including Billy, who, however, appeared on deck with a large black patch on his cheek and a handkerchief tied round his head, not certainly improving his beauty.

"Did you get any teeth knocked out?" asked Tom, as Billy passed him. "If you did, take care to pick them up and get the doctor to stick them in again, for they will grow, depend on that."

"No, I lost no teeth; I only had a piece taken out of my cheek," said Billy.

"Lucky it wasn't your nose," observed Tom; "it would have spoilt your beauty for ever." He could make no further remark, as he had to attend to his gun.

Jack had well performed the duty entrusted to him, and was expecting to remain until he had battered down the fort, when Desmond cried out that the admiral was again making signals. They were to the effect that all ships of the squadron were to get under way and form line of battle before the town.

Accordingly Jack, leaving the sorely battered fort, steamed away to take up his position in the line. The weather, which had long been threatening, came on much worse as the crews stood ready at their guns. A heavy squall blew across the gulf, and at the same instant a downfall of rain came on.

Suddenly the whole of the batteries opened on the squadron; still the ships did not return the fire. Immediately the squall cleared away, the signal was seen flying from the flag-ship, directing the prizes to be destroyed and the vessels which had them in charge to join the line of battle. The flag-ship, which was leading, was for some time, owing to the heavy gale which was blowing, exposed to the fire of several batteries, which killed two of her officers and wounded a considerable number of men.

As soon as the weather would allow, the other ships got up and lost not a moment in opening with their guns on the batteries. The ships had not long been engaged, when the effects of their fire became visible from the battered state to which the fort was reduced, while flames were seen bursting out in different parts of the town. Every moment the weather was getting worse. The wind had increased almost to a hurricane. The sky was overcast with dark and gloomy clouds, rendering more than usually vivid the flashes of the guns as they poured forth their death-dealing shot into the town. At length it became difficult to work them, and the admiral gave the signal to discontinue the action.

Five large junks lay to the southward of the town, which the Japanese might have hoped would have escaped, but they were mistaken in supposing that the prince was not to receive the full punishment due to him. These vessels were his private property. The admiral ordered one of the smaller ships to proceed immediately and set fire to the junks, as there was no possibility of carrying them off. One after the other they were quickly blazing up, and the flames, fanned by the rising gale, soon destroyed them.

The steamer also threw her shells into an arsenal and among a number of large storehouses, which soon, sharing the fate of the junks, were left furiously blazing away.

The squadron now stood off from the batteries and returned to their former anchorage. Scarcely were their anchors down than the hurricane came on with greater fury than before. The night was as dark as pitch, heavy thunder-clouds rolling overhead; but the wind was off the land, though it was a question whether it might not change, and should any of the ships be driven ashore, their crews could expect but little mercy from the hands of the Japanese.

The *Empress* was one of the outermost of the squadron. It had just gone four bells in the first watch when the third lieutenant reported that the ship was dragging her anchors. More cable was veered out, but she was by this time exposed to the full blast of gale. The lead was hove, and sixty fathoms reported; that she could hold the ground now was, therefore, impossible. The captain ordered the cable to be slipped, and the steam having been kept up, she drifted slowly away, still endeavouring to regain her lost position. Every moment she became more and more exposed to the force of the hurricane. All on board were well aware of her danger, although she might bring up on the opposite side of the bay; she would then be on a lee shore, and should her anchors not hold, her loss was almost inevitable, although some hours might pass before her fate was sealed.

All hands remained on deck. Jack had been in many a dangerous position; but in those days he had no wife to care for, and he had not the responsibilities of command. The night passed slowly away. When morning broke, the gale continued blowing as fiercely as ever, while the land to leeward looked unpleasantly near. Still steam was kept up, and the trusty screw was doing its best to drive the gallant ship ahead. The instant the hurricane moderated she began to make way, and soon again got up to her anchorage with the rest of the squadron.

Desmond was turning his telescope towards the shore, where, at the top of a hill overlooking the anchorage, among a grove of thick trees, he saw a number of Japanese working away with picks and shovels, and a little further on he caught a glimpse of a heavy gun, dragged by a number of horses, coming along the road, and then another and another. It was very clear that the Japanese intended, from the advantageous position they held, to open fire on the smaller vessels lying within pistol-shot of the shore. The admiral, on discovering this, ordered the squadron to weigh, and his ship leading they steamed through the channel in line, passing the batteries on either side, which they saluted as they glided by with a hot fire, bestowing particular attention on the palace of the prince, teaching him a lesson he was not likely soon to forget. The batteries replied, but feebly and without damage to any one of the ships.

The squadron now returned to the anchorage they had taken up on first entering the bay, where their crews had plenty of work to do in repairing damages; fishing spars and refitting before proceeding to sea.

Returning to Yokohama, they had the satisfaction of learning that their proceedings having brought the prince to reason, the whole of the sum demanded had been paid and ample apologies offered. The undertaking, however, had been a costly one. Two gallant officers and eleven men had been killed and forty-eight wounded.

Friendly relations were ultimately established with Prince Satsuma, who expressed his intention of sending several of his young nobility to England to be educated, while the Tycoon despatched a special envoy to congratulate the British *chargé d'affaires* on the satisfactory termination of all difficulties, and to express a hope that in future amicable relations would exist between the two nations.

Chapter Ten.

The Empress sails for the Fiji Islands—Picks up two
Papuans—Calls off the coast of New Guinea—The wreck
seen—Two boats go on shore—What have become of the
crew?—Lieutenant Norman ascends a hill—Tom Desmond
and their party push on—The lieutenant attacked by the
natives—Retreats—Tom and Desmond missing—After a
severe fight, regains the boats—Captain Rogers lands, to
recover his brother and his companions—Unsuccessful
march—Native village burnt—Boats sent in again—Gale
comes on, and the ship stands off the land—Returns—No
traces of the midshipmen—Continues her voyage—Long
stay at Fiji—Empress and Orion sail for Sydney—A wreck
seen.

The Japanese difficulty having been satisfactorily settled, the ships of
the squadron separated to proceed to their various destinations. The
Empress, while lying in Victoria Harbour, received orders to proceed
to the Fiji Islands, with directions to touch on her way at the
northern coast of New Guinea in search of the crew of a merchant
vessel said to have been lost thereabouts. Captain Rogers was
afterwards to visit Sydney and other Australian ports before
returning home.

All hands were well pleased at the thoughts of the number of places
they were to visit, and the curious people they were to see.

The *Empress* was once more at sea. Passing by the north of the
Philippine Islands into the Pacific, she steered to the southward until
she sighted the Pelew Islands, about eight degrees north of the
equator. As they are surrounded by a reef, she did not stand close in.
Several well-built canoes, however, came off, manned by the dark-
skinned race who inhabit the group. They brought tropical fruits and
vegetables, and appeared eager to trade. Hills covered with trees,
and fruitful valleys with streams trickling down them, could be seen.
The distance to the shore, however, was too great to allow of a
landing being made, and further intercourse being opened up with
the people.

The natives, having disposed of the cargoes of their canoes, were
about to return, when another canoe came off, having on board two

black men with frizzly heads of hair, evidently not Pelew Islanders. Having come on board, they made signs that they wished to go to some country to the southward. The captain on this placed a chart before them, pointing to the islands off which the ship then was. After regarding it for some time, one of them drew his finger along the chart until it reached the coast of New Guinea. On a picture of a group of Papuans being then exhibited to him he seemed at once to recognise it; indeed, on looking at his features and then at the picture, Jack was himself convinced that his two visitors were themselves Papuans. One of the Papuans, who had been on board a whaler for some months and could speak a little English, confirmed this. Jack accordingly, without hesitation, undertook to carry the men to their native land. Their names, they informed Pat Casey, who took to them at once and managed by some means or other to understand what they said, were Nicho and Picho, and forthwith they were dubbed Nick and Pipes.

Nick was a curious-looking little fellow, scarcely four feet high, but with broad shoulders, and as strong as Hercules, his face being as hideous as could be well imagined. Pipes was taller by a foot or more, and was intelligent and not so desperately ill-looking as his companion, though far from a beauty. They rapidly acquired a knowledge of English, and Pat took great pains to teach them. They were evidently accustomed to a ship, and he discovered that they had been brought off from their native land by a whaler, on board which they had picked up some knowledge of the language.

Captain Rogers hoped that they would make themselves useful in communicating with their countrymen. He would indeed gladly have had them on board for some weeks, in order that they might express themselves better than they now did. However, Pat understood them, and so did Tom and Gerald, who were constantly talking to the men. The ship continued her course under sail in order to spare the coals, but as the wind was light she made but little way. At length, however, the coast of New Guinea was sighted, ranges of lofty mountains appearing in the distance, while the ground from their base was of a more level character, and thickly covered with trees down to the water's edge. The ship stood along the coast, sending her boats frequently on shore, but nothing of the wreck was seen, nor could Nick or Pipes manage to communicate with any of their countrymen, whom they described as "bad mans," and made gestures significant of knocking on the head any intruders. Captain Rogers began to fear that such had been the fate of the crew of the

Fair Imogene, the vessel of which they were in search. The ship occasionally came to an anchor, but the two Papuans invariably gave the same character to the inhabitants.

She was running along one afternoon before a light breeze under easy sail, the lead going, and the fires banked ready to get up steam should it be necessary, when the master, who was standing on the bridge, with his glass turned towards the coast, exclaimed—

"I see a wreck close in shore, though her masts are gone; but that's a ship's hull, or I'm a Dutchman."

Several glasses were pointed in the same direction, and all came to the conclusion that the master was right. The ship was accordingly hove to with her head off shore, and two boats were sent in, the second lieutenant going in one to command the expedition, and having Billy Blueblazes with him, Tom having charge of the other with Desmond, Pat Casey, and Peter the black, with Nick and Pipes. The sea was perfectly smooth, so that they were able to get alongside the wreck. A cursory examination left no doubt that she was the vessel of which they were in search. She was in a fearfully battered condition. Her after-cabin had been knocked to pieces, and the whole of her cargo washed out of her; still it was possible that her crew might have escaped to the shore, and not have been destroyed by the natives. Pipes asserted that they were "good mans," but Nick was evidently doubtful about the matter. On reaching the beach the party from the boats landed without difficulty, and two men being left in charge of each, the rest proceeded in search of any signs of the *Fair Imogene's* crew. Mr Norman said he thought they might probably have built a hut on the shore with part of the wreck, or erected a flag-staff to make signals to any passing vessel. Not far off was a stream of fresh water, which would have enabled them to remain on the spot.

Birds innumerable, of gay plumage, and the traces of four-footed animals, showed that they could have been in no want of food. A search of an hour and a half or more, however, convinced Mr Norman that if the crew had landed there, they must have soon taken their departure, either inland or along the coast, for not the slightest sign of them could be found. The next thing was to discover some natives with whom to try and open up a communication. Not far off to the right was a rocky hill partly covered with trees. Mr Norman, taking two of his men with him, climbed to the top, hoping from thence to be able to obtain a good view over the country, and to ascertain if any human habitation existed in the   neighbourhood. Tom and Gerald, with their party, accompanied by the natives, had, perhaps imprudently, pushed further inland, intending to return to meet the lieutenant, who had neglected to give them any directions to remain stationary until he had come down from the hill. This was considerably higher than he had supposed, and occupied him a much longer time than he had expected in gaining the summit. He obtained, however, a much more extensive view than he had thought possible. Although the shore was fringed with trees, which made it appear as if the whole country was covered with them, there were here and there plantations or open grassy spaces, as also numerous huts, built apparently like those of the Malays, on piles. He had been for some time noting these and various other objects, when he caught sight below the hill, to the westward, of a considerable body of men, some armed with muskets, others with bows, spears, and swords. As they were making directly for the hill, he had but little doubt that he had been observed; and as they might cut him and his companions off from the rest of the party, he considered it prudent instantly to descend. Just as he got to the bottom, he caught sight between the trees of a body of natives advancing towards him.

"Where are Mr Rogers and his men?" he inquired.

"They went in that direction," was the answer.

"It is possible, sir, that they have got back to the boats by some other way," said Bird. "We fancied we caught sight of them between the trees in the distance."

Mr Norman, however, not satisfied that such was the case, was about to lead forward his men in the direction which Tom, Desmond, and his companions had taken, when the natives in considerable numbers spread out in front of him, evidently intending to dispute his advance. As the captain had given him strict orders on no account to show any hostility to the inhabitants, he considered it his duty to halt and make signs of friendship. This, however, produced no effect on the natives. Had either Nick or Pipes been with him he might have opened a communication, but they had gone on with Tom Rogers, and he had no means of making the natives understand that he wished to be on friendly terms with them.

They soon showed their hostility by firing several shots. The lieutenant, therefore, felt it his duty to call his men together and to retreat in order to the boats, hoping to find that Tom and his party had already reached them. As soon as they began to retreat the enemy pressed on. He now gave the order to fire in return, but no sooner did the seamen lift their muskets to their shoulders than the natives got under cover, and although the shot must have passed close to them, no one apparently was hurt. As others were seen coming up, Mr Norman continued to retreat.

The enemy now grew bolder, and showers of arrows fell around the seamen, in addition to the bullets which whistled past their ears. The moment they halted to fire, the natives again dodged behind the trees, though they did not altogether escape, and two or three were seen to fall. The enemy, increasing in numbers, rushed boldly on, and only stopped when the sailors turned round to fire at them. Mr Norman was wounded in the arm by a bullet, and an arrow struck him in the side. Calling on his men again to halt and fire, he succeeded in pulling it out and continued to retire. Four of his men were shortly afterwards wounded, either by bullets or arrows, but happily as yet none had fallen.

At length he could see the boats in the distance. He hoped that Tom Rogers and his men would come to his assistance, but he looked in vain. Except the two men in the boats, who must have heard the firing and were standing up with their muskets ready for service, no one was to be seen. His great object was now to prevent the enemy getting between him and the water. Continuing his retreat, he ordered his men to reload and fire as rapidly as they could, and then to push on for the boats. From the courage and hostility of the people, he doubted very much that they were Papuans, and was convinced that they were Malays who had taken possession of that part of the country. One thing was certain, that they must have had constant intercourse with white men to have obtained so large a supply of firearms and powder.

Not seeing Tom and Desmond, nor any of the men who accompanied them, he began to fear that they must have been cut off by another party of the natives. He determined, however, on reaching the boats, should the enemy advance, to shove off to a distance, and there await the possible reappearance of the midshipmen, or, should they not return, to go off to the ship for reinforcements, and if they had escaped with their lives, to endeavour to rescue them.

It was a serious question, however, whether he should succeed in reaching the boats. He called on his men to fight to the last, and to sell their lives dearly. A hearty cheer was the reply, and the seamen fired a well-directed volley, which knocked over several of their enemies; but before they could reload, the natives were upon them, and a hand-to-hand fight ensued. Animated by the voice of their officer, they got their bayonets fixed and charged the enemy. Two poor fellows had dropped, shot through the heart. Besides those already wounded, another close to Mr Norman had his brains knocked out. The survivors making a desperate effort, finally succeeded in reaching the boats.

Scarcely, however, had they got on board than the enemy regaining courage rushed down upon them, and not without a severe struggle did they manage to shove off, so many being wounded that it was with the greatest difficulty they could man the oars. Scarcely had Mr Norman taken his seat in the stern sheets than he sank down fainting. He recovered somewhat as the boats got beyond the reach of shot from the shore; and although he wished to put himself and the other wounded men under the care of the surgeon, he felt a great unwillingness to pull off without having ascertained the fate of the midshipmen.

"Did any one see them?" he asked.

"No, sir," answered Jerry Bird in a mournful tone. "Not a glimpse of them. I have been listening in case they should fire, but I have not heard a shot from the direction I've an idea they took."

"Give way, then, lads," said the lieutenant, putting the boat's head round; the other following his example, they pulled back to the ship.

The sound of the firing having been heard, the captain had just ordered three boats to be got ready, and a party of marines and blue-jackets well armed to go in and help their shipmates, when the boats were seen coming off. As it was supposed that all had returned in them, the order was countermanded. On hearing from Mr Norman what had occurred, the boats were immediately ordered off, the captain himself taking command, the third lieutenant and the senior mate having charge of the other boats, with two or three other midshipmen and master's assistants, who were all eager to recover their lost messmates.

No one would believe that they had been actually cut off, and fully expected to find them either defending themselves in some strong position, or on the beach, having cut their way through their enemies. The boats drew near the shore, but no natives were to be seen, nor were the missing party. On landing, Jack ordered the marines to form, and threw out skirmishers in front and on either side, to feel the way, fully expecting every moment to come in sight of a large body of the natives. Still on they went, but no one appeared. On getting to the foot of the knoll from which Lieutenant Norman had obtained a view of the country round, the captain and a party of men climbed up to the summit. Not a native was to be seen. In vain Jack turned his glass in every direction, hoping to see his brother's party. No human being was visible, not even among the huts in the distance which Lieutenant Norman had discovered. To be sure, there might be natives close to them, yet concealed by the dense growth of the trees.

Jerry Bird, who had returned in the captain's boat, and was as anxious as any one to recover the young officers, expressed his opinion that they had gone to the southward or south-west, and Jack resolved to make his way in that direction, in the hopes of coming upon their "trail," as the expression is in North America. Desirous as he was of recovering the lost ones, he did not forget his duty to his ship. He felt that he must not run the risk of being drawn into a trap and surrounded by a superior force of the enemy, while it was incumbent on him to return to the boats before nightfall. The party could advance but slowly through the thick brushwood, in many places having to hew away with their cutlasses, every instant expecting to see the enemy start up before them. There were traces of blood on the ground and bushes, showing where some of the natives had fallen by the bullets fired by Mr Norman's party, but the bodies of those killed had been carried off. Indeed, savage as these Papuans appeared to be, they apparently considered that "discretion is the best part of valour," and seeing a superior force landing, had beat a retreat into their inland fastnesses.

Jack began to feel sick at heart as hour after hour went by, and several miles of ground had been passed over, without any traces of Tom and his companions having been discovered. The heat was intense, and the men began to show signs of fatigue, though they endeavoured to keep up as well as they could. Jack, finding a tolerably open space with a rivulet of fresh water running through it, called a halt. He considered that here there was no risk of surprise, as by placing men on the watch, there would be time to stand on the defensive before they were attacked. The rest, with food and fresh water, restored the men, and they were eager once more to push forward. The "bush" in front was becoming thicker than ever; should they once work their way well into it, they might find it a difficult matter to get out again. He accordingly ordered them to fire off their muskets and to give a good hearty British cheer, so that should the missing party be anywhere in the neighbourhood they might hear it. They waited in silence; no reply came. Jack looked at his watch. There would be barely time to reach the boats before dark, and should the enemy get between them and the shore, they would have to cut their way through them.

With a heavy heart the captain at last gave the order to retire.

"What! are we going off without punishing the rascals for the opposition they have shown us?" Jack overheard one of the officers remark. "They will consider that they have gained the day, and will behave in the same fashion to any who may pay them another visit."

Jack's thoughts had been so completely engaged about Tom and the other midshipmen that the necessity of inflicting punishment on the natives had not occurred to him. Perhaps, after all, should their friends not have been killed, they might have been carried prisoners to the village he had seen from the height. He accordingly directed his march towards it, and as the country was pretty open in that direction, the party made good progress.

The huts were reached; they were of considerable size, raised above the ground on piles, and were constructed chiefly of bamboos and thatched with palm leaves. The first they entered was deserted. They went on from house to house. Not a human being was to be found, even the old people and children had been removed. As the only means of punishing the people for the uninvited attack they had made on the boats' crews, Jack ordered the whole village to be given to the flames. By igniting a few handfuls of dried leaves which were thrown into the houses, they quickly blazed up from one end to the other. They were left burning so furiously that even should the inhabitants return, they could not possibly extinguish the fire.

Even this necessary act did not induce the enemy to come from their hiding-places, nor did they appear even in the distance as the party marched back to the boats. It was a bitter disappointment not to have recovered the midshipmen and their companions, while, from not having got hold of any of the natives, it had been impossible to ascertain their fate.

Night was approaching. Jack felt it his duty to return to the ship, but he resolved on leaving one of the boats under Mr Hanson, the third lieutenant, who volunteered to remain. He was to keep close in shore, prepared to shove off at any moment, should he be attacked by a superior force of the enemy.

Much regret was expressed when the captain returned on board, that Tom and his companions had not been recovered. The ship remained hove to all night, and many hoped and believed that the boat would return with the missing ones in the morning.

When the morning came, however, no boat appeared. Jack accordingly pulled in with two other boats, intending to relieve Lieutenant Hanson. The latter was seen coming out to meet them. He had remained at his post, he said, all night, and although he was not attacked, he heard the natives shouting and occasionally firing off muskets, so that even had the midshipmen attempted to do so, they could not have succeeded in making their way to the beach without fighting.

Jack, unwilling to give up all hope of getting Tom back, again landed with his whole force and marched inland, but, as on the preceding day, the enemy retreated and hid themselves, being evidently conscious that they were unable to cope with so strong a party. The difficult nature of the country rendered it impossible for them to advance further than they had done on the previous day, and Captain Rogers was again compelled to return to the boats, without having effected anything. He left another boat under Mr Tomkinson, the senior mate, with the same directions he had given to the lieutenant. In addition, however, he instructed him that should the natives approach, if possible to get hold of one or more of them, charging him on no account to fire, unless attacked. Once more the boats pulled back to the ship. On getting on board, Jack, finding that the barometer was falling slightly, though the sky looked as serene as ever, considered it prudent to get a better offing than on the previous night, intending to stand back in the morning to pick up Mr

Tomkinson's boat. He talked over with his first lieutenant the possibility of penetrating further into the country with a larger number of men than he had before landed. Much would depend on the state of the weather; should it continue calm the larger boats might go in with guns in their bows, and securely hold the beach against any number of the inhabitants who might appear, so that a party landing might advance a considerable distance without fear of being attacked in the rear.

Their plans were, however, defeated. As the night drew on the weather began sensibly to change, and fears now began to be entertained that Mr Tomkinson's boat would not succeed in regaining the ship. Should the expected gale blow on the shore, it would be necessary for the ship to gain a good offing as soon as possible. Steam was got up, and her head was put towards the shore; she slowly made her way back, so as to be as close in as possible, in the expectation that Mr Tomkinson would, seeing the change in the weather, pull off to meet her. The lead was kept going, that she might run no risk of getting into too shallow water. Just before daylight the captain ordered a gun to be fired, and another shortly afterwards, which Mr Tomkinson would, of course, understand as a signal of recall. When at length the gloom of night had cleared away, the boat was seen pulling off as fast as the crew could lay their backs to the oars. The ship's head, in the meantime, was put round, as it would have been dangerous for her to approach nearer. Mr Tomkinson reported, as Mr Hanson had done, that the natives had continued making a noise the whole night and firing, but that they had carefully kept out of the way, so that he had been unable to catch hold of any of them. Scarcely had the boat been hoisted up, than a heavy squall struck the ship, and it became necessary to put on all the steam to enable her to obtain a sufficient offing from the land. As the wind continued to get up and the sea to increase, all hopes of communicating with the shore for some days to come, had to be abandoned. Jack still would not believe that his midshipmen had been killed, though it was generally supposed on board that such had been their fate.

The surgeon, Dr McGauley, however, was inclined to hold with the captain. "Dinna fash yourself, Captain Rogers," he observed, "midshipmen have nine lives, like cats, and it is hard if the three together don't manage to get clear of the savages, although, should they be addicted to cannibalism, master Billy will run a good chance of being eaten."

"It is said, however, that the Papuans are not cannibals, and the fellows we encountered are certainly not the sort of savages I supposed we should meet. My hope is that they have either made prisoners of the midshipmen and the other men, or that our people have managed to escape to the southward, and perhaps we may pick them up further along the coast," observed the captain.

There was, however, no abatement of the gale; on the contrary, it had become a perfect hurricane, and as reefs abound along the coast of New Guinea, it was necessary for the safety of the ship to stand out to sea. For nearly ten days the bad weather continued, and upwards of two weeks elapsed before the *Empress* could get back to the coast. Boats were sent on shore as before, but the natives took good care not to appear. The ship then slowly steamed to the southward, firing guns and making signals, and, whenever possible, sending the boats in on two or three occasions the natives were seen, but without an interpreter it was found impossible to hold intercourse with them.

At length Jack was reluctantly compelled to give up all hope of recovering his midshipmen and the men with them. He felt bound to continue his voyage and to visit the islands at which he was directed to call, before going to Fiji.

Several places were touched at in New Ireland, the Solomon Islands, Santa Cruz and New Hebrides. One of the duties Captain Rogers had to perform was to overhaul vessels suspected of unlawfully having islanders on board for the purpose of taking them to work in Queensland or Fiji. Several were met with, but their papers were regular and their passengers appeared to be willingly on board; but at the same time, as there was no one to interpret for them, the latter point remained doubtful.

The *Empress* continued her voyage, touching at numerous places, until she reached the Fiji group, which has since passed into the possession of England. Here she fell in with the *Orion*, commanded by Captain Adair; and the two old friends, after spending some time in visiting the various chiefs, sailed for Sydney, their ultimate destination. A visit was paid to Noumea, the French settlement in New Caledonia, and the ships also touched at Norfolk Island, no longer a convict establishment, but now the habitation of the Pitcairn Islanders, and the head-quarters of the Melanesian mission.

The ships had been at sea five days after leaving Norfolk Island, being under sail, when the look-out from the mast-head of the *Empress* announced that he saw what looked like a dead whale away on the starboard bow.

"A whale does not float so high out of the water as that," remarked Mr Hanson, who went up the rigging with his glass. "That's a vessel of some sort, and a good large one, on her beam ends. Possibly her crew may have escaped, and are clinging on to her."

On returning on deck he made his report, and the captain ordering the yards to be braced up, the ship stood in the direction of the wreck.

Chapter Eleven.

Tom and Desmond with their party retreat into the interior—Nick sets out to scout—Returns—Tom goes out and brings unsatisfactory intelligence—The party reach the river—Embark in a canoe—Pursued—Escape up the river—Moor to a tree for the night—A plentiful breakfast—Through a forest—Tom and Pipes visit the shore—See the ship sail—A storm—Return to their companions—Commence journey to the southward—Escape observation of natives—Numerous dangers—Peter seized by a tiger—Beautiful flowers—Birds of gay plumage shot—Billy narrowly escapes from a crocodile—Attacked by monkeys—Cross a wide prairie—Want of water—Find water-melons—Buffaloes killed—Sight a snowy mountain—Deer killed, and a fight with a tiger—Crossing the mountains—See a volcano—An eruption—Serpents—A large lake—A friendly chief—Journey continued—The coast reached—An English brig in the harbour.

The party consisting of Tom Rogers, Gerald Desmond, and Billy Blueblazes, with Casey, Peter, and the two Papuans, Nick and Pipes, had penetrated a considerable distance to the south-west, when they heard the sound of hot firing in the rear. The midshipmen proposed at once returning to rejoin their friends, but Pipes, in great alarm, pointed out the probability that the Papuans had got between them and the English, and that they would to a certainty, should such be the case, be attacked and killed before they could regain the beach. Nick joined his entreaties to those of his countryman, and offered to steal forward and ascertain the position of the two parties, begging his friends to remain concealed behind some rocks and thick bushes until his return. The sound of firing continued. From the nature of the volleys it was evident that two parties were engaged, and that the Papuans must possess a considerable number of muskets. Tom, therefore, thought it prudent to agree to Nick's proposal. He and his companions accordingly concealed themselves in the spot proposed, while Nick hurried forward in the direction of the firing. Tom and Desmond considered that it must have been further off than they had at first supposed. As Nick did not re-appear, they at last began to fear that he had been caught by the enemy, or had perhaps deserted to them. They suggested this to Pipes, who replied, "No, no; he good man; come back!"

"I wish that we had run for it, and tried to reach the shore," said Desmond.

"We might have been knocked on the head had we made the attempt," answered Tom; "but should we be discovered by the enemy we will sell our lives dearly, if we can but get possession of one of those rocks near us and hold it until our ammunition is expended."

"Oh dear? how dreadful!" exclaimed Billy. "I'm thankful to say, however, that I brought away a powder flask quite full, and an ammunition pouch, so that we may hold out for some hours; and I hope by that time our friends will come to our rescue."

They waited for nearly an hour longer. Again there came the sound of even sharper firing than before, though it seemed further off. Pipes now and then crept out of his hiding-place to ascertain if any one was approaching, a proceeding, had such been the case, which would very likely have betrayed him.

"Here come Nick! Him sure!" exclaimed Pipes at last.

"I hope it is," said Tom. "But silence, all of you, in case it should prove an enemy who might betray our hiding-place."

It was Nick, however. He looked very much alarmed. His report, as far as could be understood, was that the Papuans, having collected from other villages, had taken up positions some little distance from the coast, whence they could watch the proceedings of the white men, and that it would be impossible to get down to the shore without being discovered.

Tom and Desmond, on this, proposed fighting their way through. Casey and Peter were ready enough to do so, or anything else they wished; but Nick and Pipes objected strongly to such a proceeding, affirming that they should be discovered and shot down were they to make the attempt.

"Wait; by-and-by mans go away!" said Pipes.

Tom, not satisfied with this, determined to go out and scout for himself. Desmond and Billy wanted to go with him.

"One is enough to run the risk," he answered. "Two are more likely to be observed. I will not go far, and keep well under cover."

Desmond and Billy felt very anxious while Tom was away, lest he should fall into the hands of the Papuans.

"If they get him they will cut off his head," said Billy, "and we shall never see him again."

"Tom knows what he is about; and unless the enemy suspect that we are in their rear, and are looking about, there is not much risk of his being discovered," answered Desmond.

"It would have been better to have sent one of the black fellows," observed Billy. "I say, Desmond, what are we to do for grub? I'm getting very sharp set, in spite of my feelings."

"I suspect we shall get nothing to-night," answered Desmond. "If we were to fire we should betray ourselves, and have the enemy down upon us. Perhaps Tom will report that they have moved away, and we shall after all be able to reach the beach. Lieutenant Norman is sure not to go away without us."

"But he won't stop if he fancies that we are killed; and that will be his opinion, depend upon it," said Billy, in a melancholy tone.

"Hark! I hear some one coming," said Desmond. "Keep quiet!" It proved to be Tom, who looked unusually grave.

"I have been a considerable distance," he said, "and have had a sharp run for it to keep ahead of the enemy. They are coming this way, and I question whether this will prove a secure hiding-place; for, as I watched them, they seemed to be stowing themselves away between trees or behind hillocks and rocks, and some of them are sure to pop in here."

Nick and Pipes appeared quickly to understand what he was saying. "Den we go on higher," said Nick, pointing towards the bank of the river.

It at once occurred to Tom that the Papuan expected to find a canoe by which they might escape down the river and get out to sea. He accordingly without hesitation followed Nick's advice; and the party set out, following the two Papuans as fast as they could run, hoping to avoid being seen by the enemy. Instead, however, of keeping down the stream, as Tom expected they would do, they proceeded up it.

"I suppose they think we shall find a canoe in that direction more likely than below," said Tom to Desmond, "but it won't do to turn back."

They continued along the bank in the direction their guides led them, thus getting further and further from the coast. They had gone on some way when Tom asked Nick whether he was sure they should find a canoe.

"Yes, yes, sure," was the answer.

"We shall soon get back with the current," observed Desmond. "It won't make much difference, indeed it will be sufficient if we wait until dark, and then we shall run but little risk of being seen."

The two Papuans were still positive that before long they would find a canoe. Casey was of the same opinion, although on what he grounded it, it was difficult to say. When they stopped they could hear the enemy shouting and shrieking behind them, which convinced them that it would be safer to go on than to turn back. At last, after a run of several miles along the banks of the river, they caught sight of five canoes hauled up on the shore, and not far off several huts. None of the inhabitants were visible; perhaps they had gone down to defend their shores from the expected invasion of the white men.

"Hurrah! we are all right now!" cried Desmond. "We will take the best canoe, and it might be prudent to smash the others to prevent the enemy giving chase to us."

"Let us get our own into the water first, and see about that afterwards," said Tom, looking about for paddles. He found enough for each of his party, and a couple besides, which were carried off.

It took some little time to launch the canoe, which was somewhat heavy and drawn up at a distance from the water. Tom seated himself aft to steer. Desmond and Billy sat next to him, Casey and Peter next, and the two Papuans in the bows to use the two foremost paddles. Pipes was still on shore prepared to shove off the bow of the canoe before he stepped on board, when pointing to the eastward, he exclaimed "Here come!" The midshipmen, looking in that direction, saw a large body of men approaching.

"Jump in, Pipes, jump in!" exclaimed Tom. "We must get down the stream before the enemy reach the banks, or they may be peppering us more warmly than we may find pleasant."

Tom was about to turn the head of the canoe in that direction, when Desmond exclaimed —

"Look there, look there! what are those fellows about?" Three canoes full of men were seen darting from behind some thick bushes out of another small river which had not before been observed. They would effectually prevent the escape of the midshipmen's canoe.

"We shall have a desperate fight with those fellows before: we can get down the river," cried Desmond, "and they will have the assistance of their friends on shore."

While Desmond was speaking and Tom was considering what was best to be done, several men flourishing paddles in their hands were seen to rush out of the huts.

"Dat way, dat way!" exclaimed both Nick and Pipes at the same time, pointing up the river.

The sun was by this time on the point of setting, and Tom considered that if they could keep ahead of their enemies until darkness set in, they might then either find some place of concealment, or paddle silently down during the night and escape observation. There was no time to consider the plan proposed; they must either follow it at once, or prepare for a desperate encounter.

"It is the only thing to be done," observed Desmond; and Tom, turning the head of the canoe up the river, told his crew to paddle away for their lives. They had scarcely got good way on the canoe, before the men from the village began to launch theirs. More natives appeared, and in two or three minutes the whole of the native fleet was in the water.

"They don't appear to have firearms, but they have got bows and arrows," said Tom, looking astern. "If we had a good English boat, the whole fleet should not make us fly, but they might quickly capsize this canoe and have us in their power. I fear that more than their arms. Paddle, paddle, lads!" he shouted.

His crew did paddle, probably harder than they had ever done in their lives. Poor Billy exerted himself until he was red in the face, "puffing and blowing," as Desmond declared, "like a grampus;" for in spite of the danger they were in, he amused himself by quizzing his companion.

"We are gaining on them at all events," said Tom. "If we do not encounter any more higher up the river, we shall distance them by the time it is dark, and then we shall have a good chance of getting clear."

The river continued broad, and as the current was not very strong, the canoe made good headway. They kept in the centre, to run no risk of being attacked by the natives on the shore. Here and there among the trees huts were seen, but the inhabitants either did not perceive them or supposed that they were Papuans, for although they saw several canoes drawn up on the banks, no attempt was made to launch them.

Thus they went on without relaxing their efforts for an instant until sunset, when the shades of night quickly crept over the scene. Tom felt very unwilling to go further from the coast, and proposed looking out for some creek or bay, shaded by trees, where they could remain concealed until their enemies were likely to be no longer watching the river, and they might steal down unobserved. No such spot, however, could they discover, and when at last wearied by their exertions they stopped paddling, they heard the shrieks of their pursuers in the distance.

"They have not given up the chase yet," observed Desmond. "The fact of their following us shows that they fear we may escape them by some other way. Perhaps we may find a branch with another outlet to the sea."

"Oh, do let us paddle on," cried Billy. "I don't like the thoughts of being caught and eaten by the savages."

"Whether they eat men or not, they will knock us on the head, and it will come to much the same thing," said Casey; "so that we had better keep ahead of them until they give up the chase, and very likely, when they don't find us, they will fancy that we have landed, and turn back to where they come from."

The paddles were accordingly plied with as much vigour as before. Tom had a pocket compass, but it was too dark to see it; he however judged by the stars overhead that the river was running from the southward, and he hoped, by landing on the right bank, to be able to strike eastward across the country and regain the sea-shore. Had he known the nature of the task, he would have considered the undertaking far more difficult than he now supposed it to be. In vain he and his companions looked out for another branch of the river which they might descend. No opening appeared either on one side or the other. After paddling on for another hour, they again stopped. At first no sounds were heard except the cries of night birds and the strange shrieks of animals in the forest.

"We might pull in now to one bank or the other, and rest until it is time to slip down again," observed Desmond.

They were on the point of doing as proposed, when again the sound of the natives' voices was heard coming up the stream. The enemy had probably by this time been joined by the other canoes which had been seen on the banks, and Tom confessed that he considered the risk of attempting to escape by the way they had come very great. The only thing they could therefore do was to keep on until Tom and Desmond had good reason to believe that they had completely distanced their pursuers, and then as soon as it was daylight they might hope to strike across the country and regain the coast, where they were sure that the boats would be on the look-out for them.

For some time they had seen no lights on the banks or other indications that the country was inhabited, and the further they got up the river the less risk there was of being discovered. They had not correctly calculated the distance they had gone. There had been for some time little or no current against them, but this they had not discovered while they were paddling on. The tide was setting up the river, and had thus sent them on much faster than they had supposed. Nick and Pipes urged them to continue their course.

"All right; we get away!" cried Nick.

"No fear," cried Pipes. "Paddle, boys, paddle!" Thus hour after hour they paddled on, until Tom declared that it would be folly to go further, and that they must either land or else secure the canoe to the trunk of a tree and wait in her until daylight. The latter plan was adopted. Steering to the right bank, where some thick branches overhung the stream, they secured the canoe to the stem of a small tree.

"We must keep watch," said Tom, "or we may receive a visit from a wild beast, or be found napping by the natives, and be made prisoners or killed without an opportunity of defending ourselves."

Gerald agreed to keep the first watch for a couple of hours, and then to call Tom.

"I wish we had something to eat," said Billy. "I shall grow as thin as a whipping-post, and never be able to march all the way to the coast, which must be very far off, I suspect."

"Never fear, Billy; you had better get some sleep, and forget all about the matter. In the morning we shall probably be able to kill some birds, or find some wild fruit," answered Tom.

Billy, with a groan, lay down in the bottom of the canoe, in which the rest of the party had stretched themselves as well as they could, although there was not much room for their legs.

Desmond sat up with his musket in his hands, keeping an eye down the river, and occasionally peering in among the trees on the shore. Mournful sounds ever and anon came out of the forest, but he could detect no human voices; and he therefore hoped that the enemy had given up the pursuit. He had a hard matter to keep awake, the murmur of the water, as it passed by, tending much to lull him to sleep. He contrived, however, to keep his eyes open. He knew that in that region such disagreeable creatures existed as anacondas, tigers, huge baboons, and alligators, and that one or the other of them might suddenly make its appearance. He had stood his watch, as near as he could calculate, about a couple of hours, when feeling that, notwithstanding the danger to be apprehended, he could not hold out much longer, he roused up Tom, who, after his two hours' sound sleep, was soon wide awake.

"I have been thinking of all sorts of horrible creatures who may chance to be in the neighbourhood. Take care you do not let any of them get hold of us," said Gerald.

"No fear of that," answered Tom, taking Gerald's musket; "I will try and give a good account of any beast which comes near us."

Tom sat, as Desmond had done, with his rifle ready for immediate action. It had hitherto been too dark to look at his watch, and he thought it imprudent to strike a light for the purpose. He had, therefore, no notion of how time went by. Greatly to his surprise he very shortly saw the streaks of dawn in the sky, and ere long a rich glow, heralding the rising sun, appeared to the eastward, shedding a ruddy tint over the calm surface of the river.

He had now to decide what was next to be done. To attempt to descend the river during the daytime would expose them to certain capture. He was anxious to try and reach the coast as early as possible. Taking out his compass, he ascertained that it lay due east, and that the course of the river was south-west and north-east; but how far off the shore was it was difficult to say. Nick and Pipes evidently did not like the thoughts of having to proceed in that direction, and, pointing towards the south, said that that was where their native village was situated.

"We must go to the coast, at all events," said Tom. "If they desert us we cannot help it."

"Since that matter is settled, let us have some breakfast," exclaimed Billy. "I wish you would knock over a few birds. There are plenty of them. Here are some small shot. I thought it would be useful."

There were parrots, paraquets, doves, and several other birds of exquisite plumage, flying about; and Tom, who was a very good shot, even with a ship's musket, in a few minutes shot as many as would serve the party for breakfast. The men then set to work to pluck them, caring very little for their fine feathers. An open space, where they could venture to light a fire, was soon found. Nick and Pipes had in the mean time been hunting about for wild fruit, and quickly brought in a good supply.

"There's no fear of starving in this country; that's one comfort," observed Billy, as he began to munch away at his share of a parrot.

The fruits were very refreshing. They ate them without fear, although they did not know their names, as Nick and Pipes assured them they were good.

The meal over, the party prepared to set out. They first, however, drew up the canoe, and concealed it as closely as possible under the bushes, that they might again make use of it if necessary. Nick and Pipes, when they understood what Tom required, offered to go in front and scout, but gave him to understand that should they fall in with an enemy they would retreat, and that he must be prepared to halt or turn back again, as they might deem necessary.

They soon found themselves in a very dense forest, through which it was a hard matter to make their way. Wherever there was an open space the ground was covered with a profusion of flowers; and birds of gay plumage flew amid the trees, and monkeys of various sizes leaped from branch to branch. Occasionally they had to make their way with their cutlasses, but it was a somewhat slow business, and fatiguing into the bargain. In many places Nick and Pipes were no more able to get through than they were, and they were also constantly afraid that they might come suddenly upon some natives and betray themselves. At last, coming to a brook, from sheer fatigue they were compelled to halt and eat the remainder of the provisions they had cooked in the morning. After resting they again pushed on, but their progress was not more rapid than at first. Towards evening Tom, in hopes of getting a sight of the ocean, climbed a tree taller than most of its fellows. Having his spy-glass, he could see to a great distance.

"How far off is it?" inquired Desmond, when Tom came down.

"Shall we get there to-night?" asked Billy.

"Not for a week if we do not make better way than we have done this morning," answered Tom. "I could make out the sea in the distance, and I fancied some huts and plantations between us and the shore. We must try to pass by them without being discovered by the inhabitants."

The heat had been excessive, and the midshipmen were glad to rest until the following morning. During the night it was utterly impossible to make their way through the wood. As no huts had been seen near, they ventured to light a fire, watching carefully that it should not spread, when, as Billy observed, their provisions would have been very much overdone.

After camping, the first thing they had to do was to look out for food. The parrots, for some reason or other, were rather shy, but a troop of inquisitive monkeys came near to ascertain what the strangers were about.

Pipes, who accompanied Tom, urged him to shoot.

"Him very good, very good," he said.

Tom had of course heard that the creatures were eaten, although he had never tasted monkey. He accordingly fired, and brought down two who were sitting together grinning at him. The rest on this came chattering and screeching to the boughs close above his head, and began to throw down sticks and nuts, some of the latter of which they had been eating, and to spit at him in the most furious fashion.

"Kill more, kill more!" cried Pipes.

Tom again fired, and two others fell to the ground, when the remainder ran shrieking away through the forest. Pipes, taking possession of the game, marched back to the camp with a well-satisfied air.

"You do not mean to say we are to feed on these creatures?" exclaimed Desmond.

"I can't shoot anything else, and better eat them than starve," answered Tom.

"Ah! let's try them," cried Billy. "Anything better than an empty stomach."

By the time the monkeys had been cooked the appetites of all the party had considerably increased. Although the midshipmen made some wry faces at first, after a few mouthfuls they went on eating monkey as if they had been accustomed to it all their lives. Nick and Pipes advised that they should keep up the fire all night, as otherwise they might find that somebody had been carried off by a huge species of tiger which they said infested the woods and forests of their country. Their advice was followed, and all hands took it by turns to remain on watch. Billy called up his companions twice, declaring that he saw the head of a huge tiger peering from between the bushes, but he did not fire, as he was afraid of missing. Though Desmond grumbled at being roused up, it was proved that Billy was right by the marks the tiger had left on the ground.

They had not got far the next day when their scouts came back and urged them not to proceed. As to reaching the shore without being discovered, they said that it was impossible, as the country was thickly inhabited and open, their only chance being to pass through it at night. Should they advance much further they would run great risk of being seen.

After searching about Pipes and his companion discovered a good hiding-place, very similar to the one in which they had before concealed themselves. Towards night they could tell, by the soughing of the wind in the trees and the appearance of the sky, that there was a change in the weather.

"I am sure the boats won't leave us while there is a chance," observed Tom. "I will make my way alone, with the help of Pipes, and see what has become of them. If I do not come back you will know that I am caught, and I would advise you to try and get to the southward, where you may perhaps find the inhabitants more friendly, and be able to get across to Australia."

Desmond begged Tom to let him go instead; but Tom had made up his mind to undertake the excursion, and as soon as it was dark he set off with Pipes, who had agreed to go, although he evidently did not like the work. Tom and his faithful attendant set off. They had a long distance to go, and detours to make. Occasionally they heard dogs bark, and saw lights in the windows of huts; but they kept clear of them, and made good progress. They had one or two narrow escapes; and on one occasion both tumbled into a water-course. They, however, scrambled out again, with only the inconvenience of a wetting, which, considering the warmth of the weather, was of no great consequence, even to Tom; and Pipes had only to rub himself over with his hand, and he was dry again in a few minutes. It was nearly daylight, however, before the beach was reached, when they hunted about and found shelter under some rocks, which would prevent their being seen by the people on shore.

Here they waited until daylight, when Tom eagerly looked out for the ship.

"There she is!" he cried out, as the gloom of night clearing away he saw her standing in towards the land, though at some distance to the northward of where he was. Presently a gun was fired, followed shortly afterwards by another. He was about to set off to try and make his way along the beach, feeling sure that the guns were fired as signals to some of the crew on shore, when he saw through his telescope a boat pull out from behind a point and make her way towards the ship, which at the same time swept round until her head was off shore. He had no means of making a signal. Even should he fire his rifle, it would not be heard. To shout would be of no avail. He watched the boat until she was alongside, when she was hoisted up and the ship steamed away. It was high time that she should get off the shore, for a heavy gale had sprung up, sending the heavy breakers with fury against the rock-bound coast.

"There is no chance of our getting off if this continues," said Tom to himself; "we are left to our own resources, I see that. The best thing would be to start to the southward, as Pipes recommends."

Tom was eager to return and consult with Desmond, but Pipes earnestly entreated him to remain concealed during the day, and then at night there would be but little difficulty in making their way back to their companions.

It was a melancholy day, as he sat on the sea-shore under the rocks, watching the departing ship. A few shell-fish was the only food he and Pipes could procure. As soon as night came on and the inhabitants had returned to their huts, he and his faithful companion set out. As the storm was howling and making a tremendous noise, there was little danger of being discovered.

Desmond and Billy had become very anxious and were thankful to see them, although Billy uttered a deep groan when he heard that the ship had sailed away, and that he would have some hundreds of miles to trudge through the country. None of them indeed knew what they were about to undertake, and, with the exception of Billy, looked upon the journey as a pleasant excursion.

As Tom had had plenty of time to rest during the previous day, he was ready to set off early in the morning.

Guided by Tom's pocket compass, they steered westward of south, which was the direction Nick and Pipes wished them to take.

The two Papuans explained that they would have to go out of their way to reach the river, and advised them to keep in the direction they were now pursuing.

During the day they travelled on without stopping, anxious to get away from the sea-board. It was evidently the most thickly populated part of the country, while, judging from what they had seen, there were few or no inhabitants in the interior. In the afternoon, as they were moving on, Pipes, who had been scouting in front, came back and made a sign to them all to get under the cover of some bushes, which he pointed out close at hand.

Scarcely had they crouched down, when they heard the voices of a party of natives who passed close by without discovering them. Further on they came upon a plantation, with a number of women working on it. By turning aside in time, they escaped observation. They were, however, afraid of lighting a fire that night, lest it might betray their whereabouts to the natives. They had, fortunately, preserved some of the cooked meat before starting, and had enough for supper, with the help of some fruit. Tom urged all hands, each man in his turn, to keep a strict watch; for having no fire there would be a great risk of being attacked by wild beasts. All promised to obey his injunctions.

Tom intended to take the first watch, Casey the next, Desmond the third, and Billy—who, it was hoped, after a good sleep, would keep awake—the fourth. The three first had carefully kept their watches, moving round and round their sleeping companions, so that no savage beast could approach unperceived. Desmond, however, fancied that he saw some object moving amid the trees in the gloom. At last he called up Billy, and charged him to keep a bright look-out. "If you don't, depend upon it you or some of us will be carried off by one of those beasts of tigers," he said, with much emphasis. "I have not felt so uncomfortable for a long time as I have been during the time I have been on the watch."

Billy promised to remain broad awake and to keep his weather eye open.

"Mind you do!" said Desmond, as he lay down.

The whole camp was awakened by a fearful shriek and a loud cry from Billy, and starting to their feet, they saw by the light of the day, which had just broken, a huge animal carrying off Peter, the black, in its jaws, while Billy lay sprawling on the ground where he had fallen, his foot having caught in a supple jack, as he was making chase after the depredator. The whole party followed, but the tiger, if tiger it was, quickly bounded out of sight. Tom and the other midshipmen had a sincere regard for honest Peter, and were grieved to think that they had lost him. Rushing on, they caught sight of Peter in the monster's jaws. But the black was not inactive, for having been seized by the left shoulder, with his right hand, which was free, he was punching the tiger furiously in the eyes. Tom was afraid of firing, lest he should hit Peter; at the same time it seemed scarcely possible that the poor fellow would escape being torn to pieces. Suddenly, however, the tiger gave a spring forward, when the midshipmen saw that Peter was no longer in the creature's mouth. Tom and Desmond both fired together, but the tiger bounded away. On getting up, what was their surprise to find Peter rising to his feet, and, although his left shoulder was very much torn and he looked somewhat confused, he was well able to accompany them back to the camp. He knew no more about the matter than they did. Suddenly he had felt himself carried off in the jaws of a big animal, and as he said, "naturally made the best use of his fists to get free."

Billy looked very much ashamed of himself, and was compelled to acknowledge that he must have been dozing, as he certainly did not see the tiger coming.

"It shows that we must keep very wide awake, or none of us will reach the end of our journey," said Tom. "Now, the sooner we get away from this the better; for the sound of our shots may have attracted the attention of the natives in the neighbourhood."

Casey, who had been accustomed to see all sorts of wounds, assisted to bind up the hurt of poor Peter, who declared that he was perfectly ready to continue the march. As they were afraid of lighting a fire and had no food, they pushed on during the cool hours of the morning, intending to take a substantial meal as soon as it was too hot to proceed. They had no little difficulty, however, in making their way amid the creepers and climbing plants, which, hanging from tree to tree, interlaced each other in a perfect network. They often, therefore, had to hunt about until they could discover a more open place, through which they could advance.

They calculated that they had pushed forward about ten miles, when they reached a stream, arched over by tall trees, from which hung numberless flowers, bearing climbers of great beauty and of varied and brilliant colours. Many of them were convolvulus-shaped, and of prodigious size, some white and yellow, spotted with red, others of a pale violet. There were scarlet flowers, blue, and sulphur-coloured flowers, and others of similar tints, striped and spotted in the most curious way. But far more interesting to the hungry travellers were the numberless water-fowl, which flew up and down the stream, and Tom and Desmond in a few minutes had knocked over several kingfishers, storks, and ducks, amply sufficient to supply all hands with food.

The two natives had, in the mean time, been searching for honey and nuts, of which they brought in a supply. The latter grew on some enormous trees at no great distance. The natives had picked them up from the ground to which they had fallen, having been bitten off by the parrots. The outer shell was black and hard, about the size and shape of a lemon, and the kernel, enclosed in a thick inner covering, was white and hard, resembling chestnuts when roasted.

"Hurrah!" cried Billy. "We shall run no risk of starving, at all events. These nuts will serve us for bread, and with the honey will stay our appetites."

The fire was quickly blazing up, and the birds, plucked and spitted, placed before it. A sharp look-out was kept on every side for natives, snakes, tigers, or any other wild beasts which might be tempted to pay them a visit. Tom urged his friends to keep together as much as possible, and always to have their arms ready. After a good rest they again pushed on, and encamped in the evening on the bank of a large river, no doubt the one up which they had come in the canoe.

While Casey and Peter were lighting the fire, the two Papuans were looking out for honey, and Tom and Desmond were shooting some birds for supper, Billy went down to the water to fill a large gourd which Pipes had procured for them. Just as he was about to dip it in, a long snout appeared above the surface, the possessor of which—a huge crocodile—made directly at him. Billy, throwing down the gourd, scampered off. Fortunately for him the monster stopped for an instant to pick up the gourd, which it crushed in its huge jaws, and thus Billy was able to increase his distance.

Pat Casey and Peter, on hearing his cries, started up with their rifles, and as they ran forward uttered loud shouts to distract the attention of the crocodile. Still, so determined was the monster to seize poor Billy, that it did not seem to heed them.

"Jump on one side, sir, jump on one side!" cried Casey to Billy, who followed the advice, and the seaman, levelling his rifle, poured the contents down the crocodile's throat. It immediately rolled over, and after a few struggles lay dead.

Tom and Desmond considered it advisable on their return to move further away from the river. Fortunately they did so, for while they were sitting round the fire cooking their game, a dozen crocodiles crept out of the water and came towards them. The whole party, starting to their feet, shouted and shrieked, but not until Tom and Desmond had fired down the throats of a couple of the saurians did the rest turn tail, when, plunging into the water, they disappeared beneath the surface.

"If we don't keep a bright look-out during the night one or other of us will be carried off, depend upon that," observed Tom.

His warning had a good effect, and it was agreed that two of the party should keep watch together, as they had to risk an attack from crocodiles on one side and tigers on the other, not to speak of big serpents and other creatures. The most dangerous of these were scorpions, several of which were seen five and six inches long, with stings which the natives asserted would deprive a person of life in the course of an hour or less.

"Oh dear, oh dear!" sighed Billy. "I knew the journey would be fatiguing enough, but I little thought the trouble all these horrid beasts would cause us."

For several days they travelled on along the course of the river, but taking care not to camp near enough to the bank to be surprised by a hungry crocodile. On several occasions they caught sight of tigers, and three were shot which came nearer to them than was pleasant. Among the vast numbers of the feathered tribe which perched in the trees, or flitted amid the boughs, or soared high into the air, were the beautiful birds of paradise, of brilliant colours and graceful forms, which Tom and Desmond agreed it was a shame to kill when they could obtain as much game of a different species as they required. Monkeys of various sizes were seen, some not larger than cats and others half as big as a man. The travellers were moving on, Nick and Pipes scouting in front, the three midshipmen following, Casey and the black bringing up the rear. Presently they heard a loud chattering overhead, and down came a shower of nuts, one of which hit Billy on the nose. The pain made him cry out, when his voice was replied to by shrieks of laughter from overhead, followed by another volley. On looking up they caught sight of a large troop of big monkeys scampering from bough to bough, some of them descending as close as possible in order to get nearer the intruders of their domain.

One old fellow spat right at Desmond, and when he saw that the shot had been successful, shrieked and chuckled with laughter as he climbed back to a more secure part of the bough. The monkeys on this, emboldened by success and increased in numbers, discharged volleys of missiles of all descriptions, some of a very disagreeable character, so that the three midshipmen with their followers were fairly put to flight, the monkeys pursuing them, chattering and shrieking until they made their escape from the forest, which here fortunately came to a termination.

"I'll pay you off for this!" cried Desmond, who had been a sufferer with Billy, and, firing, he brought down one of the monkeys, on which the rest set up the most fearful cries, shaking their fists and making all sorts of defiant grimaces.

They now entered on a region totally different to any they had hitherto passed through. It was a vast open prairie, covered in many places with long grass, amid which snakes of large size were seen creeping, but Nick assured Tom that they were not venomous, and would afford a meal at any time, should game not be abundant. The difficulty of walking over this grass was considerable, as they had to lift their feet high at every step, while they were exposed to the rays of the sun. Having hitherto obtained as much water as they required, it did not occur to them that they might fail to procure it. They caught sight of herds of buffalo and deer, but none during the day came near enough to be shot. All day they trudged on without water, and were well nigh ready to drop from thirst.

"I shall die if I don't get something to drink," cried poor Billy.

Tom got Casey and Peter to lift him up on their shoulders that he might obtain thereby a wider view, but nowhere was a stream or lake to be seen. He, however, caught sight of several round yellow objects on the ground, and on getting nearer, great was the joy of the party to discover that they were melons, the produce of a creeper with ivy-shaped leaves.

The fruit proved even more refreshing than water, and enabled them to march on for several hours during the night. This they did in the hopes of reaching some clump of trees the next day before the sun had attained its greatest height. At last, overcome with fatigue, they were compelled to camp on the open prairie without afire. They were afraid of lighting one lest it should ignite the grass. After a few hours' rest they again moved on. Already the sun had risen and every moment it was gaining strength, when they saw before them a grove of palm trees rising out of the plain. Although they hastened their steps and went on for some time, they still seemed a long way off, but happily they found an abundance of water melons, which quenched their thirst. Without them they must have perished. They were also getting very hungry, and in the open country no honey or nuts were to be procured, nor did birds come near them. A flight of parrots passed over their heads, but too high up for a shot, Billy was crying out that he should die, when a herd of buffaloes were seen scampering across the plain towards them.

"Down, down!" cried the two Papuans; "dey no see us den."

The whole party hid themselves in the tall grass, with their rifles ready for action. There seemed great likelihood, however, that the buffaloes would trample them to death as they came rushing furiously on not dreaming of danger. The leading animals were close upon them when Nick and Pipes jumped up and waved their hands, shouting loudly at the same time. This turned the herd slightly, and as they swept by the animals presented a good shot, when their concealed foes, Tom and Gerald, fired, and two young bulls rolled over. The rest were not so successful, and before the first two who had fired had time to re-load, the herd were out of range. The two buffaloes shot were, however, more than sufficient for their wants, and in an instant Casey and Peter, aided by the Papuans, were engaged with their long knives in flaying the two beasts, and cutting off such pieces of flesh as they could carry. Here was a supply of food which would last them as long as it would keep good. The midshipmen did not fancy eating it raw, but the rest of the party were not so fastidious, and cut off favourite bits, which they clapped into their mouths with evident satisfaction. They were, in consequence, better able to bear their loads of meat than the midshipmen, who had satisfied themselves with two or three water melons apiece. At length the clump of trees was reached.

The party seated in the shade enjoyed the cool air which played among the tall stems. Having cleared away the grass in front of them, they lighted a fire and cooked a part of their meat, the rest being cut into strips and hung up in the sun to dry. It was fortunate for them that they took this precaution. For two days or more they travelled on without meeting with a drop of water, but existed as before on water melons, which prevented them suffering from thirst—as valuable to them as the plant of a similar species which exists on the arid sands of Africa is to many a weary traveller, as well as to the wild beasts who roam over those sandy regions.

They were keeping a look-out ahead for some prominent object by which to steer, when, as the sun rose one day, after they had been marching all night, his rays fell on what seemed like a white cone rising out of the plain. As they pushed on and on it rose higher and higher, although it seemed as far off as ever.

"Why, it must be a snow-covered mountain!" exclaimed Tom.

"I hope we shall not have to climb it, although I should not object to a good roll in the snow just to cool myself," said Billy.

In spite of their eagerness they were compelled to rest as before at the first wood they reached, near the banks of a stream. As most of the party lay fast asleep in the shade, Tom, who was on the watch, observed a herd of small deer apparently coming down to drink. He roused up Desmond, and taking their rifles they crept behind two trees. The deer came on in single file. They were graceful little animals of a dark drab colour on their backs and sides, and white underneath, and pretty large antlers. Without hesitation they at once began to cross the stream, passing along close to where the midshipmen were concealed. Tom selected one animal and Gerald another, and both firing brought the two to the ground. The rest of the deer looked about very much astonished, but did not take to flight. Those who had crossed still continued the same course as before. This gave Tom and Gerald time to re-load, and they brought down two more animals. Not until this did the herd bound off in confusion. The firing had roused up the rest of the party. Tom and Desmond were eagerly rushing out to despatch one deer which was not quite dead, when they saw before them a large tiger, which had been following the herd, and was now going to seize hold of one of the slain deer. The beast looked at them, and seemed about to spring. Neither of them had re-loaded his rifle, Tom immediately began to do so, keeping his eyes on the tiger.

"Don't move, Desmond," he cried out, "or the brute will spring on you!" Desmond, imitating Tom's coolness, also began to load, the tiger in the mean time lashing his tail and showing his huge teeth, while he kept a paw on one of the deer, which he seemed to claim as his prize.

"Now!" cried Tom. "I'll fire at his head, you at his shoulder."

Just as the tiger was about to make a spring which might have proved fatal to one of the party, Tom fired and hit him in the head. The creature gave a bound into the air. Desmond's bullet struck him at the same moment and he rolled over dead.

"Well done, your honour!" cried Casey, who had just come up; "that was a fine shot."

"Hurrah! we shall have some venison now," exclaimed Billy, who followed him.

"We shall want it," said Tom, "if we have to climb those mountains ahead, for very likely we shall find no food there."

The deer were collected, and without delay all hands set to work to cook some of the fresh flesh and to dry the remainder.

Three days after this they found themselves at the foot of a large and lofty mountain, which if they were to get to the south must be crossed. Each man cut a stout stick, the end of which he pointed in the fire. Their dried meat held out; fortunately they shot a couple more deer out of a herd which came to drink at a pool near their camp, and thus the next morning at daybreak, with their provisions strapped on their backs, they commenced the ascent. The cone which they had seen in the distance rose high on their left hand, but they discovered a passage lower down. Up and up they climbed, feeling the cold increase, and suffering intensely after the heat of the plain. At length they could with difficulty breathe, and a desire to sleep seized all the party. Tom, knowing the danger of giving way to it, urged his companions to keep moving. Once Peter sat down, declaring that he could go no further. Tom and Desmond dragged him up, and told Casey to prick him on with the point of his stick if he attempted to stop again. Poor Billy puffed and panted, and at last declared that "he must have a snooze."

"It won't be until you are over the other side," cried Desmond. "Haul him along! Do you want to leave your bones here, or come with us? Just think of the venison pasties and the parrot pies we will have when we get down into a more civilised country!" Thus urged, Billy exerted himself afresh. None of them could afterwards describe the way they got over the mountain. For several miles they dragged themselves over the snow, with the fear of sinking down into some crevice or hollow, while fearful precipices yawned now on one side, now on the other. The two Papuans held on bravely, and, considering their scanty clothing, this was surprising. For a considerable time the whole party moved on without speaking, staggering as if in sleep. Their eyes were dazzled with the whiteness of the snow, which now surrounded them on all sides. Above their heads hung icicles of fantastic shapes, ornamenting cliff and crag.

At length the summit of the pass was gained, and they commenced their descent, less painful because they knew that soon they would get into a warmer region. By nightfall they reached a valley, where the trees afforded them fuel to light a fire, round which they gathered, its genial blaze restoring warmth to their frozen limbs. For two days more they continued among the mountains, but gradually attained a lower altitude, until at last they once more found themselves in a tolerably level country. As far as they could see to the south, rose here and there ranges of hills, but they hoped, by skirting round their bases, to avoid the sufferings they had lately endured. The cooler air of this region enabled them to make longer journeys than before. They had been travelling along a range of hills, which shut out the country to the south from their view. Having crossed these, they encamped one evening on some rocky ground, from whence they saw away to their left conical mountains, several thousand feet in height, of which they had only just before obtained a view. There appeared to be clouds rising above their summits, of which they, however, took but little notice, as they were busy preparing for the night. Tom and Desmond, as usual, were hunting for game. They had shot several birds and a couple of monkeys, which they immediately brought into the camp to be cooked.

After the heat they had endured, finding the night chilly, they piled up some pieces of rock and slabs of bark to form a shelter from the wind. They had all stretched themselves to sleep, with the exception of Casey, who had to keep the first watch, when they were aroused by a loud exclamation uttered by him, and at the same time by a thundering sound and by feeling the earth shake beneath them. Starting to their feet, their eyes were attracted by a bright light, which rose from the mountain, where shooting upwards, it increased in size, until it assumed a mushroom appearance, the top extending far and wide round the mountain. It was a volcano which had suddenly burst forth. No lava, however, was seen descending its sides, but they felt a shower of fine ashes falling on their heads. The screen they had put up, however, partially sheltered them from it. Nothing further could be done, so they resolved to remain where they were, hoping that the eruption would not increase.

Further sleep was out of the question; all night long they watched the fearful flames, expecting every moment to find a fiery shower falling upon them.

"It might have been much worse," said Tom. "We might have been close under it, and here, at all events, we only get a little peppered."

Towards morning the eruption began to subside, and by daylight dense smoke only was seen ascending out of the crater. In spite of their want of sleep, they at once continued their march, hoping to get well to the southward. As none of the party had pocket-books, they were unable to note down a description of the curious creatures they met with and the wonderful scenery they passed through. They frequently saw serpents of fifteen or twenty feet in length, and huge apes, upwards of five feet in height, with hideous features, of almost human shape. They were thankful when they got out of the volcanic region, although they had again to endure the heat of the plains. What was their joy, after ascending a low ridge, to see before them a wide expanse of water, glittering in the sun.

"The sea! the sea!" exclaimed Billy.

Casey and Peter echoed the cry. Had they truly reached the termination of their journey? Tom doubted it. Looking through his telescope, he discovered both to the east and west, a low shore. It might be an estuary extending a long way inland, but they might still be many days' journey from the coast. Whether it was really the sea or a fresh water lake, could only be determined by getting down to it and tasting its waters.

With stout hearts they marched on. They were now well supplied with food. Seldom many hours passed without their meeting herds of deer and buffalo, from which they obtained an ample supply of food. Smaller game, such as monkeys and parrots, were in abundance in the woods, while there were plenty of streams and lakelets of pure water, in which they often took a refreshing bath.

Billy, whose spirits had risen with the expectation of reaching the coast, insisted to the last that the water they had seen from the height was the sea. Casey and the black agreed with him. At last they got close to it. They all hurried forward. Fortunately the bank they reached was hard, and they without difficulty got down to the water. Billy dipped in his hand.

"It's fresh!" he exclaimed, as he tasted it.

"I was sure of that," said Tom. "It's a lake, and a good big one too. We are a couple of hundred miles yet from the coast."

They continued their course along the western shore of the lake, and as they spent fully four days before they reached the southern end, calculating by the rate at which they travelled it must have been between seventy and eighty miles long.

After this they had another range of mountains to pass, which, though wild and rugged in the extreme, were of less elevation than those to the north. Once more they were on a level country, covered with tall grass. They crossed several streams, in wading through one of which a huge crocodile made a dash at them and very nearly caught poor Billy.

Nick and Pipes now began to examine the country with more curious eyes than before, and at last led them into a native path.

"Friends there!" said Pipes, pointing ahead, and they saw through an opening in the trees several huts.

The two Papuans hurried on, begging their friends to sit down in the shade. In a short time they returned with a large party of natives, who, ugly as they were, had smiling faces. One of them who seemed to be the chief, advanced to Tom and made him a speech, which Pipes, who had accompanied him, interpreted as an invitation to the strangers to come to his village.

"Good mans!" said Pipes. "Plenty food!" The invitation was, of course, accepted. The chief, taking Tom by the hand and signing to the rest to follow, led him towards the village, which consisted of a number of large huts composed of wooden frames covered with mats, with which the floor was also spread. The chief begged his visitors to sit down, and ordered food to be brought in. A number of yellow-skinned damsels in a short time appeared, bearing boiled rice and messes of roasted and stewed monkey and yams. Whatever the midshipmen might formerly have thought of such a repast, they acknowledged that this was delicious. Calabashes full of toddy, prepared from the sap of the cocoa-nut tree, were then introduced.

"I say!" said Tom, after he had drunk two or three cups, "we had better not take too much of this, or we shall find ourselves fou."

They wisely declined a pressing invitation of the chief to imbibe any more of the apparently harmless liquor, but their two Papuan friends, after their long absence, seemed to enjoy it, and were in a short time perfectly drunk. This was a misfortune, as they could no longer communicate with the friendly chief. However, he made signs to them to lie down on their mats. Feeling confident of his honesty, they willingly complied with his request.

After a day's rest, which all the party greatly required, Nick and Pipes having recovered, they set off for a village on the coast, about thirty miles distant.

Here the two Papuans found friends and relatives, who welcomed them cordially, having long given them up for lost. The chief of the village, to whom Nick and Pipes were related, requested the midshipmen to take up their abode in his hut. It was situated in the midst of a grove of magnificent trees, and near it was a garden, in which were growing yams, bananas, pumpkins, and many other vegetables and fruits. They were glad to accept the invitation, as the hut was of considerable size, the floor spread neatly with mats, and perfectly clean. The reception over, they made their way down to the shores of the harbour, where, among several Chinese and other strange craft, what was their satisfaction to see an English brig.

Chapter Twelve.

The master of the Fox—Bargain for a passage—Trading with the natives—Farewell to friends—The skipper's rascally trick—The Fox with the midshipmen on board at sea—Bad fare—Fishing—A shark captured, and the skipper knocked over—Short of water—The Fox struck by a squall—Capsized—The midshipmen hold on to the side of the brig—In a desperate condition—A sail—Taken off by a boat from the Empress—Fox founders—Welcomed on board—Sydney reached—A pleasant visit on shore—Bound for New Zealand.

While the midshipmen were standing on the shore of the harbour a boat put off from the brig, and came towards them. She was pulled by four hands, two of whom were blacks and two Malays. A stout white man, in a broad-brimmed straw hat, evidently the skipper, sat in the stern sheets. On landing, the latter, looking hard at them, and surveying their travel-stained, tattered uniforms, inquired—

"Where in the world do you come from?"

"From the other side of New Guinea," answered Tom. He briefly narrated their adventures. "We want to get on to Sydney, where we expect to find our ship. Can you take us there?" he added.

"That depends on circumstances," answered the skipper. "Can you pay for your passage?"

"We can work it, at all events, and I have no doubt that our captain will pay any sum we agree to," said Tom.

Tom did not like either the manner or appearance of the skipper. Of course he did not express his opinion, either by words or looks.

"Are you bound for Sydney?" inquired Tom; "for, if so, we may come to terms."

"As to that, I should not mind putting in there, provided you will pay the expenses. I was thinking of going further south, but I have not quite made up my mind," was the answer. "The Fox is a fine craft, and you will not have another chance of getting to Sydney, or to any other English port for many months to come. Few British traders touch here."

"I see several Chinese junks and Malay proas. We may have a chance of getting to Banda, or to some Dutch port, or Singapore," said Tom, determined not to be done, if he could help it, by the master of the *Fox*.

"You will wish yourself on board the *Fox* if you sail in one of those craft, I can tell you," said the skipper. "Come, you had better close with me, and I'll undertake to land you at Sydney. What do you say now to 30 pounds a head, and payment for such provisions and liquors as you consume? It will be a mighty deal better than sweltering on here in this hot place, with a chance of being knocked on the head, or being brought down by fever."

Tom thought the charge exorbitant, as probably no small sum would be added for provisions. He drew Desmond and Billy aside to consult with them. They were of opinion that the captain would certainly be unwilling to pay so large an amount. They soon returned to where the master of the *Fox* was standing watching them.

"May I ask your name?" said Tom.

"Yes; it's Stubbins; I've no reason to be ashamed of it."

"Well, Captain Stubbins, we will pay you twenty pounds a-head for ourselves, and fifteen for each of our men, besides a pound a day for provisions."

"You are sharp young gentlemen, I've an opinion," said the skipper. "If you don't like my terms you will stay here until you wish you had accepted them. I shall not be away for a fortnight or more, for I only came in yesterday, and have to get rid of my cargo and take a fresh one on board."

Accompanied by Captain Stubbins they returned to the hut of the chief, who was, they found, the principal trader in the place. He and the skipper appeared to be well acquainted, and arrangements for trading were soon concluded. The *Fox* had brought a cargo of very miscellaneous articles, consisting of gorgeously coloured calicoes of patterns such as to attract the savage taste—firearms, powder and shot, axes, knives, other articles of ironware, and no small amount of execrable rum and other spirits. The skipper invited the natives on board, and took good care to ply them with liquor before he commenced trading. The chief and his people had stores collected for the purpose, consisting of birds of paradise, and monkey skins, pearls, various kinds of wood and bark and gums, drugs and spices, besides cocoa-nuts, and other fruit and vegetables.

They showed themselves keen traders; and it was evident that, should they meet with a certain sale and obtain fair prices, they would be ready to collect a large amount of valuable produce, such as there can be no doubt their country furnishes.

Captain Stubbins, having obtained all the produce which had been collected by the natives, urged them to obtain a supply from other villages in the interior; and parties set off in various directions with the goods they had brought to make purchases. Thus the midshipmen were detained a month instead of a fortnight; and, as Captain Stubbins would not abate his demands, they were finally compelled to accept them. Immediately they had agreed to his terms, the skipper's manner changed. He appeared to be anxious to accommodate them in every way in his power. He persuaded them to come and live on board, as they would be more comfortable than in the hut of the chief, and he would be ready, should the wind come fair, to put to sea at any moment, without having to wait for them. The midshipmen agreed to his proposal, carrying with them several monkeys, and cages full of birds, which the hospitable chief had given them. In return for all his kindness they presented him with their own rifles, while they gave to Nick and Pipes two seamen's muskets, and such other articles as they could spare, promising to send the honest fellows more should an opportunity occur of forwarding the things from Sydney, as a reward for their fidelity. The two Papuans and their chief were highly delighted and grateful for the gifts, which they looked upon as an ample return for the services they had rendered.

The brig looked like a menagerie, with the number of creatures which the captain and crew were taking, mostly monkeys and birds, such as were not to be found in Australia.

The natives now returned with a considerable amount of produce, which the skipper received on board, promising to send the goods in payment on shore. In the mean time he presented, with apparent generosity, some kegs of spirits to the chief and his people.

The midshipmen, Casey, and Peter had turned in for the night, which was very dark, with the wind off shore. They heard the skipper go on deck, but were soon asleep again. Not long after this they were awakened by the sound of the windlass.

"Why they must be weighing anchor!" exclaimed Tom.

He and Desmond dressed, and went on deck. The brig was already under way, standing out of the harbour.

"Why, Captain Stubbins, you've forgotten to send the goods on shore, in return for the produce which came off yesterday!"

"Bless my heart! so I have!" answered the skipper, with a hoarse laugh. "I'll pay the people the next time I come here; but they are too drunk by this time to know whether I have paid or not; and, knowing that you were in a hurry to get to Sydney, as the wind was fair, I could not resist the temptation of putting to sea."

Tom made no reply, but he had a very strong suspicion that the skipper had intended to cheat the poor natives, and such, indeed, he found to be the case.

When morning dawned, the *Fox* was far beyond the possibility of pursuit by the natives, even had the chiefs been in a condition to follow her, which in all probability they were not, owing to the cunningly bestowed kegs of liquor. The breeze continued, and the *Fox* made good way. The skipper and his mate were constantly on the look-out to avoid the rocks and shoals which so thickly dot the entrance to Torres Straits. The brig then stood to the eastward, so as to run well clear of the coral reefs which fringe the north-eastern portion of Australia. Tom and his companions were thankful at length to find themselves, after all the dangers and toils they had gone through, on their way to a place where they could hope to meet with their ship; at the same time, there was little comfort to boast of on board. Their berths were narrow recesses on either side of the little cabin, which was close in the extreme, and swarmed, moreover, with cockroaches and other creeping things, scorpions and centipedes, which had come on board with the cargo and occasionally made their appearance.

"I don't care for the beasts, hungry as they are, but it is not pleasant to know that one may be stung at any moment by them," said Desmond, as he brought his knife down on one which had fallen on the breakfast table.

As long as their fresh provisions lasted, they fared pretty well, but when these were exhausted, they were reduced to very short commons, and, as Desmond observed, "very bad of its sort." Salt junk, which had made, perhaps, more than one voyage round the world, and mouldy biscuit, constituted the chief ingredients of their meals. The midshipmen complained, but the skipper replied that he gave them the best he had. Billy especially declared that he should die of inanition. "Salt junk never agreed with me at the best of times, and this is more like old horse than beef," he groaned, as he turned about a piece of black-looking stuff at the end of his fork.

The men were quite as ill off—they could not be worse; but when they found their officers faring as badly as they were, they could not complain. The old brig sailed like a tub even in a breeze, and at last the wind dropped and they lay becalmed day after day with the sun striking down on their heads. They had found it hot enough very frequently in travelling through the country; it was here sometimes even hotter. On their journey they had had at all events abundance of food, refreshing fruits, and clear water, while now they had only tepid, thick, brackish liquid to drink. When they made faces as they poured it out at meal time, the skipper remarked with a grin—

"You're better off than if we had none, and if we are many weeks longer on the voyage maybe we shall be in that condition."

Tom suggested that as soon as a breeze sprang up, they should steer for Brisbane, or one of the northern Australian ports, but the skipper would not listen to any such proposal. He preferred keeping the open sea, free of the reefs which existed nearer in with the land. Tom observed that they were already much further to the eastward than was necessary, but Captain Stubbins, though he was evidently no great navigator, declared that he knew his way as well as any naval officer, and refused to lend Tom his quadrant to make an observation.

Billy looked very melancholy, and declared that should the voyage continue much longer he should give up the ghost.

"If we could catch some fish we should do better," said Tom. "Suppose you ask the skipper if he has got any hooks and lines."

"I doubt whether the old fellow will take the trouble to look them out if he has," observed Desmond.

Billy applied as was proposed, and greatly to his delight the mats produced a shark hook and several others of smaller size, with a supply of lines. In a few minutes all hands were busy with lines overboard with bits of pork and beef for bait. Several curious fish were hauled up, but the native crew pronounced them poisonous, and declared that those who ate them would die. This was tantalising.

While they were engaged in the sport, Toby—Desmond's favourite monkey, whom he had taught all sorts of tricks—hopped on the bulwarks to see what they were about.

"Take care what you are doing, Master Toby," sang out Desmond, springing forward to catch the monkey, who was in dangerous proximity to the shark hook line. Toby, expecting to be caught, made a spring, but having no rope to take hold of, lost his balance, and over he went into the water.

Desmond, who was fond of the little animal, threw a line, calling to him to catch hold of it, but the monkey, finding itself in the water, was too much alarmed to obey his directions.

"I'll go after him," cried Desmond, and was on the point of leaping overboard, when Toby uttered a cry of agony, a black snout was seen to rise for an instant, the white of a shark's belly glanced in the water, and Toby disappeared beneath the surface.

"The horrid brute!" exclaimed Desmond; "we will pay him off for this if we can."

The fishermen persevered, and Desmond caught a good-looking fish and Tom another.

"I've got one!" cried Billy, pulling away. "Here, Desmond, come and help me haul it in—he must be a big fellow."

They hauled away at the line, which suddenly came up very rapidly, when a shark's nose appeared above the water; it was but for a moment, and the next Billy and Desmond were sprawling on the deck with the hook bitten off some way above the shank.

"Bad luck to the beast! It's the same which ate up poor Toby," cried Desmond, as he picked himself up.

"I only hope he will not run away with any more of our hooks," said Tom. "It will be as well to haul them in before he gets hold of them."

Directly afterwards the line with the shark hook attached was seen to be pulled violently.

"Hurrah! the voracious brute has got hold of the hook intended for him," cried Tom. "Let's haul him in before he breaks clear."

All hands ran to the line. Casey made a bowline round the line, ready to slip over the shark's head as soon as it should appear above water. Could it once be got round its body, its capture would be certain.

Peter, in the mean time, got another ready to slip over its tail. The mate and some of the Malays came to the assistance of the midshipmen. Keeping a steady pull on the line, they soon brought the head of the big shark to the surface. It had bolted the hook, and was biting away at the chain secured to the shank.

"He'll be through it if we don't make haste!" cried Tom. "Quick, quick, Casey! slip the bowline round him!"

The seaman managed dexterously to do this, and the rest of the crew, hauling away, at length got its body out of the water. It was a huge creature, ten feet long. It struggled desperately, beating the water into foam alongside, so that it was some time before Peter could get a rope round its tail. That done it was a close prisoner.

"Keep all the lines taut, or he'll be wriggling through them and carry off the hook and line!" cried Tom. At last it was got up flush with the bulwarks, when down it came, knocking over poor Billy and two of the native crew. Had not Tom and Desmond rushed forward and hauled Billy out of the way, he would have been beaten into a mummy by the furious lashing of the creature's tail. For several moments it had possession of the deck, until at length Casey and Peter, having got hold of an axe apiece, rushed up and each dealt him a blow across the tail, springing back the next instant out of its way. Again and again they had to repeat their blows. It was some time before the struggles of the monster ceased.

"I shouldn't like to be in the way of that fellow's jaws," exclaimed Billy, as he examined the shark's head.

Just then the creature gave a heave, and Billy sprang back, knocking over Peter, who, in his turn, tumbling against the skipper, brought him sprawling to the deck. Captain Stubbins, getting up, furiously attacked poor Peter, as if he had tumbled against him intentionally, and, seizing a rope, began to belabour him severely. This excited Tom's and Desmond's indignation.

"You've no business to treat the poor fellow in that way," exclaimed Tom; "and I'll not allow it!"

"Who are you?" said the skipper. "This is mutiny, and I'll clap you and your companions in irons as soon as look at you."

"We are Queen's officers, and cannot allow a man under our charge to be treated as you have this poor fellow," answered Tom, in a determined tone.

The skipper, muttering a furious oath, without another word retired to his cabin, and presently re-appeared with a pistol in his hand, and another sticking out of his pocket.

Tom fixed his eye calmly upon him. "We do not fear your threats, Captain Stubbins," he said. "If you were to kill one of us, you would be guilty of murder, and would be hung to a certainty. Let me advise you, then, to take those pistols back to your cabin. We have no wish to insult you or to dispute your authority. Our messmate, who was the cause of the black's falling against you, is ready to apologise: I hope that will satisfy you."

"Really, Captain Stubbins, I am very sorry for what has happened," exclaimed Billy; "and I am sure the shark would be if he could speak, for he, after all, was the cause of your misfortune. Had he not given so unexpected a plunge, I should not have tumbled down nor knocked over Peter, and Peter would not have knocked over you. I promise you it shall not occur again, for I'll keep clear of him until we have a few delicately browned slices placed on the table. I never ate shark, but I'll undertake that it shall be better than the salt beef we have on board."

By the time Billy had finished his apology the skipper's anger had somewhat cooled down, but he still walked the deck with a pistol in his hand, and Tom and Desmond kept an eye upon him lest he should all of a sudden take it into his head to fire at one of them. At last, greatly to their satisfaction, he went below, and replaced the pistols in his berth.

Several other fish were caught after this, so that the midshipmen were not reduced to eat the shark. On cutting it open, poor Toby was discovered within, and served as a *bonne bouche* to the crew, the midshipmen contenting themselves with the fish.

As long as the calm lasted, and fish could be obtained, the passengers and crew of the *Fox* did not fare ill; but as the midshipmen were anxious to get over a disagreeable passage and rejoin their ship, they would gladly have gone on short commons and made a quick passage. The water every day became worse and diminished in quantity, and they had serious apprehensions of what might be the result.

"If we could manage to construct such a still as our friend the American doctor formed on the sand-bank, we might obtain fresh water," observed Tom.

"I'm sure I don't know exactly how it was done," answered Desmond, "but I remember the principle, and feel pretty sure that I could manage it if any one on board understands blacksmith's work. Steam we can produce fast enough from the largest tea-kettle on board; the chief difficulty will be the condenser."

When, however, Tom mentioned his idea to Captain Stubbins, the skipper laughed at him, and declared that he could not do it if he tried, as there was no blacksmith on board. A breeze springing up made it less necessary for Tom to try his experiment, and the skipper asserted that the water would hold out until they could get into Sydney. He was, however, all this time keeping much further to the eastward than was necessary. Tom and Desmond agreed that he was not aware how far off he was from land, though he would find out his mistake when he came to haul to the westward.

"Well, I do wish this voyage was over," exclaimed poor Billy, on whom the hard fare was beginning to tell, though he had wonderfully withstood the long journey across the country. "I shall be losing the number of my mess if this horrid brig doesn't make better way than she has hitherto been doing."

There seemed every probability of the voyage being prolonged. Now the wind was contrary, now it again fell calm; and even with a fair wind the tub of a brig seldom made more than five or six knots an hour. The heat of the cabin was such that the midshipmen never remained below longer than they could help, and much of the night was spent on deck. The skipper, on the contrary, seemed seasoned to any amount of heat, and was constantly below.

One night, after a supper of hard, cold, salt beef, which they could only eat by cutting it into the thinnest of slices—mouldy biscuit, rum and muddy water—they went on deck, where they found Casey and Peter, who had been taking a meal of the same description. Excepting the watch, the rest of the crew were below.

"Any chance of our getting in, sir?" asked Casey of Tom. "It is pretty well time we should be there, for I've been trying to learn what quantity of water we have got on board. As far as I can make out, we've not got a gallon at the most, and that won't keep our tongues moist for more than a couple of days."

"I doubt whether the master himself is aware of this," said Tom, "for he takes the matter very easy, and he ought to have put all hands on an allowance before this. He must do so, or we shall be dying of thirst before we drop anchor in Sydney harbour."

The brig was at this time under all sail, but the wind was light, and she was making little way. Suddenly her sails gave a loud flap against the mast.

"We are going to have another calm, I fear," said Desmond.

"I'm not quite so sure of that," said Casey. "I've been watching the sky, and it seems to me as if a thick gloom was spreading over it. I've observed a dark bank rising rapidly to the southward and eastward. Look, sir, you cannot see a star in that quarter. If I was the mate, I'd shorten sail at once."

Tom and Desmond took a survey of the horizon in the quarter to which Casey was pointing. The bank was rising rapidly; it looked, indeed, as if a dark curtain was being drawn over the sky.

"I'll point it out to the mate," said Tom.

On going aft, Tom found the mate seated close to the taffrail. Instead of keeping a look-out, he was fast asleep. Tom roused him up, and pointed out the appearance of the sky.

"I don't think it's anything," he observed, rubbing his eyes.

"It is, though," cried Tom. "Listen to that roar."

At that moment a dull rushing sound was heard, and a long streak of white was seen extending from east to south-west across the ocean.

"Turn the hands up! shorten sail!" cried Tom.

The mate repeated the order. The midshipmen sprang to the main-topsail halyards, Casey and Peter to the fore-topsail; but almost before a rope could be let go, a fierce blast struck the brig. In vain the mate tried to put the helm up. Over she heeled more and more, until the yardarms touched the water. Tom and Desmond seized hold of Billy, who had just before dropped off to sleep, and scrambled up to the weather bulwarks. Casey and Peter had been doing the same. Another instant and the brig was on her beam ends, with the water rising up to the combings of the hatchway.

Believing that the brig was going over, the midshipmen and their companions got on to the outside of the bulwarks, holding on to the main-chains. As the lee side of the sails was already under water, there was no probability that the brig would rise again. Every moment, indeed, it seemed as if she must go down. Their position was truly a fearful one.

The mate and the man at the helm had apparently slipped off into the water, as they were nowhere visible. Of the two men forward, one only succeeded in gaining the bulwarks, the other had probably shared the fate of the mate. The condition of those below was terrible. Unable to gain the deck, they were probably drowned in their berths. Although the main hatchway was closed, the fore and companion hatches were open.

The wind howled over the doomed brig; the sea was getting up. The midshipmen believed that she must quickly founder and their fate be sealed.

"We have gone through many a danger together," said Tom, to Desmond; "but I believe our time has come at last. I wish my brother Jack could have known our fate. He will be very sorry for us, and so will those at home."

"It cannot be helped," said Desmond. "I should have liked to live longer, and we are better off than the poor fellows drowning in their berths."

"What! Do you think the brig is going down?" cried Billy. "Dear me, how dreadful; can't we get something to float upon?"

"As the water is rushing into her fearfully fast, I don't see what chance there is of her floating," answered Tom. "However, we will not give up all hope while she remains above water. Perhaps, when the squall is passed over, we may manage to scramble out along the masts and cut away the topgallant yards, and get hold of some of the gratings or spare spars to form a raft."

"We must be quick about it, then," observed Desmond; "for the old craft may go down at any moment."

"While the wind is blowing as it is now, there is no use making the attempt," said Tom. "She does not appear to me to have sunk lower than she did when she first went over. She has a light cargo, and will float longer than a vessel heavily laden."

The midshipmen, however, could not talk much, for it was a difficult matter to make each other hear, what with the sound of the wind, and the sea dashing against the hull of the brig, while showers of spray fell over them. They could distinguish the figures of Casey and Peter, with another man holding on to the fore-rigging, but as yet they had been unable to exchange words with them, and were afraid to let go their hold, lest they should be washed off by the sea. The gale continued to blow furiously, and for two hours a perfect hurricane raged. It suddenly ceased, and the sea—though not so rapidly—began to go down. On this their hopes revived. Tom was anxious to ascertain Casey's opinion, and made his way to the fore-rigging.

"I'd stick to the hull, sir," answered Pat. "The brig has floated so long; she may float longer, and we had better wait until daylight before we attempt to make a raft. We may chance to slip off into the sea, or one of those savage sharks may be watching a chance to get hold of us."

Tom followed Casey's advice, and without much difficulty regained his former position. Never had a night appeared so long to any of the party. Notwithstanding their position, however, Billy was constantly dropping off to sleep, and Tom and Desmond had to hold him on, or he would to a certainty have fallen into the water. As the morning approached, the sea became perfectly calm. They would have been thankful for the breeze, which might bring some vessel to their succour. What hope could they have of surviving many hours on the bottom of the brig? The sun rose. Almost exhausted, the midshipmen could with difficulty hold on. As they turned their weary eyes in all directions, not an object was in sight.

"No land to be seen?" asked poor Billy.

"That may be a couple of hundred miles away, I fear," answered Tom.

"Any vessel coming to our help?" again inquired Billy, who, stretched on the rigging, could not lift his head.

"Without a breath of air, there is no chance of that," said Desmond; "but cheer up, Billy, perhaps a steamer will be coming this way."

"There are not many likely to be cruising in this direction," observed Tom. "However, as I have said all along, we will hope for the best."

"Oh! I'm so hungry; so thirsty," moaned the younger midshipman. "Can't you get me something to eat?"

"If we were to go into the cabin, we should find nothing," said Desmond. "The last cask of water was on the starboard side, with the hung out, and must be full of salt water by this time."

The midshipmen again relapsed into silence.

The sun rose higher and higher, its beams striking down with fury on their heads; even Tom, who was the strongest, felt that they could not hold out much longer. Hour after hour went by; still, if they were not to perish, something must be done. He asked Casey and the other men whether they had by chance any fish-hooks in their pockets? They searched, but in vain, and as to going below to look for them, they all declared that it would be impossible. The brig, however, continued to float; that was something, but Tom could not help acknowledging that they would be unable to hold out another night. Even he, as he felt the pangs of hunger and his mouth parched with thirst, began to despair. Desmond and Billy were already far gone. He gazed at the countenances of his two messmates. "They'll never see another sun rise, and shall I?" Tom began seriously to consider how best to prepare himself for his inevitable fate.

Just then Casey sang out, "A breeze! a breeze! I felt it on my cheek, a moment ago!" He endeavoured to wet his finger with his parched tongue, but could hardly do so. He held up his hand. "It's from the southward, and if we can manage to build a raft, we may yet reach the land, or get into the line of vessels running between Sydney and the northern ports."

These exclamations aroused Tom; even Desmond looked up.

"A breeze! Yes, indeed, there is, and a sail too. She is standing towards us!" He pointed to the southward. A patch of white canvas, on which the sun was shining brightly, appeared on the blue ocean. Casey, at at the same time, caught sight of it.

"Hurrah! hurrah! we are saved; she cannot fail to see us."

The cheer was taken up by his companions in misfortune. Even Billy lifted up his head.

"Is it true, Rogers, that you see a sail?" he asked.

"As true as that we are here, but we must not make too sure of being discovered," replied Tom.

"Sure, they would not be after passing us, if they once get sight of the wreck," said Desmond.

"That's just what they may not happen to do," answered Tom, who had become much less sanguine than formerly, and, hungry and worn out, was inclined to look on the dark side of things.

The breeze increased, the stranger drew nearer and nearer. Tom and Desmond were both of opinion that she was a man-of-war. Casey thought the same. The question was, however, whether she would pass them by. She was steering due west, and an object so low in the water as the hull of the brig now was, might not be visible. On she came, until she was about south-east of them, and as yet it was evident that those on board had not seen the wreck, though she herself was easily made out to be a large man-of-war steamer. Proudly she was gliding on, when her yards were braced up and she stood towards the brig.

"Thank Heaven, there is no longer any doubt about it!" cried Tom. "Rouse up, Billy, rouse up, my boy! We are all right! Here comes the steamer to our assistance, and more than that, I'm very sure that she is the *Empress*, or a craft so like her that it would be difficult to distinguish one from the other."

Poor Billy could only raise his head and smile faintly, as he ejaculated, "Thank Heaven, too!"

Tom was undoubtedly right. In a few minutes more the *Empress* was almost within hail, a boat was lowered, and with rapid strokes came pulling towards them. Mr Norman, from whom they had last parted on the coast of Papua, was in her, but he evidently did not recognise them, supposing them to be part of the brig's crew.

"Slide down, and we will catch you," he cried out, as the boat pulled close to the keel of the brig, the rigging preventing her approaching the deck side.

"Billy shall go first," said Tom, and making a rope fast round their messmate, he and Desmond lowered him down.

"Handsomely, handsomely!" cried the lieutenant, "or that boy's skin will be torn off his back. Why! who have we here?" exclaimed Mr Norman in astonishment, looking at Billy's haggard countenance and recognising him rather by his faded and tattered uniform than by his features.

"Don't you know me, sir?" asked Billy, in a faint voice. He could say no more.

"Bless my heart, is it you? and are those Rogers and Desmond?"

"Here we are, to answer for ourselves," said Tom, who, with Desmond, had managed with the aid of the rope to get down close to the boat, into which they were helped by the men, although in their weak state, so overcome were they by the exertion they had made, that they could hardly stand. They were handed into the stern sheets, and the boat then moving on took off the other three men in the same fashion. Scarcely were they dear of the brig than she righted, and as she did so began rapidly to settle down.

The midshipmen and their companions were received with hearty congratulations on board the *Empress*, by no one more so than by her captain, who was truly thankful to get back his younger brother, about whose fate he had long been intensely anxious. The *Orion*, which had been astern, now came up, and Adair was informed that his nephew was safe, although apparently in a precarious condition.

It was several days before the midshipmen could give an account of their adventures. When once they were able to use their tongues, they had very little rest, for every one was eager to know what they had done and seen, and it must be acknowledged that sometimes they were inclined to indulge their hearers with travellers' tales.

By the time they reached Sydney they were well enough to come on deck and have a look at the magnificent scenery of that superb harbour.

Of their stay there, although full of interest to themselves, but a brief account alone can be given. They were received in the kindest way by the inhabitants, and spent some weeks at the house of an old friend of the Rogers' family.

Their friends, Mr and Mrs Calvert, had several daughters, who contributed not a little to make their stay agreeable. On their first arrival the young gentlemen were compelled to keep their rooms, as it was considered that they had not sufficiently recovered to bear the excitement of society. They were not allowed to starve, however. A handsome repast had been sent up to them, and they were pledging each other in glasses of light Australian wine, which they found very refreshing, when the two captains entered the room.

"I congratulate you," said Jack, as he handed two official-looking letters, the one to Tom and the other to Desmond, respectively addressed Lieutenant Thomas Rogers and Lieutenant Gerald Desmond.

The envelopes contained their commissions.

"Those papers, I suspect, will do more to set you up than anything else," said Jack.

"Indeed they will, although they have been long enough in coming," answered Tom.

"Faith! I could get up and dance a jig forthwith," exclaimed Desmond.

"You'd better not, in case the ladies should arrive to congratulate you," observed his uncle.

"Is there no letter for me? I wonder when I shall get promoted!" asked Billy from his corner of the room.

"All in good time," answered Jack. "Perhaps you will have an opportunity before long of doing something to distinguish yourself."

Next morning the two lieutenants and Billy were able to come downstairs. Their promotion had had a wonderful effect on Tom and Desmond, who talked and joked at a great rate with their fair hostesses. As might be supposed, the young lieutenants lost their hearts, and even Billy Blueblazes, though still a midshipman, became more sentimental than he was ever before known to have been, the most juvenile of the ladies being the object of his adoration. A copy of verses, which he had begun to compose in her praise, though as yet he had not got very far in them, afforded a subject of amusement to his messmates.

Their visit on shore was, however, brought abruptly to an end, in consequence of the two ships being ordered off to New Zealand.

Chapter Thirteen.

Warfare in New Zealand—Blue-jackets from Empress and Orion land—A desperate attack on a pah—The pah captured—A night march—The party lose their way—Gain the top of a hill—Bivouac—Attacked by a large party of Maoris—A gallant defence—Many killed—Tom wounded— Nearly overwhelmed—Jack holds out bravely—Succoured in time by Adair and Desmond—Assault on the pah— Deserted by the garrison—A night march to attack a village—Desperate defence of the inhabitants—The old chief's granddaughter—Tim proposes to splice her offhand—The end of the contest—Homeward bound—Billy struck by moon-blindness—A thunderstorm—Billy restored to sight—The Orion lost sight of—The Empress reaches Spithead.

Each of the two ships carried a party of volunteers, who had been raised to assist the New Zealand colonists and regular troops in putting down the Maori rebellion, which had some time before broken out.

The part of the northern island of New Zealand in which the natives had taken up arms, is a region of mountains, hills, and valleys, with lakes and streams, and several rivers of considerable size, the Thames and the Waikato being the largest. The ground is either covered with dense forest or scrub, or long grass, and the thickly growing flax plant, which afforded cover to the Maoris in their engagements with the British troops. The rebels had frequently been defeated, but had fought bravely on all occasions, and sometimes successfully defended themselves.

The commander-in-chief had resolved to attack a strong pah, in which one of the principal chiefs, with a large body of followers, held out, and the ships of war were ordered round, that the men of the larger ones might be landed to co-operate with the troops, while the smaller vessels and gun-boats proceeded up the river to bombard the enemy's fortifications before they were assaulted. The Maoris had already shown themselves to be both brave and intelligent foes, and that, savages though they were called, they were in no way to be despised.

Jack and Adair were dining together on board the *Empress*. They intended to land next day with about eighty men and several officers, to assist the troops in the attack on the pah. It was situated on a hill some way up the river. The smaller steamers and gun-boats were to convey the troops and tow the men-of-war's boats with the blue-jackets on board. Besides the pah, strong entrenchments had been thrown up by the Maoris, reaching from the right bank of the river to a lake on the opposite side of the pah, thus completely blocking up the road. In addition to these fortifications, were two lines of rifle-pits, the most dangerous style of defence to attack in the hands of a desperate enemy. Both soldiers and sailors knew that it was no child's play in which they were to be engaged, and that, savage as was the foe, many a life might be lost before he would be compelled to succumb.

Jack was unusually grave. Adair laughed and joked, as was his custom.

"If I fall to-morrow," said Jack, "tell Julia how I longed to return home to be with her. There is a letter for her, which I wrote last night, in my desk. I have left you my executor. My worldly affairs are in good order, so that you will not have much trouble. My letter contains chiefly expressions of my devoted affection and a few directions."

"Of course I will do everything you wish, should such a misfortune happen, but I do not believe that the bullet is cast that is to deprive you of life, Jack," answered Adair. "You'll get your flag, as I hope to get mine one of these days; although I know it is possible that a bit of lead may find me out, yet the chances are if it does it won't hit a vital part. Still, in case such a thing should happen, you will bear my affectionate farewells to Lucy, though she knows that I love her as the 'apple of my eye.'"

Gerald had come on board to see Tom, and the four relatives spent the evening together. The two young lieutenants were to join in the attack.

At an early hour the next morning the expedition commenced the ascent of the river. It was sufficiently wide and deep to float steamers of considerable size, but as the current was very strong, it greatly impeded their progress. It had been arranged that simultaneous attacks should be made both above the fortifications and below them. The steamers which carried the troops destined to assault the southern end of the pah proceeded up the river.

Jack and Terence with their men, having landed on the north side of the fortifications, were directed to proceed close to the neck of land, and sweeping round, left shoulders foremost, to attack the entrenchments at the part they would then reach.

Their guide conducted them until they reached the foot of a low ridge just beyond gunshot of the enemy. Here they were to remain until a signal was made for them to commence the action.

Jack and Tom climbed up among some low brushwood which lined the top of the ridge, whence they could see into the pah about to be attacked. It was a formidable-looking place, with a deep ditch in front, and strong palisades, which must be pulled down or escaladed before it could be entered. Through his glass Jack observed a line of dark heads with musket barrels shining in the sun. These were only the outer defences; within were other entrenchments and pits, all probably concealing a host of determined enemies, for it had been reported that the pah was held by nearly a thousand men.

The blue-jackets cared very little for the difficulties and dangers before them. They were laughing and joking as usual, eagerly looking forward for the signal to assault the works. In the mean time the troops, having landed, were marching up to their destined positions, the object of the general being so completely to surround the pah that none of the garrison could escape and give further trouble.

Just then an officer arrived, directing Captain Rogers to keep his men in reserve. This was disappointment, as all hoped to be among the first in the fort.

At length the gun-boats, which had got into position, opened fire on the fort. Their shot, however, produced but little effect in the wide open space into which they fell, the enemy having numberless pits and holes in which they could protect themselves. The larger steamers were impeded by the current, and unable to get into position from whence they could discharge their shot at the pah.

At length a rocket flew up from a hill at the north end above the river, as a signal to attack. It was answered by another at the south end, when the troops, rising from behind the cover which had concealed them from the enemy, rushed forward towards the pah, those who had just landed joining them on their right. They were received by a withering fire from the fortifications, which brought many to the ground, but, nothing daunted, they pushed forward to plant their scaling ladders against the palisades. The first line was quickly gained. More soldiers, as they landed, joined the first assailants, when the enemy retreated to the centre of the redoubt, where they seemed determined to defend themselves. The troops on the south side were at the same time fighting their way across the lines of rifle-pits, from which the enemy were firing at them with deadly effect. One pit after another was taken, the occupants of some being bayoneted, while those of others, losing heart, leaped out and endeavoured to make their escape across the lake to the east, the only outlet which now remained for them.

The main body of the enemy held out in their centre fortification, which was of the strongest description. In vain the most desperate attack was made on it by a gallant party of artillery. So high were the palisades that the scaling ladders could not reach the summit. Their commanding officer, in searching for a spot through which an entrance might be made, was brought mortally wounded to the ground. Other officers fell; at length the soldiers had to retire.

"Now, Captain Rogers, will you see what you can do?" said an *aide-de-camp*, who had been despatched by the general.

"On, lads!" cried Jack. He and Adair led the way, followed at hot speed by their men. Terence had brought a number of hand-grenades, which were carried by a party under Desmond's command. It was hoped, by throwing them in, the enemy would be driven from the spot, and time allowed for the seamen to climb over the palisades. The naval party were received with as hot a fire as had met the troops. The brave Maoris, disconcerted by the repeated attacks made on them, began to waver.

Jack, in leading on his men, was struck down, and Tom, who took his place, was wounded in the left shoulder, but still continued at the head of his men.

Desmond, in the mean time, was endeavouring to throw in his hand-grenades. Although they burst in the midst of the enemy, and must have wounded several, others springing forward occupied their places, and nearly a score of blue jackets being killed or wounded, Captain Adair was obliged to retire.

Just then Jack, who had been stunned by a bullet which had grazed his head, inflicting a scalp wound, recovered, and, calling on his men to follow, led them up once more to the assault.

Adair, imitating his example, and observing that some of the palisades had been shattered by the hand-grenades, attacked them with a party of his men who carried axes. While the Maoris hurried to defend the spot thus threatened by Adair, Jack and Tom, quickly followed by the *Empress's* men, mounting their ladders, climbed over the palisades, and were inside before the enemy perceived them. Although there was yet another fortification in which the Maoris might have held out for a short time longer, finding that they were overpowered, they hoisted a white flag as a sign that they were ready to capitulate.

The troops who had been advancing to the support of the blue-jackets joined their shouts to the hearty cheers of the victors. Not another shot was fired. Several hundred Maoris, many of them being chiefs, laid down their arms. Some of the warriors declared that when they saw an officer whom they thought killed get up and lead on his men as bravely as before, it was time to give in.

The victory, however, had been dearly purchased: upwards of forty men had been killed, including four officers, and nearly a hundred wounded, while the Maoris must have lost a much larger number. Two or three hundred of the enemy, who had been unable to escape, yielded themselves prisoners of war, promising never again to take up arms against the British. They were kindly treated, and at once became on very good terms with the soldiers and blue-jackets. It was curious to see them mingling with the men round their camp fires, talking in broken English, and apparently on the most friendly terms with their late enemies. As they were totally unarmed, and their chiefs remained as hostages well guarded, there was no fear of their attempting any treachery.

A redoubt was now commenced on the captured position. Soldiers and sailors laboured together in its construction, the latter especially in bringing up the guns, ammunition, and stores required by the garrison.

Another important pah, one of the principal strongholds of the enemy, further in the interior, had now to be attacked. The steamers proceeded up the river as far as the depth of water would allow, and the troops landed, with several bodies of blue-jackets from the different ships, under their respective officers.

Jack had his second lieutenant with him, Mr Norman, his brother, Billy Blueblazes, and about sixty men, among whom were Jerry and Tim Nolan. Adair was accompanied by Desmond, his second lieutenant, and about the same number of men. While the main body of the troops were to assault the pah in front, other parties were sent round to attack it in the rear, as also to cut off the retreat of the enemy.

Jack had secured the services of a guide, a friendly native, who professed to know the country, and undertook to conduct him to a position whence he could observe the fort, and either move on to attack it, or, should the Maoris take to flight, capture or shoot them down if they refused to yield. The force destined to attack the enemy in reverse, which had furthest to go, started from the camp late in the evening. The men had had their supper, and were ready for any amount of fatigue they might be called on to endure. Tom marched alongside Jack for the first part of the distance. There was no necessity for keeping silence, as no enemy was near.

"I wish this business was over," said Tom. "There is little honour or glory to be gained. It is excessively fatiguing and unsatisfactory work."

"It has to be done, at all events," observed Jack. "As to honour and glory, these Maoris are no despicable foes, and fight as bravely as any men can do, though not always in the most civilised fashion, it must be allowed. It is to be hoped that they will in time discover the hopelessness of their cause, and sue for peace. It is sad to think how many brave officers and men have already lost their lives, and if the enemy holds out many more, too, probably will be killed. I am sorry, too, for the Maoris themselves, who, from their ignorance of our power, venture so boldly to resist it."

"It is satisfactory, at all events, to find that when they discover how hopeless is resistance, that they are inclined to become friends, as they have just shown," observed Tom.

The party were marching along a native path towards the south-east. On the left were hills covered with brushwood; on the right a more level country, partly wooded, with wide open spaces, in which grew in rich profusion the tall New Zealand flax. The shades of evening were gradually closing around. Jack was well aware that should the enemy discover the advance of his party, his position might become critical in the extreme. He therefore kept his men well together, and pushed forward as rapidly as the nature of the ground and the darkness would allow. Having proceeded some distance, he ordered them to maintain perfect silence, and to tread as lightly as possible, so that their footsteps might not be heard at a distance. He sent Tom with four men ahead, directing him to fall back should an enemy appear. Thus the little band marched on, climbing hills, diving into valleys, now crossing open spaces, now making their way through the dense scrub.

At length Jack began to suspect that they had marched much longer than was necessary to gain the desired position. He interrogated the guide, who, in his replies, showed some hesitation, and at length confessed that a considerable period had elapsed since he had come that road.

"I was afraid so," said Jack. "We must look out for a spot where we can encamp until daylight, when we shall be able to ascertain our true position. If we march further we may get beyond the pah, and be too late for the assault."

The party were then in a small valley, commanded on the left side by a wooded hill, from whence an enemy might fire down with impunity upon them. The guide asserted there was no risk of this, and advised Jack to advance for a short time longer, assuring him that they should soon reach the position he wished to gain.

He was so confident in his manner that Jack allowed him to continue ahead to lead the way. As they advanced, however, the valley narrowed so that the party might be assaulted on both sides. Still, as no enemy appeared, his belief in the guide's honesty returned. Again the valley opened out; a hill appeared on the left side, sloping gradually up from the valley. Jack determined to take possession of it, and to remain there until daylight. He accordingly sent Tim Nolan on to Tom, who had charge of the guide, directing him to halt until the main body came up, when he hoped the guide would find a path by which the hill might be ascended. Tim quickly returned, reporting that the guide had disappeared and although two of Tom's men had instantly set off in pursuit, they had been unable to find him. This looked suspicious, and made Jack more than ever anxious to get into a secure position. A path was found leading up the hill. He determined to pursue it, though steep and narrow, directing the men to be prepared for an attack, as he thought it possible that the hill might be in possession of the Maoris. In perfect silence they proceeded, two men abreast, for the path would allow of no more. At any moment they might hear the crack of the enemy's rifles, and a shower of bullets might come rattling about their ears. Still they went boldly on.

Up and up they ascended among the tall trees. It was too dark to see more than a few yards ahead; and Jack issued orders that should the enemy appear, his men were to fire a volley and charge, when he had little doubt but that the Maoris would give way. The path made several bends to avoid the steeper portions of the hill. It might easily have been defended by a determined body of natives. As none showed themselves, Jack began to hope that he should gain the position without fighting. Suddenly looking upwards, he discovered that there were no tall trees rising above him, and directly afterwards he found himself in an open space, destitute even of brushwood, on the summit of the hill. A line of palisades, partly broken down on the opposite side, convinced him that the ground was the site of an ancient pah or village; and, as it was of considerable elevation, he hoped at daylight, by obtaining a good view over the country, to ascertain the direction he must then take. It was not, he was certain, the position he had been directed to occupy, and was, he thought, a considerable way beyond it. That, however, without a guide, could only be ascertained in the morning. It was more secure than would have been a spot covered with trees, but at the same time the enemy might steal close up to it without being discovered. He therefore saw the necessity of keeping a vigilant look-out.

A short time before a detachment of military, after a long march, having halted, had become scattered, the officers going to a distance from their men, when the Maoris, who had been on the watch, fell upon them, killed one of the officers, wounded another, and killed or wounded upwards of a dozen men. To avoid a like misfortune, Jack kept his men together in the centre of the space, and placed sentries all round. The rest he allowed to lie down with their arms by their sides. As they had had supper before marching, they were not hungry. Many cried out for water, but unfortunately none had been brought. Although there was no moon the stars were bright, and enabled objects to be seen from the hill-tops at a considerable distance. Jack, though he sat down, did not venture to go to sleep, keeping his eyes and ears open. Occasionally he and Tom made a circuit of the ground, stopping every now and then to listen, but no sounds reached their ears.

"I really don't think the enemy can have discovered us," observed Tom; "or if they know where we are, they consider it too hazardous to attack us."

Jack was inclined to be of Tom's opinion; so, directing the look-out men to keep a vigilant watch, they retired to the centre of the open space, and sat down close to the rest of the people.

"It has occurred to me," said Tom, at length, "that if our guide means treachery, he will find out the Maoris and bring down a body upon us; and it is quite possible that we may even now be attacked before morning."

"I have little doubt that he did intend treachery; and that he thought, on deserting us in the valley, that we should bivouac where we then were, from failing to discover this hill. If so, the Maoris will be disappointed," answered Jack. "Whether they will venture to attack us when they find that we have gained this position, is the question."

Scarcely half an hour had passed after these remarks had been made, when suddenly, from amid the dark wood on every side, bright flashes of flame burst forth. The crack of rifles was heard, and bullets came flying over where the men lay. The sentries returned the fire. Two of them the next instant were seen to fall. Had the rest of the men been standing up, many of them must have been hit.

The sound of musketry made the party spring to their feet; and Jack, directing Mr Norman and Tom to hold their ground with half the men, led the other half towards the side of the hill from whence the firing appeared to be thickest. As he gained it he ordered half of those with him to fire a volley down the hill, aiming at any objects they could see moving, then to lie down or seek cover behind trees. As soon as the smoke had cleared away he caught sight of a number of dark forms advancing up the hill.

"Now is your time, my lads!" he sang out.

The men in reserve, while the first half were re-loading, fired at the approaching foe. Several must have been hit, but the next instant not a man was to be seen, they having evidently sought cover by springing behind the trees.

What has now been described occupied scarcely a minute of time. Jack did not forget that the enemy were on the right and left of him, and might at any moment gain the level ground and get between him and the rest of his party. He therefore thought it prudent to fall back, intending to hold the position on the side where the hill was steepest, and which might be defended by a few men, while the main body were occupied by the enemy in front.

His position was dangerous in the extreme. Completely surrounded as he was by apparently a large force, he might find it difficult to hold out until the arrival of reinforcements; indeed, it was a question whether they would be sent to him. Before he could get across the open space to the spot he had determined to hold, the enemy again appeared, this time coming boldly from under the cover of the trees, firing as they did so. They must have been somewhat surprised by the volley they received in return, as they must have supposed that the small number of men they first encountered formed the whole of the party. Still several of the seamen had been hit, and two more poor fellows killed outright. It wanted yet an hour to dawn, but it was doubtful whether Jack's position would be improved by daylight. The enemy would be able to take better aim from behind the trees at his men, exposed in the open. Had there been time he would have pulled down the old palisades and made a breastwork, which would have afforded some protection to his people, but now the Maoris had got behind the palisades and fired from thence. To attempt to leave the position would be madness. He could not hope to gain a better without having to pass through the thick of the forest, while his men would have been exposed to the fire of an almost invisible foe. His chief hope was that the Maoris would discover that the other pah was to be attacked and would retreat to assist in its defence. This, however, was only likely provided they were at no great distance from the fortification. The warm way in which he received the enemy whenever they appeared kept them in check, and sometimes, for several minutes together, it was hoped that they had retreated, but again and again they came on, though they must have suffered severely.

Many more seamen would have been hit had not Jack made them lie down and only rise on their knees to fire. It was satisfactory to him to think that it was owing to his vigilance that his whole party had not been surprised. It was very evident that they were far out-numbered by the enemy, who still seemed resolved to persevere in the attack. Dawn at length broke, and as daylight increased Jack knew that the diminished numbers of his party would be discovered by the Maoris. For some time, however, no attack was made, nor could an enemy be seen. Hopes were entertained that they really had retreated. The wounded were crying out for water, and as at some distance at the bottom of the hill, a stream could be discerned, Jerry Bird and several of the men volunteered to go down and fetch it.

Jack, of course, could not allow them to do this until he had ascertained whether the enemy had left the neighbourhood. Taking, therefore, a dozen men with him, he was making his way across the open to examine the side of the hill, when a hundred dark forms sprang from behind the brushwood, where they had concealed themselves, and opened a hot fire on him and his small party.

"Give them a volley in return, lads, and retreat!" cried out Jack.

He was promptly obeyed by all but three, who had been struck down. He and his men then rapidly retreated, re-loading as they went.

Seeing what had occurred, Tom, with a dozen more men, rushed forward to succour the captain, and greatly contributed to keep back the Maoris, who, on seeing the retreat of the first party, had begun to advance. Jack was on the point of giving the order for the whole of his party to charge, when a volley fired in his rear by a number of the enemy who had climbed up the steep sides of the hill, made him order the men to halt and deal with the fresh party of the foe. Though the latter climbed up with the greatest courage, they were unable to avoid exposing themselves. Several being shot, the rest sprang down the steep side of the hill, seeking such shelter as they could find.

More of the seamen had been wounded, and even now from behind rocks and trunks of trees the Maoris continued to fire from the foot of the hill at any of the sailors who exposed themselves. Jack was casting a look round his diminished band, when to his grief he saw Tom fall. He sent Jerry Bird to ascertain the nature of his brother's wound. Jerry, stooping down, bound up Tom's side, and directly afterwards Lieutenant Norman, who was bravely repelling, with half-a-dozen men, another assault on that side of the hill, was struck in the head by a bullet. In a short time Bird rejoined him.

"Lieutenant Rogers is badly hurt, sir; but I don't think he is mortally wounded, and as I've managed to stop the bleeding, if he can get the help of the doctor I think he'll do well, but I'm sorry to say, sir, poor Mr Norman is done for. He never moved after he fell. We've lost a good officer, sir."

"You speak the truth, Bird, but I wish you would stay by Lieutenant Rogers while you are able, and defend him to the last, should the enemy gain the hill. We must keep in check those in front. If it were not for our wounded, who would be exposed to destruction, I would charge and drive them down the hill."

A short time after this the hard-pressed band were left at peace, and the wounded who lay on the ground were lifted up and brought together, so that a small party could defend them. The sun rose, and the heat, even on the summit of the hill, became excessive. The poor wounded fellows cried out loudly for water.

"I think, sir, I might get down, and by keeping among the trees, be back with a couple of hats full before the enemy find me out," said Jerry.

"I wish, my brave fellow, that I dare let you go," answered Jack. "I feel confident that you would be discovered and shot."

It was very tantalising to see the water glittering in the distance and yet not to be able to get to it. That Jack was right was soon shown by the enemy suddenly appearing. They must have observed how many of the seamen had already been shot down, and felt confident of ultimate success. They were received with the same steady fire as before, and several were killed. Jack at last began to lose all hope of escaping, but he determined to hold out while a man remained alive. He had often been in dangerous positions, but at no time had he seen the prospect of death so near for himself and his followers. As long as his ammunition held out, however, he might still hope to keep the enemy at bay, as they appeared to have no inclination to come to close quarters. Scarcely a man of his party had escaped without one or more bullets having pierced his clothes or hat, while on each occasion, when attacked, several had fallen.

A longer pause than before ensued, when the Maoris, with loud shouts, sprang up the hill, as if resolved to surround and overwhelm the small party of seamen. Jack could not help feeling that they would too probably succeed. He, notwithstanding, cheered on his men and urged them to deliver their fire steadily at the foe.

Just then a cheer was heard at the bottom of the hill. The advancing Maoris stopped and looked over their right shoulders. The next instant a volley was fired among them, which brought several to the ground, while the rest turned and fled away to the left, many throwing down their muskets as they rushed through the brushwood. In a few minutes a party of seamen were seen coming up the hill, and Adair and Desmond dashed across the open to meet Jack with his men. Their greeting was but short, as Adair considered that the enemy should be followed and severely punished. Jack advised him not to go far lest he might fall into an ambush.

Happily Adair's party was accompanied by an assistant surgeon, who at once hastened to attend to the wounded. He gave a favourable report of Tom, whose wound he had dressed, as well as most of the other men who were wounded. The hill being cleared of the enemy, Bird with a party set off to obtain water for them, for all, even those unhurt, were suffering fearfully from thirst.

In a short time Adair returned, having found it impracticable to force his way through the bush in pursuit of the enemy. He brought in a number of muskets and pouches, showing that a panic must have seized the Maoris, who evidently fancied that the whole of the

British force was upon them. He, like Jack, had lost his way, and hearing the firing, had directed his course to the spot whence it came.

From the summit of the hill they were now able with their glasses to distinguish the pah it was intended to attack, which had been passed at a considerable distance. Stretchers were at once made for the wounded, and as it was impossible to carry the dead, graves were dug at the top of the hill, where the bodies were interred. As far as they could judge, the attack on the fort had not commenced, and they would still be in time to perform the duty assigned to them. Jack's people, though hungry and weary, and mourning for their shipmates, were still eager for the fight.

Taking a survey of the country from the hill, they were able to select a more open path than that by which they had come, towards the pah, which could be seen in the far distance. They of course had to keep a bright look-out, and to send out scouts on either hand to avoid a surprise should the natives rally and again attack them. They were at length much relieved by falling in with a body of troops sent round to join in the assault on the rear of the fort. As the road to the river was perfectly safe, the wounded were carried down to the boats to be conveyed on board the ships of war, where they could be better attended to than on shore.

Jack and Terence learned from the officer commanding the troops that the attack on the pah had been postponed, and that they were still in time to take part in it. They accordingly pushed forward until they got just beyond gunshot, where they halted, expecting the signal from the opposite side for commencing the assault. Jack and Terence advanced, under cover of the trees, to a point whence they could obtain a good survey of the whole pah through their glasses.

"Very strange!" observed Jack. "I see no people moving about, nor any in the entrenchments."

"We must not, however, be too sure of that," answered Terence. "They may show themselves fast enough when we commence the assault."

They were now joined by the major commanding the troops, and together they settled the part of the works on which to direct the chief attack.

Scarcely was this done when up went the signal rocket, and hurrying back to their men they led them forward, expecting every moment to be exposed to the enemy's fire, but still not a black head appeared, not a gun barrel was to be seen. As soon as the ground would permit, the blue-jackets and soldiers advanced at the double, creating a dust which completely surrounded them. On reaching the palisades the seamen began to climb over, while the soldiers with their axes commenced opening a space through which they could force their way. Still not a shot had been fired. They could see that the troops at the other side of the pah were engaged in similar work, and almost at the same moment both parties forced an entrance. Great was their surprise and disappointment to discover that the space was deserted. There could be no doubt that the Maoris who had attacked Jack formed part of the garrison, and that finding the formidable preparations made for their destruction, they had deserted the pah, and falling in with him on their retreat, had intended to revenge themselves by attempting to cut him off.

The general now resolved to attack two other important positions to the south of the province of Auckland, which prevented a free communication between that province and Taranki. Jack had much wished to return on board the *Empress* to ascertain how Tom was getting on, but finding that more work was to be done, he overcame his fraternal feelings, though Tom's wound caused him considerable anxiety.

The object on most occasions throughout the warfare waged with the rebel tribes was to out-flank and take the enemy in the rear. The success of these movements of course depended greatly upon the secrecy with which they were conducted. The force was now strengthened by three guns, two Armstrong six-pounders, and a naval six-pounder which Terence had brought from his ship. The tents were allowed to stand until after nightfall, and no signs were made in the British camp that the troops were about to move. Soon after dark, however, the tents were struck and the troops being paraded without sound of bugle, moved silently forward. Among them were the seamen and marines landed from the *Empress* and *Orion*. Jack and Terence marched with their men, who dragged along their gun, which from the careful way they handled it, they evidently regarded with the greatest affection.

After marching for a couple of hours, and crossing a river by a ford, they approached the enemy's position, into the rear of which it was necessary to get without being discovered. So perfect was the discipline of the troops that not a sound was uttered as they moved along, and the Maoris—not dreaming that they were in the neighbourhood—were heard calling out as usual to evince their alertness—

"I see you, ye dogs, come on and fight! come on!"

A low chuckle from the seamen was the only reply. It was not the intention of the general to attack this position, which would, by its supplies being cut off, become untenable when turned, and the column, therefore, marched on to capture a large Maori village in which were considerable stores, the whole neighbourhood being also under cultivation. The advance guard consisted of a body of forest rangers, a colonial cavalry corps. They were followed by the seamen, who, lightly clad, managed to keep up with them. For several miles they marched along a path with high ferns on either side, the country beyond being completely shut out from their view. By pushing the cavalry and light troops forward it was hoped that the village might be surrounded, and the inhabitants prevented from making their escape. Whether they would attempt to defend themselves was doubtful. It was hoped that they would see the uselessness of doing so, and orders were issued to treat them— should they yield—with all kindness and consideration. Ascending a slight elevation, the village, covering a wide extent of ground, could be seen, not a quarter of a mile away. No lights were visible in any of the huts, nor were any of the people moving about. Not a dog barked—not a sound was heard. The rangers were ordered to push forward and enter the village on one side, while the seamen and marines closed it in on the other, so that should the inhabitants take to flight they must fall into the hands of the troops who were coming up over the ridge. As the seamen were advancing, not supposing that they were even discovered, suddenly a line of fire opened on them from a range of huts in their front, the Maoris running their muskets through the walls. The defenders in the smaller huts were soon disposed of, but from a large hut in the centre a most determined resistance was made. One of the seamen had got close up to the door, when it was opened and he was hauled inside before his comrades could rescue him. There could be little doubt but that he was instantly put to death. There being nothing at hand to break in the door, the seamen again and again attempted to force an entrance, while the defenders continued to fire through the walls.

"We must not let those fellows keep us back," cried Jack, dashing forward at the head of his men, when all at once flames burst forth so furiously from every part of the building that no one could approach it.

Not another shot was fired; probably the defenders had exhausted their ammunition. Just as Jack was about to order his men to move on and attack another part of the village, the door opened and a tall Maori stalked forth, his blanket over his head to defend himself from the flames. With a dignified step he advanced towards Jack, and presenting his war axe, he yielded himself up as a prisoner. No others came out, and the roof of the hut directly afterwards fell in. For a moment the seamen stopped, gazing at the catastrophe; then the impulse seized them to rush forward and attempt to rescue their fellow-creatures, but it was too late: for an instant a blackened head rose amidst the burning embers, and in another place an arm and shoulder appeared, but directly after sank down. Not a groan, not a sound proceeded from the building. All within it had perished, together with the unfortunate seaman who had been dragged inside.

In the mean time the resistance offered in the other parts of the village had been overcome. A hut near the centre still remained, however, from which shots were fired at the assailants. Jack led on his men to attack it. As the door was closed they fired, knowing that their bullets would penetrate the walls. After the first discharge Jack called to the inmates to surrender themselves. A shout of defiance was the only reply, followed by several shots. Again the seamen fired, when dashing forward they burst open the door. No further resistance was then offered. On the ground lay stretched four Maoris, still grasping their muskets, while at the other end sat a young girl, supporting in her lap the head of an old warrior, who had been shot through the chest and who was apparently dying. Three other men—the remainder of the garrison—having thrown down their weapons, stood ready to deliver themselves up.

As Jack, followed by Bird, Nolan, and other men, approached the young girl, she said in broken English, pointing to the old warrior, "He grandfather! Soon die! No hurt him!"

"That we won't, my pretty maiden. I am sorry that he should have been wounded. We will see what the doctor can do for him."

The girl shook her head. Jack saw that not only was blood flowing from the wound in the old man's breast, but that it came gushing out from his mouth. He despatched one of his men for the surgeon, and had the old warrior lifted out of the hut, which felt hot and stifling, in the hopes that the fresh air might revive him. The girl followed and again seated herself on the ground beside her aged relative.

"Sure! isn't she a beauty!" exclaimed Tim Nolan, who had assisted in carrying the old man, and now stood regarding the girl with an expression of admiration in his countenance. "If she'd be after having me, I'd lave the sarvice and settle down in this beautiful country."

"May be she wouldn't have you, me boy," observed Jerry Bird. "If she is a chief's daughter she'll be looking after an officer."

Tim gave a hitch to his trousers. "Though I'm not an officer I'm a British seaman, and a mighty deal better looking than many an officer, no disrespect to my superiors, and I don't see why a Maori girl should turn up her nose at me or at any one like me. I'll ask the captain's lave to splice her off hand."

The surgeon soon arrived and at once pronounced the old chiefs wound mortal; indeed, before many minutes elapsed he had breathed his last.

The poor girl was inconsolable. Her mother, she said, was dead, and her father had gone off to defend a pah which it was supposed would be attacked by the British. Jack promised to protect her to the best of his power. She seemed inclined to trust him. He was greatly puzzled, however, how to act, and Tim, who made the offer to "splice her forthwith," in no way relieved him. While Jack was in this dilemma the surgeon suggested that a missionary, who had accompanied the forces as interpreter, would be the best person to whom to consign her. The excellent man, when appealed to, gladly undertook the task, promising to send her at once to his station, where she would be looked after by his wife with some other chiefs' daughters of the same age. Whether the young lady was pleased or not with this arrangement, it was difficult to say. She had been overcome with grief at the death of her relative, and she was still seen every now and then to give way to tears. Poor Tim was in despair.

"I told you so," observed Jerry Bird. "She's a young lady born, though she's not rigged out in silks and furbelows, and she's not for such as you or me. If you are a wise man you'll wait for an English or an Irish girl, for though she may have a cock-up nose, and weigh three times as much as this young beauty, she'll make you a far better wife."

The expedition was successful. The strong posts of the Maoris being captured, and the inhabitants of the whole of that part of the country having sent in their submission, the seamen and marines were able to return to their ships.

Jack and Terence, after this, were engaged in several other expeditions on shore, in which, though successful, several officers and a large number of men lost their lives. At length the Maoris discovered, what they might have known from the first, had they not been instigated by the knavish foes of England, who kept well in the background, that it was useless to contend against the power of Britain. Most of the rebel chiefs losing heart, tendered their submission, and promised in future to be faithful subjects of Queen Victoria.

The regular forces were consequently withdrawn, and the protection of the provinces left to the care of the colonial troops. Jack and Terence, greatly to their satisfaction and to that of their officers and crews, received orders to return home. They agreed, as far as they were able, to keep together, although they would have few opportunities of communicating, except by signal. They were of course to proceed under sail, except in the event of continued calms, when they would put on steam. They had filled up their bunkers with coal at Auckland, and they hoped to avoid the necessity of touching at Rio, or any other place for fuel. The *Empress* taking the lead, the two men-of-war steamed together out of Auckland harbour, when, having gained a good offing and a fair breeze springing up, all sail was made and they stood together on their homeward course.

Tom Rogers, having completely recovered, was able to resume his duty. Though he had often made Billy Blueblazes his butt, he had a sincere regard for the midshipman, who was placed in his watch.

He was one night, soon after leaving New Zealand, walking the deck, on which the full moon shone down with even more than its usual brilliancy, when he missed Billy. Leaving the poop he walked forward, when he found that he had slipped down with his back leaning against the bulwarks, just behind a gun, and was fast asleep with his eyes open.

"Well, Billy, what sort of a night is it?" he asked.

Billy, starting up, rubbed his eyes. "Very dark, sir; I've been looking out for some time, but can see nothing."

Tom was somewhat astonished at this answer.

"What's the matter with you?" he asked. "I don't like to suppose that you were asleep, but it did look like it."

"Oh, no, sir," answered Billy. "I never go to sleep if I can help it, at all events on duty. It is a dark night, although some time ago I know the moon was shining very brightly."

"You must be joking," said Tom; "why the moon is shining as brightly as ever I saw it in my life."

"On my word, I cannot see that or any thing else," answered Billy. "It seems to me that I have not been ten minutes on deck."

Just then it struck seven bells of the first watch. Again poor Billy rubbed his eyes.

"I'm very sorry, but if I've been asleep I didn't know it," he said, putting out his hands instinctively before him. "Do you know, I'm afraid I'm blind."

"I very much fear that you are," said Tom. "I'll send you below and you'd better turn in and have the doctor to see you in the morning;

maybe that your eyes are only a little dazzled just now, and you will be all to rights by that time."

Tom called another midshipman and directed him to help Billy into his hammock and let him know how he was.

From the way poor Billy walked, it was very evident that he could not see an inch before his nose, although, when he had once got his feet on the after hatchway ladder, he easily made his way to his hammock. He felt about, however, where to place his clothes, and required some assistance in turning in. When there, he heaved a deep sigh. His messmates heard him murmur, "Oh, dear me! am I going to be blind all my life?"

"I hope not Billy, but Mr Rogers says that he thinks you have been struck by moon-blindness, from sleeping with your eyes open, gazing too long at Dame Luna. You would have got in a precious scrape if that had not happened. I suppose Mr Rogers won't report you now."

Again Billy groaned. He had much rather have been reported and punished than have lost his sight, as he now supposed was the case. As soon as Tom's watch was over, he came down to see Billy, who was still groaning at the thoughts of having lost his sight. Tom did not think matters so serious. Intending to comfort Billy, he told him that in consideration of what had happened, the captain would not be severe on him.

Billy at last groaned himself to sleep. He awoke just before daylight. All was as dark as ever, but, though he began to groan again, he very soon once more dropped off to sleep. At last he was aroused by hearing the hammocks piped up. He instinctively tumbled out of his, when what was his surprise to find that he could see as well as ever, though his eyes ached a little, and he felt an uncomfortable smarting about them.

He hastily dressed and went on deck. The discovery that he could see threw him into high spirits. He began to tell every one of his wonderful recovery. In a short time the doctor heard of what had happened, and called him up to hear about it and to examine his eyes.

"I don't wish to damp your spirits, but you must not be too sure of retaining your sight," observed the surgeon.

Still Billy would not believe this, and was perfectly satisfied that he was all right. At night, however, what was his disappointment when, directly the sun set, he became blind and had to be led below to his hammock. In vain the doctor applied remedies—none of them had the slightest effect. Poor Billy was under the impression that he should have to leave the service without a chance of becoming one of England's admirals, or even obtaining his lieutenancy.

The two ships, still keeping in company, had a long spell of fine weather, but at length one evening it came on to blow hard. The wind increased during the night, and on the following day a terrific storm of thunder and lightning burst over the ship. The *Orion*, which had hitherto kept company, was lost sight off. The thunder rolled and rattled, and flash succeeded flash, each more vivid than the first. Several times it appeared as if the ship herself would be struck, as the forked lightning, bursting from the mass of dark clouds above, went zig-zagging over the summits of the waves. It was Tom's watch. Billy, who, in the day time, could do duty as well as ever, was on deck, as indeed were most of the officers, who had come up to witness the terrific strife of the elements. Billy was standing by himself, when a flash, darting through the air, passed so close to him that it appeared as if he had been struck. It was seen to flash across the deck and to lose itself in the foaming ocean. Billy uttered a cry and put his hands to his eyes. Tom asked him if anything had happened.

He answered, "No, only the lightning looked very bright. I thought I was struck."

The gale continued. No one thought of leaving the deck. Night came on, yet Billy remained moving about as he had not done for several weeks past.

"Why, Billy, you seem, to be able to see your way as well as ever," said Tom, who observed him.

"So I do; although, between the flashes, the night is dark enough, I can make out objects as well as I ever could."

Though the gale continued, the thunderstorm blew over before midnight, and Billy, with the rest of the watch below, turned in. The next evening he found to his infinite satisfaction that his moon blindness no longer existed, and the doctor and all who pretended to any scientific knowledge, were of opinion that it had been cured by the electric fluid, which had glanced across his face.

"Another half-inch, however, and we might have had a different tale to tell of you," observed the doctor.

"How so?" inquired Billy.

"Why, that you would have been turned into a piece of charcoal, instead of being restored to sight. There is something to think of, my boy, for the rest of your days."

A look-out was kept for the *Orion*. Although the gale had ceased, and the horizon was clear, she was nowhere to be seen.

"I hope they've not been after killing a pig aboard," remarked Pat. "They may not get off so cheap as we have."

"What do you mean?" asked Tim Nolan.

"Why, for what we can tell, one of them zig-zag flashes may have struck her, and sent her down to Davy's locker, or fired her magazine and blown her up sky high."

"I hope that's not Captain Adair's fate," observed Jerry Bird. "I've sailed with him many a day, and a better officer and a nicer gentleman does not command one of her Majesty's ships. When I have been on shore with him, he has been kind and friendly like, and looked after the interests of his men, seeing that they have plenty of grub when it was to be got. Never made us work when there was no necessity for it, and I should be sorry indeed if any harm happened to him."

When, however, day after day went by, and the *Orion* was not seen, even Jack began to feel somewhat anxious. She was not likely to have gone ahead of the *Empress*, which was the faster ship of the two, nor could she have dropped so far astern as to be altogether out of sight in so short a time. Still, as Jack observed to Tom, "They had often, during their early days, been inclined to give each other up for lost, and always met again," and he still hoped that such would be the case. At last, however, when the shores of Old England appeared in sight, he began to dread having to tell his sister Lucy his anxiety about her husband. Proceeding up Channel, Spithead was reached, and the *Empress* immediately received orders to go into harbour to be paid off.

Jack wisely, when writing to his wife, who, with Lucy, was staying at Lady Rogers', did not speak of his anxiety about Adair, but merely said that he had parted from him at sea and hoped the *Orion*, which had proved herself rather a slower ship than the *Empress*, would soon make her appearance at Spithead. Murray and Stella, with their children, were, he learned, at Bercaldine, for which he was sorry, as he thought he might have had the satisfaction of meeting them in the south. Some days must elapse before he could pay off his ship; he fully expected that Julia and Lucy would forthwith come down with their elder girls to Southsea, though he felt very much inclined to advise them to wait. Tom was glad to find that Archie Gordon had been promoted for more than a year, and was now serving in the Channel squadron, so that he was very likely to fall in with him before long. As Jack had expected, scarcely two days had passed since the *Empress* had dropped anchor, before Julia and Lucy arrived at Southsea, each with a little girl, the very image of their mothers. Jack had the happiness of hearing that a little Jack had been born a few months after he had left England, and was grown into a fine chubby fellow, and that if the small Lucy was the image of her mamma, still more so was young Jack that of his papa. Poor Lucy began to look very sorrowful, when day after day went by, and the *Orion* did not appear.

Chapter Fourteen.

A visit to the grave of an old friend—The three old shipmates meet—Desmond in Ireland—Lays claim to a title and estate—The post captains take to yachting—Cruises on board the Stella—A naval review—Down Channel—A gale—A run up the Irish Sea—Dublin reached—Gerald Desmond has become Viscount Saint Maur—Pleasant excursions round Dublin—Counsellor McMahon and his fair daughters—The Stella again sails, with Lord Saint Maur on board—Becalmed in the chops of the English Channel—The yacht run down by a big ship—Saint Maur disappears—Anxiety as to his fate—Dangerous condition of the yacht—Falmouth reached—Dick Stokes gives an account of the collision—Return to Ryde—The Stella sails northward—Jack appointed to the Bellona, Adair to the Empress.

Two gentlemen, who might at a glance have been known as naval officers, were walking arm-in-arm towards a church in the midst of a burial ground, standing on the summit of a hill surrounded by woods in the Isle of Wight, overlooking the Solent. The trees were green with the bright leaves of early summer, the birds flew here and there, carrying food to their young, and chirping merrily. In several places openings had been cut, affording a view of the blue water down the Channel in the direction of Calshot Castle and towards Spithead and the entrance of Portsmouth harbour.

One of the gentlemen was strongly built, of middle height, with an open, well-bronzed countenance, a few grey hairs showing themselves amid his bushy whiskers, proving that he was getting on in life. The other was tall and of slender proportions, but had equally the air and bearing of a son of the ocean.

Passing though a wicket gate, they went along a well-kept gravel path, and stopped before two monuments, side by side, one of granite, the other of white marble. On the first, surmounted by a naval crown, was engraved— "To the memory of Admiral Triton;" and on the other was inscribed the name of Deborah Triton, daughter of the late Captain Triton, RN, and sister of Admiral Triton, who lies interred by her side.

At a little distance followed two ladies, with a party of girls and boys, who had been laughing, chatting, and joking, as they ran in and out among each other, skipping and jumping, and darting here and there. Their voices were, however, hushed as they approached the wicket gate and discovered that they had arrived at the churchyard.

"I'm glad that my directions have been carried out," said Captain Adair, the taller of the two gentlemen. "It is but a poor mark, after all, of the gratitude and affection I owe to my kind old friends, by whom I have been so largely benefited. What do you think of them, Jack?"

"They are very much to my taste, and are exactly such as I should have wished to put up," answered Captain Rogers. "We shall hear what Julia and Lucy say."

Their two wives, who now arrived, were equally pleased. The elder girls, who had brought wreaths of flowers, placed them on the graves as a token of their visit—an idea of their mothers, though it is probable that neither Jack nor Terence would have thought of doing such a thing. They were still looking at the monuments when carriage wheels were heard, and a gentleman and lady soon afterwards appeared from the other side of the churchyard, and approached them, accompanied by a fine-looking lad in a midshipman's uniform.

"Why, Murray! My dear fellow! I little expected to see you here!" exclaimed Jack, hurrying forward to greet them, Adair following.

Captain Murray introduced his son, who had just left the *Britannia*, and expected every day to be appointed to a ship.

"But where have you come from, and where are you staying?" asked Jack.

"From Bercaldine, on board the *Stella*, but not the *Stella* you know. Our family having considerably increased, we had outgrown the old craft, so I purchased a fine schooner in Greenock, aboard which we arrived only yesterday evening. Finding you were staying at Ryde, we went to your house and there heard that you had gone in this direction. Guessing your object, we drove on here in the hopes of meeting you."

This of course gave Jack and Terence and their wives the greatest satisfaction. Thus the three old shipmates were again united, and together they stood round the grave of the friend they had known from their youth upwards. Of course they had a great deal to talk about, and Murray, sending away his carriage, walked back with his friends to Ryde.

Young Alick, as may be supposed, made himself agreeable to Miss Julia Rogers and Miss Lucy Adair—for both girls were christened after their mothers. He was a fine handsome boy, full of life and spirits, without a particle of bashfulness. Murray inquired after Tom and Desmond. Tom was at sea on board the *Roarer*, a lately launched composite frigate, which was expected to perform wonders both under sail and steam, but she had already had to put back twice into Plymouth with broken-down machinery and other injuries. It was hoped, however, now that she had undergone a thorough repair, that she would at all events be able to keep above water, although she might not succeed in running after a smaller enemy, or in running away from a big one.

"And where is your nephew Desmond?" asked Murray.

"In Dublin, closeted every day, he writes me word, with a lawyer, poring over papers, writing and receiving letters, and seeing witnesses. Our friend McMahon assures me that he is certain ultimately to succeed his father's relative, Viscount Saint Maur, a fifth, sixth, or seventh cousin, I believe, who has died lately. Several other persons, however, having laid claim to the title and estates, McMahon was somehow or other induced to look into the case, and became convinced that Gerald was the rightful heir. I thought that it was better while he was at sea not to unsettle his mind by holding out any great prospect of success."

"I heartily hope that he will succeed," said Jack. "He is a fine young fellow; although he has not particularly distinguished himself in the service, I'm sure he will, should he have an opportunity. I hope he'll stick to it even although he should become Viscount Saint Maur."

"I'm not very confident about his doing that, even should the Lords of the Admiralty offer to promote him," said Terence, laughing. "He may possibly imitate the example of our old school-fellow, Johnny Grant, who had been a mate eight or ten years, when, on his coming into a title, my lords wrote, offering at once to promote him and appoint him to a ship. He politely replied, that though hitherto overlooked, he was bound to thank them, but declined their noble offer. I suspect that Gerald also will prefer remaining at home looking after his property, and probably taking to himself a wife."

"Not one of our Australian friends?" asked Jack. "I didn't think he was so far gone as that."

"Oh no; he is as heart-sound as ever, but an Irishman with a title and good property is not likely to be allowed to remain in single blessedness. If he gains his cause at the trial, which is to come off shortly, I hope that he will come over and pay us a visit while the old house is undergoing repairs; we shall then probably go and stay with him during the winter. I wish that you and Murray would come and see us at Ballymacree—including, of course, Mrs Murray and Mrs Rogers and all your belongings. We have had the place put to rights, and I've bought back some of the dirty acres surrounding it which my poor father let slip through his fingers, so that it has regained some of its pristine greatness or glory, although we do not intend to carry on as was the custom in days of yore, when half-a-dozen hogsheads of claret were on tap at once, and anybody who asked for it got the key."

The young ladies were, perhaps, not quite so much interested with the account Adair gave of his nephew as were their parents, or in the prospect of seeing the future viscount. Murray feared that he should be unable to visit Ballymacree.

"We are due at Bercaldine in the autumn," he observed. "We are unwilling to disappoint the people there, who always look forward to our return, and we have been so many years absent that we do not like to remain away oftener than is necessary."

"You'll be getting your flag soon," observed Adair. "Then if you have an appointment offered you, surely you would not wish to decline it. It will be some time before Jack and I become admirals, although I shall scarcely feel myself neglected if I do not get a ship.

In the mean time, I have paid several visits to the Admiralty lately to ascertain by ocular demonstration what are my prospects, and, judging by appearances, they are not so bad as may be supposed. By my calculations, you will have your flag in a couple of years at the outside."

"How is that?" asked Mrs Murray.

"Why, I will tell you. Your husband, as well as Rogers, well knows the waiting-room to which officers are ushered, who desire to pay their respects to the First Lord of the Admiralty, to obtain anything they can out of him. When I see a number of old post-captains collected, I generally drop a remark that I have not come to ask for employment, but to inquire how soon I am likely to obtain my flag. Some one is sure to think I'm cracked, and to beg that I will say how I can possibly learn that? My reply is that I watch the way in which my seniors go upstairs. If they run nimbly up when summoned, I am pretty sure that they are likely to remain on the books as long as I am, and become admirals. But if they drag their legs up after them, and ascend at a slow pace, I feel certain that they will be placed on the retired list, or perhaps go out of the world altogether. On hearing this my respected seniors have generally cast angry looks at me; and when they are summoned I follow them out. The first few steps they go up nimbly enough, but by the fourth or fifth they drag their legs slower. Before they are out of sight I see them creeping on, and often blowing like grampuses with the unusual exertion they have made. I generally pull out my watch too, and time them, making a note also of their mode of progress. In nine cases out of ten I have found that I have been right. Since the idea first occurred to me fifty at least have gone off the list."

Mrs Murray looked somewhat grave. "I had rather Alick remained a captain than see a number of officers put aside or die to make room for him," she answered.

"Why, my dear Mrs Murray, it's all we have to look to," answered Terence. "We must grow old, it's certain; and we wish to become admirals before we are laid up with the gout, or become too decrepit to go to sea. I hear the Admiralty are taking the matter into consideration, and intend to increase the retired list, so that we juvenile captains may have a better chance of our flags."

Jack and Terence accompanied Murray and Stella down to the pier, where their boat was waiting to take them off to the yacht, which lay among several other fine craft a short distance from it. Both promised to go on board with their wives and children the next morning.

"Have you got Ben Snatchblock as master?" asked Jack.

"No, no," said Murray, laughing. "He modestly declined taking so responsible a charge, and I thought he was right, so he has subsided into the more retiring character of boatswain or second mate. I brought the craft round myself, but I intend to look out for a Cowes man as first mate and pilot, as I wish to have no anxieties, and be able to send the vessel anywhere I wish, without going in her. I propose engaging a couple of good men as master and mate, if they are to be found at this season of the year. Most of the well-known men are, of course, already engaged."

Next morning Jack and Terence, with their belongings, went down to the pier, where the *Stella's* boat, with the young Alick, was waiting to receive them with oars in the air. Young Alick gave the word to shove off in a very officer-like way, and the blades dropping flat on the water, scarcely making a splash, the boat with rapid strokes was pulled alongside the yacht. Even to Jack's critical eye she was as neat and trim as any craft could be, and, moreover, a thoroughly comfortable, wholesome vessel, as are most of the Scotch yachts.

Captain Murray stood in the gangway to hand in his guests, who were soon seated in easy camp chairs, on cloaks and cushions round the skylight. The anchor was hove up. The vessel's head, under her jib and foresail, payed round before a light air from the eastward, and the mainsail being hoisted, she stood away with several other yachts, which got under way at the same time, standing to the westward. The sky was blue and clear, and the sun shone brightly on the glittering water, just rippled over by the breeze, on the polished sides of the yacht, on the burnished brass work, and on the sails white as snow.

As the *Stella's* squaresail was set, she ran by several of the yachts, showing that, although a comfortable craft, she was no laggard. Every thing on board was perfect. The men in their white duck trousers, blue shirts, their hats having a band on which the name of the yacht was inscribed in gold letters, the decks without a spot, the ropes neatly flemished down, the bulwarks of a pale salmon colour, the stanchions, belaying-pins, and other brass work burnished to a nicety, all betokened a thoroughly well-ordered yacht, Murray himself setting the example in his own person. The yacht soon glided by the wooded heights of Binsted. The royal domain of Osborne, surrounded by trees, with its green lawn, was passed, Cowes Point rounded, and its harbour opened out full of yachts of every size and rig, some at anchor, others just getting under way. Its club house and picturesque villas, amid its groves of trees and bright lawns, were seen close on the port side; while on the opposite shore, at the mouth of Southampton Water, could be distinguished Calshot Castle, once the residence of a general well known in the Peninsular War, the predecessor in the command of the British army of Sir Arthur Wellesley. Beyond Calshot rose the tower of Eaglehurst, and to the west of it, reaching to the shore, the outskirts of the New Forest. Then further on could be seen the town of Lymington, at the end of a river meandering through mud flats, with Jack-in-the-basket at its mouth; on the Isle of Wight shore the village of Newton, peeping out amongst the thick foliage, with a line of downs rising far beyond it, extending to the extreme west of the island; and Yarmouth, with its long street and sturdy little castle at one end, a church tower rising in its midst; and Freshwater, with its attractive-looking residences, perched on the hillside; and to the west of it, its formidable but unpicturesque-looking forts, scientifically placed on heights commanding the entrance to the Solent. On the right, at the end of a long spit of sand, were the red light-houses, and the castle, and newly erected batteries of Hurst, such as no hostile fleet would dare to encounter; outside of which could be distinguished, by the broken water, the dangerous shoal of the Shingles, well marked also by its huge black buoys.

"How beautiful and curious those cliffs are coloured!" exclaimed the children in chorus, pointing to a bay in the Isle of Wight shore, a short distance inside the white Needle rocks.

"That is Alum Bay," answered Captain Murray. "The cliffs are composed of fine sand of different colours, as you see. You shall land there some day, when we will come down on purpose; and you can collect specimens for your museum. There are tints sufficient for forming a picture, and you may try who can produce the prettiest landscape with them."

Beyond Alum Bay the cliffs rose to a great height, continuing to the very end of the island, where the white Needle rocks ran out into the blue waters. The most northern one had been scarped so as to form a platform, on which a granite light-house had been built, instead of one on the downs, which, frequently shrouded by mists, was not to be seen in thick weather by vessels entering from the westward. The Needle rocks were soon rounded, while the tide was still ebbing, and Scratchel's Bay was opened out, its perpendicular cliff rising sheer out of the water several hundred feet. The pilot Murray had engaged narrated how once upon a time a transport on a dark night ran in on the rocks, and the crew and passengers escaped over the fallen masts, and succeeded in scrambling up the more accessible part of the cliff; when the morning broke the white rocks looked as if sprinkled over by lady-birds, as the soldiers in their red jackets attempted to make their way to the summit.

The yacht stood on until Christchurch Head was passed, and Bournemouth, peeping out amid pine groves, and Studland Bay, and the pretty little town of Swanage appeared, when she hauled her wind to save the tide back, as with a light breeze she would require every inch of it to reach Ryde before nightfall.

The ladies, who had never sailed down the Solent before, were delighted with the scenery. Even the three captains, who had so often come in and out through the Needle passage, declared that they enjoyed the views more than they had ever done before. The sea was so smooth that there was no necessity to bring up for luncheon, while before dinner-time the *Stella* was again inside the Isle of Wight.

It was the first of several pleasant trips the three old friends with their young people took on board the *Stella*. The captains declared that they felt like boys again, and that it was the happiest time in their lives. They had picnics at Alum Bay, Netley Abbey, on the shores of Southampton Water; they pulled up Beaulieu River in the boats, and several times sailed round the Isle of Wight.

Adair received a letter from his nephew Gerald, giving a hopeful account of his prospects.

"What do you say to a trip round to Dublin to congratulate him if he succeeds, or to console the poor fellow if he fails?" said Murray.

"You will come, I am sure, and I dare say Jack will have no objection to the trip."

Both Adair and Jack were perfectly ready to accept the invitation. Mrs Rogers expressed her readiness, and Lucy undertook to remain at Ryde to look after the children. It was finally settled that the eldest Miss Murray and Miss Rogers should go with the yacht, with, of course, young Alick, while the rest remained behind. It was arranged that the *Stella* should sail as soon as a grand review of the fleet, which was about to take place, was over. The review was in honour of a visit paid to the Queen by the Sultan of Turkey and the Pasha of Egypt, or rather to exhibit Britannia's might and power to the two Eastern potentates. Murray had invited several friends of his own, as well as of Jack's and Adair's, to see the fleet. As soon as they were on board, the *Stella* got under way, and making sail ran down the two lines, the one composed of lofty line-of-battle ships and frigates, relics of days gone by, consisting of the *Victory*, the *Duke of Wellington*, the *Donegal*, the *Revenge*, the *Saint Vincent*, the *Royal George*, the *Saint George*, the *Dauntless*, and many others, whose names recalled the proudest days of England's glory, but which were probably three or four times the size of the old ships, with a weight of metal immensely surpassing their predecessors. In the other line were cupola or turret-ships; iron-clads, with four or five huge guns, armoured screw frigates, and screw corvettes, and rams—hideous to look at, but formidable monsters—and gun-boats innumerable, like huge beetles turned on their backs, each with a single gun capable of dealing destruction on the proudest of the ancient line-of-battle ships.

The fleet getting under way stood to the eastward, when they formed in perfect order, the sailing ships taking the port line, the iron-clads the starboard. The *Stella*, having stood back to Spithead, saw them approaching, presenting a magnificent spectacle as they gradually emerged from the broad wreaths of smoke issuing from their funnels.

"Gaze at yonder sight, ladies and gentlemen; it will probably be the last time you will see the ancient and modern fleets of Great Britain placed in juxtaposition. All those magnificent three-deckers will be cut down into turret-ships, as the *Royal Sovereign* has been treated, or be broken up as useless, unable to contend with the smallest gun-boat afloat." Jack heaved a deep sigh as he spoke, adding, "I cannot help wishing at times that things had remained as they were, and that smoke-jacks and iron-clads, and rams and torpedoes, and other diabolical inventions had never been thought of; but we must take them as they are and make the best use of them in our power. In the next naval war, whenever it takes place, there will be some extraordinary naval events to be recorded. Instead of stately ships and light frigates, with their white canvas reaching to the skies, the ocean will be covered with low black monsters, darting here and there seeking for antagonists, others ramming, and some sending their vile torpedoes beneath an enemy's keel; others thundering away from their monster guns; not a few blowing up and foundering with all hands on board."

"You do not draw a pleasant picture of the battles of the future," observed Adair, laughing. "My idea is that if the British fleet is kept up as it should be, no enemy will venture out to attack it."

A strong south-westerly gale kept the *Stella* in Cowes harbour for some days, but the weather again clearing, and promising to continue fine, she sailed with a northerly breeze down Channel. By this time the ladies had got so well accustomed to the yacht that they felt themselves perfectly at home. Murray had a good supply of books, and a box from Mudie's was added to the store, with creature comforts of all sorts on board.

"After all, though we are somewhat closer packed than we should be on board a line-of-battle ship, I must say that yachting is a mighty pleasant way of spending the time," exclaimed Adair.

"Lucy, I suspect, will be well content if you are satisfied with indulging your nautical propensities in this way, instead of going afloat for three or four long years," observed Julia.

"It's as well not to think about the future. If the Lords of the Admiralty insist on my taking the command of a ship, unless I make up my mind to give up the service, I must accept their offer. However, at present, as they do not know where to find me, I am not likely to hear about the matter, even should they offer me a ship, so let's be happy while we can, and drive dull care away."

The fine weather continued until the *Stella* had got to the westward of the Eddystone, when it came on to blow pretty hard from the southward. Murray proposed running into Falmouth for the sake of the ladies.

"Will there be any danger if we continue the voyage?" asked his wife.

"Not the slightest; at the utmost we need only expect a summer gale, and though we may have a heavy sea when doubling the Lizard, once round it there will be a fair wind for us," was the answer.

The ladies were unanimous in their desire to keep at sea, so the yacht stood on her course. They certainly did repent of their resolve when the beacon on the Wolf Rock appeared on the starboard hand, and the gale came down with redoubled force, while a heavy sea got up, such as those who have often been in the chops of the Channel have experienced to their cost. The ladies, however, showed not a shadow of fear.

The yacht behaved beautifully. Murray knew that he could trust to her spars and rigging, for Ben had superintended the fitting out of the vessel, and set up each shroud and stay, and carefully examined every inch of her masts and yards, so that he felt confident that not a flaw existed. In a short time the helm was put up and the yacht stood for the passage between the Land's End and the Scilly Isles, guided by the two magnificent lights, the Longships on the starboard bow and those of the light vessel off the Seven Stones on the port.

"Why, I expected that we should have a terrible night of it; how suddenly the gale has gone down!" exclaimed Julia, not aware that the yacht had been just put before the wind, as she and the other ladies were seated on the sofas in the luxurious cabin.

The yacht, instead of heeling over as she had hitherto been doing, was on a tolerably even keel, though she gave now and then a little playful roll or pitch into the seas as she rapidly clove her way over them.

Jack came down and invited them to come on deck and see the two lights, which now appeared before them on each bow.

"Before the light vessel on the port bow was stationed there, no ship on a dark night and bad weather would willingly run through this channel," he observed. "But now it can be done as safely as in the broadest daylight, or indeed even more so."

"But I see two lights close together," said Julia.

"Yes," answered Jack, "one is at each mast-head of the vessel. It can thus be distinguished from the larger light of the Longships, which is a single light of much greater power. We can also thus distinguish the Longships from the revolving light of Saint Agnes, on the southern rocks of Scilly. You can see it low down over the port quarter. Now you see it is hidden, but it will appear again in another minute, whereas the Longships light is fixed and is always visible."

As Murray had prognosticated, the wind moderated, and the *Stella* had a pleasant run across the mouth of the Bristol Channel, sighting the Smalls light-house the next forenoon to the westward of Milford Haven on the starboard hand, the revolving Tuscar lights off the Irish coast being seen over the port quarter as it grew dark.

The wind now fell, and not until next morning did a light breeze spring up, which wafted the *Stella* along the Wicklow coast. Just before dark she brought up in the beautiful Bay of Dublin, the wind not allowing her to get into Kingstown harbour. Adair being especially anxious to go on shore to learn how it fared with Desmond, the boat was manned, and Jack accompanied him on shore, the ladies preferring to remain on board.

The eventful day of the trial was over, and already it had been decided whether Gerald Desmond was to remain a poor lieutenant with his half-pay alone to depend upon, or become the owner of a handsome estate—albeit somewhat encumbered—and the possessor of a title, at all events worth something, whatever cynics might think about the matter. Jack felt almost as much interested as Adair, and could talk of nothing else during their passage up to Dublin. The crew seemed to guess there was something in the wind, and gave way with a will. On arriving at Dublin, having sent the boat back to the yacht, they hastened up to the residence of the Counsellor McMahon, with whom Desmond was staying. They intended to sleep that night in Dublin, and to return the next morning by way of Kingstown to the *Stella*.

Captain Adair, excited by his feelings, pulled the bell with more than his usual vehemence.

"Is Counsellor McMahon at home?" he asked.

"No, your honour, the master, with the lieutenant, is out, but they'll not be long before they're home," was the answer.

Adair thought the term lieutenant augured ill. Surely the servant would speak of Desmond as the young lord if he had gained his cause. He, however, considered that it would be undignified to put the question.

"Are any of the family at home?" asked Jack, as he and Adair tendered their cards.

"Sure, yes, capt'ns; the mistress and the young ladies are at home, and they'll be mighty glad to see ye."

"Take up our cards, at all events," said Adair, "and we will wait in the hall."

The servant hurried off, while Jack and Adair stood waiting his return. The man soon returned.

"Come up, come up, capt'ns; the mistress will be mighty pleased to see you," he said, beginning, in a way no English servant would have thought of doing, to relieve them of their hats.

"Sure, I'll just take charge of these; they'll be after incommoding you in the drawing-room," he said, taking possession of their beavers by gentle force.

Adair smiled, but made no objection, although Jack was very unwilling to give up his hat.

They were ushered into a handsome drawing-room, and the lady of the house—a buxom dame—came smiling forward, while three young damsels rose and put down the work on which they had been engaged.

"The Counsellor must have had good hope of success, or he would scarcely have invited the young lieutenant to remain at his house with three such attractive girls as those are," thought Jack, as he cast a glance at the young ladies, while he advanced across the room.

Mrs McMahon received them with Irish cordiality and begged them to be seated. "I'm expecting the counsellor back every moment, and I conclude that our young friend, Lord Saint Maur, will return with him; for so I may call Lieutenant Desmond, as only a few technicalities have to be gone through before he can properly assume the title."

"Has he really gained the cause?" exclaimed Adair. "I am delighted, and grateful to Counsellor McMahon, without whose aid he would have had no chance of success."

"The counsellor has done his best, and his success has afforded him as much satisfaction as it can any one else," answered the lady, bowing. "Indeed, it is a pleasure to have been of service to so excellent and delightful a young man as your nephew, Captain Adair."

Jack looked round to see whether any of the young ladies gave responsive looks to the encomiums passed on Gerald. They all three smiled sweetly, with precisely the same expression, so that it would have required a better physiognomist than was Captain Rogers to have discovered what was passing in their innocent minds.

"I fully believe that the counsellor was disinterested in the efforts he made to forward Desmond's cause," he thought to himself.

There was not much time for conversation before Counsellor McMahon, a round, ruddy-faced, white-haired, bright-eyed man, accompanied by Desmond, entered the room. He took Adair's hand in both his own and shook it cordially, saying in a hearty tone—

"I congratulate you, my dear captain, on your nephew's success."

"Oh, don't thank me; I merely took care justice was done—that's all a lawyer has to do, from his client's point of view at all events. We triumphed, as I knew we should, notwithstanding the forgeries, the falsehood, and the perjury brought in array against us. It was truly a satisfaction to fight in the cause of your nephew, who bore his blushing honours with so much equanimity. I believe that had he lost, he would again have gone to sea and done his duty with as much zeal as ever. Whether or not he will now return to tempt once more the tempest and the waves, not to speak of round shot and bullets, is more than I can say. I only know that if I were in his place I should stick to *terra firma*. But I never much admired a life on the ocean wave, albeit feeling the deepest respect for its gallant sons who hazard their lives in their country's cause."

The lawyer ran on, scarcely allowing Jack or Adair to get in a word. At last, however, they had an opportunity of congratulating Desmond on his good fortune.

He spoke very sensibly, and was evidently in no way unduly elated by his success. Jack rightly thought that he had been too busy to dream of making love to the lawyer's fair daughters, attractive as one and all of them were.

In a few minutes supper was announced, and Jack, as the senior officer, handed down the lady of the house, Desmond modestly slipping behind and refusing to move.

Mrs McMahon was affability itself, the counsellor brimful of jokes and good humour, laughing and talking for everybody else. On hearing that Jack and Adair had part of their families on board, he insisted that they should come on shore, and allow his wife to show them the lions of Dublin and its neighbourhood. "You'll not be going away without taking a drive into Wicklow, the most perfect paradise on the surface of the globe in my opinion," he added. "Carriages shall be in waiting for the ladies, and I'll take all the trouble off your hands."

So pressing an invitation was not to be refused. The various excursions Mrs McMahon and her friends made on shore need not be described. They were delighted with all they saw of the country, if not of Dublin itself and the Misses Murray at once declared that they should be perfectly ready to come and live in Ireland, though they had seen no spot which could equal Bercaldine.

As Captain Murray had to return to Ryde to take on board his younger children, before returning to Scotland, his stay in Dublin could not be prolonged. "We can give you a berth, Saint Maur, if you are inclined to take a trip to sea again, although we will not make you keep watch unless you specially wish it," he said, scarcely expecting, however, that the invitation would be accepted.

"I shall be delighted," answered Desmond; "I can spare a couple of weeks, as McMahon will not immediately require my signature and will do all that is necessary in the mean time. I feel as fond of the sea as ever, though I shall certainly not seek for employment, and may possibly retire and start a yacht next year if I can afford it, although on that score I am not very sanguine, as the old house, I understand, requires extensive repairs, and there is much to be done on the estate: decent cottages, instead of pigsties, to be built; land to be drained and fences put up—the tenantry must be looked after."

Murray, as the only way of returning the attentions he had received from Counsellor McMahon, took him, his wife, and daughters, a trip on board the *Stella*, their cruise being along the Wicklow coast, and highly delighted the young ladies were, though the counsellor acknowledged that he was much happier when the *Stella* brought up in Kingstown Harbour, and he found himself at the dinner table in the comfortable cabin at perfect rest.

"It may be very pleasant for you young people to be tumbled and tossed about while you are gazing at the scenery of our incomparable mountains, but I confess that I can only enjoy the beauties of nature while I find my feet securely placed on *terra firma*," he remarked.

The following day, with a spanking breeze from the westward, the *Stella* sailed on her return to the Isle of Wight. The fine weather continued until she had got clear of Scilly. While she was still in the chops of the Channel it fell a dead calm, and a thick fog came on. There the *Stella* lay, drifted slowly up by one tide and to the westward again by the other. Night came on. The officers agreed that they had never been in the Channel with such perfect darkness as hung over the water. Lights were hoisted, and a look-out kept for any steamers which might be coming up or down the Channel, although to get out of their way was impossible.

Captain Murray and his friends felt far more anxiety than they would have experienced had it been blowing a strong gale. The evening was unusually chilly. Moisture dropped from the sails and rigging, preventing the ladies from remaining on deck. Adair went below, as he said, to amuse them; but Murray, Jack, and Desmond remained looking out, ready to shout should they see a steamer approaching. Of sailing vessels there was no fear, for they, as was the *Stella*, would be becalmed.

"Oh, those horrible steam-kettles! I never before so heartily hated them as I do now. If one of them was to come thundering along now, without a bright look-out, she might be into us before our lights could be seen, or our warning shouts heard!" exclaimed Adair.

"Yes, indeed," answered Murray. "I'm almost inclined to get the ladies on deck and to have a boat lowered, in case a steamer should run into us. We should have a better hope of saving their lives, for the sides of a yacht are but ill able to withstand a blow from a steamer going at even a moderate speed; and some of those steam-boat skippers, provided they make a fast passage, care very little what damage they may do to small craft in their way."

Murray, however, kept all fast. He felt ashamed of making preparations for a catastrophe which might never occur. Hour after hour passed by, while they paced the deck with their hands in their pockets, whistling for a breeze. It was very trying, as they were in a hurry to get back.

"You had better go below, Saint Maur," said Murray; "there is no necessity for us all to remain on deck."

"Thank you; but I would rather assist in keeping a look-out, while either you or Captain Rogers turn in. I'll keep moving, though, for I feel it rather cold;" and Desmond continued walking up and down at a quick pace.

Captain Rogers at last said he would go below to see what the ladies were about, and to advise them to turn in.

Scarcely had his head descended below the companion hatch than Murray exclaimed—

"Here's a breeze at last! Its dead ahead though; but it will blow away the fog, I hope, and we shall be able to keep the yacht moving."

312

Two or three minutes, however, passed before the vessel's sails, feeling the influence of the wind, enabled her to gather way. Contrary to Murray's expectations, the fog still hung as thickly as before above the water.

"Here, Murray, the ladies want you to settle a knotty point," exclaimed Jack, from the foot of the companion ladder.

Murray, seeing that the schooner had now got way on her, dived below. Not a minute after, a crash was heard. He, followed by Jack, sprang on deck, when they saw a large dark hull, with a pyramid of canvas, rising above the deck, over the after part of which a long projecting bowsprit made a rapid sweep, tearing a hole through the mainsail, and carrying away the leech. They both instinctively sprang aft to the helm, the man at which had been knocked down. In another instant the schooner was clear, and the stranger had disappeared in the darkness.

Jack, taking the helm, kept it up, for the blow had brought the vessel to the wind, while Murray hastened to ascertain what damage had been done.

"She has only torn away our bulwarks, sir," cried Ben. "Try the well," said Murray.

Ben reported—

"She's making no water, but I don't know what she may do when we go on t'other tack."

"Clear the boats ready for lowering," exclaimed Murray.

That on the port side, however, was found to have been carried away, with the davits, and now hung crushed to pieces, held by the falls. The darkness prevented all the damage which had been done from being discovered for some time. Adair had remained a minute behind his friends, to quiet the alarm of the ladies, who were naturally somewhat agitated at hearing the sound caused by the collision. He now sprang on deck, just as Murray was ordering a boat to be lowered.

"Here, Desmond," he sang out, "lend me a hand at the after falls."

"Hold on!" cried Murray; "there's no necessity for lowering a boat. There's no great damage done, after all, I hope; though it would have been the same to that big fellow, for no one on board him even hailed to know whether we required assistance."

The breeze was every instant freshening. The schooner heeled over to starboard.

"Where are you, Desmond?" exclaimed Adair.

No one answered.

"Good Heavens! where's Saint Maur?" cried Jack. "Can he have gone below?"

"That's not likely. Alick, where are you?" cried Captain Murray, the fearful idea occurring to him that some accident might have happened to his son.

"Here, sir," cried Alick, who had been forward talking to Ben Snatchblock.

Murray uttered his thanks to Heaven. "Bring a light here, and look round the deck," he exclaimed. "He may have been struck down."

The search was in vain. The man who had been at the helm seemed to have been seriously injured, as he was found senseless close to the taffrail. It became too sadly evident that the young lord had been carried overboard.

He must have been struck on the head; for no cry had been heard, and, owing to the pitchy darkness, no one had seen him. The crew, with the exception of the helmsman, having been gathered forward, they were now mustered to ascertain if any one else had been carried overboard, but all answered to their names.

Murray and Jack blamed themselves bitterly for having left the deck when they ought to have been on the look-out; but even had they remained, the collision might not have been avoided, so suddenly had the stranger appeared running down before the wind. Adair could scarcely restrain his grief for the loss of his nephew. Murray immediately put the schooner about, and then kept away, so as to pass over the spot where the accident had occurred. Desmond might possibly have recovered his senses, and kept himself afloat, either by swimming or holding on to the fragments of the boat. Every eye was strained in looking ahead and on both sides, in the possibility of discovering him; but no voice replied to their repeated shouts, and nothing was seen floating on the water. Hands were stationed at the falls to lower the boat, should it become necessary. The schooner was frequently tacked, so that every inch of water was explored; but the search was in vain.

Murray considered that it would be useless to attempt to overtake the stranger, to ascertain who she was, and to demand reparation for the damage inflicted. At length the search was abandoned as hopeless; and the yacht once more hauled her wind. She was destined, to all appearance, to have a long beat up Channel.

Jack undertook to convey the sad intelligence to his wife and Mrs Murray, who had remained below, wondering what had occurred.

It was a sad event in the trip, which had otherwise been so agreeable. The wind continued to increase, and Murray felt too anxious to go below. The schooner had been put about and was now standing to the northward. He had made up his mind to run into Falmouth to wait for a fair wind, should the weather not improve. Ben Snatchblock came aft.

"I'm afraid, sir, that the craft's making more water than she should. We'll man the pumps, if you please. She got more damage than I had supposed. The chief injury seems to be amidships, and I should not be surprised if the water wasn't coming in through one of the side berths."

Jack and Adair went below to examine into the state of affairs. One of the berths on the port side had been occupied by Desmond. On entering it, by the light from the main cabin, they saw the water gushing in every time the schooner heeled over. The ladies naturally cried out with alarm.

"It might have been far worse," said Jack. "We can soon stop this. We must shorten sail and keep as much as possible on an even keel."

The carpenter came below with some tools and planks, and set to work to try and stop the leak. The pumps were, in the mean time, kept actively going, and Ben reported that the water was decreasing. Still, the injury might be more serious than was at first apprehended, and no little anxiety was felt by all on board. It might be many hours before Falmouth could be reached.

The damage having been partially repaired, the yacht was put about. The leak in the side was anxiously watched, to ascertain if the water still came in. A small quantity was evidently forcing its way through the seams, but Murray hoped that it would not prove of much consequence, and that the pumps might easily keep the vessel clear. Still he was aware that at any moment the plank nailed on might be forced in. It seemed a wonder indeed that the yacht had not been sunk at once by the blow she had received.

"The wind's coming a point or two more to the south'ard, sir," observed Ben Snatchblock, who had been looking at the binnacle. "Half a point or so more, and we shall weather the Lizard. There are the lights, sir. I thought we should see them before long."

The mist clearing away, the fixed lights of the Lizard were seen on the port bow. Gradually the wind allowed the vessel's head to be turned more to the eastward, when they appeared broad on the bow. The schooner, by keeping close to the wind, was able to steer a course direct for Falmouth Harbour, and away she went slashing through the seas at a great rate. Just before dawn it again grew unusually dark and thick, so that even the bright lights of the Lizard could be seen but dimly. They served, however, to show that she was at a sufficient distance from the shore, but that shore was a lee one, and should any accident happen, she would be placed in great peril.

"Luff all you can," said Murray to the helmsman, for he naturally dreaded, should the wind increase, to find himself with a rocky coast under his lee, though he had confidence in his craft.

Day dawned, and the Cornish land appeared stretching along from north to south, and much nearer than had been supposed. Breakers were seen dashing over the dangerous rocks of the Manacles, close under their lee. Just then a heavy squall struck the yacht; over she heeled, and the water rushed half up her deck, pouring in through crevices which had hitherto not been discovered. To keep her away was impossible. By luffing up she ran the risk of getting into the wind. To shorten sail would have been equally hazardous. She must stand on at all risks. The yacht flew through the water, plunging into the seas like a being struggling for life. Falmouth Harbour appeared directly ahead, with Saint Anthony's light-house on the east side of the entrance. In a short time the vessel would be safe. She shot by close to the buoy of the Manacles. Murray knew that it was placed some distance outside the rocks. He drew his breath when he saw it astern; still no one looking at him would have suspected the anxiety which had weighed on his heart.

By keeping the pumps going the water did not gain sufficiently to cause much alarm, but the *Stella* had already more in her hold than was pleasant, and her stores, at all events, were likely to suffer. Murray was infinitely relieved when he was able to let go the anchor, and the yacht rode safely in the beautiful harbour of Falmouth, among numerous other craft, of various rig and size. The vessel once at rest, the water was soon pumped out, and, breakfast over, Murray and Adair went on shore to obtain a carpenter capable of thoroughly repairing the damages the vessel had received, as also to ascertain whether she had received any injury below water. Meantime Ben was engaged in mending the mainsail.

The ladies did not feel disposed to go on shore. They were, fortunately, not fully aware of the danger in which the yacht had been placed, and had as much confidence in her as ever. The carpenter and his assistants set to work without delay, and, wonderful to relate, undertook to have all damages repaired by the following day. A doctor was also sent for to attend to poor Dick Stokes, who had remained senseless since he was taken below. After some treatment, however, he recovered sufficiently to speak and to give an account of what he recollected from the moment he saw the stranger gliding stem on towards the *Stella's* beam.

"She seemed to be coming just as it were out of a fog, like a big ice mountain, and I thought it was all over with us," he said. "I'd just time to put the helm down, hoping to scrape clear of her, when I heard a crash and saw her bowsprit come sweeping along over our deck, tearing away the luff of the mainsail and knocking the port quarter-boat to pieces. I thought I saw some one hanging on to her bobstay, and the next moment that or something else struck me on the head and shoulders, and I thought I was going overboard. It seemed as if I heard a cry, but whether it was my own shout or some one else's is more than I can tell. You see, sir, it was so dark I could not make out anything more, so whether it was really a man I caught sight of or not I cannot tell. To my mind, where the schooner was struck, she bounded off from the ship, or we should have been sent to the bottom. That she was a sailing ship and not a steamer I am pretty certain, for I had time to see her canvas rising up above us."

Dick's statement, as far as the appearance of the ship was concerned, was corroborated by the rest of the crew, but so dark was it that only two had actually seen her before she was again clear of the schooner and running past astern. Dick's statement slightly raised the hopes of Adair and his friends, that Lord Saint Maur might have escaped, but why, if he had got safely on board the ship, she did not heave to to allow the yacht to speak with her was surprising. The only supposition was that she was a foreigner, and that he could not make himself understood, or that the officer of the watch, supposing that the schooner had sunk, was afraid to heave to lest he might be made answerable for the catastrophe.

Such utter disregard for human life had before been exhibited on more than one occasion, and this might be another instance. However, conjectures were useless. If Saint Maur had been saved they would hear of him again. He would either get on board a homeward-bound vessel, or land at the first port at which the ship touched. The sad subject was discussed over and over again.

"I cannot believe that Lord Saint Maur is dead," said Miss Julia Rogers, Jack's eldest daughter—who had looked the picture of woe since the accident, although she had said nothing—when she heard Dick's statement. "He was telling me of the numerous dangers he and Tom had been in, and how they had got out of them all, and I don't see why he should not have escaped from this one. Dick Stokes thinks he saw a human being clinging on to the bowsprit rigging, and that must have been Lord Saint Maur, and he being a sailor could easily have climbed up and got on board. I have been picturing to myself his doing so, and how astonished the sailors must have been when they saw him, though it was very, very cruel of them not to heave to and wait for us to receive him back again."

Stella smiled sadly at young Julia's remark. Murray was not so sanguine as his friends. He suspected that Dick had been nodding at the helm, and that had he had his eyes open, he would at all events have given the alarm before the stranger had struck the yacht. The latter, it should have been said, was sailing on a course diagonal to the ship, or she would have been more severely damaged.

The bad weather being over, the *Stella* once more sailed for the Isle of Wight. Adair had written to Counsellor McMahon an account of the accident. He had posted the letter before Dick had come to his senses, and he then expressed no hopes that his nephew had escaped. As the winds were light, the *Stella* was three days getting up the Channel, and it was not till late at night that she brought up off Ryde. The party, therefore, did not go on shore until the following morning. His aunt and young cousins were deeply grieved at hearing of Desmond's possible fate.

"It will be a sad blow for Tom and Archie when they hear of it," observed Jack to Adair. "They have as great an affection for him as we three had for each other."

Murray remained at Ryde some days longer, taking trips in various directions, and then the captain and his family, bidding adieu to their old friends, sailed, intending to go homewards along the east coast and round the north of Scotland. Young Alick, who had not yet been appointed to a ship, accompanied his father and mother.

Next morning, as Jack and Adair were seated at breakfast, Adair remarked, as he was overlooking a new navy list, just sent in from the library—

"I had no idea that Murray was so near his flag. I see that Sir Benjamin Blowhard, old Grummet, poor Marlin, and Kelson, Lord Figgins, as we used to call him, Dick Dotheboys, and Oakum, have gone the way of all flesh. I saw by yesterday's paper that Bulkhead had died in the West Indies, and two other captains senior to Murray are very ill."

"I shall rejoice at Murray's promotion," said Jack; "there is no man better suited to command a fleet."

"I cannot say that I wish for such a responsibility," observed Adair, "nor am I in any special hurry to become an admiral, though Lucy may think it a very fine thing, especially if I am made a KCB, of which, however, there is not the slightest probability. I'm much more

319

likely to be kicked off to sea and sent to the East Indies or West Coast of Africa to sun myself."

While this conversation was going forward, two long official-looking letters were received. Julia and Lucy looked at them suspiciously.

"Those very affectionate gentlemen, the Lords of the Admiralty, request that I will do them the favour of taking command of the *Bellona,* Murray's old ship," said Jack; "but whether to serve on the home station or to go out to the Antipodes they do not explain."

He handed the letter to his wife, who put her hand to her heart, as if she felt a sudden pain there.

"Oh, Jack, I did not think they would send you off again!" she said, with a deep sigh.

"And what is your despatch about?" asked Lucy, in a trembling voice.

"Of the same tenor as Jack's. Those dear old fellows offer me the command of the *Empress,* but leave me as much in the dark as Jack is as to where I am to go."

Lucy always behaved better than her sister-in-law on such occasions, although she certainly did not love her husband a bit the less.

"I hope if you are sent out to a foreign station where the children and I can live, that you will let us go too," said Lucy; "either to North America, or the Mediterranean, or Australia, or the Cape. I'm sure it will be one of these."

Julia was equally pressing to be allowed to go out to any part of the world to which the *Bellona* might be sent, but Jack would wisely make no promises.

"Well, we must go over to-morrow or the next day to commission the old tubs, I suppose," said Adair, laughing, as if the appointment was anything but satisfactory, although in reality he felt proud at being again sent to sea.

This event almost banished poor Desmond for a short time from his mind, until he received a letter from Counsellor McMahon:— "I cannot believe that our young friend has gone, after all the efforts we made to obtain his rights for him. I would rather suppose that he was even now swimming about somewhere in the chops of the Channel, or was carried off by the ship which so abominably attempted to run you down. I have always heard that midshipmen have as many lives as a cat, and though he had become a lieutenant, he had not abandoned the privilege he enjoyed in his youth. I don't believe he is lost, and I do not intend to let either of the other claimants get hold of the property, or assume his title, until I have stronger evidence of his death than your letter supplies. I remember only a short time ago, one of the Lords of the Admiralty, or some high official in the Marine Department, was carried off by a stranger running into the vessel he was on board, and it was not until several days after that he was discovered, having clung to what is called the dolphin striker—although to what part of a ship's rigging that instrument belongs I do not know, but conclude that it must be at the end of the bowsprit—and that his lordship was hooked up by the breeks, from which disagreeable position he was rescued by the sympathising crew of the vessel which had run into his."

The lawyer's confidence, although, perhaps, arising from insufficient grounds, greatly restored Adair's spirits, and he and Jack the next day went over to Portsmouth to assume command of their respective ships.

Jack applied for his brother, and the Lords of the Admiralty graciously granted his request. He was very glad to obtain Archie Gordon as his first lieutenant. He at once wrote to Murray, saying how delighted he should be to have young Alick. His letter found the *Stella* lying in Leith Roads, she having put into the Firth of Forth to remain a few days. In less than twenty-four hours young Alick appeared with a letter from his father, requesting Jack to obtain the necessary articles for his outfit. Orders were received to get both ships ready for sea with all possible expedition, and the two captains found that they were to proceed round the Cape of Good Hope to Aden, to which place further orders were to be transmitted to them.

Chapter Fifteen.

The Bellona and Empress sail for Aden—Part company—
Bellona falls in with a merchantman in distress—A gleam of
hope—Touches at the Cape and Aden, and proceeds up the
Red Sea—The Bellona reaches Annesley Bay—Jack and Tom
land at Zulla—Visit the British camp—Extensive operations
going forward—March commenced—Interview between Sir
Robert Napier and the Prince of Tigré—The British army
advances to attack Magdala—Encounters Theodore's
forces—Defeat of the Abyssinians—Theodore sends
Lieutenant Prideaux to Sir Robert—Anxious negotiations—
The captives released—Most of Theodore's troops lay down
their arms—The king holds out—Magdala stormed—
Theodore shoots himself—The fortress destroyed—Return
march—The Bellona sails for Aden.

The *Bellona* and *Empress* had been for some time at sea on their
voyage round the Cape of Good Hope. Adair had, to the last
moment before leaving England, expected to hear of his nephew,
Lord Saint Maur, but although he had instituted every possible
inquiry, no news had come of him.

He had hoped, should Gerald have been carried off by the ship
which ran down the yacht, that he would have got on board some
homeward-bound vessel or have landed at some port from whence
he could send word of his safety, which he would certainly have
done, knowing the deep anxiety which must be felt about him, not
only by his uncle, but by his many other friends.

Though sailing in company, Jack and Adair were seldom able to
communicate except by signal. They had, before crossing the line,
met with a heavy gale, during which they lost sight of each other,
though they fully expected to meet again before long, as their course
was the same and both ships sailed or steamed at a pretty equal rate.
On board the *Bellona*, which ship we must accompany, a look-out
was kept for the *Empress*, as Jack had no doubt that she was ahead.
But day after day the sun rose and set and she did not appear. The
Bellona had reached almost to the latitude of Saint Helena, when it
came on a dead calm, and as there appeared every prospect of its
continuance, Jack unwillingly—as he had been charged to husband

his coal—got up steam, and the ship clove her rapid way through the calm water.

Just as morning dawned, the look-out from the mast-head announced a vessel in sight on the starboard bow. Archie Gordon, who, as first lieutenant, was paddling about with his trousers tucked up and his feet bare, superintending the process of holystoning and washing decks, inquired the appearance of the stranger, hoping that she might prove to be the *Empress*.

"She looks as if she had met with bad weather, sir; her foremast and two topmasts are gone. She has just hoisted a signal of distress half mast high."

Tom at that moment came on deck, and on hearing this went aloft with his spy-glass to have a look at the stranger. Being satisfied that she was really in distress, on coming down, he sent young Alick to inform the captain, and asked leave to steer for her.

Jack, quickly coming on deck, ordered the ship to be headed up towards the stranger. As the *Bellona* approached, her battered condition became more clearly visible; her boats were gone, her bulwarks stove in, and she lay a mere wreck on the water; a few people only were seen on her deck, and even through the telescopes directed at them, their countenances appeared worn and haggard as they stood leaning over the bulwarks gazing at the approaching man-of-war. The *Bellona's* way was stopped, and a boat being lowered, Tom was soon alongside the wreck.

"What ship is that?" he asked, as he pulled up.

"The *Argo*, Captain Robson, from Hong-kong. In Heaven's Dame, I trust you can render us assistance," said the man, in a hollow voice. "We are short of provisions, and consumed our last drop of water yesterday. We are dying of thirst, and scarcely strong enough to keep the pumps going."

"We will give you all the help we can," said Tom, climbing up on deck, where the spectacle which met his view convinced him of the truth of the master's statement. Five of the hands, whose countenances showed the sufferings they had endured, were working away at the pumps with all the strength they possessed, the clear stream which issued from the side showing the large amount of water the vessel must be making; while several others lay about the deck, exhausted from their previous exertions. A few only remained on foot, who looked ready to sink.

Tom, on seeing this, without further inquiries sent young Alick back in the boat with a report of the state of the ship, requesting that the carpenter and his crew and some hands might return, to assist in repairing as far as possible the damages, as also that a supply of water and provisions might quickly be sent.

"Water! oh, water! Let us have water first!" cried the master.

The men bent to their oars, and quickly reached the *Bellona*. Two other boats were immediately lowered, and into Alick's, which was the first ready, a cask of water was at once put, with which he and several additional hands returned to the merchantman.

The fresh hands jumped on board and hoisted up the cask of water, at the sight of which the thirsty crew rushed aft. Tom, who stood by while the contents were drawn up, was about to hand the cup to the master. He took it and hurried below.

"It's for his wife," observed one of the men; "she's very bad."

Two boys, whose looks betrayed their sufferings, came forward, heaving deep sighs as they poured the refreshing liquid down their throats. The other men followed in turn. By this time the master returned and eagerly drank a draught of water.

"Thank Heaven!" he ejaculated. "It has restored new strength to me, but we must not let the pumps be idle, or the water will gain upon us more rapidly than it has been doing."

"Let your men rest," said Tom, leading the way to the pumps, which he with his people manned.

Meantime Alick took his place at the cask and served out more water to the master and his men, who appeared still far from satisfied.

Jack, hearing of the condition of the merchantman's crew, sent the doctor, who now stepped on board.

"Stop, my lads!" he cried, on seeing the quantity of water the men were drinking. "You may have too much of such a simple thing as pure water."

"Will you come below and see my poor wife, sir?" said the master, in an anxious tone.

The doctor at once descended with him. Meantime the provisions were handed up; some cans of hot cocoa and biscuit. The crew stood round like school children, waiting to be supplied with their food, with difficulty restraining their eagerness until the cups of cocoa were handed to them.

The food had a magical effect, and even those stretched on the deck now managed to move about.

Some spars had been towed off from the *Bellona*, and Tom at once set about fitting up a jury-mast, while the carpenter and his crew went below to try and find the leak, and see what could be done to stop it. The energetic pumping of the man-of-war's men soon reduced the water in the hold. After a long search the carpenter sent up to say he had discovered the worst leak and was already at work stopping it.

Expressions of thankfulness escaped from the crew as they heard this, and they turned to with a vigour they had not hitherto shown, to assist in the repairs going forward.

"Your wife will do very well," said the doctor, as he accompanied the master on deck. "Proper food is all she wants, and Captain Rogers will do his utmost to supply you."

"I shall be very grateful," said the master. "My poor wife would not take more than her share when she found how the men were suffering, nor touch any of mine, and, being delicate, she was almost succumbing."

The doctor having now examined the most suffering of the crew, returned on board to report their condition, and obtain the medicines he considered necessary.

Jack liberally supplied the ship with such provisions as were required to take them home. As he was anxious to lose as little time as possible, he also sent Mr Large, the boatswain, with more men on board, who, working assiduously, soon got up a fore jury-mast, repaired the bowsprit, set up topmasts, with their rigging, and bent fresh sails, all of which had been carried away.

The carpenter, having stopped the leak, set to work to patch up the bulwarks, a task the diminished crew of the *Argo* were unable to accomplish.

Captain Robson gave a sad account of their sufferings. Two men had died of fever, while three had been washed overboard during a previous gale, which had well-nigh sent her to the bottom. "By-the-by, sir," he said to Tom, "we spoke a ship just as it was commencing, but there was too much sea on to allow us to board her. She was under Dutch colours, bound out to Batavia. She began to signalise us, but all I could make out was what seemed to be 'British officer, take him on board, say'; but before I could distinguish the other flags, the gale came down on us, and we had too much to do to look after his signals, which probably did not concern us."

"Could you make out anybody on the stranger's deck?" asked Tom, eagerly.

"No, sir, for evening was coming on, and we were too far off for that. She was a big ship, high out of the water for one outward bound. However, I did not further note her, and she was soon out of sight. That very night we lost a man overboard, but it was not until some weeks later, after we had been becalmed for ten days or more, that we fell in with the gale which reduced us to the wrecked state in which you found us."

"I wish you could have made out the signal," said Tom. "Are you certain that the first part was 'British officer'?"

"No doubt about that," answered Captain Robson, "and I am certain as to the other words."

"That's strange," thought Tom. "I wonder whether Desmond could have been on board. If so, we may hear of him from Batavia, or one of the Spice Islands, to which the stranger was bound."

Tom, as he surveyed the still haggard-looking crew and their commander, felt how unfit they were to continue the voyage to England, and proposed that he should request the captain of the *Bellona* to strengthen her crew, and assist in navigating her to Saint Helena, or back to the Cape.

"No, thank you, sir," replied the stout-hearted master, "you have set me to rights, and given me food and water, and I will touch at Saint Helena or Ascension for more, if necessary, and hope, with God's providence, to find my way safe up the Mersey. I have been in a worse plight than this, and provided the leak doesn't break out again, or my men fall sick, and we don't run short of provisions and water, we shall get home in time. You will come below, sir, before you leave, and let my wife thank you. She is grateful for all you have done for us. It is the only return we can make, under present circumstances."

Tom accepted the invitation, and found the master's wife seated on sofa, and a very ladylike person she seemed to be, though she looked dreadfully ill.

"I shall be better soon, I trust, now that I have some wholesome food; but we are in God's hands. He knows best what is good for us, and we must not repine. You and your men, sir, have saved our lives, for we could not have held out many hours longer; and accept our gratitude. Our prayers will be offered for your safety wherever you go."

Tom could remain but a couple of minutes. His men having performed their tasks, had returned to the ship, and his boat was the only one alongside. He jumped into her, feeling very doubtful whether the *Argo* would ever reach home in safety.

"Go ahead!" cried the captain, as Tom's boat was hoisted up, and the *Bellona* soon left the unfortunate *Argo* astern. In a few hours, however, they met a strong breeze, which they hoped would fill her sails and waft her on her way.

In consequence of the expenditure of so much coal, the *Bellona* had to touch at the Cape. Jack and Tom made every possible inquiry for Lord Saint Maur, but they could gain no tidings of the Dutch ship.

"He must, then, have gone on to Batavia. I was in hopes that he might have put in here," observed Tom.

Jack was surprised that the *Empress* had not got in, as he thought that she could have done so before him, in consequence of his delay in assisting the *Argo*. Some time was occupied in taking in coal and fresh water and provisions, to make up for the stores supplied to the merchant vessel. He waited until the last moment he felt justified in doing, but still the *Empress* did not appear, and he then had to continue his course up the Mozambique Channel, with which he and Green were so well acquainted, and onwards to Aden.

Here he found numerous ships of war, and several transports and store ships. The troops were to proceed up the Red Sea to Massowah, a port belonging to the Egyptians, at which the Foreign Office had obtained permission for the disembarkation of the forces destined to march to the rescue of the British prisoners held captive by Theodore, the tyrant King of Abyssinia. Colliers also were arriving with coal to supply motive power, both for the transit of troops and also for the purpose of condensing from the sea fresh water for the use of men and animals.

The *Bellona*, in company with numerous other ships, now proceeded up the Red Sea. On their arrival in the neighbourhood of their destined port, they found that a convenient landing-place had been selected at Zulla, on the shore of Annesley Bay.

The *Bellona* steamed slowly in amid the vast number of vessels already arrived, and at length came to an anchor. About fourteen miles off rose the lofty mountains of Abyssinia, which it was the destined task of the British soldiers to scale. Between these mountains and the sea extended a wide plain, on which could be seen a large collection of white canvas tents, glittering in the tropical sun. Among them red dots represented the British soldiers moving about; while the banner of England floated from a tall flag-staff in their midst. A long wharf had been constructed, extending into the sea, and on both sides of it were lighters, discharging munitions of war and stores of all descriptions, while countless other boats pulled backwards and forwards between the vessels and the pier.

On shore, thousands of labourers of every hue were employed like ants, carrying the stores as they were landed to the commissariat depôts. Steam-engines were at work, rendering help of all sorts; some condensing the salt water, and, when turned into fresh fit for drinking, forcing it through pipes to the shore.

Nearly every hour fresh vessels were arriving, both from Suez and Aden, the former bringing mules and horses in vast numbers, to be employed in the transport service, the latter camels and even elephants, attended by swarthy drivers, sent out from India.

Jack, accompanied by his brother, hastened on shore to report his arrival and request to know from the commander-in-chief what service he could render. He was not a little pleased to find that a naval brigade was to be formed, and that there was a prospect of seeing some fighting and more of the wild mountainous region which rose before them, about which people in general seemed to know very little. (See note 1.)

Of course the expected warfare was the subject of conversation in the ward room, and various opinions were hazarded as to the result.

"We shall know more about it in the course of a few days, when the march is commenced," observed the first lieutenant. "The question is whether Theodore will murder his prisoners and fight to the last, or whether, when he sees the approach of so formidable a force as ours, he will deliver them up and apologise for his conduct."

"At all events we will do our best to help the soldiers," said Tom, and this sentiment was very general throughout the squadron, for never did soldiers and sailors work more cordially together.

The next morning Tom and his men, with Billy Blueblazes and Dicky Duff, now senior mate, and Alick Murray as midshipman, went on shore to join the Naval Brigade, to which, to their infinite satisfaction, they had been appointed. It was under the command of Captain Fellows. They had been but two days encamped when the order to commence the march was issued.

The army, in detachments, moved forward for the front, for which the commander-in-chief had started on the 25th of January. The first post was Senáffe, high up among the mountains, 7000 feet above the level of the sea. It was situated about two miles in front of the issue of the Komayli defile, on elevated rocky ground. To the east and west rose lofty cliffs, and in front extended a wide plain. The scenery was magnificent. Here rose masses of jagged rock, topped with acacia and juniper trees, deep valleys intervened with rushing streams, while heights extended as far as the eye could range over a vast extent of country. Tom fancied that the army was to push on without stopping, but he found that each post had to be fortified and garrisoned, for it was evident that as the expedition showed strength, so in proportion it obtained the confidence of the savage rulers of the country.

In spite, however, of the toil the army had to undergo, the men were in high spirits, the seamen especially laughing and joking as they marched along. They could carry but a small amount of provisions; and every article of baggage which could be dispensed with was left behind. In regard to provisions, they hoped that, on arriving at the next post, they would be amply provided.

Billy groaned as he went puffing and blowing up the hills.

"I believe, Mr Rogers, that we are worse off than we were when making our way through Papua."

"I can't agree with you there," answered Tom, laughing. "We found it pretty hard work, to be sure, crossing the mountains, and where for several days we had to go on short allowance of food and water, but I expect that things will mend as we advance, when we shall get into a more fertile region."

Tom was right. At length the army emerged into a broader but still barren portion of the pass, the road winding steeply for several miles along a snowy water-course, whence they passed over a plain, which, from the number of guinea fowls found there, obtained the name of "Guinea Fowl Plain." Here were seen tulip trees of enormous size, and graceful acacias, while the cactus, with its stiff, prickly leaves, grew in profusion among the rocks. Antelopes frequently bounded across the road, and it was said at no great distance elephants and wild boars were to be found. Birds of all sizes, some of the most gorgeous plumage, flashed here and there in the sunlight. Monkeys and baboons appeared scrambling among the rocks, or leaping from tree to tree, jabbering at the strangers visiting their territory.

"Those beasts remind me of Papua, though they have a very different appearance," observed Billy. "We should astonish some of our friends if we were to shoot and cook a big monkey for dinner. I shouldn't mind eating one, I know."

The monkeys, however, were generally too wary to come within gunshot; and Billy had not an opportunity of astonishing his friends, which he certainly would have done. The country through which they passed continued rugged and barren in the extreme. The villages consisted of groups of mud hovels, generally pitched on high ground, originally for defence. The inhabitants were tall, with fine figures, the men dressed in a single robe of cotton, seldom washed, their black hair plaited and covered with rancid butter. Their arms generally consisted of a crooked sword and spear, as well as a club. Such were the weapons used for ages by their ancestors; but many had matchlocks, and others even double-barrelled guns. The discipline of the army was strict, so that no plundering took place; and the inhabitants were everywhere treated with kindness. Negotiations were now opened with the Prince of Tigré, who professed a friendship for the British. Nothing created so much astonishment as the appearance of the elephants, which were followed by crowds of wondering natives, who had been under the impression that no elephant could be tamed. The arrival of a battery of Armstrong guns created equal surprise.

Notwithstanding the difficulties of the road, the gunners succeeded in carrying their guns to Adigerat. Step by step the army advanced, until Anotolo was reached, on the 2nd of March. Anotolo may be said to be half-way between Zulla and Magdala. Letters were received from the prisoners, stating that Theodore was still engaged in efforts to get up his ordnance and heavy baggage to Magdala; but, impeded by his mortar, it was not likely that he could reach that stronghold until the first week in March.

News was now brought that Kassai, Prince of Tigré, was advancing, to seek an interview with the British general, and Sir Robert accordingly marched forward, taking advantage of the cool hours of the morning to meet him on the banks of the Diab.

The force, which was accompanied by several guns, pitched their camp about half a mile from the eastern bank of the river, which it was arranged should divide the two armies.

The scenery around was magnificent, the ground sloping up gradually from the western bank of the Diab, where the Tigréan army was to be posted. The sun shone out brilliantly. The heat was excessive. About eleven o'clock the vanguard of Kassai's army was seen approaching, and a body of men hurriedly coming forward, pitched a red tent on the slope opposite to that of the strangers' camp. Just before midday the whole of the Tigréan army, with drums beating and standards flying, consisting of about 4000 men, advanced down the slope towards the river, two yellow and red flags fluttering high above their heads showing the position of the chief and his principal officers. Sir Robert had directed a tent to be raised close to the bank of the river, where the meeting was to take place.

As soon as the Abyssinians were seen advancing, the English forces got under arms. The commander-in-chief, mounted on an elephant, and followed by his staff, rode forward. The appearance of the elephant undoubtedly greatly impressed the Abyssinians, it being supposed that their own African elephants are untameable. On getting near the stream Sir Robert descended from his elephant, and mounted a horse, on which the Abyssinian line opened; and Kassai, surrounded by his chiefs and mounted on a white mule, with a crimson umbrella borne over his head, came forward, and at once fording the river approached Sir Robert. The Abyssinian chief wore a white robe embroidered with crimson round his body, and a flowered silk shirt; his black hair, carefully plaited, was drawn back from his forehead, and tied behind his neck with a ribbon. He was still in the prime of manhood. His complexion was of a dark olive hue, his countenance intellectual; but he looked careworn and anxious.

After the usual civilities had been gone through, Sir Robert conducted his guest to the tent, where a guard of honour drawn up fired a salute, evidently causing no small alarm in the chiefs mind and in that of his followers, who probably expected that the strangers would set upon them and shoot them down. On dismounting Sir Robert led the chief into the tent, when their respective officers arranged themselves on either side, the Abyssinians squatting down on the ground.

The conversation was for some time commonplace. Then the presents which had been brought were offered, among which was a fine Arab horse, the gift of Sir Robert himself. Port wine was then served out, greatly to the satisfaction of the chiefs, when all, with the exception of two of the principal officers of both parties, having retired, serious matters were entered into between Sir Robert and Kassai, who was assured that if he showed a friendly disposition and would send grain to the army, he would be handsomely rewarded.

After the prince had rested, a review of the forces took place. The regiments, whose uniforms were very picturesque, among them being seen the light blue and silver of the Bombay cavalry, the scarlet of the King's Own, the dark blue and red facings of the artillery, and the scarlet coats and white turbans of the Tenth Native Infantry, went through various manoeuvres. Now they skirmished, now formed square for receiving cavalry, and then the cavalry charged furiously at a supposed foe. The prince appeared to take especial interest in the rifled guns, and complimented the British on possessing, as he called it, "so inestimable a blessing."

Sir Robert returned the visit later in the day, and with his staff crossed the stream to the Abyssinian camp. The uniform of the soldiers of Tigré was picturesque, if not quite according to European notions. Their heads were bare, except such covering as their plaited hair afforded. They wore long white robes, embroidered with scarlet, and the greater number possessed firearms, either matchlocks or double-barrelled percussion guns, some even had double-barrelled rifles, many had pistols, and all wore long, crooked swords on the right side. A comparative few were armed with sword, spear, and shield. The cavalry, to the number of about 400 men, were mounted on shaggy ponies or mules. The discipline of the men was, however, very good, and they went through a number of movements in a most creditable manner.

The general and his staff descended close to Kassai's tent; inside it was a couch, covered with silk, on which the prince placed Sir Robert by his side. Several richly and variously dressed officers also were present, while the evening sun, shining through the red tent on the group, produced a most picturesque and scenic effect. Girls soon afterwards came in, bearing baskets with bread and curry. They were followed by others carrying huge jugs, filled with tedj, a beverage manufactured from fermented honey. Each guest was expected to drink several flasks, but as it tasted somewhat like bad small beer, they had no great satisfaction in performing the necessary ceremony. Shortly afterwards a band of six musicians, playing on long pipes, performed a wild piece of music; then a minstrel sang a war song, in which all the Abyssinians joined.

The entertainment being now considered at an end, the chief insisted on presenting Sir Robert with the gifts he had prepared. The first consisted of a silver gilt armlet, the sign of a great warrior, which was clasped round the general's arm. Then a lion's skin and mane, the mark of a fierce fighter in battle, was thrown over his shoulder, a sword was next girt on his side, and a spear and shield, intended for his use, handed to one of the *aides-de-camp*, who acted for the nonce as his armour bearer. In this guise the general had to ride back to his own camp on a mule, but fortunately by this time the shades of evening having closed in, he was prevented from exhibiting himself in so antique a guise to his troops.

Notwithstanding all the professions of friendship and promises of assistance he received, Sir Robert very wisely did not put perfect faith in the prince, but determined to fortify his posts and guard his advance, as if he was passing through the country of an enemy.

At Anotolo the army was re-distributed in divisions, to each of which a separate duty was assigned. Tom and his men marched with the second brigade of the first division. Communication was kept up the whole of the way with Zulla, and a telegraph wire laid down. On the 20th of March Sir Robert led forward his forces to Tat. From this station he began a rapid advance on Magdala. Hitherto every movement had been in preparation for that undertaking.

By the 31st March the army was at no great distance from the line of Theodore's advance posts, and scouts were frequently seen on horseback, but were too nimble to be captured. Precautions were taken against a night attack, which it was supposed Theodore would make. Several of the enemy's deserted camps were passed. The inhabitants had hitherto been universally friendly, and the Gallas, who were now gained over in consequence of the barbarous treatment they had received from Theodore, undertook to guard the passes by which the tyrant could make his way eastward.

Young Alick Murray had bravely endured the fatigues of the march; he generally kept by the side of Tom, who, indeed, was unwilling to have him out of his sight. As they and the other officers of the Naval Brigade sat round the camp fire at night, many a yarn was spun and many a merry song sung, while during the day, as they marched on, jokes were constantly cracked by the seamen, whose spirits never flagged. They were always meeting objects of some sort to interest them, while the scenery itself through which their route lay was often magnificent in the extreme. At length the Delanta Heights were reached with the river of Bashilo flowing beneath them on its course westward, hereafter to swell the waters of the mighty Nile, of which it is one of the numberless tributaries.

On either side of the valley through which the river flowed rose a series of rugged heights forming a crescent, on the eastern horn of which stood the fortress of Magdala, Theodore's supposed impregnable stronghold, while on the west was the rugged hill of Fahla, mid-way between it and the lofty plateau of Selassie. Magdala and Selassie were seen to be connected by a ridge, known as the Saddle of Islamgi, while the ridge joining Selassie to Fahla was called the Saddle of Fahla. The plateau on which Magdala stood rose to a height of upwards of 9000 feet above the sea, and 3000 above the ravines immediately surrounding it. The sides were so steep and scarped by nature that it seemed as if it would be impossible to scale them, but a closer inspection showed that two causeways led to the plateau, one from Islamgi and one from Sangalat.

Theodore's army, its size and strength unknown, was seen encamped on the spit of Islamgi. A deep ravine led into the wide valley beneath the heights occupied by the Abyssinians. Over-looking the plain of Arogi was a spur, bearing in different parts the names of Gumbaji and Afficho, which Sir Robert had resolved to occupy, so that he could operate on either side of Fahla, evidently the key of Theodore's position. The army was encamped above the Bashilo, the troops in high spirits at the thoughts that at length they were about to meet the enemy whom they had marched so many miles to encounter.

Sir Robert and his staff having crossed the river and reconnoitred the ground, at early dawn on the 10th of April the advance was ordered. As no water was to be procured between the river and the fortress, except under the enemy's fire, a band of carriers had been organised for transporting a supply for the troops, while another band marched in the rear with stretchers for the removal of the wounded.

While the greater part of the troops were toiling slowly up the steep slopes of the Gumbaji spur, which they were destined to occupy, the

Naval Brigade and a party of artillery, with the baggage of the first brigade, were making their way through the pass of the Wurki Waha valley, which it had been the intention of the general to secure by a body of infantry, and to form a road from thence up the Gumbaji spur. The latter task, through a mistake, had not been performed, nor was the issue of the pass secured. The day had been threatening, already showers of rain had begun to fall, while roars of thunder and flashes of lightning burst from the clouds. The mules of the artillery and the Rocket Brigade had just emerged from the valley, when, echoing the roar of the thunder, the report of a gun was heard, fired from the heights on which Theodore's army was posted, from whence, at the same moment, a body of warriors was seen descending, evidently with the intention of attacking the artillery. The small body of British immediately prepared for the expected encounter. Most of the enemy were on foot, though some, evidently chiefs, from their gorgeous scarlet costumes, were mounted. The Naval Brigade, hastening up the Afficho plateau, got their rocket tubes into position to receive the advancing mass of the foe. Their position was critical in the extreme. Should the Abyssinians push forward they might be overwhelmed by numbers. Without thinking of that, however, they began blazing away with their rockets, every missile telling fearfully among the crowded ranks of Theodore's troops, who, brave as they were, appeared to be thrown into confusion. Tom looked round to see what support was coming. At first the thought flashed upon him that he and his companions must be annihilated by the overwhelming hordes of barbarians rapidly approaching. Young Alick was thinking much the same thing, but no sign of fear was exhibited in his countenance.

"I suppose, Mr Rogers, we shall have a pretty hard fight for it?" he remarked; "but we won't let them take our rocket tubes at all events."

"No fear of that," answered Tom. "See, the troops are advancing."

While he was speaking, one party of the Abyssinians was seen coming towards the artillery and baggage guard, who were, however, prepared to receive them, while another larger party, taking a different course, hurried on to battle, for now over the rugged ground the red coats of the British were seen making their way as skirmishers in front, the rapid crack of their rifles being heard as they got within range of the enemy.

The troops now engaged consisted of the King's Own Regiment, with the Belochees, and a detachment of the Royal Engineers and Bombay Sappers, the men cheering lustily as they saw their enemy before them. At the same time two companies of the 4th Regiment, with a body of pioneers, attacked the enemy on their flank, pouring in rapid discharges from their Snider rifles, the rockets whizzing again and again through their ranks, while the artillery produced equal havoc.

All this time the enemy's guns had been playing on the British columns, but, owing to their elevated position, their fire was plunging, while their shot, from the use of too heavy charges of powder, ranged too far to do any harm. The seamen continued to fire their rockets among the mass of Abyssinians until the infantry, advancing, drove back the enemy, when the rockets were directed upon the summit of Fahla, where Theodore and his staff were still posted. So good was their practice, that they caused confusion and dismay, and one, it was afterwards ascertained, very nearly killed the king as he was superintending the fire of his guns.

Though defeated at all quarters again and again, the Abyssinians advanced. Masses of slain and wounded covered the plain. For three hours the contest continued, when, in spite of their heroic courage, the dark-skinned warriors were compelled to retire, at first slowly and steadily up the heights, but a panic at length appeared to seize them as they cast an eye over the ground on which they had fought, covered by heaps of their men, when the larger number took to flight. The pursuit continued for some way, but Sir Robert wisely prevented his troops from advancing too far, lest by the British having to retire, the Abyssinians might regain their courage. Wet and weary with the exertions they had gone through, the troops bivouacked for the night at the mouth of the ravine.

"I can't say I admire campaigning," observed Billy Blueblazes, as they were sitting round their camp fire on the wet ground, the lofty hills rising up above them, while the cries of the wounded Abyssinians could still be heard from various parts of the plain where they had fallen.

The British camp was kept constantly on the alert for lights were seen passing over the plain; but at length it was discovered that they were borne by Abyssinians searching for their wounded or dead countrymen.

The British wounded amounted only to twenty men. They were soon brought in. Most of them were suffering from spear wounds, received during the desperate attempt of the Abyssinians to capture the baggage. Such of the wounded Abyssinians as could be found were also brought into the British camp to be attended to by the surgeons.

Next morning Tom, with several other officers, went over the battle-field, which exhibited a scene of horror in every direction. At the entrance of the ravine, men and horses were heaped together, shot down or pierced through with sword or bayonet, ten or twelve together. Further on could be seen tracks of blood, where the wounded had attempted to crawl back to their friends or to gain the shelter of some rock or bush. Almost in the middle of the field lay the dead body of Theodore's chief general, arrayed in a splendid scarlet dress, surrounded by no less than seven chiefs who had fallen with him. Further to the right, where the firing had been at long ranges, there were fewer dead, but numbers were stretched wounded on the ground. The points towards which the rockets had been chiefly directed could be discovered by the charred masses, showing the awful death the missiles carried wherever they sped their devastating course.

The British army, having taken up their position, were again advancing to attack the enemy, when, in the far distance, a white flag was made out, borne aloft in the midst of a small party of horsemen, who came winding down the mountain path to meet them.

As they approached nearer, the uniform of a British officer was seen among them. Amid joyful cheers Lieutenant Prideaux and the missionary, Mr Flad, rode through the outposts towards Sir Robert Napier's tent. They came with a verbal message only from the king. He acknowledged that heretofore he had considered himself the most important personage in the world, but having now discovered that there were others more powerful, he consequently desired to be reconciled to his sister sovereign, the Queen of England.

Sir Robert replied that he must come and put himself into the power of her general, and that no other terms could be accepted. The British lieutenant and the missionary, with the courage of heroes, returned with this answer in writing, knowing perfectly well that the tyrant in his rage might put them to death.

Some time elapsed, when they returned with a written answer from Theodore, in which he declared it had been his intention to conquer the whole world, and that, among other things, he hoped to lead an army against Jerusalem and expel the Turks from it; consequently he was not inclined to yield to the British arms.

To this absurd missive Sir Robert sent back the answer he had returned in the morning by Lieutenant Prideaux and Mr Flad, who owned that their apprehensions of being put to death were very naturally increased. Intense was their joy and that of many others who had accompanied them on part of their journey to see a large band of persons approaching the camp, who turned out to be the envoy Mr Rassam, Consul Cameron, Doctor Blanc, and several others.

"The king," they said, "convinced that he was defeated, had put a pistol to his head and attempted to destroy himself. On it being wrested from him, he had at once ordered the release of the captives, who immediately took advantage of his permission to get out of his power." During the day a herd of cattle arrived at the outpost, sent by the savage king as a peace offering, but the animals were returned by Sir Robert, who saw the importance of exhibiting no signs of wavering. Not only was it necessary to vindicate the honour of England, but, in justice to those tribes who had assisted the British on their march, it was absolutely necessary to remove Theodore from the country, for, had he escaped, he would not have failed to have revenged himself on those who had sided with his foes.

Some of his troops had now again gathered round him, and, his spirits reviving, he led them into Magdala. The larger portion, however, deserted him, and thousands were flying from the fortress.

Sir Robert had meantime so posted his forces that, with the aid of the Gallas, no outlet for escape was left for Theodore. The second brigade occupied the heights of Selassie, when the king's troops who had not entered Magdala were ordered to lay down their arms. This they immediately did, to the number of about 10,000 men, besides whom there were 15,000 or 20,000 women and children, who had fled with their husbands and fathers from the fortress. They now hurried as fast as the narrow path would allow to the plain below, where they remained to watch the issue of the contest.

A curious scene was enacted on the Islamgi Saddle, which was occupied by a detachment of cavalry as well as by a company of infantry. Between it and Magdala, Theodore had posted his six guns. A party from the fortress issued out and dragged off two of these, but before the other four could be removed, they were completely under the fire of the British rifles. Theodore himself appeared mounted on a handsome charger, when, riding towards his foes, he began careering about, boasting of his mighty deeds, and occasionally firing off his rifle, shouting in a loud voice to any of the British officers who would come forth and meet him. He took good care, however, not to have his retreat to the fortress cut off, and all that could be done was to prevent him and his followers from making their escape down the other side of the Saddle.

Tom, with a party of his men, had joined the infantry thus engaged. As they were moving along the top of the cliff, their noses were assailed by a most fearful odour. Looking down, what was their horror to see, at the foot of the precipice to the right, a mass of human bodies in a dreadful state of corruption, some chained together, others manacled, many among them being those of old men, women, and children. They were some unfortunate prisoners who had been carried off by a party from the fortress some time before, and had been put to death in a drunken fit by Theodore the day he heard of the approach of the British. It was, in truth, a fearful sight, and increased the desire of the soldiers and sailors to inflict condign punishment on the author of the atrocity.

The end was now approaching. Sir Robert had occupied with his troops the nearest level spot to the principal gate of Magdala, and, planting his artillery and rocket battery in commanding positions, he prepared for the assault. Beyond this point, known as the Saddle of Islamgi, the rock on which the fortress stood rose 300 feet in height, with precipitous sides, a narrow, steep, and winding path leading up to it, with two lines of defence, in each of which was a narrow gateway. It was thus difficult to get a sight of the defenders, yet occasionally armed men were seen moving about, and a stubborn resistance was expected.

With a humanity worthy of imitation, Sir Robert so placed his guns that they should only act upon the gate, without running the risk of hurting the women and children still within the fortress. The two brigades now advanced, the storming party leading, and, covered by their fire, up the steep path they climbed with scaling-ladders fixed, and crowbars to burst open the gates. They were met by a hot fire from the garrison, not a man of whom could be seen. Before the stormers was a wall, surrounded by a strong and thick barricade of stout stakes, with a narrow stone gateway. On reaching this gateway the engineers, finding that the powder-bags were not forthcoming, immediately set to work with their crowbars and burst it in, when, what was their disappointment to discover a pile of large stones, twelve feet in height, and a still greater breadth, directly in front of them.

All this time they were exposed to the fire of the garrison. In vain they endeavoured to surmount a formidable barricade, but at length a party of the 33rd Regiment, turning to the right, discovered a lower part of the wall, against which a scaling-ladder was placed. Immediately mounting, they reached the top of the wall, and, leaping down, forming as they did so, attacked the garrison, who, seeing that their fortress was entered, took to flight towards the second defence. The whole regiment was quickly in, and, pressing after the fugitives, rushed through the second gateway, when, the summit of the fortress being gained, the British flag was quickly flying above it. On this the Abyssinians, throwing down their arms, asked for quarter, which was at once granted.

But what had become of the unhappy king, who had been the chief cause of the misery and suffering endured by his unhappy subjects for so many years? Stretched on the ground leading to the second gateway to the palace his body was found, with a pistol-bullet through his head, the weapon with which he had shot himself still by his side. Near the outward gateway lay several of his devoted chiefs, while the rest of his officers, throwing down their arms, endeavoured to escape. They all, however, before long, having been driven back by the Gallas, who were watching for them on the other side, were compelled to return to the fortress, where they delivered themselves up.

Taking possession of Magdala, Sir Robert, having made a hasty survey of it, collected all the Abyssinians in the centre space, and placed a strong guard over them. An anxious night now commenced, as at any moment the numberless thatched buildings which covered the heights might have been set on fire and a heavy loss of life have ensued. The two gates were carefully watched, and, owing to the admirable arrangements, no disturbance occurred. The inhabitants were desired to take their departure, while the body of

Theodore was delivered up to his unhappy queen, and was interred two days afterwards in the church of Magdala. The queen and her son then came into the British camp, where they received honourable treatment, while the inhabitants were escorted as far as was necessary towards the district where they had friends.

The fortress was afterwards destroyed, the buildings within set on fire, and the guns which had been captured were also burst into fragments. As the British army retired they could see for many a league the dense clouds of smoke which rose to the sky and hung like a funeral pall over the stronghold of the tyrant king.

"I'm thankful that we've done it, and done it well," exclaimed Tom, as he, with his blue jackets, commenced their march towards Annesley Bay.

"So am I," answered Billy Blueblazes. "For my part, I don't like this campaigning business. It may be very pleasant over a tolerable good road and plenty to eat, but I don't like having to climb these hills and to exist on short commons."

The return march was not without its dangers, for the rebel tribes were on the watch to attack any weak convoy, tempted by the plunder they hoped to obtain, and aware that the British were not likely to follow them far into their mountain fastnesses; indeed, several persons who had incautiously wandered out of the line of march were cut off and murdered.

The events of the return march need not be described. It was managed with the same skill as the advance, although the troops suffered somewhat from the storms of rain to which they were exposed.

With no small satisfaction the men of the Naval Brigade returned to their respective ships, whose crews, however, had to remain to assist in the embarkation of the troops and stores.

"Why, Mr Blewitt, you appear to have lost two stone in weight!" observed the first lieutenant when Billy made his appearance on board.

"Yes, sir," answered Billy, with a rueful countenance. "I believe I've lost three stone; but I intend to do my best to make up for it now I've got back to the ship."

Billy did not fail to keep to his intentions, and the rest of the mess declared that he ought to pay a double subscription, as he certainly consumed more than any two others among them.

"So would you if you fellows had gone through what I have done," answered Billy, and he gave, not for the first time, an account of the hardships he had endured, the weight he had carried on his shoulders, his hard fare, the steep hills he had climbed, and the abrupt descents down which he had had to make his way.

The *Bellona* remained with other ships of war until the troops had gone and the last of the stores had been embarked, when once more Annesley Bay was left to itself, in its original solitude. With a cheerful song the crew tramped round and round at the capstan, steam was got up, and the *Bellona*, proceeding out of the bay, steered for Aden, where Captain Rogers hoped to obtain intelligence of the *Empress*.

Note 1. An account of the origin of the war, and of many interesting particulars connected with it, will be found in "Our Soldiers, or Anecdotes of the Campaigns and Gallant Deeds of the British Army," published by Griffith and Farran.

Chapter Sixteen.

The Bellona proceeds down the African coast—Overhauls a suspicious dhow—Tom finds his old acquaintance Pango on board, and the dhow is condemned—After touching at Zanzibar, the Bellona proceeds to Simon's Bay—Takes troops on board for Caffraria—Major Bubsby and his family—A storm in the cabin—Billy in love—A heavy surf on the coast—Machinery gives way—Ship on a lee shore— Attempt to beat off—Billy and Angelica fall out—The Bellona anchors—In great danger—Has to stand off shore— A man on a raft picked up—Interesting information—A fire breaks out on board—The major's family lowered into a boat—He is detained by Angelica—The boat dropped astern—The fire is extinguished—The major coldly received by his officers—The troops landed—The major begs to return in the Bellona—Jack refuses, and sends him on shore—The stranger picked up reports having seen a signal on a lone rock—The Bellona reaches Simon's Bay, and sails in search of the Empress.

Jack had some hopes on touching at Aden that he might hear something of the *Empress*, but not a word had been received there of her. Taking in coal at that sandy and most unattractive of England's possessions, the *Bellona* sailed for the Cape. She actually did sail, for the wind was fair, and Jack, in common with other officers, had received orders to consume as little coal as possible. A bright lookout was kept for slavers, and several suspicious-looking craft were overhauled, but as the black-looking individuals found on board appeared to be either part of the crew or passengers, they were allowed to proceed on their voyage.

Some time before Zanzibar was reached, a dhow was seen early one morning becalmed. Some hours previously the *Bellona* had got up her steam, and was cleaving her way rapidly through the smooth water. By altering her course slightly she was thus able to pass close enough to the dhow to ascertain her character. As the sun rose, a breeze sprang up, and the dhow was seen to hoist her largest sail and to stand away for the coast. As this looked suspicious, a gun was fired, as a signal to her to heave to. The breeze was increasing, and she might lead the *Bellona* a considerable distance out of her course. She took no notice of the signal, but continued standing on as before, her crew possibly ignorant of the rate at which the dark-looking stranger could go. Full speed was put on, and the steamer gained on the chase, while Captain Rogers continued throwing shot on either side of her, with no more effect, however, than at first. As, however, the *Bellona* must ere long come up with the dhow, he refrained from firing a shot into her, which he felt very much inclined to do. At length, when the Arabs saw that they could not possibly reach the shore before they were overtaken, they lowered their huge sail, and the *Bellona* was quickly up to them.

A boat being lowered, Tom and Alick soon pulled up alongside the dhow. As Tom had no interpreter, and knew as much about Arabic as he did about the ancient Chaldean, he could only judge of the character of the craft by the appearance of things. Her crew were very picturesque gentlemen, but, judging by their looks, cut-throats every one of them, and without any ceremony would have stuck their long daggers into the English officers had they dared. But the sight of the yardarm of a man-of-war, not to speak of her guns, has a wonderful effect in keeping such gentry in order. Along the decks were arranged a party of ladies and gentlemen, most of them jet black, dressed out in a variety of fanciful costumes. Some in pink and checked shirts, others with blankets over their shoulders, and others in loose trousers and vests, but it was easy to see that they were destitute of under garments.

Nearly a score of naked fellows, with clothes only round their waists, were standing round the halyards, to which they were holding on as if they were part of the crew.

Tom inquired of the savage-looking fellow who came forward in the character of captain, where they came from.

"Zanzibar," was the answer.

"And where bound for?"

The captain pointed to the north-east, and pronounced some name not on the chart.

"Of how many men does your ship's company consist?" asked Tom, making signs by hauling away with his hands, then pretending to be rowing, and then holding up his fingers and pretending to count.

The skipper pointed to the black fellows forward and then to the Arabs, who were, indeed, alone quite sufficient for navigating the craft.

"Who are these ebony-coloured ladies and gentlemen who sit so demurely about the deck?" asked Tom, pointing to them.

The Arab replied by signs that they had paid money into his hands for their passage, and by putting his head down, as if to sleep, that they had no work to do.

"So they are passengers," observed Tom. "I understand that, and now my fine fellow, we will have a look below."

In the cabin were seated nearly a dozen young women and girls, dressed up in somewhat more elegant costumes than those on deck.

"Who are these?" asked Tom.

The captain signified that they were his wives.

"What! all of them, you old wretch?" cried Tom.

The captain smiled in return, and pressed his hand on his heart, either to signify that he was speaking the truth or that they reigned there supreme.

"We will now have a peep into the hold."

Tom, telling Alick to look out on deck, descended with two hands below. As little light reached that region, it appeared at first to be entirely empty. The odour was not very pleasant. Tom was on the point of returning on deck when he heard a groan, and hurrying to the fore part, by the dim light which came down, he distinguished a human form lying on the deck. Blood was streaming from the poor fellow's head. Tom and his men lifted him up, and discovering no one else, they carried him under the main hatchway. He quickly revived in the fresher air, and gazed with astonishment at the lieutenant and his men.

"Who are you, my poor fellow?" asked Tom, not expecting an answer.

"Me Pango; served board English man-war."

"Pango!" exclaimed Tom, remembering the black who had been rescued at Zanzibar by the *Opal*, and who, after serving on board of her for some time, was lost sight of. "I recollect all about you, and if you wish it you shall come on board again, but I want first to know who all those people are."

"All slavy, slavy," answered Pango. "Dey jus' dress up, an' when I tell cap'n dat trick no do, he cut me down an' try to kill me."

"There is no time to be lost; take him up on deck, and we will soon show the skipper that you speak the truth," said Tom.

The Arab captain looked very much taken aback, while he cast savage glances at poor Pango; he saw, however, that the game was up, and that it was useless any longer to attempt deceiving the English officer.

Tom immediately ordered him and several of his crew to get into the boat, which conveyed them on board the *Bellona*, under charge of Alick. Another boat being lowered, Pango was taken on board, with the remainder of the Arab crew, that the surgeon might look to him. Tom then returned to the *Bellona*.

Jack decided on taking all the supposed passengers on board. As soon as Pango was sufficiently recovered to act as interpreter, they were examined, when they said that they had been forced to dress up, and threatened that should they not do so they would be thrown overboard. It was ascertained that most of them had been carried away from the coast not many days before, and that they had come a long journey from the interior. Pango had been picked up from a canoe while fishing off the shore, and carried away.

The evidence was so clear that Jack, without hesitation, destroyed the dhow, which could not be towed all the way to Zanzibar, resolving to risk all the consequences.

During the passage several other dhows were met with, but although there were blacks on board, there was not sufficient evidence to prove that they were slaves. It convinced Jack, however, that the abominable trade was still carried on, that thousands of Africans were carried off to Arabia, Persia, and other parts of Asia, to toil in hopeless slavery for the remainder of their lives, and that it would be necessary to make yet more strenuous efforts than before if it was to be effectually put down. He remembered, too, all the horrors he had witnessed and heard of in connection with the slave trade in the interior, when whole villages and districts were depopulated, and numbers were killed or perished from hunger, besides those captured by the Arabs.

Pango was of assistance in enabling him to condemn two dhows, besides those he was compelled to let escape. The black improved rapidly in English, or rather recovered what he had lost. Jack asked where he wished to be put on shore.

"Me no go shore 'gain," answered Pango. "May be slave fellow take me 'gain. Me go where ship go. Me stay board. Pango now sailor man."

He was accordingly entered as one of the crew, greatly to his delight.

Jack inquired for his brother Bango.

Pango's countenance became very sad. "Do slavy man take him. Me tinke cut him troat. Me not see him now five years;" and poor Pango burst into tears as he thought of the fate which had overtaken Bango, showing that some Africans, at all events, have as great an affection for their relatives as have white men for theirs.

On arriving at Zanzibar, Jack handed over the Arab crew to the authorities, to be dealt with for their infraction of the law; and the slaves were placed on board another man-of-war, to be carried to the Seychelle Islands, where they might enjoy liberty and a climate suited to their constitutions.

Jack was again disappointed at not gaining at Zanzibar any tidings of the *Empress*. Running through the Mozambique Channel, he continued his course for Cape Town, where he arrived without any further adventure. His first inquiry was for the *Empress*. No tidings, however, had been received, and serious apprehensions were felt for her safety.

"It is supposed that she must have foundered in a typhoon in the Indian seas, if she ever got there; or that she has been cast away and gone to pieces on some unknown rock," was the answer received.

"Poor Adair! is such your end?" exclaimed Jack, sorrowfully. "I won't believe it, however. I trust that Lucy will not hear these reports."

A day after his arrival the mail from England came in, bringing letters for him from Julia and Murray, who had just gained his rank as an admiral.

"As there are so many good officers seeking for employment, I conclude that I shall be virtually shelved, although for my boy's sake I would gladly have gone to sea again," wrote Murray. "His mother and I are looking out anxiously for tidings of him. His last letter gave us an account of the commencement of the Abyssinian expedition, and that he was to go up the country with the Naval Brigade. It is important that a youngster should see service on shore as well as afloat, although we naturally feel anxious lest he should have suffered from the hardships to which he must of necessity have been exposed. We are, therefore, eagerly looking forward to his next letter. Our girls are well, and we hear good accounts from Julia of yours; but Lucy is naturally in a sad state of anxiety. No tidings have reached England of the *Empress*, nor has anything been heard of Saint Maur. I am continuing to make all possible inquiries, and have written to agents at various seaports to ascertain from the masters of ships trading foreign to endeavour to find some clue to his fate."

The remainder of the letter referred to private matters. The *Bellona* remained some time in Simon's Bay, and all on board were in hopes of being sent home, when, no transport being ready, Captain Rogers was requested to proceed with a wing of the — Regiment to the coast of Caffraria, where they were immediately wanted to put down a serious outbreak of the natives. It was far from a satisfactory or pleasant task, for the *Bellona* had no accommodation for officers or men; but Captain Rogers was not a person to throw difficulties in the way when a service could be rendered to the country. He had lately, during his constant intercourse with military men, got on without a dispute; and he hoped that such would be the case at present. All hands were busily employed in taking the baggage on board and embarking the men, so that neither he nor his officers had much time to attend to their guests. The last person to arrive on board was Major Bubsby, commanding the troops; and Jack was not a little taken aback when he found that he had brought his wife and two tall daughters on board. The lady was almost twice the height of her better half, and the daughters promised to grow into the same proportions. The major was undoubtedly a short man, although not a small one either in girth or in his own estimation. He had a rubicund countenance, huge mustachios, and small, ferrety eyes.

"I was not aware that we should have ladies, or I should have advised you not to bring them, although, as they have come, I will endeavour to provide the best accommodation I can for them," said Jack, with his usual politeness.

"You must understand, Captain Rogers, that I never move anywhere without Mrs Bubsby and my daughters. They are accustomed to camp life, and like it; and should I be wounded or fall sick, I should have them at hand to nurse me. I require care, for I am not so young as I once was, though still strong and active;" and the major twirled his mustachios and gave a loud "Ahem!"

"I am afraid that the ladies will be put to much inconvenience, both on board and on shore; for, should the regiment have to advance into the interior, I don't know what will become of them," observed Jack. "And if you will take my advice—though, as I have said, I am perfectly ready to accommodate them—you will leave them at Cape Town to await your return."

"Never! Captain Rogers, never!" exclaimed Major Bubsby. "If I do I shall not know what they are about."

"But should you be killed, and there may be some sharp fighting, what then will become of your wife and daughters?" observed Jack, eyeing the stout little major.

"Then, Captain Rogers, I must beg that you will have the kindness so far to oblige me as to take them back to Cape Town," answered the major, looking evidently as if he did not quite like the remark. "I have now been in the service thirty years, and have no intention that the Caffres or any other savages should take my life. They are a contemptible lot. Why, a glance from my eye alone would be sufficient to put a whole host of the niggers to flight!"

"As you please, Major Bubsby," said Jack. "I shall be ready to appropriate a portion of my after cabin to your wife and daughters, and I will direct the carpenter to put up a screen, that they may live in private if they wish to do so."

"Ah, that will do, that will do," answered the major.

This conversation took place out of earshot of Mrs Bubsby, who was not aware of Jack's kind intentions towards her. Jack, approaching with a bow, requested her and her daughters to remain on deck until the cabin was fitted up for their accommodation. "We do things rapidly on board, and shall not detain you long," he added.

"I am surprised that the major did not intimate his intention to bring us; but it is very like him," answered Mrs Bubsby. "He is a worthy man, and devotedly attached to me and my daughters. Allow me to introduce them. Eugenia, my eldest, and Angelica, my second daughter. They look forward with greater pleasure to the voyage and life in the bush than I do, I confess. They are good-hearted girls, and would be ready to follow their father into the field, if required."

"Ah, yes; we do not care where we go, or what we do," said Eugenia. "We are never so happy as when on horseback or living under canvas."

"I delight in the sea, and I love seamen," said Angelica, smiling sweetly at the captain.

She was not aware that Jack possessed a wife and family. He had now to quit the ladies to attend to the duty of the ship.

"Blue Peter" had been flying for some time, and a gun was fired to hurry off those on shore. The anchor was weighed, and the *Bellona* with her living freight steamed majestically out of the harbour.

As soon as things had been got somewhat to rights, the baggage stowed away, and the soldiers berthed, Jack and his lieutenants had time to look after the officers.

Directly the ladies' cabin was ready, Jack escorted them below. Mrs Bubsby cast a somewhat indignant glance at the canvas screen which had been put up, but said nothing. But Eugenia exclaimed—

"How nice! we shall hear everything that is said outside, and you'll hear us, so we must take care what we talk about."

"I'm sure that we shall hear nothing but what is pleasant and sensible and right," said Jack, with less veracity than it was his wont to speak.

Mrs Bubsby gave a "hem!" and Jack, bowing, left the cabin in possession of his fair guests.

The major was pacing the deck, fussing and fuming. Something had gone wrong with him. Jack kept out of his way. He had already got hold of one of his own junior officers, to whom he was explaining what had happened. At last he came up to Jack.

"I must beg you, Captain Rogers, to put back. My dressing-case, with valuables to a large amount, has been left behind; and it will to a certainty be stolen. I cannot do without it while campaigning; and it will be a fearful inconvenience not to have it on board. I will give you a written request, if you think it necessary to have one."

"I cannot return to harbour for such a purpose, even with a written request from you," answered Jack, scarcely able to restrain his laughter. "Perhaps the case in question has been brought on board after all. If not, anything I possess I shall be happy to place at your disposal."

"You do not possess what I require, I am sure," answered the major.

"But tell me what it is that your case contains which I cannot supply!" said Jack.

The major took Jack by the arm and led him out of earshot of his officers. "My second set of teeth," he whispered. "I confide the fact to you; I shall never masticate my food without them; I shall die of indigestion."

Jack could not help giving way to his inclination to laugh. "I own, major, I do not possess a second set of teeth of any description, but we will try the doctor; he is a clever man, and although such things are not supplied among our medical stores, he may possibly have some."

"I shall be most grateful if he can furnish me," answered the major, in the same tone as before; "but if you will not return into port, I must request you to institute a search for the dressing-case. You will not speak of its contents?"

Jack promised to do as the major requested, and directed Tom to learn if any case belonging to one of the officers had been carried forward or stowed away by mistake.

The major having allowed his "woman kind," as he called them, time to shake into their berths, went below. He had not been there long before Jack, who had gone to his cabin, heard a low whispering from within. He caught the words—

"It was your fault!"

"It was yours!"

"I tell you it was not. I looked after everything entrusted to me. Sniggins should have kept a better eye on your baggage."

"No; he was not to blame. It was your business to look after the smaller articles; for what other reason do I carry you and your daughters about?"

"I'm sure I don't want to go. You and the girls made me."

"I made you? I never made you do anything in your life which you did not like. My beloved, you are losing your temper!"

"I tell you I am as cool as a cucumber!" answered the lady, the tone of her voice belying the assertion.

"Don't fall out about it, papa," said a younger voice. "You are inclined to be aggravating."

"My dear, I am as calm as your mamma," said the major.

"Then why do you come here and accuse me of doing what I didn't?" cried the lady. "I will not stand such treatment. It is all your fault!"

"It's your fault, I say! Why was that case left behind?"

"It was not my fault," exclaimed Mrs Bubsby. "I'll teach you not to repeat such falsehoods!" There was a slight scream from Eugenia, echoed by Angelica, while some sounds greatly resembling those produced when a person is having his ears boxed, proceeded through the canvas. Directly afterwards the major, with a flushed countenance and a bald head, rushed out at the door, followed by a wig sent as a missile after him. On seeing Captain Rogers reading at the further corner of the cabin, he tried to pick it up, but the vessel giving a gentle roll at the time, sent him flying into the middle of the cabin before he had succeeded in his object. Pulling out his handkerchief in a vain endeavour to conceal his shaven crown, he uttered a groan. Jack tried not to look at him, but believing that he had been hurt, was compelled at length to inquire what was the matter.

"I confessed to you, Captain Rogers, that I made use of some false teeth in addition to my own natural ones, and now you have discovered that I wear a wig. But you will not, I trust, make it known to my officers, or they may lose the respect they now entertain for me."

A scornful laugh from within showed that the major's last observation had been overheard, and that some one did not agree with it.

Jack, however, kindly rising from his seat, picked up the major's wig, and having handed it to him, helped him to get on his legs.

"Do you wish to return to your cabin?" asked Jack.

The major shook his head. "Not at present," he whispered; "I'll wait until the storm has blown over. She is a good woman," pointing with his thumb to where it might be supposed Mrs Bubsby was standing; "but she's a little hasty, as you see, at times. I would have left her behind, but I could not bring my girls without a chaperon, besides which she would come, whether I liked it or not. I am frank with you, Captain Rogers; but I am frank by nature."

"Would you like to walk on deck, Major Bubsby?" asked Jack, not wishing to make any remark in the presence of the lady, aware that every word he uttered would reach her ears.

"Yes, indeed, I would," answered the major; "a little fresh air would greatly restore me. These fits are apt to unman me for a time, but I quickly recover, and soon resume the command of my amazon forces."

Jack heard another scornful laugh from within, as the major hurried into the main cabin. The captain good-naturedly paced the deck with him for some minutes, listening to the account of his domestic woes, arising from Mrs Bubsby's somewhat uncertain temper.

"She is in the main, however, a charming creature, charming when I married her—a perfect angel. Still charming, though less angelic, I'll allow, at times."

Jack could not help smiling. The major observed him.

"You doubt my assertion! Wait until you have been married as long as I have, thirty years or more, and you'll understand what's what. You are not married, I conclude, Captain Rogers?"

"I have the happiness of being so, although we poor sailors are not allowed to carry our wives and families with us, as you military men have the privilege of doing."

"That will be a disappointment to Eugenia and Angelica," observed the major, apparently speaking to himself. "They fully speculated on your being a bachelor. You have some bachelor officers, however, captain?"

"Oh, yes," answered Jack laughing; "my three lieutenants are all unmarried, and so are the rest of the officers, with the exception of the doctor and paymaster."

"That's some consolation, at all events. If there's one thing I have at heart more than another, it is to see my charming daughters well married."

"I wish you every success in so laudable an object," said Jack, "but it is a matter in which I should decline to interfere with respect to my officers. Indeed they are all too young to take upon themselves the responsibilities of married life. In my opinion a naval officer should not venture to fall in love until he is thirty at least, if he intends to get on in the service, and it would be much better to wait a few years beyond that."

"Ah, but my daughters would not consider them too young," said the major. "Angelica once engaged herself to a young gentleman of seventeen, and would have married him too had not his father, who objected to the match, sent him off up the country, and the poor girl for a month at least could not hold up her head. It was not until a fresh regiment arrived that she in any way recovered her usual buoyant spirits, and had no less than three admirers at once dangling after her. One was so old that she could not make up her mind to accept him. Another was over head and ears in debt, and asked me to pay his bills, on condition that he would take my daughter off my hands, and a third had, I found out, an unacknowledged wife. So you see my sweet Angelica is perfectly free to give her heart and hand to the first person who asks her."

The major, as he made these revelations, did not appear at all aware of the effect they were likely to produce on his auditor, who, as may be supposed, found it difficult to offer any remark on some of them.

"I think I may now venture below, as time has been given for the storm which raged in a certain region to calm down," said the major, who was beginning to feel a little tired from so long pacing the deck.

Jack advised him by all means to return to his cabin. He wanted, indeed, to enjoy a good hearty fit of laughter by himself, as he felt every instant ready to explode. He somewhat astonished Tom, who was on deck, when he at length gave way to his feelings as the major's head disappeared below the deck.

Tom, on hearing the account of the major's expulsion from the cabin, as may be supposed, joined his brother Jack in his merriment, and it was with difficulty for hours afterwards that he could refrain from bursting into fits of laughter.

The *Bellona* steamed on; not at full speed, however, for the engineer found something amiss with the machinery, and begged the captain, as soon as the wind should shift, to proceed under sail, that he might have an opportunity of repairing the defect.

The young ladies were constantly on deck, endeavouring to make themselves as charming as possible. Archie Gordon and Tom were respectfully polite, and took care not to commit themselves by any undue attentions. Billy Blueblazes was far less cautious. Whenever he could find a spare minute, he was sure to make his way to the side of the fair Angelica.

At last, one night, while Tom was on watch, he was surprised to find Billy walk up to him.

"I thought you'd turned in," remarked Tom.

"It wouldn't have been of any use; I couldn't have slept had I tried," answered Billy, with a sigh. "I want, Tom, to confide a secret to you."

"What is it?" inquired Tom. "You have had no quarrel with any of those military officers, I hope?"

"Oh, no, no," answered Billy. "I know, Rogers, that you were once susceptible of the tender passion, and I want to make you my confidant. I am in love, irretrievably, hopelessly in love, and the fair object of my affections returns it, she assures me, with the same ardour. But, you know, my income is small. At present I have nothing but my pay, and that will only keep me and allow me a few pounds to spend on tarts and jellies and ice creams, and I should have to give those up at all events, which would be a terrible sacrifice. And then the major, her father, is evidently a hard-hearted, stubborn old fogey, and the mother's a she-dragon. The adorable creature insists that I shall marry her on the first opportunity. She, indeed, proposes that the chaplain should perform the ceremony on board, but I am afraid the captain would not allow that, and I am in a fearful state of perplexity."

"Which of them is it?" asked Tom; "for you appeared equally attentive to both whenever I have seen you together."

"Ah! but you have not observed the glances Angelica has cast at me, nor the blush which mantles on her cheek when I approach. I thought that every one must have observed it, though I desired to keep the matter a secret in my own breast until I confided it to you. We have been shipmates for many years, so that I felt sure I could trust you."

"Indeed you can," answered Tom. "I'll give you the best advice I can. Don't say anything to any one else for a few days; at all events restrain your ardour, do not commit yourself while the lady remains on board. You can write to her, you know, at any time, when she's safe on shore, then the captain would not interfere. Perhaps, after a little absence, you may find your affection cool; for, from the way you describe her parents, I am, as a friend, bound to tell you that there are some objections to the match, and I am sure the captain would see them."

"I am sure that I shall never love her less than I do now," answered Billy. "I have been thinking of composing some verses to present to her. As you know, I am something of a poet, but I should like to show them to you before I give them."

"Didn't you once begin some to a young lady in Sydney?" asked Tom, slily. "I don't think you ever finished them."

"No, nor did I; still, I thought of completing them now. You must remember that the young lady there gave me no encouragement, but at present I know that they will be received, and my poetic genius will be stimulated. Oh, Tom! it is very delightful to be in love, but it sadly unhinges a man, you know that from experience."

"Bosh! If I ever was in love, it is so long ago and I was such a boy at the time, that I have forgotten all about it," answered Tom, not quits liking Billy's remark. "But what about the verses?" he asked.

"I have them in my pocket, as far as I have gone. I would read them by the binnacle lamp but that the helmsman would overhear me. I think, however, I can recollect them. They begin—

"'Angelica, my own beloved,
An earhly angel thou!'

"I forget the third line, but the fourth is—

"'Before thy shrine I bow.

"'The jasmine, lily, and the rose,
In thee are all entwined.'

"Those third lines bother me, but the fourth I thought of terminating with 'combined.' Perhaps you can help me, Tom?"

"Couldn't you put in something about a sunflower or a poplar," suggested Tom. "The lady in question rather brings to my mind some of the taller productions of nature. You must have remarked she's a head and a half taller than you are, Billy, and Mrs Bubsby even more than that above the major."

"I might begin, 'Tall art thou as the stately pine,' but I think I should be bothered if I had to introduce the sunflower," observed Billy.

"Give them to me," said Tom, "and I will look them over; perhaps I may get the paymaster to help me—he's a capital hand with his pen."

Billy, pulling a paper out of his pocket, gave it to Tom, and after pacing the deck for a few minutes longer went below to turn in, though, he averred, not to sleep. It should have been mentioned that Billy had been promoted before leaving England, and was now junior lieutenant of the ship.

Tom, however, had no opportunity of looking at the verses. The following night the ship was five or six miles from Waterloo Bay, but Jack deemed it prudent to wait until next morning to stand in.

Billy was very miserable at the thoughts of having so soon to part from Angelica.

"I say, Rogers, do you think the captain would let me go on shore just for a day or two? The ship is sure to remain here for some time."

"I'm not so certain of that, and you cannot be spared," answered Tom. "The captain would smell a rat; depend upon that. He's too sharp-sighted not to have observed what has been going on. I don't think he altogether admires the young lady as much as you do."

"Have you read the remainder of the verses?" asked Billy. "Some of the lines want endings, and some of the verses want lines and rhymes. My ideas are very grand, but I am apt to break down for want of appropriate rhymes."

"I'll find them for you," said Tom. "I've got a dictionary, and I'll run my eye down it, and select as many as you can want."

"I should like to have finished them before she goes on shore," said Billy.

"I don't see how that can be managed," observed Tom. "You can send them to her before we again put to sea; it will be a last tender mark of your affection, and she will appreciate it. If you will write the address on an envelope I will get it sent with the captain's letters."

Billy was contented with this proposal, and turned in until his watch on deck came round. At daylight the *Bellona* slowly steamed in for the land, for it was very nearly a calm, though heavy undulations rolled on beneath the ship towards the shore. On approaching it the loud roar of the surf was heard. It soon became evident that it would be utterly impossible to land the troops. Jack made a signal to ask how long this state of things would last. The answer was unsatisfactory. It might be for a week or ten days. The troops were greatly wanted, but it would be impossible for them to land, and Captain Rogers was requested to keep close to the coast, that no opportunity might be lost in case the surf should unexpectedly cease. He accordingly put the ship's head round, and was steaming off, when suddenly the engines stopped.

The anchor, of course, was now the only resource, as there was not sufficient wind to enable the ship to claw off the land. As rapidly as possible the anchor was let go. No sooner had it caught the ground, and the cable run out, than the influence of the rollers began sensibly to be felt and the ship began pitching in a very unsatisfactory manner. Astern was the threatening, barren-looking coast, with a broad line of white breakers dashing savagely on it. On trying the current, it was found setting west by north at the rate of a mile and a half an hour, which, with the swell, would soon have placed the ship in a most dangerous position. Jack himself went below to ascertain the amount of damage to the machinery, and to urge the engineers to work with all speed. The chief engineer looked grave.

"We ought to be in harbour, with smooth water, to accomplish this work," he observed; "but we will do our best, sir."

"Should a breeze spring up, we will get under way, and the ship will be far more steady than she is now," answered Jack. "What was the cause of the accident?"

"A flaw, sir, which ought to have been discovered. It is only a wonder that it did not give way before, and I cannot account for its going now. However, as I said, sir, we will do our best."

"You can do no more, Mr Rivett," answered Jack. "Send for as many hands as you want, if they can assist you."

"Our own people are enough at present, but we may want them by-and-by," was the answer.

Jack returned on deck to find his principal guest looking rather pale. The major had been often enough at sea to know that a ship caught on a lee shore, with the chance of a heavy gale springing up, was not in a pleasant position. He felt also somewhat physically upset by the unusual motion. The ship was indeed riding uneasily, pulling at her cable as if at any instant she might haul the anchor from the bottom. Jack ordered another cable to be ranged in case of accident, for, should the bower anchor be carried away, there would be no time to lose in bringing up.

It is an ill wind that blows nobody good; and Billy was congratulating himself on the happiness of spending a few more days in the society of Angelica, but the motion of the ship had produced the same effect on her as it had on her papa, and when at length she did appear on deck, Tom remarked that she looked wonderfully yellow about the region of the mouth.

"I say, Billy," he observed, mischievously, "I think it would be very appropriate to compare her to the sunflower now."

In vain Billy tried to console her; she was too miserable to speak. He at length had to lead her below to the door of her cabin.

The calm continued all night, though the weather looked very threatening. In vain the engineers toiled on without ceasing. It might take two or three days even now before the damage could be repaired. The night came on. The captain, first lieutenant, and master felt too uneasy to turn in. Either the second or third lieutenant remained on the forecastle, ready to issue the necessary orders for letting go the other cable, should the first give way. It held on, however, until morning, but still the same heavy surf as before rolled on the shore, from whence, in answer to Jack's signals, the reply came, "Troops cannot yet land."

"I think, sir, before long, we shall have a breeze," said the master. "I hope it won't come due south; and from the look of the sky I should say that we shall have it from the south-west, or perhaps from the westward."

"I trust, if we do get it, that it will be from a quarter which will enable us to make sail," answered Jack.

Still hour after hour went by, and no breeze came. At length, towards night, a few ripples were seen on the water. They became more frequent. The dog vanes blew out.

"Hurrah! here comes a breeze!" cried the master. "We shall have it strong enough presently to make sail," he added. "We may then get that ironwork of ours to rights."

The capstan was manned. Scarcely had the men commenced tramping round than a loud report was heard. The messenger had given way, when the cable ran out to the clench, carrying away the stoppers, and running through both compressors. By great exertions, however, the messenger was again shackled together and the anchor hove up. No sooner did it appear above water than Tom, who was on the forecastle, exclaimed —

"Both flukes carried away, sir; nothing but the shank and stock remaining."

Sail was now made; but the ship was evidently drifting to the westward, by which she approached nearer and nearer the shore. Every stitch of canvas that could be set was hoisted. The wind shifted to the very worst quarter from which it could blow. The ship stood on, however, close-hauled, first on the starboard tack, and then, the wind shifting half a point or so, for the purpose of taking advantage of it, she was put about. Every sheet and brace was flattened aft; still, judging by the roar of the breakers, she was no further off the threatening coast than at first.

Many an eye was turned to leeward in an endeavour to discover the line of the coast, which, through the gloom, could dimly be distinguished below the bright sky.

"We still hold our own," said Jack to Archie Gordon, who was walking the deck. "If we can continue to do that until the sea goes down, we may still do well; and we must hope, if we should let drop an anchor, that it will prove sounder than the last. Probably the engineers will by that time have accomplished their task, and we shall be able to get steam on the ship. She doesn't sail close-hauled as well as I expected, and we never before have had an opportunity of testing her as we are now doing."

"I suspect that it is the current carrying her to leeward," observed Archie. "Possibly the wind may increase before daylight, and we shall then be better able to claw off the land."

All night long the captain, endeavouring to take advantage of every change of wind, frequently put the ship about, anxiously wishing for daylight, to be able to judge better than he could during the darkness of her distance from the land. The lead kept going showed no increase of depth, which ranged from thirty-five to forty fathoms. As morning approached, the water shallowed, showing that she was nearer than she had been when night closed in.

"By the deep, twenty," sang out the man in the chains. A short time afterwards, "fifteen fathom," then "twelve." Just at daylight she was in ten fathoms of water. As the sun rose, the marks denoting the entrance to Waterloo Bay were seen under the lee. The bay afforded no shelter with the wind blowing, as it then did, directly into it. Jack hoisted the signals, "Can the troops land?" The answer run up on shore was, "Not until the weather moderates."

In a short time a pilot came off in a surf-boat, and the ship was brought up in nine fathoms, about a mile and a half from the shore. A spring was also got on the cable, in case of requiring to slip, and a bow-rope for a slip-rope, while the spare anchor was shifted to the cathead, in lieu of the one carried away, that everything might be ready in case of necessity.

The pilot, on discovering that the machinery had given way, looked grave. He had been accustomed to sailing vessels all his life, and had no love for steamers.

"I hope your engineers will look sharp and get their work done," he observed to the master. "This is a queer place when the wind is as it is, though well enough when it's off shore."

After breakfast, the major and his family came on deck. Angelica, looking about her, inquired why they could not land.

"Because the boats would be upset and rolled over and over in these breakers, and you, my sweet girl, would be gobbled up by a shark!" answered Billy, to whom the question was put. "They would choose you first. I'm sure, if I was a shark, I shouldn't like to eat your papa or mamma!"

"Oh, what a dreadful idea!" exclaimed Angelica; yet she smiled at what she considered Billy's compliment.

Billy, who had recovered his verses from Tom, although he had not had time to look at them, thought this a good opportunity of presenting them; and, observing that the major's eyes were turned another way, took the paper out of his pocket and gave it to her.

"These lines, my dearest, will show you the depth of my affection," he said.

Angelica, with a blush, which she had the art of commanding at pleasure, took the paper. A frown, however, gathered on her brow as she read —

"'Tall as a poplar, sharp as a thorn;
I should never have missed you had you never been born.
Roses are sweet and lilies are fair,
But they lose their beauty when seen in your hair.'"

"Do you mean to insult me?" exclaimed Angelica, in an angry tone, as she continued to read on the doggerel which Tom had substituted for those Billy had given him. Just then the major, turning round, saw his daughter with a paper in her hand, and Billy standing by her side. He, supposing it to be a formal proposal which, in his paternal anxiety, he had carefully been looking for, approached with the intention of clinching the matter in the presence of witnesses, and allowing Billy no chance of escape. So convinced was he of this, that, without asking to look at the paper, he grasped Billy's hand.

"My dear fellow," he exclaimed, in his enthusiasm, "I am happy to congratulate you on your success and good taste. She will make you an admirable wife; and you will prove, I am sure, an affectionate husband. I accept your offer on my daughter's behalf and you shall have my blessing and that of Mrs Bubsby."

"But I have not made a downright offer," answered Billy.

"No, indeed he has not," exclaimed Angelica. "Look at these abominable lines he has just presented to me. What his object was I cannot divine."

The major took the paper and read the lines.

"Do you mean to insult my beloved child by putting such wretched trash as this into her hands?" exclaimed the major, with a sudden revulsion of feeling.

"I did not write them," answered Billy. "Indeed I did not. I had no wish to insult Miss Angelica; for I thought her a most charming person, and had got some beautiful lines almost ready, which I had intended to give her."

"This does not satisfy me, sir," answered the major. "The only apology you can make is to go down on your knees and beg the forgiveness of my innocent child, and offer to marry her forthwith."

"That I'll not," answered Billy, who had not at all liked the ominous frown which he had seen gather over the fair Angelica's brow, and still less the dictatorial tone of the irate major. Billy had a fair proportion of good sense, although he made a fool of himself sometimes; and was, when put on his mettle, as brave as any man. His good genius suggested to him the various remarks which Tom had made respecting the Bubsby family.

"I say that I did not intend to insult your daughter, and that I had not read the lines presented to her, nor did I compose them myself. I must beg that she will give them me back. I am ready to apologise for my unintentional mistake, and do so now."

At this juncture Mrs Bubsby and her other daughter joined the party, and at once set tooth and nail on poor Billy, not literally, but metaphorically. His spirit, however, was up. He positively refused to marry the fair Angelica, or to offer any further apology than he had already done.

"Then, sir, I must have satisfaction," exclaimed the major. "Your blood or mine must dye the soil of Africa ere many days are over!"

"Oh! my beloved husband, do not say that," exclaimed Mrs Bubsby. "He is beneath your notice. If he refuses to marry Angelica, the loss will be his. She will find ere long a far better husband."

"You wicked, deceitful, cruel, abominable young man!" exclaimed Angelica. "If you do not marry me you'll break my heart! It's not the first time I've been treated in this way. It shows me, however, more and more that you naval officers are not to be trusted."

Jack observed that something unpleasant was going on; but he was too much occupied with watching the position of the ship to interfere, as were the other officers. Billy himself also had presently to hurry forward to attend to his duties, while the major and his wife and daughters retired to their cabins to discuss the matter.

By this time heavy rollers were coming in, breaking within a cable's length of the ship on each quarter, making her position far from pleasant. There was but a light air from the southward, insufficient to enable her get under way.

Jack much regretted having come to the place, for it was evidently a far from satisfactory one for landing troops. The cutter was now lowered, and sent round the ship to sound. On her return on board the master reported only seven fathoms close to the breakers. The breeze now freshened from east-south-east, but the rollers increasing, the sea broke heavily half a cable's length from her. Everything was now prepared for making sail. On the cable being shortened in, it was discovered that it had swept over a rock about fifty fathoms from the anchor, and that at any moment it might give way.

"Stop heaving!" cried the captain. "Make ready to slip!" The sails were loosened; but as they were about to be sheeted home, the cable parted. Instantly the sheet anchor was let go. For some seconds it seemed doubtful, before it could reach the bottom, whether the ship would strike on the rocks; but it happily brought her up, though fearfully near them.

By this time it was again night; the rollers had greatly increased, and should the sheet anchor give way, it was clear that nothing could save the ship. Jack had seldom been in so anxious a position. All on board saw the danger they were in. The major's cheek lost its ruddy hue, and even Mrs Bubsby's countenance exhibited signs of alarm. Not far off lay a small vessel with both anchors down. Her master coming on board volunteered to make a hawser fast to her for the purpose of casting the man-of-war the right way.

The engineer stated that it would be some hours before steam could be got up.

"Then let me advise you, sir, to get under way forthwith," said the master of the merchantman. "Should the anchor fail to hold, the ship must inevitably strike on that reef of rocks where the surf is breaking so furiously, and where, strong as she may be, she will not hold together for an hour, while there will not be the slightest chance of saving a single human life."

Jack gladly accepted the worthy master's offer. The cutters were lowered, and hawsers carried to the vessel. The sheet anchor was then weighed, when, on its coming above water, it was found that both the flukes had gone. Her only hope of safety was on the remaining anchor. Would it hold until sail could be made? From the direction the beats were drifting it was soon seen that, in spite of all the efforts of their crews, it would be impossible to carry the hawsers to the merchantman. Jack looked anxiously at the compass and dog vanes. He knew full well that at any moment the cable might part, and, should the ship not cast the right way, she must be driven on the rocks and every soul perish.

"I would advise you to return on board your own vessel, my friend," he said to the master of the merchantman. "You will be safer on board her than here."

"Now is your chance, captain," exclaimed the master, as the wind veered a point well to the eastward.

The cable was slipped. The ship mercifully canted the right way under single-reefed topsails, topgallant sails, jib, and driver, and with a strong breeze stood out of the treacherous bay.

Jack and all on board had good reason to thank a merciful Providence that they had escaped the danger to which they had been exposed. At length the *Bellona* was clear of the land. Now came the question of what to do with the troops. There was only one anchor left. Jack considered that it would be extreme rashness to bring up again close to the shore until he had steam power on which to depend to help him off, should the wind continue to the southward. Still it was of the greatest importance that by some means or other the troops should be landed. The major, who was by this time anxious to leave the ship, insisted that "it ought to be done, and must be done."

"The *must* depends upon circumstances," answered Jack. "If I can land your men I will, without risking their lives or those of my boats' crews. By running further to the eastward, a place may be found where you can be put on shore, and you must march from thence to the place you were ordered to garrison, but until the machinery is in good working order, I must do my utmost to keep off the land."

To this the major had nothing to say.

The breeze freshened. By nightfall the *Bellona* was out of sight of land, and Jack felt much more easy than he had done for several days. Although the rough seas had greatly delayed the engineer, he was at length able to report that the machinery was again in order. The wind also had fallen considerably, and the sea having much gone down, Jack hoped that he might at length get rid of his guests. Both officers and men had behaved admirably, and had assisted on all occasions in making sail, or when pulling and hauling was required on deck. The ship was, at this time, about forty miles from the port of debarkation. After many anxious hours of watching, Jack turned in, leaving Tom, as officer of the watch, on deck.

Young Alick Murray had been placed in Tom's watch, and besides him there was a mate and another midshipman. The night was tolerably clear, the stars shining, but a mist hung above the surface of the sea, so that no object could be seen until tolerably near. Tom constantly hailed the look-outs forward to ascertain that they were keeping their eyes open, and young Alick paid frequent visits to the forecastle, sent by Tom for the same purpose. The engines were working, though not in so satisfactory a manner as was desirable. Alick was forward, when his sharp eyes discovered an object almost ahead, though slightly on the starboard bow.

"What's that?" he asked, pointing it out to Tim Nolan, who was on the watch. "A boat, a raft, or a sunken vessel?"

"It looks to me like a raft, and we must starboard the helm if we don't want to run into it," said Tim.

"A raft on the starboard bow!" shouted Alick, in his clear voice.

"Starboard the helm!"

"Starboard it is," was the answer, and presently what looked like a hen-coop and a grating with a few spars lashed together, came in sight, and an object, evidently a human being, lying on it, but whether alive or dead could not at once be ascertained. Presently, however, as the ship was abreast of the raft, a man rose on his knees and waved his hand, while he shouted out, "Ship, ahoy!" His voice sounded hollow and shrill; he apparently supposed that he had not been seen. Tom immediately ordered the engines to be stopped, and a boat to be lowered, but before this was done she had got a considerable distance from the raft. Another cry escaped the forlorn occupant of the raft, as if he fancied he was to be left to his fate. Tom hailed him, telling him that assistance would be sent. In a few minutes a boat was pulling as fast as the crew, with sturdy strokes—eager to rescue a fellow-creature—could drive her through the water. Alick had jumped into the boat, which he steered carefully up to the raft. No voice was heard as they approached. The poor man, overcome with the thought that he had been deserted, had apparently fainted or sunk down again from weakness. At first Alick thought that he was not there, but his form was seen stretched out at full length on the frail raft.

"Look out not to capsize it!" sang out Alick to his men, two of whom were about to spring on the raft. "Let one at a time get on it, and lift the man carefully into the boat."

His orders were obeyed, the man was got on board and passed along to the stern sheets, where he was laid with his head on a flag, which happened to be in the boat. Alick pulled back as hard as possible, that the stranger might be placed under charge of the doctor. The poor man breathed, and that was all. Alick was afraid that he might go off unless speedily attended to, for the boat had come away without brandy or any other restorative.

The rescued man was handed on deck with all the tenderness with which sailors are wont to treat the sick and wounded, or women and children. The doctor was immediately roused up to do what he considered necessary.

The stranger seemed by his dress to be an officer, although, whether officer or man, he would have been looked after with the same care. Tom had him at once carried to his cabin, where the doctor undressed him.

The various remedies which his case required having been applied, the stranger soon gave signs of returning animation.

"His pulse is improving," observed the doctor, "and he will do well enough after a time. No one must talk to him, however, when he comes to his senses, or try to learn how he got into the situation in which he was found."

Tom's watch being over, and having given up his cabin he was about to roll himself up in his cloak in a corner of the ward room, when the fearful cry of "Fire! fire!" was raised. He hurried on deck, where Jack and all the officers and crew quickly assembled. The drum beat to quarters. The men flew to their stations. The soldiers, who well knew the meaning of the tattoo, hastened on deck and fell in, according to their officers' orders, on either side.

During that moment of awful suspense, strict discipline prevailed. The last persons to appear were the major and Mrs Bubsby and their two tall daughters. The former, with a blanket thrown over his head, making him look very much like a young polar bear, and the lady in her nightcap, with a bonnet secured by a red woollen shawl fastened under her chin, while the costume of the young ladies showed also that they had hurriedly dressed themselves, and in a way they would not have wished to have appeared in, under ordinary circumstances, one having her papa's military cloak tied round her waist, while the other had a railway rug, of large size, covering her shoulders and hanging down behind.

"What's the matter? what's the matter?" asked the major, in a tone of agitation.

"The ship is on fire, and we, with the aid of your men, have to put it out," said Jack.

"Fire!" exclaimed Mrs Bubsby. "Oh, dear! oh, dear! what will become of us. I thought such a thing was impossible on board of a well-regulated man-of-war."

Jack had no time to reply to the lady. That the ship was on fire was too certain, as they could perceive a strong smell of burning, and although the smoke could not be seen through the darkness, its suffocating effects were felt as it ascended through the after hatchway. Jack at once ordered the first lieutenant and boatswain with a party of men to go below and ascertain the cause and extent of the fire, while the soldiers stood ready with buckets full of water in their hands, as did a party of the crew, with wet blankets and sails, to extinguish it. No sooner was the hatch taken off, however, than not only smoke but bright flames ascended. On this the soldiers, who were standing on the lower deck, were ordered to advance and heave the contents of their buckets over the spot. At first it appeared to produce but little effect. The steam pump was set to work and the hose carried aft, but scarcely had it begun to work, than the machinery by some accident gave way, and it was of no service.

The major, seeing the serious aspect of affairs, at length rushed up to Jack.

"Captain Rogers, what is to become of my wife and daughters?" he asked, in an agitated tone.

"We will lower one of the boats, and put them into it," said the captain, "with the senior mate and a midshipman."

Jack at once issued the order for the cutter to be lowered and manned. Her own crew went in her with the officers Jack had appointed.

"Murray, you go too," he said. "We will take you on board again as soon as the fire is put out."

Alick touched his cap, but was evidently very unwilling to go, though he said nothing.

"The boat is ready, major, for your wife and daughters," shouted Jack.

The accommodation ladder was lowered to enable them to descend.

"Now, my precious ones," cried the major. "Your lives shall be saved at all events, though it's my belief that the ship will burn to the water's edge and go down."

Billy was too busy attending to his duty below to assist his fair friends; indeed, he would not have been sorry to keep out of their way had he known what was taking place.

Mrs Bubsby was the first to descend, helped by two of the crew, who could for a moment be spared to assist her. The eldest daughter went next, when the major descended, supporting Angelica, who, overcome by her feelings, appeared to have fainted. When the crew offered to assist her into the boat, he exclaimed —

"No, no, hands off, I must place her in her mother's arms," and stepped in, not without a risk of pitching over into the stern sheets.

Jack, who just then looked over the side, observing that no one else remained to get into the boat, ordered her to shove off.

"But the major is in her, sir," answered Alick.

"He must not go back to the dreadful ship!" cried Mrs Bubsby, her words being echoed by her daughters, while Angelica, throwing her arms round his neck, held him down. In vain the major struggled, or appeared to struggle, to regain the accommodation ladder, but each time that he made an attempt to get on board, his wife and daughters pulled him back.

While this was going forward, the boat was veered astern by a long warp, and now and then the major attempted to shout, but his wife placed her hand over his mouth, so that his demands to be taken on board were unheeded.

At length, appearing reconciled to his fate, he subsided down and remained quietly with his wife and family, without any further effort to return to the ship.

"It can't be helped, sir," said young Alick. "They'll do very well without you, as there are quite men enough to put out the fire. I wish, though, that I was on board to help."

"Do you think there is any chance of the ship blowing up?" said Mrs Bubsby. "If it does I'm afraid we shall lose all our things."

"You may be very sure, madam, that if the ship does blow up you will lose everything, but I can't help thinking that the lives of the officers and crew, not to speak of the poor soldiers, are of more consequence than your traps," answered Alick.

"Oh dear! oh dear! will the ship blow up, do you suppose?" inquired Angelica. "And poor Lieutenant Blewitt, what will become of him?"

"I suppose that Billy must share the fate of others," answered Alick. "But I can assure you that I have no fear that she will blow up. Her crew are well-disciplined, and the soldiers appear to be equally so, judging by the way they were behaving when we left the ship, and it was only as a matter of precaution, in case of accident, that Captain

Rogers had you put into the boat, and it is probable that we shall be on board again in an hour or so, or in less time."

"Do you venture to call Lieutenant Blewitt 'Billy?'" exclaimed Angelica, in whose tender besom the full amount of affection she had ever felt had returned for our friend, on supposing that he was in peril and might be lost to her for ever.

"I beg your pardon, Miss Angelica. I forgot when I spoke that you and he were spooney on each other," answered Alick, with perfect gravity. "I confess that we always call him 'Billy' in the berth, but on duty we address him with due respect as 'Lieutenant Blewitt'; the other lieutenants, however, always speak of him as 'Billy Blueblazes,' and he likes the name, he has got so accustomed to it."

Meantime, as far as could be ascertained by those in the boat, the fire continued burning on board the ship. Sparks were seen occasionally rising above the deck, and Alick now began to entertain serious apprehensions that the ship would be destroyed. Some of her crew might escape in the boats, but he was very sure that the officers would be the last to leave her, and that it would be impossible to construct rafts to convey them all. He had been ready up to this time to joke and even to laugh. He now became very serious. The fire might reach to the magazine, though he felt sure that Captain Rogers would order it to be drowned or the powder to be thrown overboard, if such could be done.

Meantime Jack and those under his command were making every effort which men could make to extinguish the fire. It was discovered to have originated in the after bunkers, and that the flames had got hold of some of the wood-work. By persevering efforts they having been extinguished, Tom, covering up his head with a piece of wet blanket, followed by Jerry Bird and a gallant party of seamen similarly protected, made their way, buckets in hand, to the very seat of the fire.

Again and again they were driven back, and Jerry, stout-hearted as he was, was hoisted senseless on deck, overcome by the smoke; two others suffering in the same manner, Tom and the rest persevering. He was ready to perish rather than allow Jack's ship to be destroyed. More volunteers were called for. At length, by their united efforts, as one party being overcome, another taking their place, the fire was got under, when the bunk being cooled by water, the coals were scraped out.

By this time the sun was just rising above the horizon, casting a bright glare on the ship, as she slowly moved over the calm water. Jack and all the naval and military officers were still on deck, many of them with their faces and hands blackened, as well as their clothing, by the smoke, while the ship herself presented far from her usual trim appearance. The boat was hauled alongside. The first to appear was the major, still wearing his blanket, which he had forgotten to throw aside, and not recollecting the curious figure he cut. His own officers turned from him, disgusted at what they supposed his pusillanimity and his desertion of them and his men; while the naval officers only laughed at his unusual and somewhat absurd costume. He was followed by his two daughters, Mrs Major Bubsby bringing up the rear, though it might have been wiser in her to have led the van. Her curious appearance did not lessen the merriment of those who had not before seen her, and those of the crew who were standing near in no way attempted to restrain their laughter.

"What's it all about?" asked the major, in an indignant tone. He was too acute not to perceive the effect his conduct had produced on his own officers, but he determined to brazen it out. "You think I deserted you, gentlemen," he said. "You are much mistaken. I was the victim of affection. My beloved wife and daughters kept me an unwilling prisoner. I put it to you, gentlemen, how would you have behaved under similar circumstances? I made the most strenuous efforts to regain the deck, but these two dear girls of mine clung to me with frantic energy, and Mrs Bubsby held me down by main force."

"I did, I own it," exclaimed Mrs Bubsby, who, now the danger was over, saw the dubious position in which her husband was placed. "My deep affection overcame every other consideration, and all I thought of was the safety of my beloved husband. My daughters were animated by the same spirit."

"Yes, we are. We thought that you would all be burnt, or blown up, or go to the bottom, and poor dear Lieutenant Blewitt into the bargain; and we could not endure the thoughts of losing our papa, so we held him tight, though he is as brave and strong as a lion. It was a very difficult thing to keep him down, I can assure you;" and Angelica burst into tears.

Whether or not they produced any effect on the hard hearts of the captains and subalterns of the regiment it is impossible to say.

"I should advise you, major, and Mrs Bubsby to go below and turn in, or change your dress, which is not quite becoming the deck of a man-of-war, and I hope your daughters will follow your example," observed Jack, who thought that matters were proceeding too far.

It was impossible to stop the shouts of laughter which escaped the ship's company as, one after another, they managed to get a look at the curious group.

"I will take your advice, Captain Rogers," answered the major, and he, followed by his tall family, disappeared.

The ship had received less damage than might have been expected, and the machinery not having been injured, she proceeded towards her destination. Next day she came off a small, but land-locked, bay. The master, by careful pilotage, brought her in, and she anchored safely.

Jack breathed a sigh of relief as he thought that he should now get rid of the major and his family, as well as of the troops, admirably as they had behaved on board. The officers thanked him for the courtesy he had shown them. They eyed the major, who was standing at a little distance, with looks askance.

"What we shall do under such a commanding officer is more than I can tell," said the senior captain. "I am sorry, Captain Rogers, that you have had so bad a specimen of a military man on board your ship. Were any superior officers on shore, we should at once bring him to a court-martial, and you would be under the necessity of carrying him and his belongings back. As it is, in the face of an enemy, we cannot refuse to serve under him, and we can only hope that his wife and daughters will cling round his neck and keep him at head-quarters, or that a shot may disable him from active service. A very little thing would, I suspect, do that. We wish him no further ill."

"I am very willing to oblige you in everything," said Jack, laughing; "but I would rather not have the pleasure of carrying him and his 'woman kind,' as he calls them, back to Simon's Bay."

The boats were busily employed in landing the soldiers, who bade an affectionate farewell to their blue-jacket brethren. Most of the officers had landed; the major and his family still remained. He appeared to have arrived at the conclusion that he did not stand very well with those under his command. Had the ship gone down, he would have saved his life, and there would have been nobody to complain; but as it was, and there had been no real danger, he found himself placed in a very awkward position. Of this he was well aware. He came up to Jack.

"Age and infirmity have told upon me lately, Captain Rogers," he said. "Mrs Bubsby and my daughters are of the same opinion. My charming daughter Angelica is very anxious to go back with you to Cape Town. I have, therefore, come to the conclusion of resigning my command and returning home, whatever may be the consequences."

"Are you speaking seriously?" asked Jack. "Have you considered the consequences of such an act? I should have thought that you would have been anxious to retrieve your character by showing your courage the first time you had an opportunity of meeting the enemy."

"*My* courage!" exclaimed the major; "who ever doubted that? It was not my courage gave way; it was the stout arms and affectionate embraces of my beloved daughters which kept me back in the boat when they thought that the ship was going down. My courage and honour are as bright as they ever were in my best days, when I was known as a perfect fire-eater. Do you know what I did in the Crimea—how gallantly I behaved at the storming of Sevastopol? how I held the rifle-pits against a host of the enemy? how at the Alma I climbed up the heights, shouting 'Death or victory!' when my men were driven back by the showers of bullets hissing past us and might have fled? Why, sir, if any officer deserved the Victoria Cross, I did!"

"I have not heard of your brave deeds, Major Bubsby," answered Jack, "and it is my duty to land you and your wife and daughters at the nearest place to your destination. The state of the surf prevented my doing so at Waterloo Bay, and now I have only to inform you that the boat is waiting to convey you and your family on shore. Your heavy baggage has already been sent off; what remains can be carried with you."

The major looked aghast. "Surely, Captain Rogers, you do not mean to say you insist on my landing, whether I like it or not, and would compel me and my delicate wife and those fair young creatures to march thirty miles or more through the sands of Africa without conveyance for ourselves and baggage?"

"Duty is duty, major," answered Jack, who was determined not to take him back if he could help it. "Your duty is to land, mine is to put you on shore. You'll excuse me for saying this, but I intend to perform my duty."

The major, seeing that he had no help for it, made a virtue of necessity. He called out to his wife—

"We must go, my beloved, and our sweet children must be exposed to the fearful dangers of this unknown land."

On hearing this Mrs Bubsby approached Jack, who stood boldly prepared for the assault he had every reason to expect from the frown which had gathered on the lady's brow.

"Captain Rogers!" she exclaimed, in a voice which made Jack answer—

"Madam!" He had no time to say more, when she went on—

"Have you, who belong to the sister service, the barbarity to refuse a passage to my beloved husband and my delicate daughters, when the request has been made to you? For myself, I care not; I can march wherever the regiment can go. I did not expect this from you; and I'd have you know that I do not consider your conduct worthy of an officer and a gentleman."

"Madam!" again ejaculated Jack, "I must not submit to such language, even from a lady. I have simply to perform my duty, which is to land Major Bubsby and his family. If he will not go, I should be sorry to have to hoist him and you over the side; but I intend to do so."

Mrs Bubsby plucked off her gloves. Jack looked at her hands; her nails were long, but the captain of a man-of-war was not likely to be assaulted on the deck of his own ship, even by a lady. Still Jack could not tell what might be the irate dame's intention.

The fair Angelica cast a glance at Lieutenant Blewitt, who was standing at the gangway, hoping heartily to have the honour of handing her and her sister down the accommodation ladder, and of uttering a last farewell, but he averted his eyes when he saw those of his charmer fixed on him. The major now began to be seriously alarmed that his wife, of whose temper he had full experience, might proceed to extremities, and that it would be better to face the scorn of his officers and the assegais of the Caffres than be ignominiously tumbled over the side.

"Come, come, my beloved! Captain Rogers knows his duty. He fulfils it sternly, I must say; but still we must obey; so march!" In the mean time Archie Gordon, having received directions from Jack, was seeing the light baggage of the major conveyed to the boat. He sent Alick to say that all was ready. The major saw that there was no excuse for further delay.

"Farewell, Captain Rogers," he said, lifting his hat. "Farewell, gentlemen. You see a doomed man!" and he marched to the gangway.

"Oh, cruel! cruel!" uttered Mrs Bubsby, an exclamation repeated by Eugenia and Angelica.

"Give her another copy of verses," whispered Tom to Billy, "or repeat those I wrote for you."

"I forget them, or I would," said Billy.

"Good-bye, Miss Angelica," he added, as the young lady passed him with an averted countenance, not deigning a reply. The major descended into the boat. He would have been in a still greater hurry to be off had he not known what he was to expect on landing. He had some thoughts of throwing himself overboard; but the fin of a shark gliding by turned him from his intention. The ladies followed; and as they took their seats they put their handkerchiefs to their eyes, but whether to weep at parting from the naval officers or on account of their harsh treatment, it was impossible to say. Alick, who steered the boat, declared that he did not think they were crying at all. The major sat silent and moody for some time. Once he got up, "with fury in his countenance," as Alick afterwards described; but his wife and daughters pulled him down, and at length he and they were landed safe on the beach, their various articles of baggage being carried up after them to a spot where a sergeant and a party of men were standing ready to escort them to the camp which had already been pitched in an advantageous position inland. They might at any time be attacked by the Caffres; but the force was sufficient to keep at bay any number of the enemy likely to be in that part of the country.

"Have you any message to send to Lieutenant Blewitt, Miss Angelica?" asked Alick, touching his cap with perfect gravity to that lady, who was walking last; he having already wished the major and the rest "Good-bye."

"Yes; tell him he is a base deceiver," answered Angelica, "and that I hope he may catch a tartar the next time he attempts to make love to an innocent maiden by presenting her with any of his abominable verses."

"Yes, miss," answered Alick; "I'll faithfully deliver your message." And as he had been ordered to return without delay, he hurried back to the boat.

"Well, Alick, what did they say?" asked Tom, as he returned on board.

Alick described what had happened, and did not fail to repeat Miss Angelica's message to Lieutenant Blewitt.

"I would rather not deliver it myself. Perhaps you will, sir, as it may appear somewhat disrespectful coming from me," added the midshipman.

"All right," said Tom, chuckling. "I'll take care he gets it."

Tom took the opportunity, when most of the officers were collected at the mess table, to deliver Miss Angelica's message.

Billy laughed as heartily as any one. "I don't care what she called me, now that I am rid of her. I'm very much obliged to you, Rogers, for your verses, although I confess that at the time I certainly did feel considerably annoyed."

Jack, having got rid of his guests, and being anxious to repair the damage caused by the fire, without delay steamed out of the harbour and proceeded on his voyage to Simon's Bay.

The man who had been picked up just before the fire broke out had been carefully tended by the surgeon. During the whole time that efforts had been made to extinguish it, he had remained in a state of insensibility, and only recovered after the troops had landed. Tom, whose berth he occupied, visited him frequently, but found him ill able to converse or even to give any account of himself. At length, after a refreshing sleep, he awoke greatly recovered.

"I understand from the doctor, sir," he said, when Tom soon afterwards went to see him, "that you have placed me in your berth, and I wish not to keep you out of it longer than possible. I am a ruined man, and must not expect longer to enjoy any of the comforts of life, until I can retrieve my fortunes, if that can ever be done."

"Pray do not consider that you have inconvenienced me," answered Tom. "I am very happy to be of service to you. All we know is that we found you nearly perishing, and are happy to render you any aid in our power. We are naturally somewhat curious to know how you came to be floating all by yourself on a raft."

"That's very natural, sir. My story is not a long one. My name is Cooper. I was master and part owner of a fine barque, the *Flora*, trading to Hobart Town, in Tasmania. I was coming home by the southern route, when during some thick weather we sighted a rock not laid down in my chart. I call it a rock, but it was rather a small island rising in lofty precipices out of the sea. The weather clearing, somewhat to my surprise I made out a signal flying from a flag-staff, and on standing in close I could see through my glass a small hut. Believing that some shipwrecked people were there, I stood still closer in, when a sudden squall struck my vessel, and laid her on her beam ends. She righted without much damage, as far as could be discovered; but the weather coming on very bad, I was obliged to keep off the shore. I made a second attempt, but was again driven off, and soon afterwards as heavy a gale as ever I experienced coming on from the southward, having lost my main and mizzen masts, and very nearly my fore-topmast, I was compelled to run before it. I had hopes of getting into Simon's Bay, when the carpenter came to me and reported eight feet of water in the hold. I sent the crew to the pumps, but all their efforts could not free the ship, for the water kept rushing in with fearful rapidity. A butt had been started. A heavy sea was running at the time, but I hoped the boats would live. I ordered them to be lowered when the cry arose that the ship was sinking. A panic seized my crew, and all hands rushed to the sides. Some leaped into one boat, some into another. Almost immediately the boats were swamped, and I had the misery to see the poor fellows drowned before my eyes. I alone remained on deck. The ship floated longer than I expected, and I had time to lash together the imperfect raft on which you found me, get it overboard, and to leap upon it, and with only a few biscuits which I stuffed into my pockets and a bottle of water. Had I not taken them I must have perished. How I could have existed for a whole week, as I did, I know not; but I must have been very far gone, when through the mercy of Heaven you found me."

"You have indeed escaped from a terrible danger," said Tom. "But I wish that you could have given more perfect information about the rock on which you saw the signal flying, and its position."

"I noted it down at the time, sir, but my log was lost, and the events which have since occurred have put that and many other things out of my head, though I have been trying in vain to recall it. I do not remember at all clearly how many weeks' sail we were from Hobart Town, or how far I ran after sighting the rock; nor, indeed, how long I must have been on the raft, though while I retained my consciousness it seemed an age. On considering over the matter, I conclude that the gale could not have lasted much less than a week, and perhaps longer."

Tom, on obtaining this important information, at once communicated it to Jack, who immediately went to Captain Cooper, and had a conversation with him.

"It is within the range of possibilities that the *Empress* may have been lost on the rock sighted by Captain Cooper, though how she could have got so far to the east, when she should have hauled up long before for Aden, it is difficult to say," observed Jack, when afterwards talking the matter over with the lieutenant and master. "Probably her machinery broke down, as ours did."

"And meeting with a gale, she had to run before it," remarked the master. "These steam-kettles of ours can never be depended upon. I wish we could go back to the good old sailing ships. When we had them we knew what we were about, and took good care to keep off a lee shore; or, when it came on to blow, we hove the ship to and rode it out comfortably. Now we trust to the machinery, and it fails us in time of need. I shouldn't like to say that to the engineer, for he sticks up for his engines, and wonders how ships used to cross the ocean before they got steam power."

Jack smiled. The master was a thorough seaman, and he was allowed always to have his say against the "new-fangled notions of the day," as he called them. Both Gordon and Tom agreed with the master that there was a great probability that the *Empress* had been lost on the rock seen by Captain Cooper, as she had not touched at Aden nor been heard of further to the eastward. Some of her crew might have escaped, although it was too probable that many were lost, and if so that Adair was among them; he certainly would not have quitted the wreck until the last—they knew him too well to suppose that.

"The signal seen by Captain Cooper may, however, have been hoisted by the people who escaped from some other wreck," observed Tom.

"Perhaps the *Empress* went down during the gale in which we lost sight of her," said the master.

"I trust that such was not the case; she was as likely to keep afloat as we were, unless some unforeseen accident happened —"

"To the machinery," put in the master. "If the steam was shut off and Captain Adair had trusted to his stout canvas, I should have no fear on the subject."

"Heaven forbid that she should have foundered. If she did, we shall never obtain proof positive of the fact," said the captain. "I am far rather inclined to believe that she struck on some unknown reef, and that the rock or island was reached in the boats, or that the ship herself gained it, unless too much damaged to continue her voyage. One thing I am determined to do as soon as our repairs are completed, to obtain leave to go in search of her, and should any other unfortunate persons be on the rock, we shall at all events have the satisfaction of rescuing them."

Fortunately the weather continued fine, and the *Bellona*, without further misadventure, reached Simon's Bay. The repairs, however, took longer than was expected, as the damage received was far more serious than at first supposed. However, the work was such as could be accomplished while the ship was in Simon's Bay.

"Take care your machinery don't break down again, Mr Rivett," observed Mr Scales, the master, who was generally known as Gunter Scale. "We've got a ticklish part of the ocean to navigate, I can tell you, and if your engines fail just at the moment they are wanted to back astern off a coral reef, or keep the ship from being drifted on a lee shore, I shan't have much to say in their favour."

"I beg, Mr Scales, that you will not take the ship into any such position. I understood that every rock and shoal between us and the south pole was well laid down, and it will be your fault if we come upon danger without knowing it beforehand."

"You were wrongly informed, Mr Rivett; and there is many a rock, and many a shoal, and many an island, too, between us and the pole which no one alive knows anything about, although many a poor fellow has found them out too late, when his ship has run right upon them."

"What you say reminds me of the Irish pilot who told the captain of a ship he was taking to an anchorage, that he knew every rock on the coast. The captain doubted him, and five minutes afterwards the ship went crash upon one. 'Bedad! I tould your honour I knew thim, an' that's one of thim. There's many a rock I've found out in the same manner,'" said Tom, who thought it better to put an end to the discussion.

"I hope we shall find out none in that fashion," said Mr Rivett.

"That will depend on your machinery," said Mr Gunter Scale, chuckling. "We shall have to keep a bright look-out ahead and the lead going, and if your piston rods and boilers prove faithful, well and good. If not, I cannot warrant that the ship will keep out of the danger into which that screw of yours will run us. Let me have her under canvas and I'll know where I'll go and where I'll not go, and I'll answer for it that I won't run a ship under my charge into a place where her sails can't take her off again."

"Then you have not perfect confidence in my machinery?" observed Mr Rivett.

"No, I have not, and I wonder that you expect me to have. I say again, give me tough masts, sound spars, well set-up rigging, and stout canvas, with a properly built ship under my feet, and I'll keep the sea in all weathers, and carry her safely round the world."

The discussion might have continued for many hours had not both officers been summoned to their respective duties.

Jack, according to his intention, reported to the admiral the account he had received from Captain Cooper, who afterwards repeated it.

"I'm afraid that there is but little chance of your finding the missing ship, but at all events you shall go in search of her," was the answer.

The repairs at length being completed, the *Bellona* sailed in search of the *Empress*.

Chapter Seventeen.

The Empress loses sight of the Bellona—A gale—Sails blown
away—Runs before the wind—A leak—The pumps
manned—Crew set to bale—Pat's dream—Pete discovers the
leak—A thrummed sail got under the bottom—Another
leak—The gale increases—Steer for Virginia Island—All
hands spell and spell—The ship passes over a reef—False
keel carried away—The water gains on them—Adair
addresses the crew—The midshipman and ship's boy with
their water jugs—Land in sight—Reached at night—A
beacon fire appears on shore—Ship drifts from her anchor—
Surmises as to its being Fly-away Island—The ship regains
an anchorage—Two boats sent on shore—Green grasps the
hand of Lord Saint Maur—Stores and part of the crew
landed—The ship again driven off the shore.

We must now go back to the *Empress*, which we left somewhere
about the Tropic of Capricorn, in a heavy gale of wind, approaching
to a hurricane. The weather having come on very thick, she soon lost
sight of her consort, when the heavy sea which got up compelled
Captain Adair either to heave the ship to or to run before the wind.
He chose the former alternative, the steam still being kept up.
Waiting for a lull, he brought her to the wind under a close-reefed
main-topsail. Heavy ship as she was, and deep in the water with
stores and provisions of all sorts, she did not ride it out in the
comfortable fashion of an old wooden frigate. A fierce blast blew her
canvas to ribbons, and a sea striking her carried away the bulwarks
forward, and swept her deck, knocking two of her boats to pieces,
and doing other serious damage. Her screw working brought her up
again, or the consequences might have been still more serious. It
took a long time with all the strength that could be applied to set
another sail, when the ship for a time rode rather more easily.

She thus continued hove to for a couple of days, the weather in no
way moderating. Adair felt anxious about the *Bellona*, which he
hoped to have seen, not being aware that by running south he would
have got out of the gale as she did. Many a good seaman under
similar circumstances has made the same mistake. Suddenly the
engines stopped. Adair sent to inquire the cause. Part of the
machinery had got out of gear, but the engineer reported that it

would be soon again in order if the ship could be induced to remain steady for a time.

"He might as well tell us to land him and his engines and to set up a forge and shop," observed Jos Green, the master, who had no greater affection for "steam-kettles" than had old Gunter Scale, his brother master of the *Bellona*.

The ship was now in an uncomfortable position, to say the best of it another blast might blow away a second topsail, and if she fell oil it would be a difficult task to bring her to the wind again; her only resource would then be to run before the gale. The danger apprehended came upon her: the ship fell into the trough of the sea.

"Hold on, hold on, all of you for your lives!" shouted Adair, as he saw a heavy wave come rolling on. It struck the ship, the decks were again swept, and two poor fellows, who had failed to obey the captain's orders, were carried away without the slightest hope of being rescued. Adair sent below; he received the same answer as before from the engineer. Meantime an attempt was made again to set head sail. As she thus lay the sea broke over her several times, doing more damage.

The well was sounded, and the carpenter reported four feet of water in the hold. The donkey engine was immediately set to work. Fortunately, that not refusing to do its duty, after being some time in operation it gained on the water.

In the mean time another main-topsail was set and an attempt made to wear ship. Suddenly the wind shifted to the north-west, and filling the sails of the sorely battered ship she flew before it, though the heavy broken seas which rolled up astern threatened at any moment to poop her. The engineer complained bitterly of the way in which the ship tumbled about.

"Never mind it now, my good fellow," said Green; "we are under snug canvas and as much as we can carry, and your engines may have some rest. By-and-by we shall get into a calm; it will be your turn then. We seamen have the ship to ourselves at present. If we put into Simon's Bay, and there happens to be no rollers tumbling in, you will have time enough to put your gimcrack machinery to rights."

"That's just what old Gunter Scale would have said," observed the engineer, who had once served with him on the *Bellona*, and was accustomed to his satirical remarks.

The ship, however, was not destined to touch at the Cape, for one of those terrific gales which occasionally blow off the African coast caught her when within a hundred miles of land, covering her deck with a fine impalpable sand, and having only her canvas to depend upon, she was driven so far to the southward that it would have compelled her to go considerably out of her way had she hauled up again for the Cape. She then fell in with a trade wind, which carried her under all sail to the eastward, and Adair, hoping to regain the lost time, continued in that course until in the longitude of Madagascar, outside of which he intended to stand, avoiding the Mozambique Channel, and probably, if necessary, to touch at the Mauritius, where he could get his engines repaired.

Once more, however, another gale, not inferior in power to those she had already encountered, came on from the north-west. The battered *Empress* was but ill-prepared to encounter it. The donkey engine had been kept going, and the water had not hitherto considerably increased, but still it was evident that a serious leak existed somewhere, although where it was had not yet been ascertained. Adair and his lieutenant, as well as the carpenter and boatswain, had made repeated efforts to discover the exact spot. The only way to do this was to creep under the bunkers among the bilge water, an unpleasant and dangerous task. It was evident that the water must be reduced before the leak could be discovered.

The word was given to man the chain pumps, and the bilge pumps were also set in motion, while a double line of men were formed with all the buckets which could be found on board, from the main-deck to the hold, to bale out the water, one line passing down the empty buckets and the other handing up the full ones, almost as quickly as a chain pump could have done it. The men worked with a will, for they knew full well the danger to which they were exposed. Perfect discipline, however, was maintained; no one showed the slightest sign of fear, no one complained. Adair had shipped among his crew our old acquaintances Pat Casey and Peter the black, the last-named as a stoker, being better able to perform the office than most Englishmen. With one or two exceptions, the remaining stokers were either Irishmen or Germans, the latter having an aptitude for becoming stokers and sugar bakers, avocations which require the power of enduring heat.

The gale continued to increase, and in spite of all the efforts of the crew the water rushed in as furiously as before. Even had the engines been in order, it would have been impossible to steam back against the wind to the Cape, and it was a great question whether the ship could be kept afloat until the Mauritius—the nearest land—could be reached. Adair and Jos Green anxiously examined the chart.

"Should the wind shift a few points more to the westward, we might manage it under sail, but in our present circumstances the only thing to be done is to keep the ship before the gale," observed the master.

In few parts of the ocean is the sea more heavy than in the latitude in which the *Empress* now was, except, perhaps, to the southward of Cape Horn. All the other pumps were now set going, and a fresh party was told off to bale out the water with iron hand-buckets. These were hoisted up at the rate of seventy an hour.

"Set the fiddle and fife going, it will keep up the spirits of the men," said Adair to the first lieutenant, who at once issued the order. Presently merry notes were heard amid the howling of the gale, sounding strangely, and yet inspiriting the crew. Still, in spite of all that could be done, the water rose higher and higher.

"Peter," said Pat Casey to his old shipmate, when, after toiling for four hours, they knocked off to get a little rest, "it's my opinion that this is the last cruise you and I shall take together. I've been in many a mighty quare fix before now, but niver one like this. Sure, there's nothin' I hate more than a ship with a hole in her bottom, an' that's what we've got, an' a pretty big one, I'm after thinkin'."

"You no gib up, Pat," answered Peter. "We fall in with 'nother ship, or sight some land, and we get 'shore, or stop de leak. When de cap'n finds de ship make too much water, he keep her 'float by fixin' a sail under her."

"You may say what ye plaise, but before a sail could be thrummed an' passed under her keel, she'll be many fathoms down into the depths of the ocean. An' supposin' we did fall in with a ship, sure, how could we get aboard of her with this sea runnin'? Then, as to reaching land—where's the land to reach? I niver heard speak of any land away to the south'ard, except the icy pole, an' that we should niver see if we wished it ever so much."

"Dat may be de case; I nebber could make out de meanin' ob a chart, but wheneber I hab been in de Pacific, me find many islands, and tink dere mus' be some here'bout. Why you so down-hearted?"

"Down-hearted is it, sure? I'm not down-hearted, Pater; but I'll tell ye, I dreamed a dream the night the gale came on, as I lay in me hammock; the ould mither—who's gone to glory these six years—came and stood by me side, an' I saw her face as clearly as I see yours, an' says she, 'Tim, me son, I've come to wake you;' then says I, 'Mither, what's that for?' Says she, 'I can wake ye well, although I cannot give ye dacent burial.' Upon that she sit up such a howlin' I thought it would be heard all along the deck. Says I, 'Mither, just hold fast there, or you'll be afther disturbin' the whole watch below.' But she wouldn't, an' still howled on, jist as I mind th' women doin' in ould Ireland whin I was a boy. Again I sung out, 'Mither, if ye love me, hold your peace. I don't want to be waked just now,' and as I uttered the words I heard the boatswain pipe all hands on deck, when sure if the wind wasn't shrieking, an' the blocks rattling, an' the masts groaning, showin' that a dacent hurricane was blowin'. Me mither vanished immediately, an' I tumbled up on deck, more asleep thin awake, thinkin' of what the good soul had been saying to me."

Peter fell asleep while Pat was talking, and both in a brief time were again summoned to take their spell at baling. All efforts to discover the leak had been hitherto in vain. Peter went to the chief engineer.

"Pardon, sir, me tink find out de leak. If black Peter get drowned, easily find better man to take him place."

"I shall be very glad if you do, Peter, for I suspect if the leak is not found we shall all be drowned together," said the engineer. "What do you propose doing?"

"Jus' dive down under de water, wid rope round him waist, an' have a bright light held above where him go down. You see, sir, lantern no burn under de water, or me take him down."

"You might possibly succeed; but I fear you will lose your life," answered the engineer. "But you shall try if you like."

"All right, ear," said Peter, "me try, no matter what happen."

The engineer reported to the captain the offer of the black. Adair allowed him to make the attempt, and ordered the gunner to bring several blue-lights, as well as a dozen ship's lanterns, and he, with his first lieutenant, the chief engineer, the gunner, and boatswain, and three men to hold the rope, went below, where Peter stood prepared for his undertaking. The hatches overhead were taken off to allow the fumes of the blue-lights to escape.

"Now," cried Peter, "me ready," and slipping into the water, he disappeared beneath it. A blue-light was instantly ignited, the bright glare of which must, it was hoped, penetrate to the very bottom of the ship. It seemed impossible to those standing by that Peter could exist beneath the black fluid which surged over him. The seconds went slowly by, each second appearing to them almost like a minute. The doctor, who had come down, kept his watch in his hand. Adair expected him every moment to give the signal for drawing up the man.

"The poor fellow will be drowned if he stays any longer," observed Adair.

"He will endure it for twenty-five seconds more," answered the doctor. "We must have him up by that time, if he does not return."

"Haul him up," cried Adair; "he cannot stand it longer."

Just as he spoke, the black's head appeared above the water.

"Me find it next time," he said, drawing a deep breath. In a couple of minutes Peter declared himself ready again to descend. Another blue-light was burned, irradiating the depths below. As before, the doctor watched the time Peter was under the water. Two minutes had passed, when Adair ordered the man to be hauled up. It was not a moment too soon. At first, from his appearance, all supposed he was drowned, and the doctor began to prepare to resuscitate him, when he came to himself.

"All right!" he exclaimed; "de leak found, big 'nough to put him hand through."

Peter, as soon as he had regained his strength, showed the exact spot where the hole existed, through which the water was spouting as through a hose. Adair was satisfied that the black was right. The question was now how to stop it. The carpenter had got plugs ready, but Peter averred that no human power could force them in, unless the pressure of water was first taken off from the outside. The only way of doing this was by getting a thrummed sail under the ship's bottom. The engineer suggested that an iron plate should be screwed on, but the difficulty was to screw it in the proper position. He then proposed fixing an iron bar to the plate and securing the other end to a beam above it. The plate was quickly prepared as he suggested, but though it prevented the water spouting upwards as it had before done, it found an entrance notwithstanding, between the plate and the ship's bottom. Adair now gave orders to have a sail thrummed. The operation is as follows: A sail is stretched out and masses of oakum are fastened on to one side, so as to give it the appearance of a large rug of great thickness. Strong ropes are secured to the four corners; it is then dragged under the ship's bottom, when, by the force of the water rushing in, it is sucked into the leak, and although some water still finds its way through, it is calculated greatly to impede its entrance. Happily there came a lull, and during it the ropes were got over the ship's bows, and dragged on until the part where the leak existed was reached, when the thrummed sail was hauled under the bottom, and firmly secured.

A hundred more hands were now told off to bale at the different hatchways with canvas buckets, which the sailmaker's crew and other men had been employed in making to supplement the iron ones. Adair anxiously watched the result of their labours.

"If the weather improves we shall do well yet," observed Green to the first lieutenant.

"One does not see much prospect of that," was the answer.

The sky indeed was as gloomy as ever, the wind blew a perfect hurricane, while the thick mist and spray which flew over the deck wetted every one to the skin. As the hours went by there was no relaxation for the hard-worked crew. The seamen and marines, engineers, and stokers, as well as the officers, laboured away with but short intervals for rest.

No sooner were the men relieved, than, overcome by their exertions, they threw themselves down on the deck and waited until it was their turn again. The carpenter reported the water diminishing.

"We ought, howsumever, to have got more out of the ship by this time than we have," he observed. "To my mind, there must be another leak somewhere."

Adair feared that the carpenter was right, and Peter, hearing his opinion, volunteered again to do down and grope about until he could discover it. The same precautions were taken to save him from destruction.

He persevered until he was so utterly exhausted that the doctor declared him to be unfit again to go below. Though he had not succeeded, Adair thanked him for his gallant conduct, and promised that it should not be overlooked.

"Me berry happy, cap'n, if de ship get into harbour. No want reward," answered the brave negro.

Scarcely had the thrummed sail been got under the ship, than it began to blow as hard as ever. Should the gale continue for many days longer, all hope of saving the ship must be given up, and probably every soul on board would perish. Adair did not conceal this from himself, although neither by word nor look did he show what was passing in his mind. There were rocks, rather than islands, he knew to the southward, one of which might possibly be reached, but much depended on the state of the weather. Should the sea go down, the ship might be kept afloat, but he could not hope to get back to the Cape nor even to the Mauritius. At present he could steer no other course than directly before the wind.

On examining the chart, he discovered that about 200 miles off to the southward of east was a rock marked Virginia Island, but he could not find any description of it. Whether its sides were precipitous and could not be scaled, whether low and easy of access, or whether it possessed a harbour of any description, not a word was said. It might be a barren rock without water, or any means of affording sustenance to even a small number of men. He could scarcely expect it to be otherwise, for in that latitude, he knew, where exposed to the icy blasts of the southern pole, all vegetation would be stunted if not destroyed, while he could scarcely entertain a hope that springs existed. Still it was the nearest land of any description, and land is eagerly sought for by those on board a foundering ship. He was aware that other rocks in this latitude were the product of volcanic action, and that this was so likewise he had little doubt; should such be the case, it was very improbable that water would be found.

Poor Adair felt his position keenly. Through no fault of his, the lives of all entrusted to him were placed in jeopardy. Often and often his thoughts went wandering away to his dear Lucy. Although he would not have allowed any fear of losing his own life to oppress him, he could not help dreading the idea of plunging her in grief and exposing her to long months of anxious suspense. Still his officers, as they watched his calm countenance and brisk manner, fancied he was as light-hearted as ever, and some thought that he could not have realised the fearful position in which they were placed.

They were now running across a little-known sea. The chart showed dangers, but marked as somewhat uncertain. Still the storm-driven ship could pursue no other course. A hundred miles at least had yet to be accomplished before the island they hoped to sight could be reached; but even should that prove to be correctly marked on the chart, Green had some doubt about sighting it. The ship might pass it and yet it might not be seen, or the gale, continuing, might drive her on with headlong force, so that she might not be able to haul up in time to get under its lee. Twelve or fourteen hours would decide the point, perhaps even less.

The wind had begun to moderate slightly, and some of the older hands on board, accustomed to the southern ocean, prognosticated a change of weather. All prayed that it might come. Night returned, but it brought no rest to the labouring crew. Every man and boy on board, except those on the look-out, were engaged in pumping or baling, unless lying down recruiting their strength for renewed exertions. They were working spell and spell, knowing full well that unless such were done, the ship could not be kept afloat. As she had before being recommissioned undergone a thorough repair, no one could account for the leak. Many did anything but bless the ship-builders. Some declared that the outer coat of wood was rotten, and that the inner one of iron had become corroded and had just been patched up to deceive the eye of the surveyor.

"Bedad! I belave it must be one of thim big fishes with the long noses has run against us, an' drilled a hole before he could get off again," said rat Casey to his shipmate Peter; "or, maybe, the big say sarpint was swimmin' by and gave us a whisk of his tail unbeknown."

"Me tink, Massa Pat, dey make you officer, if eber we get into harbour, if you swear to dat."

"Faith, me boy, swear, is it?" observed Pat. "It's just th' sort of yarn a dockyard matey would swear to, if only to plaise his superiors; but there's one thing I believe, an' that is, that the wood an' iron are both rotten. Bad luck to thim who didn't repair the damage whin they found it out! You are of the same opinion, though it wouldn't have become ye to say so. All you'd got to do was to find out where the hole was, an' ye did it like a brave man, an' sure I'd be sorry not to get home, if it were only because you'd be afther losin' your reward."

What other reflections might have been cast on the dockyard officials it is impossible to say, when a grating sound was heard, and the ship quivered fore and aft. For a moment her way seemed to be stopped, and the cry rose from many a mouth, "We are lost! we are lost!" A tremendous sea came rolling up astern.

"Hold on, for your lives!" shouted Adair, and the order was echoed along the decks. The wave struck the vessel's stern. A portion broke over her, but the next moment she was again driven forward. That fearful, dread-inspiring sound, which tells that the keel has come in contact with a hard rock, continued. Every instant Adair dreaded that the terrific crash would come which would denote the doom of all on board. Still he stood calm, and apparently unmoved, as before.

"Keep to your stations, my lads! we will not yet let the old ship go down," shouted Adair.

The order was repeated along the deck. The magnificent discipline which prevails in the British navy, even at that terrible moment, triumphed. Not a man deserted his post, but continued pumping or baling away as if no rugged reef was beneath the ship's keel. Several times she rose and surged onwards, but it was only to feel the rock still under her. On she went. At that instant the wind began to abate, and even the sea was calmer than it had been before she had touched the reef. Still it could not be doubted that she had received a serious injury. As the howling of the tempest abated, Adair could make his voice heard along the decks.

"My lads," he said, "I know you to be true British seamen. Things may be bad enough, but we must not give way to despair. Maintain the discipline of which we are justly proud, obey your officers, and don't give in while a plank remains above water. The weather is moderating, and as soon as it is calm enough we will try and discover the amount of damage the ship has received. Stick to the pumps and buckets, and we will see if we cannot heave the water out of her faster than it comes in. Now, turn to again!" The men, while Adair was speaking, had knocked off for a few minutes. He saw, however, that he had gained time, by the energy with which they again set to work, he himself showing an example by handing along the buckets, as did all his officers. Adair and Green, however, had to knock off to try and take an observation, for the clouds gave signs of breaking, and they hoped every moment to see the sun burst forth. It was all-important indeed to ascertain the ship's exact position on the chart, that they might steer for the nearest spot where she might, if necessary, be beached, or at all events under the lee of which she might anchor, and an endeavour be made to repair damages. Whether this could be done or not could only be ascertained by a more thorough examination of her bottom than had yet been possible. The midshipmen were summoned to assist. Adair and his officers stood with their sextants in their hands ready to note the sun's altitude should he burst forth, while the first lieutenant watched the chronometer. The tossing seas rose round the labouring ship. They had already lost their leaden hue, and here and there bright green tints could be seen, while their crests no longer hissed and foamed as before. Suddenly, as if by a stroke of the magician's wand, the clouds parted, and the bright sun shone forth in a clear space of blue. The men on deck cheered as they saw it. To them it seemed an augury of safety. A satisfactory observation was taken, the exact longitude was obtained, at noon they would find the true latitude, and then, should Virginia Island have been laid down correctly, they might steer with confidence towards it. According to the chart, it was still to the eastward, and might, if the ship had not run too far south, be sighted before night.

Noon was anxiously waited for. The crew continued labouring away with the same energy as before, though in the case of some it was the energy of despair. Again Adair took his place in the line of men passing the buckets up and down. Still all their efforts did not avail to lessen the amount of water within the ship, but they kept it from increasing—that was something. As long as their strength held out, they might continue to do that. Every one knew that, should they relax in their efforts, the water would conquer them; the great point was to keep it sufficiently low to prevent the fires being put out. Should that occur and a calm come on, their case would then be desperate, even though in sight of land. Some, it is true, might be saved in the boats and others on rafts, should the ship float long enough to enable them to be constructed, but the bulk—two-thirds, probably—must be doomed to perish. Adair knew that he must be among the latter. While a soul remained on board, he could not quit his ship. Dear as life might be to him, for the sake of others it must be sacrificed. When also the trying moment should come, would discipline be maintained? Would not the crew scramble into the boats and swamp them? or leap headlong on the rafts and render them useless?

Frequently the captain and master looked at their watches. Once more they returned to the poop, with their sextants in hand. Noon was approaching. Clouds were still passing slowly across the sky; they might too probably rest between the sun and the ship, rendering it impossible to take an observation. The officers watched their progress. A large cloud was floating by; would it pass onwards before the sun gained its extreme altitude?

"Now, master!" cried Adair, in a cheerful tone.

The western edge of the cloud, tinged with a golden hue, was seen, and the sun came forth. The captain and Green with the first lieutenant had their sextants to their eyes in a moment: the sun was still rising.

"It has dipped!" cried Adair.

They carefully noted down the latitude, and Green, in a few seconds, worked out the observation on a little slip of paper, not bigger than one's thumb nail. Hurrying below, the chart was got out, and now the exact position of the ship was obtained.

"Hurrah! If this volcano of an island doesn't prove a fly-away piece of rock, we shall be up to it before sunset," exclaimed Green.

The wind had now sufficiently gone down to allow all sail to be set. The part of the crew who had knocked off from the pumps and the buckets were roused up. With the greatest alacrity, as if they had had their usual rest, they flew to their stations.

The topsails and courses, long furled, were let fall and sheeted home; staysails were hoisted, and with the screw thus aided, the ship again rushed rapidly through the water. She steered, however, with some difficulty; and Green expressed an opinion that damage had been done to her false keel, that a portion of it had been torn off, and that another part was still hanging down attached to the bottom.

"We must take that into account when we wish to bring up," observed Adair, "so that there may be no chance of running the ship on the rocks, where we do not want her to go."

The next few hours were as anxious as any that had been passed; for, although the sea was going down and the wind was moderate, the water rushed in through the leaks at a rate which required the ceaseless efforts of the crew to keep under. The youngest midshipman on board—Tommy Pratt, hitherto unknown to fame or to our readers—was observed, with one of the ship's boys, who had been considered not strong enough to handle the buckets, running up and down with two big jugs, which they emptied through the scuppers.

"Every little helps, I've heard say," answered Tommy to the first lieutenant; "and I suppose a few quarts too much would sink the ship. So I got Ned Jones, who was doing nothing, to lend me a hand; and I calculate that we have emptied two hundred gallons at least, and that's something, sir."

"Well done, my boy," answered the lieutenant. "I'll not forget you and Ned. Who knows but that you and he have kept out the last hundred gallons which might have sent her to the bottom?" Some time afterwards they were found still working away, though Tommy confessed that "his arms were aching considerably, and that he should be very glad when they could stop the leak."

Men with sharp eyes were sent to the mast-head, to look out for Virginia Island. It was uncertain whether it was a high rocky a fertile island, or little better than a sand-bank. Should it be the first and correctly laid down, the master hoped that it might at any moment be seen; but should it prove to be a low island, it might not become visible until they were close upon it. Then again came the question, was it laid down correctly? Adair, though he had assured his crew that they ought to be there before night, was not quite satisfied on that point. Hitherto the men had laboured away bravely, but some of the weaker and less spirited began to show signs of fatigue; and the instant they were relieved, threw themselves on the deck as though utterly incapable of further exertion. Some of the men, indeed, actually sank down at the pumps, but others took their places, and the doctor went round to the exhausted ones, giving them stimulants, and urging them to fresh exertions. Several, however, when it came again to their turn to pump or hand up the buckets, declared that they were unable to move. It was important to maintain discipline; at the same time the first lieutenant, who went among them, was unwilling to use harsh measures. Suddenly he recollected Tommy Pratt. Taking one of the men, he showed him where the young midshipman and his companion were still working away with their big water jugs, running up and down as nimble as squirrels.

"They have been at that work for the last eight hours, to my certain knowledge," said the lieutenant. "Are you, a big, strong man, not ashamed of yourself?"

"Yes, I am," was the answer; and, rousing up the other men, they all again set to work without further grumbling.

"I was sure the example of those youngsters would do good," observed the lieutenant to Captain Adair. "Not only have they baled out several hundred gallons, but through their gallant conduct many thousands probably will be pumped out of the ship."

As the *Empress* ran on, and no land was seen, the spirits of all began to fall lower than before. In that latitude gales were as likely to prevail as often as fine weather; and another might spring up before the ship could be carried into a harbour, or run on shore if necessary. Even Adair, who, since he had ascertained the correct position of the ship, had had his hopes revive, now felt it was too probable that the shore might never be reached.

The hours were passing by. He and Green again consulted the chart, to decide for what other spot in the ocean they should steer should Virginia Island not appear. They had just returned on deck, when the look-out aloft shouted—

"Land! land!"

"Where away?" inquired the captain. "Just over the port bow."

"Are you sure it is land?" asked the captain.

"Certain, sir. I've seen it for the last ten minutes; but there was a mist about it, and I could not make it out clearly enough."

The master and second lieutenant immediately went aloft, and took a look through their glasses at the land. On coming below they reported that there was no doubt about its being land of considerable elevation, but of no great extent, with indented shores; and that they hoped, therefore, a harbour might be found there.

The ship's course was accordingly slightly altered, and she stood towards it under sail and steam. In a short time a high, rocky island could be seen rising out of the now blue ocean, sparkling in the rays of the setting sun. It was several miles to the eastward of the spot marked on the chart.

"If it affords us shelter and the means of repairing the ship, we must be truly thankful," observed Adair.

No murmurs were now heard. Even those who had shown an inclination to skulk, laboured away with might and main. In a few more hours their safety might be secured.

The sun set. Although the land was for some time distinctly seen, it was yet a considerable distance off. Adair determined to run on and anchor under the lee of the land, and to await until daylight, when a harbour might be found.

The crew by this time might have given in, for the muscles even of the strongest ached; but one and all laboured as before. Tommy and his companion worked away with their jugs, although the poor little fellows were almost dead beat.

"Cheer up, Ned!" Tommy kept saying. "If we keep the water out of the ship, we shall see our mothers and sisters again; and if we don't, we shan't. So work away, boy, work away!" The lieutenant declared afterwards that he believed the boys would have continued heaving water overboard until the sea had got up to their necks, and the ship was going down.

As the *Empress* approached the island, sail was shortened, her way stopped, that the lead might be hove; but no soundings were found. She therefore kept at a respectful distance, cautiously steering round to the lee side, with the lead constantly going, lest she might run against any reef below the water. The outline of the island could only dimly be seen rising high out of the ocean against a clear sky. It looked barren and forlorn enough. As Adair and his officers, and indeed all who could find time, were eagerly watching it, a light was seen suddenly to burst forth. It gradually increased, until what must have been a large fire was observed blazing on a height.

"There are inhabitants, at all events," exclaimed Adair to the first lieutenant.

"There is one, any way," said the latter, "or that fire could not have been lighted. Perhaps there is a harbour, and he expects that it will serve as a beacon to us."

"He would scarcely suppose that we would venture in without some one on board who knows it, unless there are no dangers in the way," answered the captain. "Our only safe plan will be to bring up outside, and wait till daylight. We will stand in as close as we can—a dozen fathoms, if possible."

The leadsmen stood in the chains on either side, swinging the leads high in the air as they hove them. The ship appeared already very close before any bottom could be found. Slowly she stood on. The first heave showed twenty fathoms, the next fourteen, when it seemed as if the ship was directly under the cliffs. But the more experienced seamen knew that the darkness was deceptive.

"Let go!" shouted Adair, and the anchor ran out. The ship quickly brought up, and Adair hoped that, now she was at rest, the water would run in with less rapidity, though it would still be necessary to keep the crew steadily pumping away.

For the first time for several nights Adair turned in, desiring to be called should any event of importance occur. When he awoke, he had the satisfaction of hearing that the crew had gained six inches on the leak, though, from any relaxation of their efforts, the water would quickly have flowed in again.

All hands anxiously waited for daylight. The fires were kept banked up, ready at any moment should it become necessary to put on steam. It was fortunate that this precaution was taken. It had just gone two bells in the second watch, when a sudden squall, descending from the cliffs, struck the ship. The lead, which the second lieutenant, who had the watch, ordered to be hove, showed that she was drifting.

Adair was on deck in a moment. He ordered more cable to be veered out. The third lieutenant, who was in the forecastle, reported that the anchor was away. It was accordingly hove up, when it was found that it had parted close to the shank, leaving both flukes fast in the sand or rock into which it had stuck. Steam was immediately got up, although by that time the ship had drifted some distance out to sea. When the morning broke she was surrounded by a thick mist, shutting out every object half a mile off. Still, the direction of the land was known, and the engines being set to work, she soon steamed back.

"I was afther thinkin'," said Pat, "that that black rock we saw last night was but Cape Fly-away, afther all. It will be a wonder to me if we ever sight it again. But, hurrah! there's the fire we saw burning, so there must be a human being there; an' Cape Fly-away contains no living sowl except, maybe, the Flyin' Dutchman, afther he got tired of cruising about in his ould craft, an' taken to livin' on shore."

Similar ideas, although expressed in different language, were uttered by many of the other men. However, that did not prevent them from pumping away as before. All this time, it must be remembered that without a moment's cessation the whole crew were thus engaged spell and spell.

"If that's Cape Fly-away, it's not had time to fly very far," observed Pat, as the land once more came in sight and the anchor was let go in seven fathoms of water, still closer in with the shore, where it was hoped it would hold.

The engineer, however, received orders to keep the fires up, so that she might hold her own against any ordinary blast which might again strike her.

As the mist cleared away, every object on shore could be distinctly seen. The ship was found to be but a quarter of a mile distant from an almost circular line of cliffs, forming a deep basin, the only opening towards the sea. They rose in many places to the height of nearly 900 feet, extending on either side of this curious basin for about a mile. It was thus conjectured that the island was about two miles in length. That there was a bar at the entrance of the harbour was evident from the way the water broke completely across it; but, from the size of the basin, it would have contained a fleet of ships as large as the *Empress*. While they were looking at the shore, a Dutch flag was run up to the end of a staff at the end of a high rock at the southern side of the entrance.

"Sure, I thought so!" said Pat, when he saw it. "That's the Flyin' Dutchman. Before the boats reach the shore he an' his island will be off again, an' lead us a pretty chase!"

"Maybe, Massa Pat," replied Peter, "if it come on calm, we beat him by de steam. He hab always sail head to wind; but me tink dat big rock no play us dat trick."

Before sending any of the boats on shore, Adair mustered all hands.

"Now, my lads," he said, "I have to tell you what I did not think it right before to acknowledge, although you may have guessed it, that this ship will not reach Aden or the Mauritius, or any other land that I know of; and that, to save your lives, I propose running into yonder harbour and beaching her to prevent her going down; but, remember, there is one thing I must have—that is, strict discipline and obedience to orders. You will understand that I will severely punish any man who exhibits insubordination. It is as well to say that, at the same time, I know that I can trust you. You have all shown what you can do by having kept the ship afloat so long. You will, I know, work with a will, and every man must do what is necessary for the preservation of our lives. Return to the pumps until you can get the ship into harbour, or, if not, to some spot where she can sink no lower."

The crew gave three cheers, and resumed their labours. Adair immediately despatched two boats, with the first lieutenant and master, to sound the entrance of the harbour and communicate with the person or persons who had lighted the fire at night and hoisted the flag in the morning.

The master in his boat led the way, sounding as he went, until the entrance was nearly gained. Twelve feet were found, which shallowed to eight, the greatest depth over the bar. As the boats got in closer Green observed a person at the end of the point, dressed in a conical goat-skin cap, with jacket and trousers of the same material, who had been watching them closely and waving vehemently. The master, having performed the first part of his duty, steered in the direction towards which the stranger was pointing. As the boat touched the beach he sprang out, and the instant afterwards, instead of seeing a stranger, what was his surprise and delight to find his hand grasped by Gerald Desmond.

"How, by all that's wonderful, did you come here?" exclaimed the master. "We had long given you up for lost."

"I was afraid so," answered Desmond. "And, faith, I had some idea myself that I was lost, for here I've been for many a long month, with only two companions who escaped with me from the wreck of the Dutch ship which brought me thus far. But, tell me, did the *Stella* escape with my uncle and the rest of the party on board?" Green relieved Desmond's mind on that point, and astonished him not a little by adding that Captain Adair commanded the ship outside. "And who are your companions?" asked the master.

"An honest Dutch lad—Rip Van Winkle, as I call him—who was wrecked with me, and our faithful dog Snarley. They set off this morning to bring in a couple of goats to be sacrificed for your entertainment. I saw you coming in last night, and I suspected that you were an English man-of-war. You may, therefore, judge of my disappointment this morning when I found that you had disappeared. Though I guessed the truth, that you had been blown off again and would steam back, sometimes the horrible thought would occur to me that the ship had gone down; but, if such was the case, I hoped that some boats would have escaped and come on shore."

Desmond expressed his great satisfaction on receiving the information that his uncle Terence was captain of the ship which had in so extraordinary a manner been driven for refuge towards the very rock on which he had been wrecked.

"We very nearly met with the fate you supposed, and as the ship's bottom somewhat resembles a sieve, such must be her destiny if we cannot manage to get her over the bar at high water. At all events, we must run her on it, for as the men are well-nigh worn out, she cannot be kept afloat many hours longer," added Green.

"The sooner that's done the better, then," answered Desmond, "for should the gale blow heavily, either on or off this shore, and provisions and stores not have been saved, we may all quickly be reduced to starvation. Rip and I have found enough to eat with the aid of our fishing-lines, but the ship's company will be an over-abundant population for our small kingdom."

"But I am eager, Desmond, to know how you reached this said 'small kingdom' of yours," said Green.

"I'll tell you all about it as we pull off," answered Gerald, "though I am anxious to see my uncle's honest face again and to learn how things have gone on at home—whether any other claimant has taken possession of my title and estate. Poor fellow! he won't bless this island, whatever you do, for having afforded me shelter, though it may be a mighty long time before I get back to old Ireland to disappoint him and to delight the heart of our old friend, Counsellor McMahon, who will be fancying that all his toil and trouble have been thrown away, while his purse too will have suffered not a little. I have often wished that I possessed the means of tranquillising his mind on that point."

"From what Captain Adair has said, I don't think the counsellor has ever given up the idea of your safety," answered the master, "but you will hear all about it very soon."

This conversation took place as the boat was returning to the ship, after Desmond had exchanged greetings with the first lieutenant.

"Well," exclaimed Jos, "'it's an ill wind that blows nobody good,' and although I'm sorry enough to lose the ship, yet finding you goes a long way towards reconciling me to her fate, especially as I have not to pay for her."

Adair expressed himself in somewhat similar language on seeing his nephew, Saint Maur.

"I was sure that you would turn up one day or other, Gerald," he said, "and so was the counsellor, and I don't mind the court-martial and all the bother I shall have to go through, now that I have found you. Although I am anxious enough to hear how you came here, I have too much to do just now to listen to you."

Such, indeed, was the case. Before an attempt could be made to carry the ship over the bar, everything possible must be got out of her. The boats were immediately lowered and loaded with provisions and canvas for forming tents. All hands worked away with a will, young Lord Saint Maur turning to with as much energy as the rest, officers and men pulling and hauling away at the ropes. To land the stores more rapidly, Adair directed the carpenter to construct several rafts, which would be serviceable as long as the sea continued smooth, but which would be most untrustworthy should it come on to blow.

Lord Saint Maur gave the satisfactory intelligence that he had found three large boats on the island, which had apparently been left by a party who had been there for the purpose of catching whales, but for some reason or other had gone without having had time to remove them. He considered that they could be quickly repaired. He accordingly, accompanied by the carpenter's crew, returned on shore, and soon after mid-day, he and the men sent to assist him brought them off. They were soon loaded and on their way back to the shore. Not a moment was lost. The marines were at once landed to help unload the boats and carry the cargoes to the spot selected for the proposed encampment on the right side of the entrance, where there was a level space of some size at no great distance above the water. Desmond's companion, Rip Van Winkle, had, in the mean time, brought in a couple of goats, which he had killed and prepared for the refreshment of the boats' crews. No one, however, had time to do more than "fist" a piece and run back with it to the boat.

Not until it became too dark to see the entrance did the boats cease plying backwards and forwards, and even then the crew on board were engaged in hoisting up articles of all sorts from the hold, to be discharged at daybreak. The night was calm, and every hope was entertained that the next day a large portion of stores and provisions might be landed, as well as the ammunition and some of the guns. A careful watch was kept, but the greater portion of the officers and crew turned in to obtain that rest they so much needed. Those not actually on the look-out were engaged in pumping as before, for although the water ran in less furiously than at first, it would very soon otherwise have gained its previous ascendancy. Strange that men should sleep so soundly in a sinking ship, for sinking she was, slowly though gradually, and any relaxation of the efforts necessary to keep her afloat would have proved their doom. Several times during the night Captain Adair turned out, too anxious to sleep soundly. As morning approached, he feared, from the appearance of the sky, that the weather would change. His nephew, who had slept on board, joined him.

"I don't think we need fear that as yet," he observed. "I've watched the appearance of the weather ever since I landed, for every day I have been on the look-out in the hopes of seeing a ship passing and being able to attract her attention. Not long ago a vessel hove in sight, but the weather came on very bad, and although she made an attempt to near the rock, she was driven off again, and I saw no more of her."

Captain Adair was cheered up by Saint Maur's remarks. No sooner had the first streak of dawn appeared in the sky, than he roused up all hands, and the boats, which had been hoisted up, were lowered and immediately loaded with the stores which had been got ready the previous night. The other boats came off from the shore, and now as fast as they could load and unload they passed backwards and forwards between the harbour and the ship. To save the long pull, Captain Adair determined, by Saint Maur's advice, to carry her closer in. Steam was got up, and the anchor being hove from the bottom, she stood towards the shore.

As the day advanced the wind, hitherto coming off the land, shifted and began to blow much stronger than before, while a white line of surf formed across the mouth of the harbour. The boats, however, continued to pass through it, although not without risk of being swamped, while their crews on each occasion got their jackets well wetted. No one thought of that or any other danger or inconvenience. Their great object was to land stores and provisions sufficient to last them as many weeks or months, it might be, as they were to stay there, for all well knew that the old ship must go to the bottom or be knocked to pieces, unless run safely over the bar and beached inside the harbour. She had still a good store of coals on board. This was sacked and sent on shore, a small quantity only remaining, little above what was required to carry the ship over the bar. Night put an end to their labours. Besides the marines, several officers and men had been landed. As on the previous night, while part of the crew slept, the rest worked the pumps and kept a look-out.

It had just gone one bell in the middle watch, when Tommy Pratt knocked at the door of the captain's berth, and in a hurried tone exclaimed, "The wind is blowing hard; dead on shore, sir. Mr Green says the ship is drifting towards the land."

Adair sprang on deck. As he listened to the sound of the wild breakers and watched the masses of foam which appeared through the darkness leaping over the rocks, he saw that if the ship was drifting she must very soon be dashed on the wild coast under her lee. He immediately ordered steam to be got up. Small as was the amount of coal left on board, it must be employed to get the ship out of danger, when she must be carried to a safer anchorage, and some more coal brought back from the shore.

Some time elapsed, however, before steam could be got on her. She was riding to the wind with her stern to the shore, instead of, as before, with her head to it. Adair and Saint Maur anxiously paced the deck, watching the rocks under their lee. Every instant the wind was increasing. The roar of the breakers sounded louder, while masses of foam could be seen flying in sheets over the rocks.

At length the engineer announced that steam was got up, and the engines being put in motion, the cable was slipped and the still sinking ship steamed away from the only place which could afford her refuge in her last extremity. Still, with the sea there was breaking on the shore, she would to a certainty strike, and in all probability many of those on deck would be washed away, while she herself would be exposed to the full force of the waves, when ere long she would go to pieces. Adair addressed the crew, urging them to renewed exertions at the pumps. All day long she continued under steam, with her head to the wind, though still making but little way. The captain saw the importance of waiting until the spring tides, when, lightened as she was, he hoped that she would get across the bar.

That day was one of great suspense. There was too much sea for the boats to be got out, and should the bad weather continue, the coal on board would be exhausted, and she, perfectly helpless, would be driven to a distance from the land, and might be unable to regain it under sail. Saint Maur did his best to cheer up his uncle.

"I have escaped so many dangers, when I thought that all hope was gone, that I cannot say I feel as anxious as you do," he observed. "I have remarked that the wind here never blows long together from one quarter. We may have it fine and calm again to-morrow."

"I pray Heaven it may," said Adair, in a more melancholy tone than he had yet spoken in. However, to his officers and crew he kept up the same cheerful aspect as he had done all along.

Chapter Eighteen.

Lord Saint Maur narrates his adventures—Carried off by the
Dutchman—Ill-treated—Drunken skipper and mates—Rip
Van Winkle and Snarleyow—Ship strike, on a reef—Crew
desert her—Saint Maur, Rip, and Snarley get into the long-
boat—Ship goes down—Remain under the lee of the reef all
night—Make sail in the morning—No water—Virginia
Island reached—Boat capsized on the bar—Saint Maur and
Rip saved by Snarley—Their life on the island—Water
found—Goat's flesh—The Empress seen approaching the
island—Preparations for crossing the bar—Awful
suspense—Ship steams on—Strikes with a crash on the bar—
More stores landed—The jollies alarmed by a jet of steam—
Sails seen in the distance.

"By-the-by, I never told you how I came to be playing Robinson
Crusoe and his man Friday on yonder barren rock," observed Saint
Maur, as he and his uncle paced together the deck of the *Empress*.

"You remember the night I was hooked off the yacht by a stranger
which ran us down, and, as I thought, sent you to the bottom. I leave
you to judge in what a state of fear and anxiety I was left. From the
way the fellows talked when I got on board, I discovered that they
were Dutchmen. I rushed aft to the skipper and entreated him to
heave to and lower his boats to try and pick up any of you who
might be floating, but he either did not understand me or would not.
When I ran to the helm, intending to put it down, that he might the
better comprehend my meaning, he and his mates held me back. I
pitched into one fellow and knocked him over, and was about to
treat the other in the same way, when the skipper with his big fist hit
me a blow on the head which brought me to the deck.

"When I came to my senses it was broad daylight, and I knew that
long before that time, if the yacht had gone down, you must all of
you have lost your lives. I believe the Dutchman intended to
apologise for having treated me in so unceremonious a fashion, but,
as I could not understand a word he said, I am not sure. He behaved,
however, afterwards, far better than I should have expected from the
way our acquaintance had commenced. I was never a very good
hand at picking up languages, so that it was some time before I
could make myself even imperfectly understood by any one on

410

board. Strange to say, not a man among them spoke a word of English. I wanted the skipper to put into some port, but he replied that, 'Out of his course he would not go for me or any man.' I then begged him, chiefly by signs, that should we fall in with a homeward-bound ship, to put me on board of her. He nodded his head and let me understand that, providing it was during calm weather, he should have no objection, and advised me meanwhile to console myself with his schiedam, of which he had a plentiful supply. Both he and his mates indulged in it pretty largely, I found. I expected that he would touch at the Cape, but to my disgust he ran to the south'ard, in order to fall in with the westerly trades, and I found that he intended to touch nowhere until he reached Batavia.

"This was anything but consolatory, besides which I had no one to talk to, and not a book on board I could read. I tried hard to make out the few Dutch books he had on board, and used to ask him or the mates, or indeed any of the men I found at hand, to pronounce the words, when I tried to discover their meaning. I believe, had the voyage lasted longer, I should have learned to speak and read Dutch fluently; but, as the skipper was drunk half his time, and the mates the other two quarters, I could not get much out of them. The only fellow who really was of use was young Rip Van Winkle. He took a liking to me, as I did to him, from the first, and I often saved him from many a cuff and kick which he was wont to receive from the crew. He was, I confess, a sort of 'dirty Dick' on board, and so he would have continued had I not taught him to clean himself; and now he is as fond of washing as any one, except when the weather is cold, then he rather objects to it, and falls back into his bad habits. My only companion besides Rip was a large dog—no great beauty— whom I called Snarleyow, from being unable to pronounce his Dutch name, and he took to it, as he did to me, immediately, and always came when so called. I treated him as a friend, whereas, from the skipper downwards, he was accustomed to receive more kicks than ha'pence, except from poor Rip, and consequently had no great affection for his masters.

"Besides my anxiety about you, and my disappointment at not being able to take advantage of the new position into which, through Counsellor McMahon, I was placed—not that that weighed very much with me—I could not help feeling anxious about the way in which the ship was navigated. Being unable to understand the Dutch books, I could not myself work out the reckonings, though frequently I took an observation, to keep my hand in.

"I once only had a chance of communicating with England. We sighted a British ship, and as by that time I had picked up enough Dutch to use the signal-book, I hoisted the signals 'British officer on board; heave to for him.' I thought when the skipper saw the other ship heave to that he would do the same, but it was blowing hard, and he obstinately refused to lift tack or sheet or lower a boat, and you can just fancy how I felt when I saw the homeward-bound vessel standing away from us. From the temperature of the weather I now suspected that we had got a very long way to the south, when it came on to blow hard. The Dutchman shortened sail, as he generally did when there was any wind, and continued the course on which he was steering. The old ship, though a tub, was a good sea boat, and I had no reason to fear danger, provided she did not run her stem into an iceberg or strike any rocks or reefs. Blow high, blow low, the skipper walked the deck with his hands in his pockets and a huge meerschaum in his mouth, looking as composed as usual?

"One night I was about turning in, when I felt the ship strike. Of course I sprang on deck, where I was followed by the skipper and the first mate, the second mate having the watch. The crew were singing out that we were lost.

"'Do not be afraid, boys!' cried the skipper, calling for a light for his pipe, and thrusting his hands into his pockets. 'She'll drive over it. Another hand to the helm. Keep all standing!'

"I knew, by the thickness of his voice, that he was half seas over, for he never exhibited his state in any other way, except when he sank down under the table. Still, I hoped from his composure that he knew where we were, and that we should scrape clear of the sand-bank over which the sea was breaking with fearful force. Several seas, indeed, nearly pooped us; but we surged forward, touching occasionally in a way which threatened to split the ship into fragments; but she held together wonderfully. The men, however, had not the same hope that I had; for I saw them gathering on either side, near the boats, taking the falls in their hands, ready to lower them with or without orders.

"Rip came up to me. 'What's going to happen, mynheer?' he asked.

"'The ship will probably go to the bottom or get knocked to pieces; but we may perhaps escape the danger, and so at last reach Batavia,'

I answered. 'Whatever happens, stick by me, Rip, and you can lend me a hand whenever I want it, and I may perhaps save you.'

"Scarcely, however, had I spoken than the ship struck with far greater force than before, the fore and main masts going by the board, but falling clear of the deck. Still she went on; but the carpenter sounded the well, and found that the water was rushing in at a rate which precluded all possibility of keeping the ship afloat. She had gone over the edge of the reef, which rose on the starboard bow, high above the water, and broke the force of the sea. Springing aft, I put down the helm, which the man had deserted, and she rounded to under the lee of the rocks.

"The crew instantly began lowering the boats. The skipper and his first mate tumbled into one, and they with several of the men shoved off; while the second mate took possession of the other, with the rest of the crew, leaving Rip and me still on deck. So overcrowded were they, that I saw they were both likely to go down; and I determined to take my chance in the ship, which I thought, having a light cargo on board, might possibly float long enough to enable us to build a raft. The two boats quickly disappeared in the darkness, without provisions or water, which the men in their hurry forgot to take, while the skipper and his first mate were too drunk to think of it. I bethought me of examining the boat amidships, which I feared might have been crushed by the falling mast; but fortunately it had escaped. I told Rip to cut the lashings clear, reminding him that our lives depended on it—to see that not a rope remained attached to the vessel's deck. I jumped in, followed by Rip and Snarley, who had been left on board with us, and whose instinct showed him that the boat was likely to prove the only ark of safety. The oars, as well as the masts and sails, were stowed in her, with a couple of hen-coops, our last surviving pig, and a variety of other articles. Rip was about to heave the pig overboard, when I stopped him, and told him to hunt about for the plug-hole, which he had just time to stop with a bung, when I saw the water rushing over the deck. The ship did not go down immediately; and I suspect that, had all hands remained on board, we might have kept her afloat until daylight, at all events.

"We got out the oars to shove the boat clear the instant the water rushed over the deck. I do not think I ever experienced a more anxious moment in my life. At last a sea came sweeping along, round the reef, and lifted us clear, right above the bulwarks, and free of the masts and spars still hanging over the side. We pulled away for our lives, and just saw the masts dragged down as the ship went to the bottom. The mizzenmast remained the last above water. We pulled under the lee of the reef; but, having no anchor, we were compelled to hold her in her position by paddling all night. When morning broke, no land was in sight; but as the wind was from the westward, I judged that our safest plan was to steer to the northward, when we might either fall in with some ship, or make Java, or the western coast of Australia, should we not sight any island on the way. We had a small cask of water in the boat, and three empty casks, put there to be out of the way. My hope was that we should be able to fill these with rain water before we got into a more northern latitude, where we were likely to meet with a ship. The reef off which we lay ran half a mile from north to south above the water; how much further below it I could only judge by the line of white foam which extended as far as the eye could reach. As this was a place no ship was likely to approach, the sooner we got out of its latitude the better. The wind having moderated, we accordingly made sail and stood to the eastward.

"We had been three days in the boat, our small cask of water gradually diminishing, while not a drop of rain had fallen to fill our casks, when we sighted this small island. Hoping that it might afford us some shelter, and at all events that we might obtain water, we steered towards it. As we approached we saw the harbour opening out before us. Though I thought that there would be some risk in crossing the bar, yet I determined to make the attempt. Anything was better than dying of thirst. The water appearing to be smoother in the centre, I stood under all sail the boat could carry towards it, for it was still blowing fresh. The bar was reached; and I expected the next instant to be in smooth water, when an abominable roller came tumbling in, swamped our boat, and turned her over, washing Rip away. I clambered up on the bottom, when I saw Snarley, who had just come to the surface. The dog, having looked about him, made towards a point inside the harbour, and, exerting his strength, hauled Rip up. I, meantime, was tossing about on the bar, expecting every moment to be washed off, when I saw Snarley returning. Knowing that I should have his help, I sprang off and swam towards him. I twisted the fingers of my left hand in his long, shaggy hair, and he towed me through the surf safely to the shore, where I found Rip already recovered waiting for me. He threw his arms around my neck and burst into tears, exclaiming in Dutch—'I thought you had gone, mynheer, and that I was left alone; but now you are come we shall manage to live.'

"He then bestowed his caresses on Snarley for having saved me. The sun being bright and warm, we soon dried our clothes; but how we were to exist was the next question, when we had eaten up our pig, who was doomed quickly to die to satisfy our hunger. I had no fancy for raw pork, although my companions were not so particular. Suddenly I bethought me that before the wreck I put a tin box of matches in my pocket to light my pipe. I felt for it. It was there; and although the water had got in, I hoped that the sun would restore their efficiency. I laid them out carefully on the rock, and sat down to watch them, turning them over and over, while Rip set off to obtain fuel. Pieces of driftwood strewed the shore; and some, during high tide, having been thrown up to a distance from the water, were perfectly dry. Rip discovered also plenty of moss and branches of the low shrubs which grew in the hollows and level parts of the island. He had soon a sufficient supply for a good fire. I looked anxiously at the matches. I was afraid to strike one of them until I was certain that it was thoroughly dry, as I should otherwise have knocked off the end. I selected one from the middle of the box, which appeared never to have been wetted, and getting into a sheltered place, I drew it along the side of the box. To my great delight it ignited immediately; and leaving Rip to blow up the fire, I replaced the other matches in the box, which I stowed carefully away in my pocket. We had our knives, for I had got a large one on board for cutting up tobacco. We both turned our eyes on poor piggy, who was grubbing about near us, trying to find roots. In a moment Rip sprang upon him, and before he could give two grunts and a squeak he was turned into pork.

"We did not stop to singe him, but quickly had some steaks toasting before the fire, while Snarley looked wistfully on, giving a hungry sniff every now and then at piggy's carcase. It was somewhat lean, as he had been on short commons in the boat.

"'Good dog, you deserve some food,' said Rip, giving Snarley certain portions which I for one had no inclination to eat.

"While we were at our meal we saw a cask wash on shore. The pork had excited our thirst, and Rip ran down, hoping to find water in it; but it was empty. We looked about, trusting that the cask which had some still remaining in it might be sent to us, but it was nowhere to be seen.

"'Patience,' I observed; 'we may have a shower before long, and fill our cask, so bring it up where it will be safe.' The boat, I should have said, had been tumbling about on the bar. At length it was driven inside the harbour. Rip offered to swim off and tow her in. I hesitated for fear of sharks, but he declared that in that latitude they were not likely to be found. I begged him to wait until she got nearer, which she soon did, and then stripping off his clothes, he boldly plunged in.

"'You remain on shore, mynheer,' he said; 'you will better be able to help me than if you come now. Should I get tired, I can always rest on the bottom of the boat.'

"When Snarley saw him set off, he also plunged in. On reaching the boat Rip put a rope in the dog's mouth, and taking another himself, they began to tow the boat towards the beach. It was hard work, though the wind was partly in their favour, but at the same time it was sending the boat towards the foot of the cliffs opposite the entrance, against which the surf broke heavily, and would soon have knocked her to pieces. When Rip got tired, he climbed up, as he intended, on the bottom of the boat, and after resting a few seconds, again took to towing, Snarley all the time swimming bravely on. I never saw an animal exhibit so much sagacity.

"At length the boat was brought near enough to enable Rip to wade, when I going to his assistance, we dragged her up until she grounded. A slight examination showed us that without tools we should never be able to repair her, for the whole of one side was crushed in and the other was greatly damaged. We accordingly determined to break her up and build a hut with the fragments to shelter us. By this time, however, our thirst became almost unbearable.

"'Perhaps water may be found in the hollows of some of the rocks,' observed Rip.

"Snarley was apparently suffering as much as we were, and when he saw us moving away from the landing-place he ran on ahead.

"'He'll find water, if there's any to be found,' said Rip; and I had the same hope. We climbed up the rocks, and after some exertion we reached the top of the island, when Snarley dashed forward, and to

416

our great joy we saw him with his head in a hollow, evidently enjoying a draught of water. We ran on, nearly toppling on our noses in our eagerness as we made our way over the rough ground. We soon were following Snarley's example, for a pure pool of water was at our feet, while there were two others close at hand, each about a dozen yards in circumference. Although they were apparently filled with rain water, and not from a spring, there was a sufficient quantity to supply all our wants. Even could it be possible to exhaust them, they would be refilled by fresh showers.

"Having quenched our thirst we stood up to look around us, when we caught sight of several animals at no great distance off stopping to gaze at us. They were goats, and some had kids by their sides. Here was food enough to last us for years to come, though we might have a difficulty in catching them ourselves. We felt that Snarley would render us valuable aid in the matter, and that we need have no fear of starving. Refreshed, we set off to take a further survey of the island.

"As we passed along the cliffs overlooking the harbour, we caught sight in a little bay of three boats, hauled up on the beach, with a couple of huts, but no human being was to be seen. We shouted; our voices, however, might possibly not reach the spot. It was evident, at all events, that the island had at some time or other been inhabited, but at that distance we could not judge of the condition of the boats or the huts, so that it might have been years before. As we wished to be housed before night, we now returned to the landing-place, discovering on our way, among the grass, some leaves which tasted like spinach. I felt sure that they would serve as vegetable diet, which it was important to obtain. The mast, yards, and sails were still attached to the boat. Though we had not strength enough to drag her up entire, we got hold of them and put up a small tent, which served to shelter us for the night. We were thankful even for this protection, for after sunset the atmosphere became very chilly. We were in pretty good spirits, and thankful to Heaven that we had found the means of sustaining life. I thought it probable, too, that before long a vessel would appear and take us off. Snarley, who had dried himself by running about, crawled into our tent and assisted to keep us warm, while for the first part of the night we kept a large fire blazing at our feet. We did not keep watch, for our island did not certainly contain any savage inhabitants or wild beasts, so that we slept soundly with a sense of perfect security.

"Next morning, after breakfasting on pork and sorrel leaves, which we ate raw, for want of means of boiling them, we set off to examine the boats and huts. It was a long walk round to where the huts were; as we expected, we found them empty. The boats were in tolerable condition; and though they had not, we judged, been used for several months, were still serviceable. Without tools, however, we could not repair even one of them sufficiently to enable us to continue our voyage. While examining the huts, we discovered an iron pot, which was likely to prove of the greatest value to us. Rip immediately set to work to scrape it clean. On our way back we filled it with water. The rest of the day was spent in pulling to pieces the wreck of the boat, and carrying them up to the spot we had selected for our habitation, which we preferred to those we had discovered near the boats.

"As soon as we had finished our pork, which lasted us for ten days or more, we set off in search of a kid, which we felt sure Snarley would help us to catch. We were not disappointed, though its poor mother fought bravely in its defence. As she stopped until we got up, we captured her also, and soon managed to tame her sufficiently to afford us milk. We spent our time in improving our habitation, in hunting a goat when we wanted one, and in collecting sorrel, which enabled us to make some tolerable broth. Salt we got in abundance from the crevices of the rocks, and manufactured spoons out of drift-wood, and wooden platters and cups. We also brought materials from the other huts to improve our own. I think you'll say, when you see it, that it is a very respectable abode for a couple of bachelors. I own that very often I longed for a loaf of soft tack and a glass of something stronger than water. I managed to keep myself and Rip constantly employed.

"While rummaging about in the huts during one of our early visits, he discovered in a corner a bag containing a palm and sail needle, and nearly a dozen fishing-hooks and other articles. The hooks were likely to prove of great value. We immediately twisted some fishing-lines, and taking a piece of goat's flesh as bait, we scrambled out to the end of a rock, below which the water was deep, to try our luck. That day we caught ten fine fish. We had an additional cause to be thankful, for our health required a change of diet. We no longer had the slightest apprehension of starving. Still after a few months of this sort of life, I began to wish to get away. We rigged the flag-staff you saw, and hoisted the Dutch flag, one we had found in the locker of the boat.

"Day after day I looked out for a sail, but none appeared, and I began to think that I was doomed to spend the remainder of my life on this desert spot. At last our clothes wore out. To replace them I prepared some goat-skins, and we rigged ourselves out in the strange costume in which Green discovered me. I had often when a boy fancied that it would be very pleasant to live on an island by myself, or with one companion; but faith! I found the reality very different, and I would gladly have given up my title and estates to escape. 'It is an ill wind that blows no one good.' I can assure you that my heart leaped into my mouth when I saw the *Empress* approaching, not dreaming at the time of the dangerous condition to which she had been reduced. I own, however, that I shall be very glad to see her safe inside the harbour."

After some hours, the gale having moderated, the *Empress* again stood back to the mouth of the harbour, and came to an anchor as close in as Adair thought it safe to go. A boat now came off, with a sufficient supply of coal to enable her to cross the bar. Adair began to fear that it would be impossible to wait for the spring tide, as the leaks had again begun to gain on the pumps in spite of the efforts of the crew to keep the water under. The larger the quantity of water which got into the ship, the lower she would be, and the less able to cross. As the surf had considerably gone down, the boats were again employed from morning until night in landing stores. But every time they returned loaded over the bar, they ran a considerable risk of being swamped.

Adair was seated in his cabin, the day's work being over, with his nephew, when the carpenter desired to speak with him.

"The men have been doing their best, and I have done my best; but it is my opinion and my duty to express it: the ship won't swim four and twenty hours longer," said Mr Gimlet. "All hands are ready to work on at the pumps and with the buckets until we drop, but the water is rushing in faster than we can pump it out, and should it come on to blow again, no human power can keep the ship afloat."

Adair was not offended at the freedom with which the warrant officer spoke.

"You and all the hands have done your very best, Mr Gimlet," he answered. "We must manage to keep the ship from going down to-night, and to-morrow morning, at the top of high tide, we will attempt to take her over the bar. It is a question whether we shall succeed, and I am very loth to lose her, but the risk must be run."

"No doubt about that, sir," answered the carpenter. "If she once strikes on that bar, she'll never get off again, except piecemeal; but that's better than going to the bottom."

Although, besides the marines, a good many men had been landed, a sufficient number remained to work the pumps, watch and watch, and Adair and Desmond set an example by labouring with them, as they had before done. That night was as trying a one, to the captain at all events, as any yet passed. To-morrow must decide the fate of the ship, whether she would be cast a helpless wreck on the reef or be carried into smooth water and beached on a spot where it might be possible to repair her. Besides, her upper works were strong and sound, but below she was too evidently of a very different character, like many another fine-looking craft. Morning came at length. Adair urged Saint Maur to go on shore.

"I don't hide from myself that crossing the bar will be an undertaking of considerable danger—some, if not all of us, may be lost," said the captain. "I want you to return home to assume your title and property, and to enjoy your life for many years, and to benefit the peasantry on your estate by doing all the good you can. I am getting on in life, and at the best cannot expect to enjoy many more."

Nothing, however, that the captain could say would induce the young lord to quit the ship.

"I know the bar as well as any one. There exists a channel, though a narrow one, through which I think I can take her," he answered.

Adair at last consented; preparations were made for crossing the dangerous spot. Adair ordered the men to take breakfast, and then all went to their stations. The whole of the crew were on deck except the engineers, who of course had to remain below attending to the engines. There was no time to be lost, for already the water in the hold had risen higher than it had ever done before. Steam was got up. The engineer reported that all was ready below. Two of the best hands were sent to the wheel. The crew stood some forward, some aft, where most of the officers were stationed. Desmond took his post by the side of the captain, whence he could direct the helmsmen. All on board felt it to be an awful time. Some said that the ship, the moment she touched the ground, would go to pieces, and that the sea breaking over her would wash all hands from her decks. Desmond, however, assured the captain that he had no such fear; even should the ship not cross the bar, she would run far enough over it to escape the full force of the breakers, besides which, at present they were very moderate, and were not likely to injure her materially.

The anchor was now hove up, the fore-topsail only was set to assist in steering her, and she was headed in towards the mouth of the harbour. Onwards she seemed to fly towards it. Many even of the stoutest held their breath. The boats were all waiting inside the harbour's mouth, to render assistance should it be necessary. To a stranger on the shore watching the approaching ship, she appeared as trim and stout a man-of-war as need be. Nothing on deck gave indication of her rotten condition below. Pat Casey and Peter were standing together.

"Shall we get in an' put the ould boat to rights, or shall we stick on the bar an' see her knocked to pieces?" asked Pat of his companion.

"Me tink, Massa Pat, dat if de ship stick on de rocks him go to pieces, and dat it better for him to do dat dan you and all hands get drowned, 'cause we den get 'shore while him break up." Similar remarks were exchanged amongst the men generally.

"Silence, fore and aft!" sang out the captain, as the harbour's mouth was approached. All on board turned their eyes towards the white line of foam which stretched across it. Desmond pointed out to the helmsmen the exact spot for which they were to steer. He had not to give another order; no one spoke. The smooth water could be seen inside. Would the ship ever float on it?

Full steam was put on. Forward she glided like an arrow towards its mark. Already the outer barrier was reached where the water broke, hissing and foaming on either side. Onward she plunged; then there came a crash, her masts quivered, and all knew that the noble ship was devoted to destruction. A roller came sweeping on astern. It lifted her. Again she moved forward, but it was only to strike with greater force than before. Once more she floated on the buoyant water, but it was again to descend with a crash which was heard and felt from stem to stern, telling that the rocks had gone through her bottom. There she remained firmly fixed, her engines continuing to work until the rapidly rising water rushing in, put out the fires. The engineer, having thoughtfully turned off the steam to prevent the boilers from exploding, his duty done, appeared on deck to announce to the captain that the engines had stopped.

"I see that they have," said Adair, smiling, even at the moment so sad to a captain who had just seen his ship wrecked. The vessel was evidently immovable, and even had the rollers come in with sufficient force to lift her, she must have sunk immediately in deep water. Crash succeeded crash, as the rocks burst through her planks, but not a cheek blanched, not an eye quailed, not a cry was heard, not a man deserted his station.

The rollers continued to tumble in, breaking close under her stem, but failed to wash over her. Adair stood earnestly watching for what would next take place. At last he was satisfied that the lives committed to his charge were safe.

"My lads," he exclaimed, "our brave ship will never float again on the ocean; but you still form her crew, and whether on board or on shore, I am sure that you will exhibit the same good discipline you have hitherto maintained. We will now turn to again and get all we can out of her. We may be discovered and taken off in a few weeks, or we may have to remain months here. As we must be prepared for the latter alternative, we must husband our provisions and stores. I hear that the harbour is full of fish, and that there are goats on the island, and, what is of more consequence, that water is to be found, so that we need have no fear of starving. The rest all depends upon yourselves. We may be a very happy ship's company if we make the best of everything, or we may become the contrary if we grumble and are discontented. I don't expect that of you, and I'm sure we shall all work with a will and look at things on the bright side."

The crew gave three hearty cheers, and Adair directing the first lieutenant to summon the boats alongside, all hands turned to in loading them with the numberless articles which still remained on board. The most valuable things had already been got out. By the doctor's advice four main-deck tanks were landed, with the smith's forge and other apparatus pertaining to his trade, that the engineers

422

might manufacture a machine for turning salt water into fresh. The sails and ropes were also sent on shore, and indeed every article likely to prove of service which the ship contained. The captain and Desmond, with several of the principal officers, still remained on board, a careful watch being kept at night to give them due notice should a change of weather threaten and make it advisable for them to quit the ship.

Fortunately the weather continued fine and the wind mostly blew off the land, so that the boats were able to ply backwards and forwards all day long. One of the assistant-surgeons, who had only lately come to sea, declared that he should not have believed it possible that the ship could have contained the multitudinous articles he saw landed; he had no idea where they could all have been stowed away. In that latitude the winter was likely to prove severe, and as it was approaching, it was important not only to land stores and provisions, but to house the party comfortably.

For the latter purpose, Adair went on shore for the first time and laid down the plan of their town. It formed one long street, with blocks on either side, while a cross road ran at right angles with the main one. One block formed the barracks of the marines, another a hospital. The captain's own house was at the top of the street, and opposite to it one for the lieutenants, another for the rest of the ward-room officers, and a third on their side of the way for the midshipmen. Then came rows of huts, eight on each side, for the seamen. Another was put up for the petty officers, the stokers had one for themselves, and the officers' servants one. At the top of the street, so that it could be seen from the very bottom, was the officers' mess tent, with flags flying over it, and a very tasty-looking affair it was. The walls were partly composed of stone, partly of turf, roofed over with canvas. The roof of Captain Adair's house was also lined with canvas, as were the walls, and divided by partitions.

Some of the midshipmen expressed their regret that there were no ladies among them.

"The ladies are very much obliged to you," observed Charley Roy, who had joined the *Empress*, and was now senior mate on board. "I suspect that they would rather remain comfortably on shore. Perhaps you'd like a grand piano, a ball-room, and a croquet lawn?"

One building there was called the grand hotel, and it was frequented by all ranks, from the warrant officers and sergeant of marines down to the stokers and ship's boys. Liquor in very small quantities and well watered could be obtained there, as could tea and coffee, and various beverages, such as ginger beer, which the doctor continued to manufacture with certain ingredients in his possession, and which was highly appreciated in hot weather. The sergeant of marines was a temperance man, and persuaded half his own corps and fully a third of the blue-jackets to sign the pledge, which, as they had not the means of breaking, was very faithfully kept. Thus not a man ever got drunk, and many who found that they could get on as well without liquor as they could with it, became very steady, sober men. The officers did their best not only to keep the men employed, but to amuse them in a variety of ways. No grumbling was heard from any ranks. One fellow only showed signs of insubordination. He had long been known on board as "Grumpy Dick." No sooner had he set his foot on shore than he asserted that he was a free man, and would no longer work.

"Very well, my fine fellow," said the captain. "If all hands side with you, the officers and I shall have to do what you ought to do to keep you all and ourselves alive. But if not, you shall as surely taste the cat as our stout ship lies there on the rocks. Sleep upon it, and let me know what you think about it to-morrow morning."

Grumpy Dick, who was as obstinate as a pig going to market, was in the same mood the next morning, on which the captain ordered him to be triced up and to receive a dozen at the hands of the boatswain's mate. This example had a very good effect; and if any other men were inclined to follow it, they thought better of the matter, and from that time forward all worked away as well as if they had been on board. They had plenty to do in building their houses. When the men were not otherwise employed, they were engaged in pulling down the materials of the old huts, and bringing them round to strengthen the new. They were fond of boasting of the size of the town, and Pat Casey averred that it was quite large enough to send a member to Parliament, offering to be their first representative on Liberal principles.

Then water had to be brought to supply the town from the ponds Desmond and Rip had discovered at the top of the hill. It was a work mainly accomplished by means of piping of various descriptions. Some was of lead, another part was of canvas, and another portion was of wood in the form of a trough. It could be turned off at the top as was required. The apparatus for turning salt water into fresh also supplied them with such water as they required; but, on account of the fuel it consumed, it was only used when in dry weather there was a risk of the ponds becoming empty.

As soon as the town was finished, Adair had a flag-staff erected and fully rigged, in a way which Desmond, with only one assistant, had been unable to accomplish. A couple of men and a midshipman were stationed there with spy-glasses, to watch the horizon, and to hoist a flag directly a ship was seen, a hut having been built for their accommodation. A small six-pounder, used on board for signalising, was also hauled up to be fired in case of a stranger coming near enough for it to be heard. A pile of wood was also collected in order that a beacon fire should be kindled at night, and rockets and blue-lights were kept ready for letting off should a ship appear in the offing.

A hag of fish-hooks and lines had been found on board, and a party every day were told off to fish, and who never failed to return with an abundant supply.

"Our friend 'Blueblazes' would have been perfectly happy here," said Desmond, laughing, as he and the captain sat at the wardroom mess table, at which they daily dined. They had had some especial fine fish for dinner that day—indeed, they were never at that time on short commons. Of articles of luxury, as well as of meat and biscuit, which must, should they be kept there many months, ultimately come to an end, a small allowance only was of course served out. To keep up good feeling, dinner-parties were given by one mess to another. The first lieutenant invited the warrant officers and the engineers, who ranked with them, on one occasion, and the midshipmen invited them on another. Some of the seamen occasionally dined with the marines, and *vice versa*. Then they had games; though there was no ground for cricket, quoits could be played, and of course there was a fiddler on board, and hornpipes were danced. On Sunday no work was done after the first week or two, and the chaplain had service regularly twice in the day, and occasionally also on other days in the week when they became settled on the island.

Adair and Desmond had been walking a short distance from the town one afternoon, just after the men's dinner hour, when, as they came in sight of the marines' barracks, which were, as has been described, at a short distance from the high street, they heard a slight explosion, while a jet of white vapour ascended above the roof of the huts, and at the same instant the "jollies" were seen rushing out, shouting in English, Scotch, Irish, Yorkshire, and South country dialects, tumbling over each other, some sprawling on the ground, many without caps or jackets, some making their way to the town, others down to the harbour, others scrambling away up to the hill.

"What's the matter, my man?" asked Adair, as soon as he got one of them, who happened to be an Irishman, to stop.

"Arrah! your honour, captain dear, we're blown up entirely. Sure there must be a big fire or an engine of some sort under the barracks, and we would have been roasted or boiled, if it had been at night an' we had all been in our beds."

The column of steam, for Adair saw that it was not smoke, continued to ascend.

"There must be some volcanic agency at work," observed Desmond; "and I am not surprised at the fellows being frightened when it burst out suddenly in their midst."

"We'll examine it, at all events," said Adair. "If there's a vent-hole, I don't suppose we need apprehend any danger."

"Don't go near it, cap'n, it may go off again," exclaimed the Irishman, as he saw Adair and Desmond making their way into the huts.

Several of the men, who recognised their captain, shouted to their companions to stop, and the greater number came back, forming a circle round the spot, ashamed probably of their sudden flight. On examining the place, Adair found that directly under where the men's table had stood, a jet of steam had burst forth and upset it, when it must have fallen with no small force against the men seated on one side. Two poor fellows were still under the table. At first Adair feared that they were killed, but they appeared only to be stunned or frightened into unconsciousness, and in no way injured, for the table had saved them from being scalded.

The orifice was nearly a foot in diameter, and was apparently increasing, as fresh columns of steam, issuing from it, ascended high into the air, having blown off the canvas roof of the hut. The captain and Desmond summoned the men within hail, ordering them to carry their injured comrades to the hospital, where the surgeons, who had come up on hearing the noise, examined them.

The whole population had by this time turned out, and various were the surmises as to what might occur. One thing was certain, that the island was volcanic. What might ultimately happen it was impossible to say. The "croakers" feared that it was but the commencement of disasters, and that at any moment the town might be blown into the air, or the whole island itself, for what they could tell. Adair and his officers endeavoured to quiet their alarm.

The "jollies," having recovered from their fright, were ready to pull down their barracks and rebuild them at a short distance only from the vent-hole, the surgeon assuring them that they would be better off than their shipmates in the winter season, by having warm ground under their feet. As all hands turned to, the huts were shifted to another spot, a little above their former site, and before evening the work was completed.

Two days afterwards, however, a rocking motion was felt, accompanied by a low, rumbling sound, and immediately afterwards two fresh jets of steam burst forth. Day after day the rumblings were heard, and those who wandered to a distance from the town brought word that they had seen, not only jets of steam, but of smoke and fire, while certain rocks, which they had remarked rising above the water, had disappeared, and others, in different places, had come to the surface. Although Adair did not believe that any violent convulsion would take place, he naturally became more anxious than before to escape from the rock. Any spot in the neighbourhood of an active volcano is no pleasant place to live in. Still more disagreeable did the officers and ship's company of the hapless *Empress* feel it to find themselves on the side of a mountain which might at any moment be overturned or sink into the ocean, without the possibility of making their escape. As, however, Adair saw no prospect of averting the evil, should it overtake them, he endeavoured to keep up his own spirits and those of his people by persuading himself and them that such an event as they feared was highly improbable.

After a time the men got accustomed to the appearance of jets of steam, and the "jollies" even made use of them by putting their pots on them to boil their fish. At length the public mind became perfectly tranquillised, and things went on much as before. Still the captain could not help feeling it more than possible that a fresh outbreak might occur, and he found that the surgeon and first lieutenant were of the same opinion.

A sharp look-out had of course been kept for any passing sail. The royals of two ships had been seen, but the signal-gun was probably not heard; nor could the flag have been sighted. The time spent on the rock was, meanwhile, not altogether uneventful.

Week after week, however, passed by, and many by that time were perfectly reconciled to their lot; but others, especially the officers, began to grow weary of the life they were leading, and longed to get away. Trips also were taken to the ship every day, as long as anything remained on board to get out of her.

Chapter Nineteen.

Captain Adair's last visit to the Empress—Resolves to build a vessel out of the wreck—The doctor fears that the island may be blown up—A hurricane—The boats get adrift—The sea washes up the beach—A flash of lightning reveals the ship parting amidships—The masts fall—The ship breaks up—An earthquake—Rocks fail from the cliffs—Rafts constructed—The boats launched—A still more fearful convulsion than before occurs—The crew embark on the rafts and in the boats—Roy left on the cliff—Saint Maur returns to call him—A fearful rush for their lives—Reach the gig in time—The island in a terrific state of commotion—A sail in sight—Approaches the island—Proves to be the Bellona—All safe on board—Touches at the Cape—The last of Major Bubsby—Arrival at home—Happy meetings—Conclusion.

Adair and Desmond paid a visit to the *Empress* one bright morning, when the harbour was smooth as a mill pond, and scarcely a ripple even was seen over the expanse of ocean outside. She lay as firm as ever, with her masts standing, and to all appearance in as good condition as she was the day when the attempt was made to bring her into the harbour, except that when they looked below they could see the clear water washing in and out of her. At a distance she might have been supposed to be at anchor.

"I have been thinking that as no vessel has come near us since we have been here, we might have to wait for months, or perhaps years more, unless we make an attempt to get off by such means as we have at our disposal," observed Adair.

"What, you would not try to cross the Indian Ocean in the boats, would you?" asked Saint Maur.

"No; I would not thus risk the lives of my people, but we must endeavour to build a craft out of the wreck large enough to get as far as Batavia, or even Madras or Calcutta," answered Adair. "I had hopes when we first came on shore that a ship would shortly appear, or I should at once have decided on building a vessel. I have now determined to delay no longer. When we return I will draw up plan for carrying my intention into effect." Adair took several turns along the deck. "This is the third ship I have lost, and I suppose that I shall never get another," he said, with a sigh. "I shall be looked upon as an unlucky man, though in neither case could I blame myself, nor could any one blame me. We will go on shore."

He stepped down the accommodation ladder, which still remained at the side.

Some time was spent in consulting the carpenter and making the arrangements for pulling the old ship to pieces. Next morning all hands were to begin work. It was likely to prove a long undertaking, and one which no sailor likes to be engaged in. It was also doubtful if the weather would continue fine enough to enable it to be completed. During the day a slight movement of the earth was felt, and the same rumbling noise as before sounded beneath their feet, while another jet of steam burst forth from an orifice at a distance from the town. But the ship's company had become so accustomed to the sight of these spouts, that they did not trouble themselves about the matter. In the evening, while Adair and Desmond were seated together, the doctor called upon them.

"I have come, Captain Adair, to state that I have been made anxious for some days past by various phenomena which I have observed on the island. I cannot help fearing that some internal commotion is taking place beneath our feet, which may produce serious consequences. The orifices through which the steam we have observed makes its escape may prove safety valves, but what if a larger quantity of steam is engendered than they can let off?"

"You mean to say, doctor, that you fear the island may be blown up, and that we shall be blown up with it?" said Adair, laughing, though he did not feel altogether comfortable in his mind on the subject.

"Such, captain, I apprehend may be the case, but whether shortly or some time hence I cannot take it upon myself to say," observed the doctor. "I would only urge that a vessel be built in which we can all embark, for I should not like to leave a human being to run the risk of being destroyed, which would be the case were such a convulsion as I dread to take place."

"That's the very thing we are now doing as fast as possible," said Adair. "Do not, however, let the men know what you think may possibly occur, nor the officers either. The carpenter considers that it will take us two months at least to break up the ship and build a new craft out of the materials, and we can only hope that the land will remain quiet until that task is accomplished. Lord Saint Maur and I will accompany you to inspect the new vent-hole and the other phenomena you speak of; and although we would not pit our scientific knowledge against yours, yet perhaps we may make some discovery which may allay your apprehensions."

They set out at once, as there was still sufficient daylight to enable them to reach the spot to which the doctor had alluded. Adair, after making a considerable circuit, during which they discovered several spots so hot that they could scarcely touch them with their hands, thought that possibly the doctor might be correct. All that he could do, however, was to make arrangements to afford the chance of escape to portion of his people, should the island be overwhelmed.

He resolved to have all the boats fitted for sea with stores, water, and provisions. The whole of the community had turned in for the night with the exception of the sentries, who were told off to keep watch according to man-of-war fashion, although there was no enemy likely to attack them, when they were roused by the well-known sound of a furious gale blowing on the shore. It came on as suddenly as a clap of thunder, and ere long the breakers could be heard roaring as they dashed against the rocky coast. Already the wind had lashed the surface of the harbour into foam, and the water rushed up the beach, threatening to carry off the boats, the largest of which were moored a short distance off, while the others were hauled up on the sand.

The captain and officers were the first to be aroused by the sound of the gale. They hurried out, and turned up all hands to secure the boats. This was no easy matter, for two had already broken adrift, and it was necessary at all risks to go off after them. They, however, were brought back before the full fury of the hurricane burst on the island. They were at length hauled up on the beach by means of rollers placed under them and the strength of fifty hands at least applied to each. The sea continued to rise, and it became necessary to drag them still further up out of the danger of being washed away. Even in the harbour so enormous were the waves that they washed right up to the huts, threatening to destroy the whole lower part of the town, the inmates of which were compelled to carry off their goods and chattels higher up the rock. The largest of the boats still remained on the beach, and the men, headed by the captain, and accompanied by several officers, were attempting to drag her up, when a loud sound, like the report of a heavy gun, was heard.

"There goes the old ship!" cried several voices.

Adair feared that the remark was true. Scarcely had the words been uttered, when a flash of lightning revealed the ship parting asunder amidships. The mizzenmast fell at the same time, but the mainmast was seen still standing. In another minute down came the mainmast with a crash, followed shortly afterwards by the foremast and bowsprit, and, high above the roar of the surf and howling of the wind, the rending and crashing of the ship's timbers could be distinguished.

"There goes all chance of our being able to build a craft," observed Saint Maur to the captain. "The fragments which come on shore will be so battered and crushed that they will be of no use."

"I fear so, indeed," answered Adair; "but we must not show the men that we are disheartened."

The gale went on increasing, while the sad sounds of the ship breaking up continued, and huge fragments were cast by the force of the waves on the beach, several striking the stern of the large boat, and almost staving her in before she could be hauled out of danger. Though the men could do no more, they stood watching the catastrophe which, though many of them had long expected it, had come at last so suddenly upon them.

As they thus stood grouped together they felt the earth rock beneath their feet in a way it had never done before. Then came a sound far louder than any yet heard. Several of the men cried out that the island was blowing up. At that moment there was a fearful crash, and by the light of another flash of lightning a glimpse was caught of a huge mass of rock descending from the summit of the hill into the water. Another and another followed. Adair and Saint Maur remembered the doctor's prognostications, and began truly to fear that the whole island was breaking up, and that ere long it might present a mass of broken fragments or sink down bodily beneath the sea.

They endeavoured, notwithstanding, to maintain their own composure and to restore confidence to the men, many of whom were greatly alarmed.

"Whatever becomes of those high cliffs which seem to be crumbling away, I consider that we, on this level spot, have every chance of escaping," exclaimed Adair. "We must, however, keep out of the way of those rocks, which, tired of their existence up in the sky, are going to find out how they like the bottom of the sea."

By this time the night was nearly over, and when morning dawned and Adair looked out, not a particle of the ship remained entire except her engines, which, like some huge creature, could just be distinguished, surrounded by the masses of foam breaking on the bar, while over the surface of the harbour and outside along the coast could be seen fragments of wreck of every size, tossed here and there by the waves. Adair heaved a deeper sigh than he had ever done before in his life.

The storm still continued to rage as fiercely as at first, and it was impossible to secure any portions of the wreck except those which were washed ashore in the harbour, and even to do that was a service of danger, as they were tossed about, threatening to crush those who approached them. Still Adair thought that it might be possible to save wood sufficient for the building of a vessel. It would, at all events, give the men something to do and keep up their spirits with a prospect of getting off. The carpenter shook his head when he spoke to him on the subject.

"I am afraid, sir, it will be a rum sort of craft we should build, but if you will permit me to say so, I think if we were to lengthen some of the boats and rise upon them two or three feet, we should produce a better style of craft than we are likely to put together."

Adair thought the matter over, and discussed it with Saint Maur. They agreed that it was possible, and that, should some fearful convulsion of the island take place, it would be as well to have the boats thus fitted, in order that some of their lives, at all events, might be preserved.

"We will hope that some ship will come in sight before the land sinks down to the bottom of the sea," said Saint Maur, in a cheerful tone.

The captain just then remembered that the men had been on foot all that morning without breakfast.

"Pipe to breakfast, Mr Smalls," he sang out to the boatswain, who was near.

The shrill pipe of the boatswain was heard sounding above the roaring of the breakers, the howling of the wind, and the crash of the falling rocks, which still, though in smaller pieces than before, came toppling down from the summit of the cliff above into the seething waters of the harbour.

The men willingly obeyed the call, and were quickly seated at their mess tables, talking and laughing away as usual. Adair and Saint Maur returned to their cottage. The roofs of the huts had been too securely fastened down to be blown away, and all hands were soon beneath their shelter. All day long the gale raged. In spite of it, the carpenter, with the hands he required, set to work in preparing the wood they had obtained for enlarging the boats. The largest had, it must be remembered, been left just above the influence of the sea, where it was fancied she was free from danger.

In the morning, as usual, a party was sent off to the flag-staff, which was not visible from the town. Some hours had passed and a relief was proceeding to take their place, when they were observed coming down the cliffs, holding on to the rocks as they slowly made their way.

"What has happened?" asked Charley Roy, who commanded the second party.

"The flag-staff is gone and we were all well-nigh carried off with it," was the answer. "There is no ship in sight; and if there were, she would take good care not to come near this rock if she could help it, so that there is no use in your going on and running the chance of losing your lives."

"You are quite right," said Roy, and he returned to obtain further orders.

Adair, of course, told him not to go on to the hill, adding, "We must get another flag-staff ready to set up as soon as the gale is over," and he at once issued orders to the carpenter to prepare it.

When night closed in there was no appearance of a cessation of the gale; indeed, if anything, matters looked worse than they had done all day. At the usual hour all hands turned in to obtain the rest they required, while the men on watch stowed themselves away in the most sheltered corners they could find, for not a human being even during four hours could have stood exposed to the pitiless tempest.

It was about midnight when those nearest the water were aroused by a crashing sound, and before they had time to dress themselves, they found the sea washing right up to their huts, far higher than it had done the day before. Adair, who slept lightly, was also awakened by the voices and the shouts of the men as they rushed with their clothes bags and mess things out of their huts. He and Saint Maur hurried down to ascertain what was the matter, when on looking towards the beach where the large boat had been left, on which their hopes of safety depended, she was nowhere to be seen. A mass of timber and shattered fragments, surrounded by the seething water, alone marked the spot. A portion of the wreck, it was evident, had been driven against her, and the retiring sea had carried her off knocked to pieces. The remainder of the night was spent in shifting the huts exposed to the waves to a safer spot. Adair allowed no word of complaint to escape him, but he could not but dread what might next happen.

Towards morning the gale abated, and the men were employed in hauling up the fragments of spars which floated among the rocks. Some were of good size, while others were broken into small pieces, which could be of no use but to saw into planks. With the large ones the carpenter contrived, in the course of a couple of days, to build a fresh mast to supply the place of the old one. By this time the weather was again calm, and Adair and Saint Maur and several officers accompanied the party who were selected to set it up. They carried their telescopes, hoping against hope that a ship might appear. But not a sail was to be seen in the horizon, nor a wreath of smoke to indicate a passing steamer. The flag-staff was erected, the ensign run up, and the gun fired to do it honour.

But we must hasten on with the account of the adventures of the captain and crew of the unfortunate *Empress*. Day after day, week after week went by. Occasionally the earth trembled and shook, but no more jets of vapour or gas burst forth, and the orifices of those which had first appeared were stopped up. The surgeon's face grew longer and longer.

"Well, doctor," said Adair, when the latter was paying him a visit, "we are not to be blown up yet, and I hope that the old rock will stand firm enough until long after we have left it, unless we are to spend our lives here."

"That's no reason why that fearful event should not some day occur, captain," answered Dr McQuae. "I last night heard worse rumblings than have yet occurred. My bunk moved up and down in a curious fashion."

"You must have been dreaming," said Adair. "I slept but lightly, and heard no noises nor did I feel the slightest movement of the earth."

"Pardon me, Captain Adair. I was broad awake at the time, and could not be mistaken."

Adair, on making inquiries, was surprised to find that several other persons had heard noises and felt a movement, especially the sergeant of marines, who averred that he was very nearly thrown out of his bunk. His statement, however, was somewhat discredited by the warrant officers, who expressed their belief that he was addicted to romancing. Be that as it may, a very uncomfortable feeling prevailed both among the officers and men, and all were wishing themselves away from so treacherous a locality. A few days after this a commotion took place throughout the length and breadth of the island, which left the matter no longer in doubt. Vast fragments of rock came tumbling down from the summits of the cliffs, sending huge waves rolling up the beach, although the sky was serene and the wind blew gently from the northward, so that no surf broke along the mouth of the harbour.

"If this continues much longer we must launch the boats and build rafts sufficient to carry all the people, to give some of us a chance for our lives, at all events," observed Adair to Saint Maur.

"Cheer up, Uncle Terence," exclaimed Desmond; "the cliffs may tumble down, but still, as you remarked before, we may have firm ground to stand upon."

"I don't know what I should have done without you," answered Adair. "Frankly, I believe I should have broken down altogether: For my poor Lucy's sake and yours I am as anxious to escape, if I can do so with honour, as any man, but desert my people while one remains in danger I must not."

"At all events, there can be no harm in getting the rafts built," said Desmond.

"I will direct the first lieutenant to set the people about the work at once, just as a matter of precaution, so as not to alarm them," answered Adair.

There were few, however, who did not feel as anxious as the captain to get the rafts completed, and all hands set to work to collect every particle of timber they could find along the coast, and to haul it to the bay.

The carpenter, upon calculation, found that he could form six rafts, thirty feet long and twenty wide. These would carry all the crew who were not able to find room in the boats, provided the sea was tolerably smooth. A couple of rafts had been completed, and as many hands as could be employed were working away at the others, when again that ominous sound which before had alarmed them was heard, and the whole island seemed to be convulsed, as if about to be rent asunder. Although the movement ceased, it made them work away with almost frantic haste. By means of hand-spikes and rollers, the rafts, as they were finished, were launched, when the boatswain and his mates commenced rigging them in the best fashion they could, while the sail-makers were employed in cutting out the canvas, some of which had been kept in store, the rest being, taken for the roofs of the huts.

Although so much of the cliff had fallen down as to half fill the harbour, the point on which the flag-staff stood remained intact. Charley Roy was stationed there with a party of men, who kept a look-out around the horizon from sunrise to sunset. They were relieved at night by another party under the third lieutenant, who was directed to burn blue-lights and let off rockets at intervals, in case any ship should be passing.

Night brought no cessation to the toils of the crew. Torches were formed, and fresh hands laboured away at the rafts. Several times as they were thus toiling, the ground below them shook more or less violently.

"Stop a bit, an' we'll be afther gittin' off you," cried Pat Casey, who was always ready with a joke to cheer up his companions. "Jist keep quiet, me darlin', for a few hours longer, an' you an' me will part company, whin ye can trimble as much as ye like."

Whether or not the volcano would accede to his request seemed very doubtful. Towards morning the commotions increased, crash succeeded crash, and they could perceive that other portions of the cliff had given way, while there was some fear that the rafts would be swamped by the sea which the falling masses created, before they could get out of the harbour. Strange to say, in spite of the fearful danger in which they were placed, the men joked as much as ever, though they worked away in a manner which showed that they were fully conscious of the necessity of speed, the officers labouring with them as hard as any one. At the sound of the boatswain's call they scampered off to breakfast, which they bolted in a few minutes, and soon came back to their work.

The weather now became finer than it had been since they had landed on the island many months before. The sky was clear and the air pure, and there was not an invalid among them.

The sixth raft had just been completed, and the men were working it down to the water, when a rumbling sound far louder than any thunder was heard. The tall cliffs appeared as if about to fall down and fill up the whole of the harbour, the mouth evidently of an ancient crater. The rocks were seen to lift and heave; Adair stood on the shore, superintending the launching of the raft, apparently as cool and unmoved as ever.

"Now, my lads, get the boats into the water," he exclaimed. "Let their proper crews attend to them; the rest of you assist the marines in bringing down the provisions and water."

It should have been said that, under the direction of the pay-master and his assistants, all the casks had been filled with water, and all the provisions done up in packages, which could be easily transported.

Even at that moment perfect discipline prevailed; the men hurried backwards and forwards, it is true, as fast as their legs could carry them. They worked like a colony of ants, knowing exactly what they had to do. The midshipmen were ordered into the boats with their respective crews to stow the packages, and to keep the rafts off the beach. These were next loaded, and the boats being filled, the men were ordered to take their places on the rafts.

Captain Adair and Lord Saint Maur stood alone on the shore, when the sound of a gun was heard.

"I forgot Roy and the men with him," exclaimed Adair.

"I'll go for him," cried Desmond, and before he could be stopped, he darted off.

Adair now ordered the boats to take the rafts in tow, and to proceed over the bar, as it would be impossible to find a more favourable opportunity for crossing it. One boat—his own gig—with four hands in her, only remained, so that she was able to carry, in addition, Roy and his party.

Again the sound of the gun was heard, followed by a third report. All this time the cliffs above the further end of the harbour appeared crumbling away, while the ground where the marines' huts stood, as well as beyond them, was heaving in visible undulations. Adair felt that at any moment the whole island might be convulsed in such a way as to destroy all remaining on it. He anxiously looked out for the return of Saint Maur and Roy. The movements increased in violence. He saw the men in the boat turning their eyes towards the cliff, as if they were eager to be away, fearing lest they themselves would be involved in the expected destruction of the island. He drew his breath more freely when at length he saw Saint Maur appear on the top of the path leading from the hill, followed by Roy and his men. Down they rushed at headlong speed. They had not a moment to lose; already huge rents appeared in the ground, some of a width across which it seemed scarcely possible they could leap, while the rocks on either side were tumbling and leaping along, and threatening to crush the party as they made their downward way.

Adair ordered the men in the gig to come in, and he stood half in the water holding her stem. He had no need to hurry Saint Maur and the rest. One poor fellow was struck, but his companions did not wait for him; they saw at a glance that he was killed. Another narrowly escaped, and a huge block came near Saint Maur as he sprang over a wide gap. With frantic haste they dashed along, and almost breathless reached the beach.

"Spring in!" cried Adair; "I shall be the last to leave the shore!"

Roy and the other men followed. Adair now jumped on board, and made his way to the stern sheets. The bow-men shoved, off without waiting for orders, and bending to their oars the gig was soon across the bar. Saint Maur and Roy were too much out of breath to speak. Indeed, Adair himself forgot to ask the reason of the signals they had heard; as, while steering for the bar, and casting a momentary glance over his shoulders, he saw the whole island rocking to and fro, and not only steam and smoke, but flames bursting forth from several fissures. Even now neither he nor his men were in safety: for should the island sink, the rafts and boats would be drawn into the vortex; or should it blow up, as seemed very likely, the fragments would too probably fall down and crush them, or create so violent a commotion of the ocean that they would scarcely escape being overwhelmed. Steering for the heaviest raft, he joined another boat in towing her. As yet they were under the lee of the island, and their sails were of no use. Long paddles had been formed for the use of the men on the rafts, who worked energetically, as the boats, heavily laden as they were, were unable to make much headway.

Roy, who had been hitherto panting too much to speak, now recovering himself, exclaimed —

"A sail, sir! a sail! We saw her standing towards the island. She's a steamer, I think, though I could not make out her funnel. I caught sight of a wreath of white smoke hanging above her masthead."

"Too probably she's only passing," said Adair.

"No, sir, she was standing steadily this way; and the heads of her courses had already risen above the horizon. We left the flag flying, so if the hill doesn't come toppling down, she will see that, and know that there is some one on the rock. Perhaps she is coming expressly to look after us."

"Thank Heaven!" cried Adair, in a voice choking with emotion, for the first time the calm composure he had hitherto exhibited giving way. "My poor people will be saved!"

The joyful news soon spread from boat to boat and raft to raft. At length feeling the wind, sail was set, and the little squadron steered a course as close to it as was possible, not to near the ship, but to get further off from the island. As soon as they had gained what Adair considered a safe distance, he ordered the first lieutenant, who was in one of the boats, to cast off and stand towards the stranger, whose topsails by that time could be seen. He had now only earnestly to pray that the weather would continue calm until they were all on board. Meantime he had cast many an anxious glance towards the land, which seemed, at the distance they were now from it, to be at rest, though the rumbling sounds which reached them and the thick clouds of smoke and flame ascending, showed them that they had good reason to be thankful that they had escaped it.

The first lieutenant's boat was eagerly watched as she glided rapidly over the smooth water. At last her white speck of canvas disappeared beneath the horizon, and a further period elapsed.

The stranger was pronounced by the cut of her canvas to be a British man-of-war. At last she was seen to change her course, and to stand directly for the rafts. Soon afterwards the glorious ensign of England blew out at her peak. The sight was welcomed by a cheer from the whole crew. There could be no doubt that the first lieutenant had got on board. On she came until she approached, when her canvas was reduced.

"Hurrah! she's the *Bellona!*" exclaimed Saint Maur and Adair at the same moment. They both knew her, and in another minute they recognised Captain Rogers and several old friends. Adair and Desmond, springing up the side, were heartily welcomed.

"We have come expressly to look for you," said Jack, as he grasped their hands, and he told them of the information he had received from the master of the Australian trader. The *Bellona's* boats had been lowered and now approached to take off the crew from the rafts, as well as the provisions and water.

"We have arrived in the nick of time," said Jack; "but as your island now seems tolerably quiet, we may as well remove the stores, the men's bags, and your own things, which it will be a pity to lose, and I shall be glad to leave some of these boats which we cannot take away."

The *Bellona* accordingly steamed on towards the entrance of the harbour, keeping, as may be supposed, at a safe distance in case of a sudden outbreak. By this time the smoke and flames had disappeared, and the boats pulled in, piloted by Adair and his officers.

The blue-jackets were highly delighted at recovering their bags, and the marines their kits, which had of necessity been left behind. The boats which Saint Maur and Rip had found when they landed were hauled high up on the beach and covered over with canvas to protect them from the weather. The more valuable stores were carried off, though provisions and other articles were left which might afford assistance to the sufferers of any ship which might be wrecked on the island.

The *Bellona* steered directly for the Cape, in a short time, as the wind became fair, making all sail. That night the watch on deck declared that they saw a bright glare in the sky above the rock and that a low rumbling noise was heard coming from the same direction. Whether or not Virginia Island had blown up remained a matter of doubt, and Captain Rogers did not think that with two ships' companies on board it was his duty to return and ascertain the fact.

Crowded as they were, both officers and men were as happy as could be under such circumstances, and wonderful were the yarns which the crew of the *Empress* had to spin, none of the facts which had occurred losing in the narration, besides which there were many more to describe which are not chronicled in this history.

The *Bellona*, immediately on her arrival in Simon's Bay, was ordered home, where Captain Adair and his officers would have, of course, to undergo the usual court-martial for the loss of the *Empress*. Scarcely had she dropped her anchor, when, in one of the first boats which came off, was seen a stout military man, accompanied by two ladies. Shortly after, Major Bubsby and the two Misses Bubsby ascended the side. Jack, who was never wanting in politeness, whatever were his feelings, stood ready to receive them.

"My dear Captain Rogers," exclaimed the major, grasping him by the hand, "I was at the telegraph station when you made your number, and I immediately hurried down to welcome you, picking up Eugenia and Angelica on the way. Will you do me a favour?"

"What is it?" inquired Jack.

"Yes, it is a favour; I will acknowledge it as a favour if you grant it. Will you convey Mrs Bubsby and myself with our two dear daughters to England? You must know that I was compelled to resign my command, and I do not find my stay here as pleasant as I should wish."

Billy Blueblazes, who was standing behind the captain, observed Miss Angelica casting loving glances towards him. "Heaven forbid that the captain should grant the major's request," he said to himself.

He need have had no fear on that score. Jack as politely as possible declined, and did not even invite the major and the Misses Bubsby below.

"You must understand, Major Bubsby, that I have the officers and part of the ship's company of the *Empress* to carry home, so that we have not an inch to spare. I cannot turn them out of the only berths I have to offer, and you and your daughters would not like to sling up your hammocks on the lower deck."

"I did not expect this of you, Captain Rogers," said the major, an angry frown gathering on his brow.

"Hard-hearted man!" murmured Miss Angelica.

But Jack was deaf to all they could say, and felt very much inclined to order the master-at-arms to escort his visitors, *nolens volens*, down the side. They at last made a virtue of necessity, and returned to their boat.

Billy heaved a sigh of relief as he watched them pulling towards the shore. It was the last he or his captain ever saw or heard of Major Bubsby and his daughters, the major's name disappearing soon afterwards from the army list. Lord Saint Maur, of course, went home in the *Bellona*. He was accompanied by Rip and Snarley, the former begging that he might enter his service as valet. Old England was reached at last, when Captain Rogers made the pleasing discovery that he had become an admiral by seniority.

In a very short time, telegrams having conveyed the joyful intelligence of the arrival of the ship with Captain Adair and Lord Saint Maur on board, Julia and Lucy, the former accompanied by her fair daughters, arrived at Southsea, which had so often before witnessed their grievous partings and happy meetings. This, as may be supposed, was one of the happiest. Captain Adair was honourably acquitted for the loss of the *Empress*. Though he did not again obtain a ship, he accompanied the expedition to Coomassie, and took an active part in an exploit which redounded so greatly to the honour of the troops, blue-jackets, and marines engaged in it, as well as to that of its noble leader, proving what stern discipline and courage can effect, even in the most pestiferous of climates and against hosts of brave foes.

Lord Saint Maur, shortly after his return home, married Miss Lucy Rogers, and Archie Gordon became the husband of another of Jack's daughters. Tom was supposed to be a confirmed bachelor, notwithstanding his early susceptibilities to female attractions, until, on going over to pay a visit to his old shipmate at Kilcullin Castle, he there met the Misses McMahon, the youngest of whom he married. Billy Blueblazes, who came to act the part of his best man, fell head over ears in love with the eldest—not the first Englishman under similar circumstances who has been captivated by one of Erin's fair daughters, and she, discovering attractions which satisfied her, and the counsellor ascertaining that he was heir to a good estate, no objections were raised, and Billy became a happy benedict, quitting the service as a retired commander.

Tim Nolan and Pat Casey made their appearance at the castle one day, "just," as they said, "to see how his lordship was getting on."

"What are you going to do with yourselves, my good fellows?" asked Lord Saint Maur.

They twirled their hats and scraped their feet and acknowledged that they had not quite settled, except that they had made up their minds not to go to sea again.

On this Lord Saint Maur offered them cottages rent free, and employment on board his yacht in summer, and charge of his boats on the river which ran through his estate.

Jerry Bird obtained a pension and settled near Admiral Rogers, while Peter became butler to Billy Blueblazes. Indeed, a satisfactory account can be given of all the friends who have played a part in this history.

Soon after his return from Africa Captain Adair obtained his flag, and the "Three Admirals" remain, as they had been in their youth and through the whole of their career, the firmest friends, and, though they themselves are shelved, take the warmest interest in the glorious service in which they spent their lives, and in the welfare of their younger relatives and former followers.

Lightning Source UK Ltd.
Milton Keynes UK
UKHW011530090921
390292UK00001B/17